USS Lincoln

Mercy Kill

USS Hamilton Series
Book 7

Mark Wayne McGinnis

Published by: Avenstar Productions info@avenstar.net

Paperback ISBN:

• **ISBN-13** : 979-8986675275

To join Mark's mailing list, jump to:

http://eepurl.com/bs7M9r

Visit Mark Wayne McGinnis at:

http://www.markwaynemcginnis.com

 Created with Vellum

Chapter 1

Alternate Universe
USS Adams

Captain Galvin Quintos

I stood at the captain's ready room window, looking out to an inky blackness that was both alien and hostile. It wasn't my imagination; this place, this universe, if we let it would soon bring an end to the lot of us. The longer we stayed here, the more inevitable that would become. _God, I want to go home._

IT HAD BEEN three days since we'd destroyed the Ziu. Thousands upon thousands of those multiheaded, snapping-jawed little fuckers. More accurately, we destroyed their mind-controlling Ziu queen—an immense creature held up within the center-most confines of that alien mother ship. Battle weary and desperate, there was no doubt about it—we had been losing the battle—I was certain we would all die here within this horrible alternate universe.

It had come down to one last-ditch Hail Mary shot in the dark. We'd been keeping them held within a containment field —seven of the vilest creatures in existence. I'd vowed to never ever let them out. I'd seen what they could do ... witnessed first-hand via a security feed as they methodically devoured US Space-Navy personnel. Sloth forms. Virtually indestructible, each the size of a full-grown rhinoceros, they slithered more than walked on six stumpy legs. Slimy, covered with a kind of mucus, their heads were faceless, with a protruding nozzle appendage thing that could suction up a full-grown man within seconds. So, I'd broken my own resolute promise and, with Coogan's help, quansported the seven sloth forms over to the Ziu mother ship. Even now, they continued to dine on the queen's immense bulk. But I wondered. How many more Ziu mother ships were out there? We would not survive another attack like the last one. Plus, there were only so many sloth forms to go around.

Off in the distance I could just make out the Ziu mother ship's smooth, spherical hull. *What to do with it now...*

Out of view was *Boundless Wrath,* the once Varapin pris-oner ship, which was somewhat still intact and being crewed by the few surviving Symbio-Poth 2.0s... but there was another latecomer starship here within local space. I had no idea who it was being crewed by, or what they wanted.

My Jadoo comms/Quansporter ring started to vibrate. Reluctantly, I thumb-tapped the thing, bringing up the 3D projection of Hardy's oversized head.

I let out an irritated breath. "Hardy, what is it about *I don't want to be disturbed* that you didn't understand?"

"Wait... you were serious about that?"

"Just tell me what you want," I said.

"Sonya... she's—"

"Wait! Is she okay? Is she out of surgery? For shit's sake, why didn't Viv tell me?"

"Yes, yes, and I don't know... Cap, you have to know... Doc Viv is overwhelmed with more injured patients than she and her staff can handle. I offered to help; you know I do have medical train—"

I cut him off. "Uh-huh, I'm on my way. Stay there."

I accessed my Jadoo ring's projected options menu, intending to directly quansport to the corridor outside of HealthBay. Thinking better of it, I decided I'd walk... it was getting way too easy to avoid walking. I needed to be seen by the crew. I needed to be accessible.

Adjacent to the captain's ready room was the bridge. Upon entering, heads turned in my direction. Chen was at the comm station, Grimes at Helm, Bosun Johanna Polk at the bridge CIC console, and Lieutenant Akari James was at Tactical.

She stood. "I need to talk to you."

"I'm on my way to—"

She raised a palm, shaking her head. "I'll walk with you."

I noticed one of her gold piercings, this one above her left eyebrow. She'd been nervously playing with it. The skin there was still pink, looking slightly inflamed. Nerves getting to her, like the rest of us. Adding to the tat artwork down both arms, and her short and always disheveled hair, the look worked for her. Akari seemed to go out of her way to look and act irreverent —silently screaming to be both noticed and unconventional. An ace Arrow pilot in her own right, she'd settled into her post at Tactical just fine. The truth was, at least as of late, she was my most trusted bridge officer.

Leaving the bridge, she hurried to keep up with me. "We're low on... well, just about everything. Mainly spikes."

I nodded, knowing she was referring to *Adams'* rail gun ammunition, rail spikes.

"Add to that, our stock of smart missiles is getting dangerously low, and three of our plasma cannons are down; their barrels literally melted from prolonged overuse during that last battle."

I nodded but didn't comment.

"Well?" she said. "If we're attacked again ..."

"You're the tactical officer, Akari I can't do your job for you. What do you suggest, Lieutenant?"

She shrugged. "It's not as if we can jump to the closest star base, get resupplied with munitions, or have a maintenance team re-outfit our ship guns."

I looked about, then glanced up, taking in *Adams'* beautifully appointed interior. Years earlier, the USS *Hamilton* class dreadnought had been ready for the scrapyard. Then it was purchased by an investment group. Rechristened *Britannica*, she was to be the most elegant, luxurious passenger starliner in the quadrant. High above us were thirty-six oval colonnade domes, each handcrafted stained glass... nineteenth-century reproductions utilizing the age-old process of heating mixed potash and sand to over one thousand six hundred and fifty degrees Celsius and then infusing it with various metallic oxide powders to create the vibrant colors above us. The hanging chandeliers were all Waterford... each crystal had a 40 percent lead content, and there were seventy-five individual vintage incandescent lights per fixture. The vessel's interior, with her paneled mahogany bulkheads, vintage oil portraits, and gilded age opulence, was like none other, especially since she'd been reappropriated, then recommissioned, by Empress Shawlee due to ever-increasing war demands—those brought about by strategic advances coming from both the Varapin and Grish. Now this would-be starliner was also a fierce military warship.

We'd reached the bank of GravLifts. The left set of doors slid open. We both entered the lift. As with the rest of the ship, the car's interior consisted of polished brass hardware, rich mahogany paneling, and crystal wall sconces. But it was the assigned, dedicated liftman that always made me uneasy upon entering any of the lifts. The legless hover-bot was fitted with a formal tux-with-tails attire. The bot greeted us both by name as it stood vigil over the lift's virtual touchscreen controls like a guard at Buckingham Palace. I said, "HealthBay."

"Very good, Sir... leaving Deck 13 for Deck 12."

Akari and I exchanged a look.

She continued where she'd left off. "I suppose we could replicate the spikes. It's not like there's all that much to them."

"I'd get on that right away," I said. "And our low stock of smart missiles?"

She rubbed at the new piercing. "I think it's infected... does it look infected?"

I just stared at her, then hitched one shoulder. "We're headed to HealthBay. Have it looked at."

"Yeah, good point. Um, so... maybe *Boundless Wrath* has an ample stock of smart missiles. They won't be compatible, being of Varapin design, but we've jerry-rigged such compatibility issues before, right?"

I nodded, letting her ramble. My mind was onto other things. Oddly, feeling nostalgic, I missed the way things used to be. And I missed those I'd become closest to over the years, like Stephan Derrota and Gail Pristy—both, undoubtedly, were back within the secure confines of Stratham Hold. My once-pirate hideaway was nestled there, one hundred and thirty light-years' distance outside the Milky Way—on an M-class exoplanet called Genoma. It was a dangerous area of space where eight black holes had converged and, somehow, were keeping each other at bay. But all that was far away from here; hell, Genoma wasn't even within this alternate universe.

"Earth to Captain Distracted... are you even listening to me?"

I said, "Sorry," but was cut off by the overly enthusiastic liftman.

"Deck 12... please watch your step departing the lift."

We stepped out into the large, although much scaled-down version of the main Deck 13 corridor above.

"Melted gun barrels... SWM would surely have metal-working facilities onboard, right?" Akari asked.

She was referring to the ship-wide maintenance department. I nodded, stopped, and looked down at her. "You clearly had all of this figured out, Akari... you didn't need to discuss any of this with me. So, what's really going on? What's up?"

Looking caught, her cheeks reddened. "The truth?"

"Always."

"I'm worried about you, Cap. A few of us are."

Bemused, I raised my brows. I said, "I'm fine. No one should be concerned—"

"You've isolated yourself. If you're not down here in Health-Bay, you lock yourself away in that ready room of yours. Did something happen over there on that Ziu ship?"

"It's not your job to worry about me. You don't need to be concerned."

But I could see in her eyes that she was concerned. And probably others were too. Maybe something did happen to me over on the Ziu ship, or maybe it was this damn alt universe... the word that was coming to mind was "foreboding." Like it was only a matter of time for the other shoe to drop, the hammer to fall and this was the calm before the storm...

"Worry about rail spikes, low smart missile stock, and melted gun barrels. Head back to the bridge and do your job."

Chapter 2

I briefly hesitated before entering HealthBay. I'd been here a number of times over the last few days. Things continued to look crazy hectic. Inside, I saw a flurry of rushing- around medical staff and several hovering medibots. I entered the primary patient compartment. As before, the overheads had been dimmed, and each of the beds was occupied. Physiological monitoring equipment beeped and dinged, merging into a kind of constant white noise. Above several of the beds were slow-rotating 3D medical avatars. I'd make my rounds, drop by each of the patients later. For right now, I needed to check in on Sonya.

I made a left through double doors beneath a sign that read "Surgical Suite." Staff wearing pastel-colored scrubs bustled by. A harried-looking nurse noticed me.

"Captain? Um... sorry, but Doc Viv's not allowing any—"

"Sonya Winters. She's out of surgery?"

"Yes, but as I said..."

It was then that I saw Hardy lean his bulk out into the corridor. "She's in here, Cap."

I strode past the nurse. "Keep up the good work. I won't stay long."

Sonya was sitting upright but looked to be asleep. A web of tubes and wires emerged from her shoulder dressing. Rhythmic beeps of a heart monitor echoed within the quiet compartment, punctuating the stillness. Unmoving, Hardy stood tall against an adjacent bulkhead.

"How is she?" I asked.

Hardy's faceplate came alive, his holographic John Hardy face looking back at me. "She came through the surgery without any complications. Her arm was reattached at the shoulder. Prognosis... she'll be fine within several weeks. She won't be giving any high fives for a while—that, or playing badminton."

Sonya looked small and vulnerable, lying there in her pink bunny–patterned gown. Having been brought up within the Pylor pirate clan once led by the infamous pirate, Thunderballs, she'd been forced to grow up fast and fend for herself within a rough, male-dominated society. I'd only recently discovered this sixteen-year-old kid, and I had a familial genetic connection with her. I now thought of her, even if it wasn't totally true, as my niece. She was special to me. Seeing her now, lying there looking broken and helpless, well, the guilt was weighing heavy on my shoulders. She wasn't a soldier; she wasn't one of Max's Marines. She'd been insistent; nothing new there, but I should never have allowed her onto that Ziu mother ship. This was on me.

I watched as Sonya's chest rose and fell in a slow and steady rhythm.

"Are you going to just stand there and watch me? Creepy comes to mind."

Her words had come out just above a whisper.

Her eyes fluttered open. "And King Kong over there, can't you find something for him to do?"

I took a seat at the side of her bed. "How do you feel, kid?"

She didn't answer right away, and I thought she might have fallen back to sleep.

"I feel like one of those monster Ziu fuckers pulled my arm off, then tossed me around like a big chew toy."

"I'm sorry, Sonya. This is my fault."

She turned her head just enough to look at me. She made a face. "Oh God ... you're getting all sappy and mushy. Hardy, find me a bucket; my uncle's making me want to ralph."

"Knock it off. I'm allowed to be worried about you. You gave all of us, gave me, quite a scare."

"Whatever... I'm fine. When can I get out of here? I need to check on the Symbios. Both Reggie and Sadon were injured."

Symbio-Poths were bio-robotic facsimiles of various Earth lifeforms. Produced by Empress Shawlee's incredible creative people—like an onboard modern-day Disney Imagineering team —they had originally created an entire group of townspeople on USS *Hamilton,* so real, so lifelike, it was virtually impossible to distinguish them from actual human beings. I momentarily flashed back to Lori and Carl Quintos, my Symbio parents within the mock town of Clairmont. Typically situated on a ship's upper R&R decks, over the years, that same creativity had evolved into recreational games such as Convoke Wyvern and Caveman Glory games and the subsequent creation of immense dragons, prehistoric dinosaurs, even tiny flying fairies. Needless to say, the crew, hell, I myself, had gotten more than a little attached to these seemingly all-too-real creatures. But just as I had put Sonya in harm's way, I'd been forced to utilize many of the Symbio-Poths for the defense of one ship or another. Just one more thing to weigh heavy on my shoulders.

Hardy said, "Ensign Plorinne's on top of all that. No worries in that regard."

She raised her head. "Where is Plorinne? He hasn't come to see me."

I wasn't thrilled with the budding relationship between the Pleidian Weonan twenty-something Ensign and my niece. But the two did seem to care for one another. Who was I to stand in the way of young love, if that was what this was? Hell, my own love life was nonexistent.

I said, "Visitors aren't allowed back here, Sonya."

"You're here... and so is Hardy."

"Yeah, well, I'm the captain."

Hardy said, "Nurses did put up a good effort trying to keep me out. But I'm a thousand-pound ChronoBot."

The door suddenly slid open. Doc Viv stood on the threshold. "What's going on here?"

Hardy said, "Captain said it was all right for me to visit."

I ignored the robot, "I was concerned... heard Sonya was out of surgery."

Looking exasperated, Viv held up a palm, displaying her Jadoo ring. "That's what these are for, right? You could have called."

As she moved farther into the compartment, Sonya's holographic health avatar popped into view above her bed. Viv leaned forward, her legs making contact with my own.

"Want me to move?"

"Uh... no, that's okay." She proceeded to review various meta-tag-like readouts, most of which were stemming from Sonya's surgery site.

Just then, oblivious to Viv, with wings fluttering, a tiny Symbio-Poth jetted into the small compartment. Sonya, Hardy, and I all took notice of it—the fairy now circling high above Doc's head.

I GLANCED OVER TO HARDY. This was a complicated situation. I knew this particular fairy was named Tina, a Symbio-Poth that had been one of a number of fairies on board *Adams*. Truth was, I couldn't keep them all straight. They were small, but each looked distinctively different. Hardy had had a budding relationship with the Symbio fairy called Iris. They had been inseparable. In fact, she had taken up residence in his front pocket, back when Hardy wore a too-small-for-his-size biker-style leather vest. Unfortunately, Iris was no more—had died while heroically fighting the Ziu. And while this Tina fairy had relentlessly tried to tell Hardy that she was actually Iris, inhabiting the Tina fairy form, Hardy had yet to accept her as... well, Iris. I told you it was a complicated situation. What can I say? At the moment, Hardy was refusing to look up at the still-circling Symbio fairy.

Viv looked down at Sonya, offering up a crooked smile. "You seem to be doing fine. Slightly elevated temperature, but that's to be expected."

"Good, then can I get out of here?"

"Ha ha, no. Ask me again in a week."

"A week! Seriously? I have to stay in this closet of a room for a week?"

"How about if we move you out to the general patient compartment sometime tomorrow? But only if you get some rest. And no more visitors." Viv gave me a disapproving sideways glance.

Sonya nodded, her eyes heavy-lidded. "I am getting a little tired."

"You heard her. Both of you, out!" Viv said, making a two-handed *scoot* gesture toward the exit.

I stood and gave Sonya's leg a couple of pats. "I'll come see you tomorrow."

But the teenager was already asleep.

I said to Hardy, "Head back to the bridge. I'll be along shortly."

Hardy looked from me to Doc Viv and then back to me again. "Oh... you want to talk. Like without me here. Like, just the two of you—"

"Go, Hardy," I said, not in the mood for any of the robot's antics.

Once Hardy had tromped out of the compartment, I turned to Viv. Before I could say one word, she held up a palm.

"I don't have time for this, Quintos. I told you my decision; nothing's changed." She tucked blonde curls behind one ear while looking uncomfortable. "You're just making things harder... being here."

"You know, we may never find a way to leave this place, this realm."

"You'll think of something. You always do. And when you do, I'm leaving. I can't do this anymore. Look at me; I'm holding on by a thread. The constant stress and tension, the injurie the death. I want to go home. I want to be back on Earth and have a normal life."

I tried to think of something to say. Something that would change her mind. Did she know how I felt about her? I wasn't sure. Would it make a difference? I was certain it wouldn't. I was losing her and there was nothing to stop that. She looked at me, the most beautiful, intelligent, compassionate woman I had ever met, and right now I was speechless.

Just as my Jadoo ring started to vibrate, an overhead klaxon began wailing.

Overhead, Sir Calvin's British voice boomed:

Captain Quintos, your immediate presence is required on the bridge.
Captain Quintos, your immediate presence is required on the bridge.

Chapter 3

Both Hardy and I quansported back to Deck 13 just outside the bridge. Overhead, a klaxon wailed. Sir Calvin was directing ship personnel to their battle stations.

Upon entering, I saw the bridgecrew standing, all eyes locked on the forward halo display. It seemed that distant lone ship had now decided to engage—if this was a friendly, or not so friendly meet and greet, only time would tell. Seeing her up close, the vessel was triangular, or wedge-shaped, bright white with a smooth, unblemished hull. There were no visible porthole windows, tubes or cable runs, junction boxes, or hatch door accesses; this ship was as pristine and aerodynamic-looking as any spacecraft I'd ever seen.

"Lieutenant James, sitrep!"

She glanced back over one shoulder. "No clear markings, and still no attempts to make contact. Best guess, by her size, she's probably a frigate-class warship. With that said, I'm not picking up any active targeting locks or weapons alerts."

"Bosun Polk," I said. "Sensor readings?"

"*Adams'* sensors are still not where they need to be... I'm not getting much of anything off that vessel. My initial assessment, she's far higher tech than we are. I'll continue scanning."

Reaching the captain's mount, I looked to Hardy, whose own internal sensors were as sensitive as any US Space-Navy vessel, if not more so. "You picking up anything?"

The ChronoBot remained quiet for several beats before answering. "Lifeforms, perhaps two hundred. Oh, and one more thing..."

We all waited.

"Skip the dramatics, Hardy, spit it out," I said.

"I believe they're human."

"Mr. Chen, open a channel... let's see if our human friends will accept our hail."

"Aye, Sir," Chen said.

"Mr. Grimes, be prepared to get us out of here fast."

"Helm is ready, Sir."

Chen said, "Our hail was accepted, Captain."

I nodded. "Let's see who we're talking to. On display."

The halo display flickered while an abundance of static made it impossible to see who or what was on the other end of the communication. I looked to Chen.

"I'm working on it, Sir..."

The halo display suddenly went crystal clear and there stood, in 3D splendor, a human military officer. Of average height, he looked to be in his mid-forties, had dark hair with graying at the temples, a five o'clock shadow, and a weary expression. He raised his chin as if assessing me—then he offered up a measured smile. He said, "You're from Earth."

"As are you," I said. "I am Captain Galvin Quintos of USS *Adams*."

"And I am Captain Church." He made a casual sweep with one hand. "This is the *Portent*."

"Please excuse my abruptness, but what are you doing here?"

"I imagine the same thing you are—attempting to return to our own universe," he said.

"How long have you been—"

"Marooned here? Quite a while. I suggest we meet in person, Captain. We, my science personnel and others, all being a hell of a lot smarter than I am, have made some progress..." He stopped talking, narrowed his eyes. "Um, excuse me, but is that... a ChronoBot there on your bridge, Captain Quintos?"

"It is. He is. But he's not your typical three-hundred-year-old killer robot."

Church continued to stare; he didn't look convinced.

Hardy chose that moment to activate his face display—typically blacked-out glass—going with a creepy-looking circus clown and a way-too-enthusiastic smile.

Akari, who only now took notice of Hardy, stifled a laugh. She looked to Captain Church. "Hardy has a unique sense of humor."

"A ChronoBot with a sense of humor. I'm not so sure that's any more comforting," Church said.

I shrugged. "Long ago I gave up making excuses for our idiot robot. Tell me, Captain, your ship, *Portent*, is that an EUNF vessel? Perhaps US Space-Navy—"

"If we could meet, Captain, get our scientists together, perhaps we can find a way out of here. The locals, as you've discovered, are not keen on our presence. It's just a matter of time before we're discovered by the next contingent of Ziu warships."

"Very well," I said, noting the captain's non-answer. "Please make preparations to come aboard."

The halo display went black, then *Boundless Wrath,* the once Varapin prisoner ship, popped into view. She didn't look much like a starship with her thick, somewhat stumpy-looking primary superstructure and eight outlying disk or saucer-shaped appendage constructs, each adjoined to the main body by a connecting arm. Once again, I took in the total mess of a design, one that perhaps had had numerous add-ons as more prisoner detention spaces were necessary.

"Sir, we're being hailed by Captain Loggins," Chen said.

Captain Loggins was not human, nor were most of his crew. They were Pleidian Weonan Symbio-Poths, referred to as 2.0s, who looked as human as any of my own crew.

The display changed to an internal feed of Loggins standing within the *Wrath's* bridge. With his perfect posture and perfectly pressed uniform, Captain Loggins got right to it, avoiding any pleasantries. "Captain Quintos, you have contacted the other vessel, no? Would you be so kind as to enlighten me on the status of the situation?"

I relayed the details of my brief chat with Captain Church, as well as the man's dodginess when it came to him providing any real specifics.

"What I do know is this Captain Church is as desperate to get out of this alternate universe as we are. Two hours from now, we will be bringing our smartest minds together to share ideas and, hopefully, come up with a viable proposal."

"I'll be there with my own team," Loggins said.

WHILE CAPTAIN LOGGINS and his team were quansported directly over to *Adams*, Captain Church and his contingent arrived via shuttle, where Bosun Polk was waiting for them within Flight Bay.

When I arrived within the captain's conference room, Coogong, Hardy, and a chubby, freckle-faced, ginger-haired man of about forty, I remembered as being Chief Grizwald from Engineering and Propulsion, were deep in discussion.

I cleared my throat. "I take it we're the first to arrive?"

Hardy looked to the entrance, holding up a chrome forefinger. "Wait for it..."

And at that moment the hatch slid open, revealing Captain Loggins, followed by a slight wiry man—correct that, a 2.0 who looked to be still in his teens—and Loggins' second-in-command, Commander F. Stanly, tall, bald, and expressionless. I'd forgotten just how much I disliked Stanly, but let it go.

The three of them entered and found seats around the large mahogany table. Captain Loggins said, "You know my second, Commander F. Stanly... and this is my science officer, Lieutenant Trevor Mandyport."

I shot Hardy a warning look; this was no time for him to make fun of a 2.0's name.

Bosun Polk entered the compartment, followed by the *Portent* team of just two, Captain Church and a short, barrel-chested man with a mullet. Polk was still in the process of describing *Adams*, how she had been a formidable US Space-Navy dreadnought, then, at the end of her multi-decade deployment, had been saved from the scrapyard by an investment group and converted to an opulent starliner, only then to be pulled back into service once more to fight the Grish and Varapin.

Church and the short, barrel-chested man took in the lavish, wood-paneled space, along with the glistening Waterford chandelier above. Their eyes hesitated on Hardy and then fell upon Coogong.

Coogong smiled back at them. A short, stick-figured Thine alien, he wore an oversized helmet—a helmet packed full of Ambiogell, the goo-like substance necessary for Thines to breathe. Just tall enough to see over the table, Coogong said,

"Hello, I am *Adams'* Science Officer... welcome. And, speaking for myself, I am encouraged by your presence here."

Church nodded. "Uh... thank you." He gestured to the man next to him. "This is Doogan."

Hardy said, "Just Doogan?"

The squat man bristled. "That's my name. You have a problem with that, tin-man?"

I interjected, "How about we get down to business, huh?"

Commander F. Stanly said, "Personally, I think this is a waste of time. We arrived here by a fluke of nature; it's not like we're going to be able to think our way back to our own reality. We're stuck here; best we come to terms with that."

Hardy said, "Go figure... who would have thought you'd be such a bright ray of sunshine."

I closed my eyes and let out a breath. Maybe this was a bad idea.

Captain Church said, "How about I relate what we've tried thus far?"

Loggins shrugged. "Sounds like a good place to start. I'm curious, when did you, *Portent*, arrive here?"

Church and Doogan exchanged a quick glance. Church said, "Uh, well, not so long before *Adams* and..." He looked over to Captain Loggins with raised brows.

"*Boundless Wrath*," Commander Stanly interjected.

Doogan said, "It's our assumption that our manufactured wormhole was corrupted, perhaps became unbalanced. This could occur due to a number of factors, such as gravitational distortions or the unintended influence of dark matter."

Coogong nodded. "We, too, have been examining the possible introduction of gravitational waves. Gravitational waves, ripples in the fabric of space-time that may have been generated by the acceleration of, say... a massive object, such as a colliding black hole or a neutron star. By analyzing the patterns of these gravitational waves, we can potentially identify the existence and location of these anomalies."

"I think we would have noticed a colliding black hole or a neutron star," Doogan spat, dismissing the idea with the wave of a hand.

"Ah, but you're assuming I'm referring to anomalies back within our own universe. I do not believe that is the case here. In this scenario, we will consider two universes, each with its own laws of physics and properties. For the purpose of explanation, let's call them Universe A and Universe B. According to the theory of quantum mechanics, particles can exist in multiple states or locations simultaneously. It is possible that in the vast expanse of space, a rare and brief fluctuation in the quantum fields of Universe A and Universe B could occur, causing the boundaries between the two universes to temporarily weaken and overlap. During this brief period of overlap, the laws of physics and properties of each universe would mix and merge, creating a unique and unfamiliar environment. However, since the overlap is only temporary, the two universes would eventually separate again, and each would return to its original state. The consequences of such a merging could be catastrophic or transformative, depending on the specific laws of physics and properties of each universe. It could result in the formation of new particles, the creation of strange energies, or the emergence of entirely new physical laws that were not previously observed in either universe."

I said, "So you're saying the cause of this—that colliding black hole or neutron star, whatever—could have been generated within another universe? How does that help us? If anything, that seems to make this conversation even more futile."

The room went quiet.

"What if there was a record... an imprint of the course of

events leading up to and including transitioning through the wormhole?" Chief Grizwald asked. The freckled-faced man looked to Coogong and then to Doogan questioningly.

Coogong said, "Sorry, I'm not following."

Grizwald said, "While each of our three vessels has advanced MATHR-type ship artificial intelligence, that ship technology does not measure concurrent wormhole anomalies, and perhaps more importantly, track extramural influences... mainly because much of that science is either misunderstood or beyond our current technological comprehension."

Commander F. Stanly said, "I repeat, this is a waste of time."

Hardy's faceplate was now a compilation of spinning animated gears. He placed a heavy hand on Grizwald's shoulder, momentarily causing the man to wince. "We don't need to understand the science, the physics behind the wormhole influences. That would be impossible, considering we have no idea where these influences were even derived from. All we have to do is repeat them and, if I'm catching Grizzy's train of thought, *Adams'* jump drive compensator circuits will have a record. That is, unless it has been overwritten."

Coogong's face became animated. "And to take that a step further, a comparison of each of our three vessels' drive compensator circuits should have congruence!"

**Captain Quintos, your immediate presence
is required on the bridge.
Captain Quintos, your immediate presence
is required on the bridge.**

Chapter 4

I hurried onto the bridge, seeing Akari was standing in front of the captain's mount and barking off orders. "Chen, hail Captain Ryder."

The halo display was segmented into three sections, each looking nearly identical to the other. I said, "Who the hell are they?"

"My gues scout fighters."

"Ziu again?"

Bosun Polk, back at her station behind me, said, "Probably, but I'm seeing different readings. Perhaps Ziu, but not from the same clan as our previous run-ins with them."

I counted no less than thirty small ships, all coming at us from three different directions.

Chen said, "I have Captain Ryder."

"... this better be important," came the groggy-sounding voice.

"Nap time's over, Ryder," I said. "We have incoming fighters. What's the status of our Arrows? Our pilots?"

"Both are beat to shit from our last engagement. Why not use plasma guns—"

"Adams' weapons systems are a mess right now; that and our munitions stock has gone critical. Add to the fact these scout ships are tiny and lightning fast ... we'll need to engage with them one on one."

"Cripes... copy that. I'm on my way to Flight Bay now. Just have Ballbuster rally the troops for me."

"Already done, J-Dog," Akari said.

Both were using their pilot call signs. I saw the flash of envy on Akari's face. She was as badass an Arrow pilot as Ryder was. I already knew she missed her days sitting in a cockpit—fighting the enemy face to face, skill set to skill set. A part of me missed that as well. My call sign had been Brigs. As a young Arrow pilot, I had been averse to following orders and ended up in a ship's brig on a number of occasions, thus the name Brigs stuck.

My Jadoo ring vibrated; I saw it was Hardy. "What's up?"

"Both of our visiting captains want to return to their respective ships to deal with the approaching fighters."

"Fine, escort them to the bay, have them shuttled back. But first see if they'll leave their science personnel here to keep noodling with you and Coogong."

"Shit!" Akari said under her breath.

I saw them too. A second wave of Ziu scout fighters was approaching, bringing the number closer to one hundred. "Where are they coming from? Are we picking up another mother ship?"

"No ... and that's strange in and of itself. But back to the present problem. *Adams'* shields are practically nonexistent, Captain. Just one more aspect to this universe making me flippin' crazy."

Bosun Polk said, "If we can manage a short jump, there's an asteroid field not too far from our current coordinates."

"Mr. Grimes?" I said.

"I've been working on doing just that, Captain. We're dealing with alternate spatial physics here."

"Uh... so, we'd be leaving *Wrath* and *Portent* here to fend for themselves?" Chen asked.

"Good point. Okay, forget jumping for now," I said, looking to Grimes. "But get us moving just as soon as we deploy our Arrows."

I took a seat at the captain's mount. "Bosun Polk, get that asteroid field's coordinates over to Helm... and Mr. Chen, let *Wrath* and *Portent* both know our intentions. Suggest to them they keep up, so as not to get left behind."

Akari said, "I'll let J-Dog and team know they'll be on their own for a while. I'll also deploy several comms drones so we can keep abreast of the battle."

CAPTAIN WALLACE RYDER hadn't changed his uniform in two days, nor had he brushed his teeth or showered. He might have slept an hour or two. His red-rimmed eyes burned; eyelids felt like sheets of sandpaper.

"J-Dog, you're clear for takeoff," came the bay chief's voice over comms. "Go take care of business ... and watch your six out there. Over."

"Copy that, Chief. Over."

Hovering five meters off the deck, Ryder maneuvered his Arrow into position before the opened Flight Bay doors. Separated by the bay's shimmering blue energy field, the distorted, star-filled space beyond held none of its usual allure for him. This place, this universe, was just ... wrong. His eyes scanned the multiple dash displays and readouts. Behind, several dozen Arrows scrambled, jockeying for position. Not one of them was in prime operating order. With the exception of being fueled, not one of them had gone through the necessary after-flight maintenance checks. This was looking to be one more cluster-fuck deployment.

Captain Wallace Ryder punched the throttle, the sudden g-forces like a mule kick to the chest. Breaching the energy field, he quickly banked left and straightened out. Looking over his left shoulder, he saw his squadron of bright Arrow fighters shooting out from *Adams'* flight bay like bright red spikes from a rail gun. At this moment, two other squadrons would be readying for rapid deployment.

Ryder was feeling his age. Wartime Arrow pilots already didn't have a long life expectancy. In his late thirties now, he was considered an old man, ancient, perhaps even past his prime. Maybe it was time he hung up his flight suit, joined Akari and Quintos on a ship's bridge. A crooked smile pulled at his lips. *Fuck that... I'm not giving this up, at least not today.*

He spoke into the open channel. "Bogies coming up fast, Deep-Throat. You're on my wing, Court Jester; get your team ready for a flanking run. Over." Ryder continued barking off orders just as he'd done a thousand times before.

A virtual wall of Ziu scout fighters was now upon them. They moved with precision, as if operating with one mind— which, undoubtedly, they were. Undoubtedly, somewhere, not so far away, was another Ziu mother ship.

Deep-Throat said, "Engaging the enemy. Over."

The exchange of plasma fire had begun. Bright red and blue bolts of energy splintered the darkness, leaving echoes of light trails in their wake. Intense and vibrant, the blur of combating fighters was cast in a colorful glow. Arrow and Scout fighters alike darted and weaved through the barrage, their drives spewing tongues of amber and blue fire as they maneuvered. Sound cannot travel in open space, but Ryder heard it just the same—weapons fire tearing into his Arrow's energy shields. A sharp crackle, punctuated by the occasional jolt as a bolt hit its mark.

His hands moved with practiced efficiency. His thumbs moved in a constant, rhythmic cadence as he fired on the enemy. "Got you!" he said, taking out one fast-approaching scout fighter —its fireball explosion momentarily blinded him.

Deep-Throat's voice crackled over comms. "I've got company, J-Dog. Can't seem to shake the motherfucker. Over."

"Copy that, Deep-Throat. I'm coming around on your port... be ready. Over."

Ryder punched it, pulling up into a quasi-barrel roll maneuver. Once again, g-forces had him straining to breathe. Below him he saw Deep-Throat jibbing and jabbing to avoid the scout's energy fire from behind. At just twenty-three, Deep-Throat, aka Dave Plant, was a younger version of himself. He lived to fly, had grown up knowing from a young age that this was what he wanted to do. He'd sacrificed to be here, as they all had. Dave was dating another of the Arrow pilots, Selleck something or other. Pretty, and just as crazy as Dave was. Some would say it was a match made in heaven, but Ryder knew better. He'd told Dave to enjoy the moments, live for the moments, because in this line of work, that was all he, all that all of them, really had.

"Coming around, Deep-Throat... on my mark, bank to starboard. Over."

Ryder fell in behind the scout fighter and was lucky enough to get a quick weapons lock, which was confirmed by the telltale triple beep. In that instant, that nanosecond before his thumb could depress the joystick's firing pad, Ryder saw that the Ziu fighter had fired first—Deep-Throat's Arrow exploded, an incredible fireball that Ryder was forced to fly into and through.

He gulped back shock—fought mind-numbing guilt and a momentary paralysis of total disbelief. *Oh God... Dave ...*

No time for this. Fight. I can grieve later.

Ryder blinked tear-filled eyes as the vicious exchange continued—fast and furious, fighters on both sides locked in a deadly dance.

Chapter 5

Alternate Universe
USS Adams

Major Vivian Leigh

Doc Viv made her way toward her quarters from HealthBay. She shook her head as if erasing pictures from an old-fashioned Etch-a-Sketch, trying to get rid of the horror of watching crewmembers—friends—dying. She hadn't made it to Julie in time, and her friend had died as a result. A myocardial infarction. Treatable—curable, in fact. But now she was dead. Viv would have to call Julie's husband and tell him he had lost his wife, and his two teenage sons had lost their mom.

She felt as if she were walking through quicksand, each step a Herculean feat. Her head was tilted down, its weight too heavy to carry upright. She noticed a familiar scuff on the lower bulkhead, a sign that her room was just a couple of steps away.

The hatch door slid open upon her approach, her shoulders softening as she stepped into her inner sanctum. As resplendent as her quarters were, the surroundings made her feel a tad uncomfortable. An ornate gilded mirror above the inlaid mahogany Edwardian dresser held her reflection. She looked despondent. Viv jerked away, unable to accept that version of herself.

She smelled the faint scent of sage and remembered one of the crew had gone through her quarters to rid the space of Varapin ghosts.

She looked at the impressive painting with the gold-laden frame.

Ghosts don't exist, so why bother with those kinds of shenanigans?

"Don't look at me like that." She scowled at the woman depicted in muted oils. The austere lady was wearing a frilly cobalt frock, giving her a Mona Lisa smile. "I know. I know. I need to get it together.

Actually, what I really need is some sleep.

Viv threw herself on her queen-sized bed, getting lost in the gold and crimson brocade comforter. Whoever had decorated her quarters had gotten the firmness of her mattress just right. Extra soft. The tightness in her body immediately began to loosen. Eyes closed, she moaned like a dog getting its belly rubbed. Drifting off, she pushed away horrific memories from HealthBay.

WHEN SHE AWOKE, she checked her Jadoo ring messages.

Good. Got some sleep. Three hours and thirty-two minutes. I'll take it.

She sat up, positioning herself at the edge of her bed. Rubbing sleep from her eyes, she looked down at her wrinkled green scrubs. Took in the splatters of dried blood and perspiration stains. She smelled of disinfectant and sweat.

I'm disgusting.

Viv sprang up, kicked off her sensible shoes and stripped, piling her dirty clothes in a heap. She moved into the well-appointed bathroom and stepped into the shower, setting the temperature to scalding. The water burned her alabaster skin, ridding it of all the grime and ugliness of the day. After ten minutes she shut off the water and got out of the stall. After toweling herself off, her pink skin was still flushed warm.

She grabbed a stock uniform from her closet—crisp white-collared shirt, stretchy blue slacks, and a narrow black leather belt. She slipped on ankle-high boots and made her way out of the bathroom to her writing table. The desk was Edwardian, like her dresser, intricately carved mahogany. The perimeter of the desk was inlaid with delicate leaves and fruit. Viv touched the veneer with her fingertips. The style was a bit fancy for her simple taste, but she admired the artistry.

She pulled up the matching chair and pressed the button on her tablet, enabling the halo display. She was obligated to get in touch with Julie's husband, but because they were in an alternate universe, that transmission would not be possible.

She also wanted desperately to reach out to her old friend, Griffin McKenna. He had called her a couple of weeks ago, and she was looking forward to continuing their talk.

Maybe I can look at past communications.

Viv scrolled her history and pulled up the last transmission she'd had with Griffin.

As the 3-D projection took shape, she assessed a man in his early thirties. Neatly groomed sandy hair, clean-shaven, and steel-blue eyes. He had a strong jaw that went hand in hand with broad swimmer's shoulders. The image was cut off mid-chest, but she could see the top of his perfectly pressed white doctor's coat. A gold-plated name tag read *Dr. Griffin McKenna.*

"Vivian, thank you for returning my message. It was wonderful to see you again. You look stunning... as always."

Viv felt her face get hot, as if hearing his compliment for the first time.

"I really hope you will consider my offer. My practice here in Missouri is growing. I think working together would be... well, something special." He flashed her that movie-star smile. "I know Baker, Missouri, is a far cry from your intergalactic travels, but it does have its charms."

Sounds pretty amazing right about now.

"It's a town of about five thousand folks. You wouldn't know anyone except me, of course. But as you recall, we used to get along pretty well."

She remembered perfectly. Griffin had asked her to marry him right after college. Viv had loved him; she was sure of that. But she had just finished medical school and was excited about her new career as a ship's physician. He wanted to practice medicine on Earth. It simply would not work. She found out that he'd married a local beauty queen, Rebecca Rayburn. They had only been married for three years when Rebecca's AirCar had collided with another AirCar, crashing to the ground, cart-wheeling three times before rolling down a steep embankment. Three weeks later, Griffin had made the agonizing decision to take his brain-dead wife off life support.

"Well, thank you for the compliment. Means a lot coming from you."

She remembered telling him he looked good.

I hope Griffin didn't think I was flirting with him.

Viv felt heat rise in her chest. She consciously tried to stop it from reaching her face. She wasn't sure why. She was alone, after all.

If she was honest with herself, she would admit that it felt good to be told she looked beautiful, that she was wanted. Valued.

"I'm thrilled you are open to the prospect of switching gears, downshifting, I suppose, in your medical career. But the truth is, if you do decide to give small-town life a try, you can always change it back and return to space."

Yes, I will come there, live a simple life. And no, I will not change my mind. I'm tired of watching my friends die. And I'm tired of waiting for Galvin.

She remembered experiencing the small town of Clairmont —Galvin's childhood home conjured up by Shawlee as a surprise to him. The townsfolk weren't really people, just Symbio-Poths, a striking facsimile of the real deal. The soda shop, Main Street, Galvin's boyhood friends... his parents. The memories stuck with her like the embrace of a close friend.

"All right, Vivian. I'm gonna let you go. Gotta check in on Mrs. Hayden's horse. I'm currently wearing different hats. Our veterinarian died a few weeks back. It's slow here but never boring, you know." Griffin gave her a dashing wink and signed off.

"See you soon, Griffin," Viv said aloud to the dimming 3D projection. She slumped back in her chair as the hologram dissolved into nothingness.

Chapter 6

Alternate Universe
USS Adams

Captain Galvin Quintos

To sun-like stars, like distant headlights, illuminated the spectacle before us. It wasn't like any asteroid field I'd ever encountered. Gone were the telltale jagged tumbling rocks and fine mist of space dust. I turned to look at Bosun Polk.

She continued to tap at her board, and a line formed between her brows. "What the..." she glanced up. "Not an asteroid field. What we have here is a recently destroyed world."

As our squad of three spacecraft approached, more detail became apparent on the halo display.

"Clouds?" someone commented.

Polk said, "Ship's sensors are detecting a field of debris composed of various minerals and compounds. No ready indication of what caused the explosion. But whatever it was, it caused the planet's crust to rupture and break into these large chunks.

This was a water world. Ocean waters have evaporated and expanded into the cloud vapor still visible around some of the larger chunks."

"It's beautiful," Akari said.

Moving closer still, we could see the mist had somewhat diffused, spreading out from the larger chunks of debris as they moved through space. The halo display feed zoomed in to the point we could see individual droplets of water sparkling in the sunlight, creating a shimmering halo around the debris field. As *Adams* continued forward, a sudden, brilliant prismatic rainbow effect radiated throughout the field of view. So beautiful, so spectacular was the visual spectacle, no one spoke; no one so much as took a breath.

A full minute passed before Polk spoke again. Perhaps in reverence for what they had all just witnessed, her voice was soft, just above a whisper. "Sensors are detecting the chemical composition of the vapor and have determined the amount of water and other gases that were released."

"What's that?" Grimes said, pointing to an area glowing white-yellow and amber.

"What's left of the world's core?" I said, looking to Polk for verification.

She nodded, letting out a breath. "Analyzing specific minerals and materials, I'm getting a better feel for things... for the composition of the original planet. The debris field contains a mix of silicates, metals, and other compounds that were part of the planet's crust, mantle, and core. Overall, I'm finding it diffi-cult to distinguish the readings from those of Earth if she, too, had been so violently... eviscerated."

I said, "Mr. Grimes, find us a substantial, uh, segment to position *Adams* and our two sidekick vessels."

"Aye, Captain."

"Mr. Chen, transmit our coordinates to Captain Ryder."

Several moments passed. "Sir, I'm not getting a response from J-Dog. But I'll keep trying."

My Jadoo ring came alive with the projected upper body of Hardy.

"We've made some progress, Cap. Maybe you can stop by; fellas here want to give you an update."

"On my way."

"You have the conn, Lieutenant James. Keep me informed."

I LEFT the bridge feeling the weight of that destroyed world on my shoulders. The parallel wasn't lost on me. Right now, at this moment, Earth, back within another parallel universe, was in jeopardy. The Grish and the Varapin were both intent on doing something similar, something that was beyond horrific, beyond devastating. And here I was—no longer doing my part, trapped in a place that I hadn't even known existed. Next, my mind flashed to Viv. Where was she at this moment? What was she doing? Had I already lost her to a life far less daunting and traumatic?

Entering the captain's conference room, my eyes were drawn to the group huddled at one end of the table and the lone individual at the other. Commander Stanly, chair angled back, looked relaxed with his feet up on the table, brooding; his eyes followed me.

Hardy, Coogong, Doogan, Chief Grizwald, and Science Officer Trevor Mandyport were in the midst of a boisterous conversation, with Doogan being the most vocal.

I said, "I hear we may have some progress."

Doogan's sneer almost made me laugh. He and Commander Stanly should start a club.

"We're nowhere near a resolution," Doogan said. "Too dangerous. Too untested."

I looked to Coogong.

"Mr. Doogan makes a valid point, Captain—"

"Just Doogan... not Mr. Doogan."

Coogong looked momentarily flustered.

"Just tell me where things stand," I said.

Hardy interjected, "It seems Mr. Doogan here lacks any semblance of a ball sac."

"Screw you, robot, my ball sac's plenty big; hell, it hangs so low I have to tuck it into my sock."

Science Officer Trevor Mandyport giggled at that while Chief Grizwald simply shook his head.

"Seems I've wandered into a middle school gym class." I turned back to Coogong. "Please tell me what you've come up with, along with all the pros and cons."

From the other end of the table, Commander Stanly said, "I'm with Doogan on this one."

"Really? You also don't have a ball sac?" Hardy said.

"Knock it off! Coogong, just talk over them if you have to."

"Yes, Captain. Well, many of our conclusions come from Chief Grizwald and his earlier premise that *Adams'* drive compensator circuits should have a kind of rendering—not so much a data record, but an actual imprint of external gravitational as well as dark matter influences over that specific span of time while we were traversing that manufactured wormhole."

"Remember, *Adams* jumped while within that wormhole... that may have triggered or influenced the overlapping of one or more alternate universes," Hardy added.

Doogan said, "We were just about to evaluate *Adams'* drive compensator circuits. No use speculating until we know if the imprint still remains or if it's been overwritten."

Coogong was fiddling with the conference table's control panel. "One moment, please."

A large spherical 3D halo display suddenly took shape

above the center of the table. Coogong continued to tap and eventually what looked like a zoomed-in segment of a curved metal cylinder came into view.

"Ah, this is the specific area of the physical compensator that corresponds to the time frame."

It was difficult to make heads or tails of what I was looking at. It looked like faint scorch marks of various sizes, or better said, amplitudes. A virtual microscopic mountain range.

"How do you decipher—"

"Hold your horses, Cap," Hardy said.

Coogong, tapping again, now had a secondary layer superimposed onto the mountain range, a kind of data chart with lines and corresponding numbers.

"And I thought this looked complicated before," I said.

Eventually, Coogong looked up at me. A broad smile formed on his worm-like face. "Captain, I am confident I can accurately duplicate these same external influences."

I looked to Hardy, Chief Grizwald, and then the doomsayer, Doogan. Even he was nodding his head.

"How long will it take you to prepare?"

"One hour," Coogong said with confidence.

"What about *Wrath* and *Portent*?"

"The same process we just went through will need to be followed. I expect positive results on both accounts."

I nodded. "Good work, all of you. Best you get to your respective engineering department. Let's get to work."

The halo display flashed with a new feed; it was Akari's projected image coming from the bridge. "Captain, Arrows are returning to *Adams*. There have been substantial losses."

I remembered that Chen had been having trouble contacting Captain Ryder.

Chapter 7

As I paced at the front of the bridge, irritated, my temperament was like a simmering volcano; with each passing moment the pressure was building, building, building, to the point I was ready to erupt.

"What the hell is taking so long?"

No one dared speak.

I stopped, took in a breath, and let it out slowly. Taking in the bridge, I saw my crew suddenly looked away, went back to their boards—I almost laughed.

Akari said, "Not to stoke the fires, Sir... but we have three armadas closing in on our position."

"Armadas?"

She made a pained expression. "Hundreds of ships... warships, not just scout fighters this time."

"Bring us to battle stations," I said, heading for the captain's mount.

Overhead, Sir Calvin's voice boomed; a klaxon blared.

Chen said, "Both *Wrath* and *Portent* are requesting—"

"Tell them to sit tight and not to engage the enemy. At least not until I give the order."

The halo display segmented, allowing us to better see the individual armadas. "Damn, they're moving fast."

Hardy's voice to my right made me jump. "You thought a dreadnought-class vessel such as *Adams* was difficult to detect?"

"One can only hope," I said. "How long?"

"We have about five minutes before we're in firing range," Hardy said. "We could try making a run for it."

Without looking back at us, Akari said, "*Wrath's* as slow as cold molasses. Unless we leave her here—"

"Not an option, Lieutenant James," I said. "How are we doing with our rail spike replications?"

"We've had some logistical setbacks, but it's coming along. But we don't have munitions in nearly enough quantities for what's, um, coming for us."

"On a positive note, our big Phazon Pulsar cannons should all be operational soon," Hardy said.

"Mr. Chen, get me Bay Chief Mintz."

Background audio from the halo display made everyone jump. Chief Mintz looked harried and annoyed. Behind him was a kind of traffic jam of returning Arrow fighters. "Not a good time to chat, Captain."

"Well, fucking make time," I snapped back.

The older man blanched, "Sorry, Sir. It's... it's not good."

"Give me your best-guess assessment of our space force."

The man shook his head, partially turned, and gestured with a hand toward several nearby hovering Arrows. Like polka dots, blackened scorch marks dappled the craft hulls. "We lost a third of our Arrows during that last run, Captain. But many of those that have returned are fucktipated, excuse my French."

Akari had already told me as much earlier. But seeing the condition of the Arrows for myself only drove the point further home.

"How many craft are still operational? Battle ready?"

Bay Chief Mintz looked flabbergasted. He looked as if he wanted to tell me to go screw myself. "Maybe thirty, if we can get them fueled. But you'd need to find pilots that are actually flight ready."

"Get those Arrows fueled and readied for action. I'll find you the pilots."

The display blinked back to the oncoming armadas. I inwardly gasped. One of the armadas was almost upon us. There must have been fifty warships; some were dreadnought class as large as *Adams*.

"We're so fucked," came from someone behind me.

"Incoming!" Akari exclaimed. "Looks like twenty-five or so scouts coming to check us out." She looked at me. "They're approaching slowly."

"Once in range... Phazon Pulsars. Take them out."

She smiled and nodded, but before she could complete her orders, the halo display erupted in bright weapons fire.

"*Boundless Wrath* is firing on the enemy!"

"And doing so quite effectively, I might add," Hardy said.

Akari said, "That might have bought us a little time. I wouldn't count on much, though."

But I was already heading for the exit. "Lieutenant James, you have the conn."

I ARRIVED outside of HealthBay moments later, having quansported down to Deck 12. Entering HealthBay, I saw it was a madhouse of activity. Nurses, doctors, and MediBots were attending to the injured and dying. Every bed was filled; temporary field cots had been set up along the bulkheads for the overflow. In my haste to find even marginally healthy enough pilots, I'd discounted the extent of what these pilots had endured. Only now was I hearing the moans, the not-so-subtle cries for help. As I moved about the compartment, one young pilot reached out a hand, grabbing my forearm. "We got them, Sir... every last one of them."

Looking down at him, I saw that half of the man's face was blackened, charred beyond recognition. He'd been struck by an energy blast. How he'd survived the deep space atmospheric decompression, I had no idea. I saw his name below his revolving health avatar.

"Good job, pilot. Fine good job." I patted his shoulder. "Rest now... I'm proud of you, Lieutenant Craig."

I tried to move on, but the man was still grasping my arm.

"He's dead, Quintos," came a soft voice at my side. Doc Viv gently pried the pilot's fingers from my sleeve. She lowered the man back onto his bed, turned and barked off orders to a passing MediBot. "Have this body transferred to the morgue. Strip the bed for the next patient.

She turned to face me. Several blonde strands of hair had come free from her scrub cap. She impatiently swiped at them. "What are you doing here?"

"What do you mean what am I—"

"You're looking for flight-capable pilots, aren't you?" She shook her head. "You're really something, you know that? Well, take a good look. Tell me, who are you going to take? How about Madison over there? He's only lost an arm. Or how about Perkins over there in that far bed? He's quasi-brain-dead, but what the hell, he's still breathing."

"Cut him some slack, Viv," came a familiar voice behind me. "He has an impossible job. He's trying to save his ship, his crew."

Captain Wallace Ryder stood there. One arm was in a sling; his left ear was bandaged. He attempted a smile. "Come to check on me sweetheart."

Viv cursed under her breath and stormed off.

"She's right," I said. "My intentions are self-serving here."

"Yeah, well, you've always been an asshole. Think it comes with the job. Let me help make you even less popular. My totally un-medical opinion tells me we have ten, maybe twelve, pilots ready to be released soon. I've been ordered to my quarters for rest and recuperation. How's it looking in Flight Bay?"

I looked about HealthBay and then back to my friend. "Honestly? Not so different than here."

"Yeah, we've taken it in the shorts. I get that, Quintos. But we've been right here before. We'll come out of this—"

"I don't need a pep talk, Ryder. What's waiting for us beyond the remnants of that destroyed world is far more than a few Ziu scout ships. Go to your quarters, follow Viv's directives, and get some rest." I squeezed his shoulder and headed for the exit. Across the compartment, I momentarily caught Viv's eye. She looked away.

My Jadoo ring vibrated. Without looking at it, I said, "Go for Captain."

"Captain, I believe we have it worked out."

I stopped outside in the corridor. "Go on, Coogong."

"I believe we're ready..."

"You'll have to be more specific. Ready for what?"

"To jump us out of here, Captain. To return us to our own universe."

I had a lot of questions. What were the odds of success? What about *Wrath* and *Portent*? How long would it take to get things going? But instead of wasting even a moment's time, I said, "Where are you?"

"I'm on the bridge, Captain. We're all on the bridge."

"On my way."

.   .   .

HAVING JUST QUANSPORTED, I literally sprinted into the bridge. "Sitrep!" I barked, now seeing not only Coogong but also Captain Loggins and Captain Church.

Akari said, "We've been busy." She looked to Coogong to take it from there.

The Thine scientist glanced to Church and Loggins and raised his stick-figure hands, conveying I should slow down and take a breath. "The not-so-good news first. Both *Wrath's* and *Portent's* drive compensator circuits have been, for lack of a better way of putting it, overwritten."

I looked to Church and Loggins. Neither looked overly concerned. *Okay.*

Coogong continued, "With that said, *Adams* will have to make the jump for all three vessels. Together, we will make the... maneuver."

The ship suddenly shook to the point I had to reach out for the captain's mount armrest. "What was that?"

Akari said, "That would be *Boundless Wrath* cozying up to our starboard side. *Portent* is already on our portside. Mooring clamps have been secured. For all intents and purposes, we are now one ship."

I was impressed and a tad speechless.

Hardy said, "Understand, this might not work. We might tear apart from one another; we might have miscalculated things..."

"Uh ... Captain?" Grimes said from his helm station. He gestured toward the halo display. "The three armadas are moving again."

"Standing around here jabber-jawing isn't getting us anywhere," Captain Church said.

Captain Loggins nodded. "What is it you humans like to say—we're burning sunlight?"

Hardy corrected him, "That's burning daylight. But I'm more partial to the phrase 'we need to shit or get off the pot.'"

I looked at the approaching vessels. "How do we do this?"

"Everything's ready," Coogong said. "We need a bit of open space, a kind of runway to reach adequate jump speed. The manufacturing of a wormhole has already been programmed into the ship's AI."

The halo display reoriented to show grid lines, a virtual runway between large clumps of the destroyed world. I said, "Do I want to know what the odds of success are?"

No one answered me.

"Let me put it this way. Are the odds with insufficient ammo and Arrow pilots better than going up against three Ziu armadas?"

The response was unanimous. "Yes!"

I said, "Helm, swing us around and get us moving. I guess we're going to jump."

"Shit! Incoming! Captain, smart missiles inbound," Akari said, tension in her voice. "God, they're fast." She looked to Grimes. "Get us moving! Now!"

Chapter 8

I t was rare to see Coogong sitting at a console on the bridge, but here he was; even with his seat raised as high as it would go, the Thine scientist was on his knees, leaning over the console's control board. Grimes had relinquished all Helm control to Coogong. All of their fates were in the small alien's twig-like hands. The halo display was our only reference for what was happening—our three-conjoined-spacecraft monstrosity tearing through local space at incredible speeds, coming way too close to various-sized chunks of the destroyed world. For the umpteenth time I had to remind myself to trust Coogong, to have faith ... *And if I can't?* Well, we'd be screwed either way, with the Ziu fast on our heels.

Coogong said, "Ship's AI is manufacturing our wormhole in three, two, one!"

And there it was, several thousand kilometers in front of us. The spatial aberration's yawning open mouth just now forming. Stabilizing.

Akari directed my attention to a secondary feed, one that showed our relative position to that of the quickly advancing Ziu missiles. I said, "Coogong, why are we slowing?"

Coming up through the deck plates, I'd actually felt our drive vibrations reduce. Seeing the feed only confirmed my assumptions.

"Captain, we must duplicate the *Adams'* speed exactly as when we approached that wormhole prior to arriving here." He glanced at the feed, and I saw apprehension on his worm-like face. He said, "Those incoming missiles are out of my control. Do not attempt to fire on them. Any fluctuation, even by a fraction of our rate of speed could be... well, catastrophic."

I raised my palms. "This is your show, Coogong."

Overhead, Sir Calvin's British voice began a countdown. "Ten... nine... eight..."

I knew the plan was to jump the three ships at a precise moment, right into the mouth of that quickly approaching wormhole, just as *Adams* had done previously. But my confidence in the whole process was giving me pause. This was little more than an unproven experiment—an experiment where there would be no redos, no second chances. Was I really willing to risk the lives of these crewmembers all on Coogong's best-guess hunch?

"Five... four... three..."

The Ziu missiles were almost upon us. This was happening. "Two... one..."

Adams, *Portent*, and *Boundless Wrath* jumped. I closed my eyes. I held my breath.

The ship shook violently, and I was thrown to the deck; I heard a series of loud *clangs* and *bangs*. Someone yelped. Someone else cursed. The overhead crystal chandeliers swung and musically clinked like the highest piano notes.

Realizing I'd bonked my head, I brought fingertips to my forehead; they came away bloody. Those around me were getting to their feet. I felt strong hands helping me up—it was Hardy.

"You took quite a tumble there, Cap."

"I'm fine. How'd you stay on your feet?"

"Internal stabilizing servos. That and I grabbed for your captain's mount."

One glance told me the robot had severely bent and distorted the left armrest.

"That's coming out of your pay," I said, deadpan.

"Wait ... I'm supposed to be getting paid?"

Looking about the bridge, I saw the others situating themselves at their respective stations.

"Situation report. Where are we?" I looked to where Coogong had been sitting, but it was now just an empty chair. "And somebody find Coogong."

"Uh, here he is," Grimes said, bent over, looking beneath an adjacent console. With the helmsman's help, Coogong got to his feet. We all saw it—the Thine alien's helmet had a serious vertical crack running down the middle. That, and it was leaking Ambiogell goo.

"I got this," Hardy said, hurrying over to Coogong. In two long strides the ChronoBot swept Coogong up into his arms. A moment later, the two were hurrying off the bridge. Where Hardy had taken Coogong, I had no idea.

Tapping at her board, Akari answered my original question. "I have no idea where we are." She looked at me. "Most definitely not where we were... not in that same universe. If we're home, we'll need to reconfigure our sensors back to be sure."

Grimes said, "From a navigation standpoint, Captain... I have no reference for this star system. What I can tell you is EUNF US Space-Navy's celestial database is coming up blank. I do have a rough idea of what direction home is."

I looked to Bosun Polk, who shrugged. "I've got nothing for you, Sir. I can deploy a comms relay. Would increase our chances of making contact with the fleet."

"Yes, make that happen." I stared at the halo display. "Seriously... we're back inside another asteroid field?"

"Technically, we weren't in an asteroid field prior—"

I cut Akari off with a stare.

"Sir, your head. That's quite a gash you got there. If I may suggest, a few minutes in HealthBay would be a good idea."

"Thank you, Lieutenant, but I'm fine." I looked up. "Sir Calvin, damage assessment?"

Damage is minimal. *Adams'* restraining clamps 4, 7, and 9 on the portside are fractured. *Portent* has minor damage to their outer hull.

I waited for more, but none came.

Bosun Polk said, "We have injuries, Captain, but nothing all that serious being reported by HealthBay." She looked up. "A few sprained wrists and ankles," she chinned back at me, "... bonks to the head."

Hands on hips, I stared at the halo display. All seemed to be quiet. No incoming missiles, no alien ships.

"Captain?" Akari said.

I said, "Can the bridgecrew reconfigure our sensors back to normal?" Of course, I already knew the answer to that.

"Well... yes, I already said we can—"

"No. Not you, Lieutenant James, them," I said, gesturing to the others.

"Uh, I guess so," she said, looking both a little confused and hurt.

"How would you like to join me in a little spin around the neighborhood? I'm sure we can find a couple of Arrows still operational."

With a broad smile, she jumped to her feet. "Reconnaissance, right? Who needs operational sensors when two of *Adams'* finest officers can observe for themselves and make a situational assessment?"

It was close to an hour before Lieutenant James and I, along with one more very insistent *Adams* officer, Captain Wallace Ryder, were situated within our respective Arrows and waiting for clearance to deploy out into local space.

Was it wise for the ship's commanding officer to be venturing out into the great unknown? Definitely not. But I needed this, as did Akari.

The bay chief's voice came over comms, clearing us for deployment.

"Ballbuster, how about you take us on out of here. Over."

"With pleasure, Brigs. Try to keep up, old man."

And with that, a flame ignited from Akari's Arrow's aft drive, and like a bullet, she shot forward, breaching the bay's energy field. I heard Ryder chuckle over the open channel, then he too was following in her wake.

Feeling my heart rate increase in anticipation, I pulled back on the controls, felt the familiar g-force kick to my chest, and yelled out a hoot and a holler that brought me back to my early days at the academy.

Chapter 9

Captain Gail Pristy

G ail Pristy stood under the hot water, letting it pummel the muscles in her slim, strong legs and back. Being a captain came with too many responsibilities, but at least she had unlimited shower time, and today, she needed it. She'd been getting out of shape. After recent events, she'd ordered her ship's Marines to change that. They'd gleefully developed a program of running, strength training, and hand-to-hand combat that was enough to leave her aching. It did far worse to the others she'd dragged in with her: Stephan Derrota, Dr. Patty Kline, and Superintendent LaSalle. Petty Officer *Second*-Class Aubrey Laramie, twenty-two, incredibly fit, and too damn tall, took it in stride. That irritated the hell out of Pristy, especially since this whole mess was Laramie's fault.

She turned, letting the water hit her aching chest and arm muscles. Bad enough that she and her ship, USS *Hercules*, were babysitting an oversized gas station. *Sanctuary* was the only vehicle that could refuel USS *Oblivion*, once under Quintos's command. He'd given the ship up to protect a planet, if reports were true, which meant she was sitting out here for nothing. Worse, she had to do it in the Lonestar System, which hung on the ass edge of the galaxy and featured eight black holes revolving around each other in perfect synchronicity. And worst of all, now she was a time-traveling secret agent, thanks to Petty Officer then-*First*-Class Laramie.

Aubrey Laramie was obsessed with hunting, and when she went planet side, she'd snuck out to see what she could kill. Turned out it was everyone, because Laramie had brought a deadly virus back from her excursion. Or it would have been, except for General Clive Resnick, time traveler for the Grand Consortium.

They'd called General Resnick for help as the disease started spreading. Resnick gave Pristy a choice: become a Consortium agent and go back in time to stop Aubrey from getting the virus or die. Given Resnick's attitude, the second option had been tempting, but it wasn't just her own life she was playing with. So she'd done it, and discovered time travel was ridiculously complicated. They couldn't land in the same place twice, couldn't let Laramie see them, couldn't do anything that might affect other parts of the timeline. Worse, damn near everything they tried didn't work.

A shudder started at the base of Pristy's spine. She stuck her head under the steaming water, hoping to block her memory of the wild boars, called Cruggs, tearing Laramie to shreds with their foot-long tusks. Pristy and Resnick had to go back before the Crugg stampede and save her. Resnick had borrowed Bucephalus, Alexander the Great's warhorse, and Sergeant Reckless, a famous packhorse from the Korean War, for an old-fashioned roundup. Pristy smiled, remembering Resnick's face when she'd mounted Bucephalus and proved she was a far better rider than him. The two of them had redirected the stampeding Cruggs and stopped Laramie from killing everyone.

All it cost was Pristy's freedom, and the freedom of Derrota, LaSalle, Dr. Kline, and Petty Officer Second-Class Aubrey Laramie—Pristy had taken the first opportunity to bust the woman down a rank for her stupidity. It made Pristy feel better but didn't change the reality: all five of them were on call whenever Resnick needed someone to jump through time.

Which is going to be when? Pristy turned her face into the spray. Last we saw, the brass was pissed at Resnick.

In fact, the grand council of the Grand Consortium sounded furious with the man when he'd spoken to them. Given that he'd lost an entire ship and crew—not destroyed, she'd learned, but actually missing—it didn't surprise Pristy that they'd been pissed. General Resnick had spent the better part of an hour trying to persuade them to give him a new vessel. The man had used every tactic from logical arguments to outrageous flirting, but nothing worked. The grand council had simply told him to wait. They'd been smug about it, too, like they had a secret they weren't ready to tell. Which was probably true, since they regulated time travel.

No point in worrying about it. Eyes closed, Pristy shut off the water and opened the cubicle door. She reached for the towel by memory and dried her face as she stepped out of the shower. *I can stretch and sleep six hours in a row if nothing goes to shit.*

"Captain!" Resnick said. "We've got to go."

He ducked, and the bar of soap she'd thrown only grazed his military-short black hair. Impressive, considering the bathroom wasn't that big, and he was a good-sized target: six feet tall, well-muscled without being bulky, and like the last time she'd seen him, wearing black fatigues.

She held her towel in front of her, yelling. "What in the HELL do you think you're doing?"

"Saving the universe. Get dressed."

"Screw you!" Pristy barked, wrapping her towel tight around her body and tucking it in. It wouldn't stay up long, but long enough to break a knee if he didn't explain himself.

"We're also rescuing Galvin Quintos, the crew of *Adams,* and what's left of your captured shipmates," Resnick said, stepping out the bathroom door. "But we'll need the whole team, so get them together and meet me on the surface."

"Freeze!" she barked, using the voice that scared her deck officers. "No one goes anywhere until you explain what is happening here. Now talk. And face the wall until I'm dressed."

"Not how you speak to a superior officer," Resnick said, turning his back to her. "And for the record, I was aiming for your room, not your shower."

"Yeah, I'm sure." Pristy stomped out of the bathroom to her dresser. She grabbed clean, combat-worthy underwear, as well as her own black fatigues and boots. She yanked on the underwear, saying, "Talk."

"You haven't heard from Captain Quintos," Resnick said, staring at the wall, "because USS *Adams* went to another universe and ran into a nasty species called the Ziu. Giant bugs with mouths for feet. Hell of a firefight, but they eliminated a hive."

"Back it up," Pristy said, pulling her sports bra on. "What do you mean, another universe?"

"There are multiple universes," Resnick said. "Did you not take physics?"

"I know there are multiple universes," Pristy snapped. "How did they end up in one?"

"You want the two-hour lecture with the chalkboard, or the short explanation?"

"The short." You overbearing jackass.

"Something got fucked on a quantum level and when USS *Adams* and *Boundless Wrath* opened wormholes, they tore the fabric between universes and ended up somewhere else."

"And somehow they've unfucked it and come home?" Pristy asked as she pulled up her fatigues and buckled her belt.

"Not yet. *Adams* and *Boundless Wrath* returned to our universe one month from now. When they did, they ended up in one of the worst places they could. Aliens captured both ships, tortured their crews, and found enough information in their databases to launch a massive invasion."

"They're all dead?" The blood drained from Pristy's face. "No, wait, you said a month from now, they all die. How do you know?"

"Because I just checked three months in the future," Resnick said. "One billion casualties, and attacks on all human space and all our allies."

"Shit." She pulled on her shirt. "So what's the plan?"

"First, we get to the timeship and coordinate their actions with ours."

Pristy sat on the bed to put on her boots. "I thought the council wasn't giving you a timeship."

"They didn't," Resnick said. "*Portent* returned with *Adams* and *Wrath*. Remember how the council wouldn't give me a new timeship? The smug bastards knew it was coming back. Problem is, now that *Adams* and *Wrath* have seen the *Portent,* it can't just bug out. It has to wait until things resolve. So get your team together, because we need to rescue everyone. Fast."

Chapter 10

Liquilid Empire Star System
USS Adams

Captain Galvin Quintos

The asteroid field was a sea of isolated islands, big, slowly tumbling rocks, some the size of a building back on Earth, some as large as a small moon. With Akari at the pinnacle of our three-Arrow formation, we moved as one unit. Getting a feel for just how massive this field was, I realized we needed help and had Ryder call back to *Adams* for those pilots that were physically able; several more squads needed to be deployed.

We kept our comms chatter to a minimum as we swerved and dodged the celestial masses. Keeping an eye on my Arrow's sensor readings, I saw there were no signs of life, no indications of advanced technology—no alien scan pings, no distant weapon locks. I suspected we were in as remote a location as I'd ever been. Perhaps we were the first intelligent life to have ever entered this section of deep space.

That's when I saw it. A reflective glimmer of light and then it was gone. A tiny blip of illumination as we flew past one of the medium-sized asteroids. It could easily have been my imagination.

"Did either of you see that? Over."

"See what, Brigs? You catch sight of little green men? Maybe it was Big Foot in a space suit. I'm convinced we're *it* out here... all alone within the farthest reaches of space. Over," Ryder said.

"Yeah, it was just a glimmer... maybe a reflection off... something. Over," I said.

"Let's check it out," Akari said. "Take point, Brigs. Show us your glimmer of light. Over."

I moved into the point position and banked hard to port around an asteroid. Coming around it to the other side, I straightened out and slowed. "It was somewhere around here. Maybe that baby moon–sized rock up ahead. We should have a better view from this perspective—"

And there it was.

"Holy Mother of God," Ryder said.

"That's some glimmer of light, Brigs," Akari added.

I was beyond tongue-tied. It was a ship. Big. Dreadnought class for sure, and it was US Space-Navy. I recognized her profile immediately.

"Looks to be adrift. Dark... no running lights. Sensors not picking up much of anything—well, maybe some rudimentary active circuits. Okay, I'm now picking up... something. Over," Akari said.

Hardy's voice joined the open-channel conversation. He must have been listening in, back on *Adams*.

"I've been thinking I should have a callsign... How about Quicksilver? Or Metalman? Maybe—"

"Enough. You're not getting a callsign," I said. "What can you tell us about this ship?"

We had now come full circle around the vessel and were starting our second.

"She's not an old ship, ten, eleven years old at the most. As you can see, looks nothing like our typical elongated *Hamilton* Class Dreadnought. This particular vessel, a highly advanced prototype, supposed to be the first of an entirely new class of spacecraft, is one that went missing some eight years ago. This, my friend, is the long-lost, thought to have been destroyed by the Grish, EUNF's USS *Lincoln*."

Feeling exhilarated, taking in her sleek, bird-of-prey-like lines, I said, "The SpaceWing. Oh yeah, I've heard of her. Over."

"Me too," Ryder said. "Believe she was one of a kind. Never went into full production. Over."

Akari brought up the most relevant question. "So, what happened to her? She looks to be in prime condition, not so much as a scratch or blemish to her hull. Over."

"She's been well protected by this monster-sized asteroid," I said. "I'm still in disbelief we found her. Over."

"No," Ryder said. "You found her, Brigs. Maritime and celestial rules apply when it comes to finding long-lost abandoned ships—finders keepers, losers weepers. Over."

"Hardy, what else can you tell us—"

"I'm going with Quicksilver. Over."

I dragged a palm down my face. "Fine, Quicksilver, what else can you tell us about this vessel? We'll need to access her somehow."

"Captain, this is Bosun Polk. Just an update... sensors are working again, and a full sweep shows no other vessels, living beings, or movement, for that matter, in the area. Except for that warship you found, wherever we are, we're alone. Bad news:

Adams' Quansporter is down. Coogong's trying to figure out why. Over."

"Copy that, Bosun. Concentrate in-depth sensor sweeps on USS *Lincoln* here. Ready an away team with full battle suits. We should probably get Max and team involved. Over."

"Roger that, Sir. Out."

With Hardy seated at the controls, the others had been filing into the old beat-to-shit *Hub Gunther* over the last ten minutes or so. Larger than a shuttle and more equipped for battle if necessary, the old mining craft seemed to follow Quintos's crew from ship to ship. Like a loyal old dog, she might not have a lot of pep in her step these days, but she was true and steadfast.

Sergeant Max Dryer plopped down next to Hardy in the copilot's seat, while the rest of the Marines, Wanda, Grip, Ham, and Hock, settled into the seedy and threadbare seats behind. All wore combat suits, their helmet faceplates retracted.

"Smells like an old shoe in here," Wanda said from behind.

Hardy looked to the still-open hatch. "We expecting others?"

Max shook his head. "No. We have Sonya coming along virtually via our helmet comm links."

Hardy attempted a shrug and looked back at Grip. "Someone left the barn doors open."

Grip made a face. Big and ridiculously muscular, the African American Marine glowered back at him. "What you talking about, robot?"

Wanda said, "He means you're closest to the hatch. He wants you to shut it."

"Why didn't he just say that?" he said, getting up and

closing the hatch door. "What kind of rickety tin can is this that you have to manually close a hatch, anyway?"

Almost immediately there was a pounding on the hatch.

Everyone looked to Grip, who had just sat down again.

"Motherfucking tin can." He got back up and opened the hatch. Standing there were three ship-wide maintenance personnel, each holding a combat suit. Grip stared back at them blank-faced. "Uh, we're all set, boys. Kitted up with our own suits. Step away, need to shut the hatch."

"No! Wait, these are for the pilots," one of the SWM guys said.

Looking irritated, Grip glanced to Hardy and back to the three again, "Our pilot's a fucking robot; even if he needed a suit, which he doesn't, you'd never find one big enough. Now step the hell back!"

Max said, "Let them in, Grip. Those are for the captain, Akari, and Ryder."

Realization spread across Grip's face. "Oh, okay." He stepped out of the way so the three could enter. "Chop chop, you can drag your asses later when you're slopping a mop, not now."

Once the three had deposited the suits and left, Grip slammed the hatch shut and took his seat. "Can we go now?" he grumbled.

TEN MINUTES LATER, using the coordinates supplied by the captain, Hardy piloted *Hub Gunther* to within several hundred meters of the seemingly lifeless SpaceWing dreadnought.

"Will you look at that?" Max said. "She's a beauty."

"Yeah, a beauty," both Ham and Hock, the twins, parroted in unison.

The *Hub Gunther's* comms crackled. "You bring the suits,

Hardy? Over," came the captain's voice. "There's no telling if the ship still has atmosphere. Or what contaminants are present if it does."

"Quicksilver. And that's an affirmative on the suits, Cap."

"You've studied the ship schematics, I take it. We need to open up *Lincoln's* flight bay. Over."

A two-foot-tall 3D projection suddenly took shape upon the forward console. Sonya, sitting up in her hospital bed, one shoulder heavily bandaged, said, "The ship is in slumber mode. As if it was moored within a space dock for repairs. You won't be able to open the bay doors remotely."

Everyone just stared at the goliath-sized vessel.

"Well, that's embarrassing," Hardy said.

Captain Quintos audibly huffed. "Sonya, please tell us there's a workaround."

"Of course there is. All you have to say is I'm amazing and you'd all be up shit creek without a paddle without me."

"You're amazing. Now tell us how to do this. Over."

"The big problem is power. While *Lincoln's* in slumber mode, nothing is working other than the bare-bare-bare minimum ship-wide functions. Functions that do not include opening and closing the massive flight bay doors. Hardy, you'll have to make a spacewalk. Along the outside hull of the *Gunther* is a utility locker. Inside, if nobody's nicked it, there should be an intra-ship jack cable."

"Say no more, young girl wonder. I've got this," Hardy said, getting to his feet. He looked about the cabin. "I suggest you all close your helmets; it's about to get both cold and extremely hard to breathe in here." He looked to Max. "You can pilot a *Hub Gunther*, I take it?"

. . .

ONCE OUTSIDE, Hardy had found both the utility locker and the jack cable. He'd seen the three red, stationary Arrows waiting off in the distance. Now, thirty feet out from USS *Lincoln's* starboard hull, the end of the cable clutched in one hand, and having kicked off from the *Gunther* and taken up a flying Superman pose, the ChronoBot readied to make contact. Only now did he realize he'd been a tad zealous with his leap; he braced for the impending head-on collision.

His fast-moving thousand pounds of mass struck the *Lincoln* like a freight train hitting an even larger freight train. He grunted as his bulk clattered and then flopped about as he reached for any kind of handhold. "All's good here, I've got this..." he said to no one in particular.

"Dammit, you're going to topple right off the hull, Hardy!" the Captain said. "This is no time for your antics."

Remarkably still clutching the end of the jack cable, Hardy desperately reached with his other hand and found purchase, now grasping a small junction box, partially tearing it away from the hull. "Oh my... That'll need to be fixed."

"Good job, robot," Sonya said, "You're super close to the power outlet. It's two feet over your big head. You can probably reach—"

"As much as I appreciate your assistance, I do have access to the same ship schematics as you do," Hardy said.

"I'm just trying to help. You don't have to go all snotty know-it-all on me."

Hardy crab-walked, finding several solid handholds. The power outlet would have been easy to miss since it had a hinged flap over it. He lifted it, properly positioned the jack cable plug into it, and pressed. He felt it lock into place.

"That should do it... please, please... hold your applause. It was nothing."

Quintos said, "Max, flip the aux power switch. Let's see if this worked."

Hardy felt the cable come alive with thousands of volts of electricity. Within reach, also covered by a metal flap, was the ship's starboard flight bay manual access panel. He waited for a prompt to appear.

"It's going to take a few minutes before the ship's root access protocols are initialized," Sonya said.

The prompt displayed. Hardy entered a fifteen-digit access code, one that worked for all US Space-Navy vessels.

"What's going on, Hardy? Over," came the captain's less-than-patient-sounding voice.

"The bay doors should have opened," Hardy said.

"Shoulds are shit at this point. Get those doors open."

As if on cue, a near-blinding vertical swath of light, contrasting with the blackness of deep space, emanated from Hardy's left. The bay doors were indeed opening.

Chapter 11

Lost Tombstone Star System
Genoma, Stratham Hold

Captain Gail Pristy

An hour after her shower was rudely interrupted, Captain Pristy had quansported off USS *Hercules*. Stephan Derrota, Dr. Patty Kline, Superintendent LaSalle, and Petty Officer Second-Class Aubrey Laramie had already amassed within Stratham Hold's control center. All wore black combat fatigues, body armor, and their tagger sidearms.

Pristy gave them a quick overview of the situation, ending with, "Dr. Kline, stay here. If there are wounded, we'll need you ready. LaSalle, you hang with Corporal Bower. The rest, come with me."

Dr. Kline handed a medic's pack to Aubrey, who slung it over one shoulder, then the time travelers quickly headed below. They'd taken the rickety lift deep down into the rocky, cavernous base there—where the ringularity portal awaited.

Derrota had brought along his own field kit, just in case it was needed. Resnick hadn't said any of these things would be necessary, but Pristy wasn't about to put her people in jeopardy; trust of the enigmatic general only went so far. She wondered, upon their arrival below, if he'd be annoyed. He always seemed to be annoyed. Pristy would be more sympathetic if the man hadn't interrupted her shower just an hour earlier—and simply to let her know she needed to assemble her team. *Not that I would have minded something more... under different circumstances.* The thought colored her cheeks. Sure, Resnick was good looking in a rustic kind of way, well-built, and add to the fact it had been far too long since she'd...

She mentally chastised herself. He's an arrogant asshat. What are you thinking?

"Pondering something special, Captain?" Aubrey asked, derailing her train of thought. The young woman looked at her with a bemused expression. "Or maybe someone?"

"You enjoy being a petty officer?" Pristy asked.

She heard Aubrey gulp before she replied, "Yes, Captain."

"Then shut up before I bust you down to deckhand."

The others, wiser than Aubrey, didn't say anything, but kept glancing at their ChronoLinks nervously. All of them had received training, but aside from Pristy, this would be their first Time Province Intervention. Pristy had already told them what she had learned, which wasn't much, but enough to weigh them all down with worry. If they messed up, Quintos and his crew would be dead, and billions more could die in the near future.

Now, moving farther into the cavern, Pristy was certain Resnick had yet to arrive. They stopped and took in the rock-walled, dimly lit space. Above them, the ringularity loomed like a twenty-foot diameter reflective pond turned sideways and left floating in the air. The surface undulated ever so gently, as if rippled by an unseen breeze, or maybe something moving just below the surface. Pristy knew better than to stare at it too long and had warned the rest of them as well. The ringularity had its own pull, both a physical gravity, luring the unwary inside, and something else—something that felt like a hunger. A neediness. She suspected the towering aberration maintained a kind of elemental consciousness—and was certain its own self-interest would always come first. She looked away from it, saw the others had done the same.

Behind them, the lift rattled and the door opened. Resnick, wearing his own black fatigues, stepped out and looked them over. "Everyone ready?"

"No, we are not," Derrota said, his singsong Mumbai accent making the statement sound less confronting than probably intended. "We have no idea where or when we are going. Only that... what, we have to save the universe?"

"All humanity and our allies..." Resnick corrected. "The universe will continue whether we survive or not."

"Oh, so no pressure," Derrota mumbled.

Pristy said, "Where were you?"

Resnick, clearly not used to having his actions questioned, said, "Filling in Dr. Kline and Bower about the plan. Is that okay with you, Captain?"

She looked away without answering.

"Derrota, Pristy, and Aubrey, set your ChronoLinks," Resnick said, reeling off a list of coordinates. For the next few minutes, everything went silent, save for the subtle clicking of ChronoLinks being set. "You are going to a star system that is not on your charts and boarding the dreadnought USS *Lincoln*, which was captured by the Liquilids eight years ago. These devices will shield you from sensor scans."

"What are Liquilids?" Aubrey asked, and when Resnick glared at her for interrupting, added, "Sir."

"Reptilian species. Think large, thick snakes with arms. Or

long lizards. Technologically much more advanced than humanity. They use nanite technology for all their systems, including weapons. Consider all other intelligent species food, which they like to eat alive."

"Ugh."

"Very astute observation, Petty Officer," Resnick said, sarcasm dripping from his words. "Now listen up. When *Lincoln's* captain realized his ship was lost, he erased all the ship's databases to prevent the Liquilids from finding Earth and its colonies. Then he hid the records of his encounter in his safe. You three will go to his ready room, get the safe open, and make certain Quintos finds those records and backup system memory stores as quickly as possible when he reaches the bridge."

"Do you have a plan for that, Sir?" Pristy asked.

"Take this, Derrota," Resnick said, handing him a small canister. "It's a non-explosive smoke device. Put it in that bag of yours... you'll need it later."

Derrota looked at the thing with apprehension. "Uh, okay."

"Rig something smoky that completely combusts upon detonation. Have it go off when they power up the bridge systems."

Derrota nodded. "I'm not typically the go-to explosives guy."

Ignoring him, Resnick continued, "You three will be working in an oxygen-free environment," he said to Pristy. "There are combat suits in the lockers next to the control room. Get suited and ready to go in fifteen minutes. I will wait here."

Captain Pristy frowned at Resnick and didn't move. The others all looked at her, sensing something was wrong. Resnick's head tilted. "Problem?"

"Yes, Sir," Pristy said. "Why us?"

"You're here," Resnick said.

Pristy shook her head. "That's not a good reason, General.

None of us are properly trained. If this is as important as you say, why don't you have your best agents on it?"

"They're not available."

"Then why don't you go?"

"You always question your superiors?" Resnick asked.

"Only when the orders make no sense, *Sir*."

"No wonder you were posted out in the middle of nowhere."

Pristy's face heated up with rising anger. "Look, General—"

"I stay behind in case you screw up and die," Resnick said. "Which happens, especially to petty officers who haven't properly set their ChronoLinks."

"What?" Aubrey looked at her wrist, swore, and started fiddling. After a few clicks, she said, "Got it."

"And as for the rest of the agents, *Captain*," Resnick said. "When USS *Adams* got captured, its databases raided and its crew tortured and then eaten, what do you think the Liquilids found?"

"Earth's territories and our allies," Pristy snapped back. "You told me."

"I didn't tell you enough, or you would have figured out the important bit." Resnick walked past her to the ringularity. He spun on his heel and crossed his arms. "Go ahead. See if you can figure it out. I'll wait."

"Shit," Derrota said. "Time travel."

"Two points to the scientist," sarcasm laced Resnick's voice. "Now, there are no records on *Adams* of time travel, but there are records of this place, and guess where they came first? Better yet, tell me what a species... one that craves total domination and has more power than any other we've seen... would do once it acquired time travel."

Pristy sighed. "Take over everything."

"From the beginning of time."

"How long before they come here?" Derrota asked.

"Oh, they are here," Resnick said. "They're just not *now*. We've lost five hundred people securing this base. And the rest of the *real* time agents, along with the Grand Consortium's four other timeships, are fighting the Liquilids throughout time and space. So, all I have to work with are you three." He let the words sink in, then asked Aubrey, "What are the four tenets of time travel?"

She looked startled to be addressed but reeled them off like a medical resident identifying patient symptoms. "Tenet one: Top Secret. All time-travel capabilities must remain classified. Two: Uncontaminated. Leave nothing behind, especially when traveling to the past. Three: Historical Purity. Never rewrite history. Your historical timeline stability score, as measured by your ChronoLink, must be above 98.5 before the mission can be considered a success. Four: No Causal Loops. If you risk a causal loop, you must redefine your mission."

Resnick nodded his approval. "Pristy, tell everyone the current historical time stability score."

Pristy looked at her ChronoLink, and her eyes nearly bulged out of her head. "28.4 percent? What the hell?"

"Somehow, something happened which completely screwed the timeline," Resnick said. "The Grand Consortium noticed it three months from now, when the Liquilids were already destroying Earth as well as our allies. The Consortium traced it back to the arrival of *Adams, Wrath,* and *Portent* in that system. None were supposed to be there."

Aubrey looked confused, while Scientist Derrota looked intrigued. Pristy frowned. "Why can't you just stop them from arriving there, then?"

"They came from another universe. We couldn't get there to stop them from coming."

"General?" Aubrey sounded concerned, which was

completely unlike her. "You said the Liquilids are here, but not 'now,' yes?"

"Correct."

"So, when are they going to be, 'now'?"

"In about three hours," General Resnick said. "Now, if you understand the gravity of the situation, check your gear, and get back here pronto. We have a universe to save."

Chapter 12

Pristy, Derrota, and Aubrey were once more standing in front of the ringularity. They'd exchanged their fatigues for combat suits, suitable for working in zero atmosphere and gravity, each with shining bright helmet lights. Pristy swallowed hard, making a concerted effort to keep from tapping a foot.

"You nervous?" Resnick said. "Thought you were made of tougher stuff than that."

Pristy stared at him, anger fueling her next words. "Nervous, no. Am I... are we green? You bet we are, *General*."

"You're green but not stupid," Resnick said, ignoring her tone. "You think well on your feet; you've proven that. Which means you can figure out exactly how you'll, one, get that safe open, two, make certain Quintos notices it, and three, get the hell out of there without being seen. Any other issues?"

"She's just telling you we're not trained for this," Aubrey said. "And she's made a good point."

"Did I ask for your input, Petty Officer?" Resnick said, his tone hard as steel. He looked to the others. "Let's go over the plan."

"Get to the captain's ready room on *Lincoln*," Derrota said. "Open the safe so they can look inside it. Figure out how to make certain they see what's in it. Then, I guess we bug out."

"What do we do if things go FUBAR?" Aubrey asked.

"Die," Resnick said. "And probably, badly. Now get your asses moving."

As they shuffled forward, Aubrey looked back over one shoulder. "Thought you were supposed to be watching our backs, not our asses."

"I'll put my boot up yours if you don't zip it," Pristy said, then gave Resnick a *you're a pig* expression. "Comms check," she barked.

"All's green," said Bower. "We'll be here for you if you need us."

Not that it will help on the other side of the galaxy. Pristy checked her sidearm tagger one more time and said, "Right. Let's go."

They stepped through the ringularity. On the other side they found themselves within *Lincoln's* empty bridge. The overhead lights were on but substantially dimmed. Both Pristy and Aubrey drew their taggers while scanning the unattended stations. Their helmet lights swept back and forth like prison tower spotlights. Derrota slowly spun and whistled. "Looks like a major firefight took place here."

"Even still," Aubrey said, "I've never seen a bridge like this... So, well, nice ..."

As Pristy strode deeper into the compartment, she saw both of their points. Evidence of weapons fire, panic, rusty stains... despite the battle damage and in stark contrast to *Adams'* lavish —and, frankly, kind of silly—starliner opulence, the layout was no-nonsense, emphasizing efficiency and functionality above all else. Before her stretched six rows of sleekly designed consoles, and beneath the scorching, she saw state-of-the-art touchscreen control boards.

And to remind those on board that this ship still had some kind of power, several accompanying mini 3D projection displays flickered into view momentarily before disappearing just as swiftly. She ran her hand along the top of the nearest console, marveling at the technological advancement expressed in the seamless merging of form and function.

At the heart of the bridge, positioned behind the foremost row of consoles, loomed the commanding presence of the captain's mount. This elevated position offered an unobstructed view of the entire bridge and its surroundings, bestowing the captain with full authority and oversight. Drawing nearer, the armrests of the captain's mount dazzled her with an array of controls and color-coded tap buttons, each serving a specific purpose within the intricate web of the ship's operations.

Directly ahead, dominating the forefront of the bridge, stood the jaw-droppingly beautiful forward 3D projection holo display. Currently, it showcased a compilation of local space feeds, its ethereal presence almost tangible. Its pixel resolution was so refined that the projected images appeared as if the nearby asteroids were suspended in the blackness of deep space. As with all vessels in the US Space-Navy fleet, the halo display acted as the visual centerpiece of the bridge, relaying critical information and situational updates with breathtaking clarity.

Weapons, tablets, and other equipment were strewn about. Beneath Pristy's boots, the deck plates resonated with a sturdy metallic hum, underscoring the ship's robust construction. Over-head, the deckhead revealed a complex network of inlaid duct-work and precisely positioned illumination fixtures. She had to admit, the overall design flawlessly integrated functionality with aesthetics, ensuring that every inch of the bridge was optimized for both performance and visual appeal.

"Guess we should stick to the business at hand, Stephan," Pristy said, as much for herself as for them. The temptation to sit at the captain's mount was hard to ignore, but she shoved it aside. "Aubrey, on the entrance. Keep an eye out for any movement and keep track of comms. Stephan, you're with me."

She led him across the bridge to the ready room hatch door. As expected, it was locked and, unlike the rest of the bridge, seemed relatively unmolested by violence.

She stepped aside and let Derrota work his magic with the adjacent control panel with tools he'd pulled from his satchel. In less than a minute, the door slid open. "After you, Gail."

"Nice work," she said. "Now comes the fun part."

Pristy cautiously entered the captain's ready room, her helmet light piercing through the darkness, casting illuminating swaths that revealed the otherwise obscure space. The room seemed to swallow the feeble light, creating an ambience as dark and impenetrable as the depths of space itself. The captain's ready room was eerily devoid of clutter. Only a solitary desk, accompanied by a chair behind it, occupied one side of the room. The desk stood as a testament to minimalism, devoid of any personal touches or mementos. It was a functional surface, meant solely for the purpose of conducting business in the privacy of the captain's domain. On the opposite bulkhead, she could make out the faint outlines of a Murphy bed, awaiting its deployment when the captain desired proximity to the bridge without venturing too far. Its presence hinted at the relentless demands of duty, offering a momentary respite for the captain here in the relentless expanse of space.

However, despite the monastic aesthetics, the room bore evidence that the fight had indeed made it within. The room betrayed a disturbing scene, as bloodstains marred the otherwise pristine deck plates. Traces of a struggle were evident, suggesting that someone had been forcefully dragged out of the room. Seeking answers, she instinctively moved toward the bulkhead where the hidden safe would be concealed. Placing a palm up against the panel, Pristy anticipated a response, a clue to unravel the mysteries that lingered within. But to her disappointment, nothing happened. The panel remained unyielding, refusing to grant her access to its secrets.

"As I thought," Derrota said. "Let me at it; I'll get it open."

The quirky scientist once again went to work with his specialized batch of tools, but unlike the panel at the hatch door entrance, this panel was giving him trouble. After several minutes seemingly not making any progress, Pristy said, "Stephan... do you have a plan B?"

He nodded, pulled a small metallic disk from his satchel, and attached it to the bulkhead.

"Hold on there. We can't just blow it open—"

He chuckled. "Nothing so crude as that."

The disk lit up pulsing red, then orange. "Now we wait."

"How long?" Pristy asked. "... and what is that thing?"

"Portable charger," Derrota said. "But not the usual type. The ship is only partially awake. Partially powered up. This inverter device radiates the perfect power stream to any subsystems requiring power. I suppose you could jumpstart a dead Arrow if you had to. As for how long..."

"*Hub Gunther* is approaching. Hardy is about to initiate a scan of the ship." Bower's voice abruptly came over their comms. "All power off for the next two minutes."

"Oh my!" Derrota said, fumbling for the device, pulling it free, and finally turning it off. The orange band of light went dark.

"Get your helmet lights and your suits powered down too!" Pristy ordered over the open channel.

The soft whir of her air supply went silent. Beside her, Derrota powered down as well. Back within the bridge, she heard Aubrey stop walking.

One thousand one. One thousand two. The dark was stifling, the air in her suit already feeling stale, though she knew there was a sufficient amount to keep her breathing for another ten minutes at least. *One thousand three, one thousand four. One thousand five.* Pristy kept counting, knowing their lives depended on it. She could see nothing in the darkness, hear nothing but her own breathing. She kept the count going until *one thousand one hundred forty-nine, one thousand one hundred fifty.*

She whispered, "Bower... all clear?"

She waited.

"Okay, think we're clear," Bower said.

She pressed an inset button on the forearm of her suit and instantly, the power came back on within her suit. The stark band of illumination from her helmet light was almost blinding, while the whir of the air supply was a most welcome noise. A moment later, Derrota's helmet light came on.

"Let's not do that again," Aubrey's voice echoed in her ear.

"Bower, how much time?" Pristy asked.

"Twenty minutes until the next scan," he said. "But only five before *Hub Gunther* lands on the ship."

"Need to move fast," Pristy ordered, but Derrota was already attaching the disk to the panel again. It blinked red and then solid orange. For two interminable minutes they stood, waiting. The panel suddenly glowed blue, and Pristy almost jumped out of her suit. "Let's get to work on the attention-getter."

"On it, Gail," Derrota said, pulling something else from his bag.

Pristy's gloves were designed to allow for tactile feel. Perfect for a touchpad like the one currently activated. The panel beeped, and a small keypad appeared. Pristy tapped in a six-number code, and she hit enter. A red warning light appeared, and she tapped in six more. There was a pause, then a door opened beside it.

"Impressive," Derrota said from behind. "How did you know the code?"

"I didn't," Pristy said. "There's an override on every captain's safe in case of an emergency situation. Same on every ship. Can only be used if the ship cannot detect the captain's presence, and since the power's off..."

"Ooh, very smart," Aubrey said from the open hatch door. "So, can we leave yet?"

"Derrota?"

"One more minute..."

"That's all we have," Pristy said, looking back at him. "Go faster."

He was standing on the captain's desk chair, reaching both hands over his head. A vent register had been pulled down, and Derrota placed another of his devices inside. "Done."

"And it will go off when Quintos arrives?"

He repositioned the vent register and looked down at her. "That is the intent."

Pristy said, "Bower, stand by."

"Standing by."

Aubrey had moved into the compartment. The three worked their ChronoLinks, hands clumsy in their gloves.

"Thirty seconds," Bower said.

Pristy clicked the last dial into place. "Ready."

"Ready," Derrota said.

"Almost..." Aubrey said, sounding panicked. "I just have one more... got it."

"Go!"

The three vanished from the ready room and, a moment later, stepped out of the ringularity. Resnick stood where they'd left him.

"Nice work, people," Resnick said. "Now get out of those and into your regular gear. We've got a timeship to visit."

Chapter 13

**Liquilid Empire Star System
Asteroid Compound**

Commander Lu-puk

4 hours ago...

L u-puk scrutinized the Bliddit before him. As a species, Bliddits were far from imposing. They stood merely a meter tall, with rounded, bulbous bodies, short legs, and thin arms. In contrast, Liquilids, his own kind, grew six times longer, boasting powerful muscles capable of crushing any prey. Not that they had resorted to such primitive methods of obtaining food in over a thousand years, but the strength remained ingrained in their biology. Their heads formed a triangular shape, with wide mouths filled with two rows of sawblade teeth, towering two meters above the ground. The remaining four meters extended behind them in a long, red-scaled tail, offering substantial protection against most weapons. Their wiry arms terminated in four fingers, each tipped with a sharp claw.

Lu-puk emitted a hiss of amusement. Compared to the Liquilids, it seemed inconceivable that the Bliddits had survived evolution, ventured into space, and colonized hundreds of solar systems. Yet, they had built an empire. And they had proven to be worthy adversaries, cruel, even when pushed into battle. They had gone beyond the norms of battle and captured hundreds—no, thousands—of Liquilid warriors. Placing their prisoners in a deep hole, the Bliddits poured an acid-like compound on the captured warriors. Their screams could be heard from miles away. This vicious cycle of war lasted until the Liquilids discovered them, conquered them, and uncovered two intriguing revelations. First, the dozen jewel-like formations embedded in a Bliddit's skin shimmered in rainbow hues when exposed to bright light, much like the one illuminating Lu-puk's dinner table.

He reached down with his long-fingered, clawed hand. The Bliddit stared back at him defiantly, its swirling orange eyes fixed in a determined gaze. However, its body remained immobile, manipulated by the nanomachines lining its spine, trembling and quivering. Lu-puk plunged his claws into the Bliddit's flesh, delicately carving around one of the jewels. Purple blood flowed, and the Bliddit let out a screech, but the controlling nanomachines muffled the sound to a more pleasing volume for the Liquilid's sensitive ears. Delving deeper, Lu-puk continued until his claws met, and with a wrenching twist, he tore the flesh free.

Because the second thing the Liquilids had learned was that, like many species that had ventured beyond their home planets into space, Bliddits had an exceptionally delectable taste. He held the chunk of meat in front of the Bliddit's eyes as it screamed, licking the dripping blood from his claws. The

Bliddit was unable to look away or blink, thanks to the nanomachines. Yet Lu-puk could sense its fear, detecting it in the Bliddit's perspiration and observing the emanating energy. He smiled, raised the jeweled skin, and tore the meat away, akin to extracting an oyster from its shell. He relished the slow chewing, savoring the sweetness while the Bliddit continued to scream and curse. "Just wait," Lu-puk uttered, the nanomachines in the Bliddit's brain translating his words, "until I sink my teeth into your entrails."

Importing the Bliddit had cost him a week's worth of wages. He had brought it along during his six-day shift on lookout, ensuring he could devour it in solitude. His intention was to take his time, relishing every morsel of its flesh and organs, breaking its bones, savoring the marrow, and ultimately feasting upon its eyes and brain. Only once the nanomachines had eradicated the Bliddit's pain centers would it be allowed to die.

He extended his claws once again, ready to extract the next jewel. However, an alarm, low and resonant like a hammer striking a steel beam, reverberated through the room, causing his delicate ears to twitch. Emitting a hiss of annoyance, he pulled back his hand, wiping it on a blood-soaked towel before slithering toward the control panel. His inner eyelids narrowed in irritation. A wormhole had opened in the flux trap, forcing him to postpone his lunch further. He reassured himself that the Bliddit's flesh would only grow tastier with pain and fear and settled down to initiate his report.

A shiver ran from his tail to the top of his head, causing his defensive spikes to bristle. It wasn't just one ship emerging from the wormhole, but three.

Lu-puk inserted his fingers into the control orifices, allowing his nanomachines to establish a connection with the computer. He closed his eyes, enhancing his ability to comprehend the data flooding into his mind. Two of the ships appeared large and heavily armed, bearing signs of recent battle, which had likely depleted their ammunition reserves. The largest vessel carried bipedal mammalian beings, mostly adults with a lone juvenile. There were a few representatives of other species aboard, but their numbers were minimal. Although the ship's rail guns and beam weapons could pose a threat to smaller Liquilid vessels, they would have no impact on the red ships or the flux trap itself. Utilizing wormholes for interstellar travel and propulsion technology for in-system movement, it was evident that they were not embarking on a long-distance voyage.

The second ship housed artificial beings resembling the mammalians. Lu-puk's inner eyelids narrowed further. Artificials were merely a nuisance, offering little value to the Liquilids apart from the technological knowledge assimilated by their nanomachines. Leaning forward, a frown etching his features, he noticed something peculiar. The vessel they piloted was not originally designed for them. Traces of DNA found within the spattered blood indicated that another species had previously owned it. Whether the artificials had stumbled upon it or captured it, remained unknown. Nevertheless, it was of no immediate concern.

The final vessel stood apart, not only in terms of aesthetics but also in terms of technology. Its sleek outer shell concealed an arsenal more formidable and abundant than the other two ships. It possessed three distinct propulsion systems: one for standard propulsion, one for wormhole traversal, and a mysterious auxiliary system that the computer struggled to analyze. Lu-puk promptly ordered a diagnostic test, considering the possibility of an internal issue with his scanners. The crew of the third ship comprised various species, including the bipedal mammals from the first vessel, as well as a few artificial entities.

Lu-puk licked his lips and glanced back at the moaning Bliddit. Being on duty when new species stumbled into the trap meant a bonus payout. He could afford to purchase more delicacies for his mate next time, perhaps even some for their brood of twenty.

An alert appeared on the screen, causing his tail to lash harder and his spikes to bristle at full attention. If the information was correct, he would receive a significantly larger bonus than usual. Double-checking the data, he transmitted the stream to the Admiral's ship and sent a signal. Within moments, the image of Admiral Plu-tik—seven meters tall and adorned in deep red-purple hues—materialized within his mind.

"What is it, Commander?" the Admiral inquired.

"Three ships have arrived simultaneously," Lu-puk reported. "Multiple alien species, including one artificial and another that we have encountered before."

Something in his tone must have alerted Plu-tik, as the Admiral's spikes also rose. "Harvested?" he questioned.

"No, Sir. Last time, they destroyed their data before we could determine their location."

The Admiral's inner eyelids flickered back and forth, and a grin spread across his face, exposing his teeth. "Data?" he asked eagerly.

"Sent," Lu-puk replied. A moment of silence followed as the data streamed into Admiral Plu-tik. Lu-puk glanced at the Bliddit once more, contemplating whether he had time for another bite before the Admiral finished reviewing. He suspected he did, but he didn't want to risk it. Eating while conversing with a superior was an invitation for punishment, ranging from food confiscation to becoming the meal himself. He rubbed the scarred gouge on his side, a reminder of his past insolence during basic training. No, he would exercise patience and see what transpired.

"Very well," Admiral Plu-tik declared. "Why can't the computer analyze the propulsion system of the smallest ship?"

"Unknown, Sir," Lu-puk responded. "A diagnostic and sensor adjustment is underway. Shall we commence the harvest?"

The Admiral's inner eyelids closed, and he emitted a long, contemplative hiss. "Are they trapped?"

"The two larger ships, yes, Admiral. The status of the third ship is unknown, but they are not making any attempts to escape at present, only conducting scans."

"For now, leave them be," the Admiral instructed. "Monitor and report any unusual activity. And ensure your computer is functioning properly. I want to know the propulsion system of the other ships before the next cycle begins."

The image of the Admiral gradually faded from Lu-puk's mind, and he refocused his attention on the computer. He commanded a thorough scan of all the creatures aboard the ships, as well as their mechanical, electronic, and quantum systems. It would take hours to complete, affording him ample time. Slithering away from the computer, Lu-puk approached the gleaming, quivering form on the dining table. This time, he raised both hands, extending his claws and flexing them. The Bliddit shouted obscenities until the pain silenced it, leaving only its screams. Lu-puk decided to consume only half of the Bliddit for now. The remainder would taste even sweeter when he had more news to share with the Admiral.

Chapter 14

Liquilid Empire Star System
USS Adams

Captain Galvin Quintos

I was the second to breach *Lincoln's* flight bay's atmospheric energy field, Hardy being the first. To say it was an eerie feeling, entering the physical realm of this goliath-sized warship, a ghost ship, would be a gross understatement. How many years had she been here, held steadfast within an asteroid's minimal gravitational pull? I couldn't say. Below me were dozens upon dozens of bright and gleaming red Arrow fighters, all lined up like child's toys long forgotten in the corner of a room.

I brought my Arrow to a standstill thirty feet up off the deck and scanned the voluminous, football arena–sized compartment. Catching movement below, I saw Hardy waving a metallic hand.

His voice filled my helmet, "All indications thus far... The atmosphere is musky, borderline stinky, but breathable."

I proceeded forward, finding room at the back of the bay for our three Arrows to set down—taking extra care to maintain the same precision formation as *Lincoln's* other pilots had exhibited. The previous bay chief must have been some kind of hardass fusspot.

As MY ARROW's drive wound down, Akari and then Ryder put their craft down, wingtip to wingtip; they too had taken extra care to keep within proper formation.

Our canopies opened at the same time. We made eye contact.

Ryder said, "This seem creepy to you as well?"

I nodded.

Akari stood, "I don't know about you two, but I can't wait to snoop around."

Seeing Hardy's approach, I was instantly on guard. All five of his usually hidden energy guns, within his thigh, forearm, and upper shoulder compartment, had been deployed. It was times like this that the true lethality of our friendly, often goofball, ChronoBot became apparent.

"What is it, Hardy?" I said, climbing down the Arrow's hull inset ladder.

"Remember when I said the air was... stinky?"

"You weren't wrong," Akari said, making a face.

"On further examination of atmospheric particulate matter, I'm getting a sensor whiff of decomposing flesh... human flesh. I'm also picking up familiar residual ozone signatures left behind by energy weapons."

"Even after all this time?" I asked. "This ship's been here a long while, no?"

"That's a big 10-4 on that. But USS *Lincoln's* gone undisturbed for years. Added to the fact I'm amazing and, like a bloodhound, sniff out things most cannot."

"You forgot to mention how humble you are," Akari said with a roll of her eyes.

My comms crackled. Max said, "Are you four going to chitchat all day? Is there room in there for the *Gunther* or not?"

I spun around. From my perspective I couldn't see over the rows and rows of Arrows. I did remember seeing more open flight deck space farther back. *Is it enough?*

Hardy said, "There's ample room. Come on in... Uh, boys and girls, best you come out weapons hot. There's been a firefight on board. That, and I'm picking up other lifeforms."

I looked to the ChronoBot, irritated. "You might have mentioned that detail to me as well, Hardy."

KITTED UP AND WEAPONIZED, the five Marines approached. Ham and Hock carried with them three combat suits, while Wanda and Grip hefted extra shredders. Max, his own shredder raised, looked ready, if necessary, for any impending attack.

It took us another ten minutes to get fitted into our respective battle suits. With Hardy taking point and the Marines close on his heels, we moved for the nearest flight bay exit.

The double-wide hatch door slid open upon our approach.

Hardy said, "I've been systematically bringing the ship out of slumber mode. It's a monumental draw on power reserves, especially since *Lincoln's* drives are down."

Entering a lower deck of the dreadnought, and in sharp contrast to *Adams'* gilded-age wood-paneled and crystal chandelier luxury, we were immediately enveloped by an atmosphere of formidable efficiency. Though scored with tagger fire, the gleaming white SmartCoat's bulkheads exuded an air of protection, reflecting the vessel's commitment to security. The metal deck plates, worn and weathered by countless missions, resonated with a sense of durability and resilience. As we navigated the wide and spacious corridors, the stripped-down military blandness became more and more apparent, just as did the signs of an epic firefight, in particular, barricades of furniture, crates, offline bots, erected at junctions in sloppy piles, stunk of desperation and whispered of futility.

But beneath that panicked veneer, I could still see with my captain's discernment that, here, functionality reigned supreme. Every element was carefully designed to serve its purpose efficiently. This, and all other decks, would be a testament to the maximization of space, ensuring optimal utilization for personnel and equipment. Almost having to squint, I saw the stark overhead lights illuminated every corner, nook and cranny with clinical precision. Shadows were banished, leaving no room for ambiguity or hidden spaces. Not unlike the flight bay, this was an atmosphere of discipline and readiness. Military pragmatism had created an ambience that was both imposing and captivating, and something else as well. Familiar.

This was what I was used to. And strangely, I found it comforting, even calming. This was a testament to the vessel's mission—to stand as an indomitable force, capable of facing any challenge, any adversary, coming its way. *So what went wrong...*

We were coming up to a bank of GravLifts. I said, "Where, specifically, are you picking up lifeforms, Hardy?"

"This deck, further forward."

"Nothing on the decks above?"

"Nothing alive."

"Okay, we're going to split up," I said, stopping at the lifts.

Max was already shaking his head. "Bad idea, Cap... at least until we've cleared those decks."

"This vessel is as large, if not larger, than *Adams*. Some fifty decks, hundreds of thousands of square footage to clear... I'm not waiting weeks for your team to clear that kind of space. Anyway, we're well armed."

"Still a bad idea. Let's not forget, an entire crew has been wiped out here."

I looked to the five Marines. "Then give us one of your team. I need to get to the bridge, find out what the hell happened here."

"I'll go with them," Wanda said. "I'm used to watching the captain's six."

I knuckled the lift's call button. "We'll stay in contact via the open channel."

The lift doors slid open. Akari, Ryder, Wanda, and I stepped inside. Akari tapped at the destination menu display. The doors slid shut—the GravLift jostled and began accelerating away to a location basically unknown to any of us.

Ryder pursed his lips. "I'd like to head off to Engineering and Propulsion... nothing like getting eyes on the situation in there."

"Uh-uh, we need to stay together," Wanda said, leaving no doubt about her stance on the matter.

"Hardy said it himself, no living lifeforms anywhere but that lower deck," Ryder said. He moved next to Akari and studied the ship's visual representation on the display menu. "What do you know? It's on the way." He tapped at the display and the lift began to slow.

Both Akari and Wanda looked to me, as if quietly saying, *Tell him he can't do that!*

"He's a big boy. Captain Ryder doesn't need a mommy..."

"Or two mommies," Ryder said with a crooked smile.

The door opened, but before Ryder could step out, I took his arm. "You look around, you evaluate the drives, and then you get to the bridge, pronto. Got that?"

"Copy that." He winked at Akari and left.

. . .

WAITING for the GravLift's doors to open, I anticipated being disappointed. Having skippered multiple *Hamilton*-class dreadnoughts, I knew what they each had in common was a massive main deck, affectionately called Whale's Alley because of the high arching metal girders above resembling a whale's huge inner rib cage.

The lift slowed, stopped, and the doors slid open. I was the first to step out onto the main deck, which for this vessel was Deck 15.

Looking about, craning my neck to see above, I was delighted to see the Whale's Alley ship architecture was intact, even here on this SpaceWing design.

"This is one big fucking main deck," Wanda said, standing with hands on hips, appraising our surroundings.

Akari was already hurrying toward the entrance to the bridge.

"Holy shit!" we heard her say.

Upon entering the bridge, my jaw dropped open. I knew Akari wasn't commenting on the fight that went down in here. This was some command center. Far more advanced than what I was used to. There again, this was a prototype vessel of things to come. Things that had yet to materialize, other than here onboard USS *Lincoln.*

I was immediately struck by the advanced technology on display. The console stations were sleek and modern-looking, with touchscreens and holographic displays.

Akari, having found the tactical station near the front of the compartment, said, "Each station is immediately customizable to the needs of its user, with different readouts and controls depending on their role on the ship. No one-size-fits-all here, Captain." With a few taps, she gestured to the front.

It was the centerpiece of the bridge, the 3D halo display. Currently it was projecting a detailed map of the surrounding space.

"Looks like this celestial map is updating in real time. No nearby alien ships; you can see *Adams* there," Akari said, gesturing with an extended finger.

"I think the captain knows how to view a halo display, Akari," Wanda said with a smirk.

"Oh, shut up. I'm just excited."

On either side of the halo display were rows of monitors, displaying a dizzying array of data and video feeds. I could see there were sensors monitoring everything from radiation levels to gravitational fluctuations, while cameras provided live feeds from all around the ship.

Wanda, having ventured over to a bulkhead, was playing with a wall-mounted display. "Cool! The lighting here on the bridge is totally adjustable." The compartment was suddenly bathed in aqua-hued illumination. "I guess the different colors are used to indicate different levels of alert or activity."

I crossed my arms, assessing it all. Overall, the bridge of this warship was a marvel of high-tech design and well-thought-out engineering.

Akari turned and looked at me. "Well, aren't you going to try it out?"

I raised my brows. "Try what out?"

Her eyes shifted to the captain's mount. "Duuuh."

"It doesn't look anywhere near as comfortable as the one on *Adams*," I said.

"Captain, this is a true warship. No if, ands, or buts about it. And that's one badass captain's mount. If you're not going to sit in it, I am."

Before she could take one step, I was sprinting, racing toward the captain's mount.

Chapter 15

Liquilid Empire Star System
Asteroid Compound

Commander Lu-puk

L u-puk stared at his display with the eyes of a predator observing his prey. A familiar yearning, a hunger, arose within him. Little compared to fresh, vibrant quarry. *Ahh, human meat.* He swiped at saliva secretions, stringy, elastic, with a scaly forearm.

The enemy vessels' name designations were imprinted right onto their hulls. Ridiculous. Did they not remember their own ships' names? USS *Adams, Portent,* and *Boundless Wrath.*

The three ships, upon arrival, had separated and scanned local space for any credible threats—Lu-puk almost laughed —*primitives...* The superior technology of his vessel's flux trap interference had kept his ship's presence hidden. *So predictable...* Once these ridiculous humans had determined there were no immediate threats, they'd put far too much attention onto ship repairs, which only gave Lu-puk more time to scan this enemy's minimal strengths and many weaknesses. No, his red ships would take them easily, just as they'd done prior, and with far fewer casualties.

He swiped at more salivary secretions. And replenishing of meat ration stores... That could be just the thing to hand him that promotion to sector chief. What was left within that cargo hold, after so many years, was inedible.

He sat back, belched, allowing himself a few moments of self-congratulation. Lu-puk returned his attention to the squirming Bliddit, mouth agape, silently whimpering upon the table before him. Silently, because he'd instructed the nanomachines to shut off the Bliddit's vocal functions. Bliddits were highly, he'd go so far as to say, remarkably, intelligent. You could see it in their beady little eyes. They had proven themselves to be. So watchful. So calculating. Still, sometimes when Lu-puk wasn't actually eating, the sounds of the slippery little creatures would give him a throbbing headache.

He glared at his meal for a moment, calculating if he should finish the work he'd begun on the Bliddit's five-fingered left hand. Small, but so similar to those of a human. But humans were far tastier. Sentient creatures hated losing their fingers almost as much as their eyes. Probably because fingers and opposable thumbs were a hallmark of advanced civilizations. Lu-puk always began with the smallest, least useful of the digits. It gave them hope that perhaps if they could escape, they might just maintain some, even minimal, functionality. But inevitably, growing despair would fall upon them like a dark and heavy cloak as the creatures watched firsthand as digit after digit disappeared into their captor's mouth. *How delightful.* He snickered at his phrasing. *Firsthand... that and lasthand.*

Lu-puk, sated for the moment, stood, stretched, and approached the display. The humans were up to something... *Causing trouble, huh?* He glowered, seeing they'd recently deployed a small, rickety craft. Then he saw the addition of three fighters. Well, obviously they were exploring. *No!* He gasped; they'd found the other human vessel, the other dreadnought... USS *Lincoln,* another stupid human name. And with that, they'd soon discover their preserved, albeit ripening, food stores.

Lu-puk slithered back to his dining table. He caught the Bliddit's bleeding hand and, with a quick snip of his claws, cut off the second finger. The Bliddit silently shrieked. The small creature's eyes begged for mercy. *Like that would happen. After what you did to our race.* Lu-puk tossed the finger into his mouth, crunching hard.

He wiped his claws on a blood cloth and returned to his post. So easily his ship's sensors visually penetrated human vessels. The beings—three human pilots, a ginormous BattleBot, and a squad of heavily armed humans in body armor—were now stepping out of their craft there on USS *Lincoln's* flight bay. Lu-puk continued to watch. Leaving the flight bay, they moved deeper into the ship. Then, after a quick discussion, the pilots seemed to decide to separate—taking a lift up to a higher deck, perhaps the ship's bridge, while the robot and heavily armed group stuck together, moving forward within the lower corridors. It made sense. The robot was more dangerous than the rest of them. Lu-puk watched the heavily armed team search the ship. *This isn't good.*

Lu-puk hissed as he contemplated—how would he explain this? Waiting could cost him; then again, this was supposed to be the Admiral's "hebetude." Disturbing the Admiral's rest period without a definitive reason could cost him advancement, at the very least. Still, the aliens were moving quickly. Wasn't it his duty to warn his superior, hebetude or not? Lu-puk swore under his foul breath. "Computer! Contact Admiral Plu-tik."

The hail had yet to be answered, which didn't surprise Lu-puk. Back on the display, the heavily armed team moved with confidence. Lu-puk made a mental note to inform his Liquilid troops to be wary of them, especially that robot, later, when they'd be infiltrating the ship.

His hail, finally answered, took form within his cerebral implants. An image of the commander's cabin took shape, but the commander had yet to appear. Instead, one of the younger female members from the commander's brood stepped into view.

Her inner eyelids were half-closed, and her scales shone iridescent, which told Lu-puk exactly what the Admiral had been doing in his downtime.

"Ensign Kre-sith-tess answering for Admiral Plu-tik," the female said languidly. "The Admiral wants to know which of his staff values their life so little that they dare disturb him during this hebetude rest period. His own words, Commander."

"My apologies to the Admiral, *Ensign*," Lu-puk said, stressing the rank to remind her of her place. "Protocol dictated my immediate contact. It's the humans... soon, they will discover one of our food stores. Please put the Admiral on at his first convenience. I will continue to monitor the situation until he is available."

Lu-puk turned his attention back to the sensors. The humans were moving through the ship. Clearly, they had the vessel's schematics. That thought caused his fighting spikes to rise in excitement. They were definitely of the same empire as the previous, ill-fated crew. Once more, he lamented the nanomachines' inability to pull information directly from the minds of this alien species. That, and they'd yet to breach any of their ship AI's security protocols. *If only they could...* He smiled, imagining what it would be like having an entire world of humans to dine on at will.

"Commander," Admiral Plu-tik's voice and image filled his

head. The tone and the way the Admiral's fighting spikes stood out from his skin confirmed how displeased he was at the interruption. "You say the aliens have progressed into the humans' warship?"

"Yes, Sir. They launched ships upon arrival, discovered the other ship from their species, and have a team exploring it. They will reach both the bridge and our food stores within minutes."

The Admiral's annoyed hiss made Lu-puk's spine go rigid, but the Admiral did not seem to be angry with him in particular. Behind Plu-tik, the Ensign slithered out of the cabin, perhaps wanting to avoid any wrath turning in her direction. The Admiral's spikes flared higher. "It was only a matter of time... but they are ahead of schedule. Thus, we must be too. Send out the signal! Order our Slisset fighters to attack. We must test their defenses."

"Excellent idea, Admiral," Lu-puk said, forcing himself not to roll his eyes.

Commander Lu-puk stabbed the button with an extended claw, instantly sending a coded message out to the very fringes of the star system. He knew that the dozens of Liquilid frigates would receive the signal, convey the warnings to their reactive crews: *Aliens present in-system. Make preparations.*

Lu-puk surmised none of the captains would hurry. They all knew the proper battle order. Slissets went first, then the Liquilids gathered the data from their interactions with the enemy, their weapons and shields ensuring maximized efficiency. Only then would they begin the second wave.

The red ships felt the pulse as well, and their captains began the slow, ponderous process of bringing their engines to life and their crews to the ready. A red ship was as large as a small moon and capable of fragmenting planets into asteroids. Even mighty gas giants blew apart under the destructive power of massed red ships. Hundreds of systems and dozens of alien species had learned this to their detriment.

The pulse reverberated over every lifeless asteroid in the system, and their surfaces started vibrating. Billions of nanomachines, dormant until summoned, shook to life, rose up, and sought out one another. They came together, first around the *plitissetec* ore that lay scattered over the asteroids. Plitissetec ore held incredible amounts of accessible energy. As the plitissetec energy flowed into them, the nanomachines formed into Slisset fighters.

Slissets looked like giant insects. A cone of exploration sensors dominated the nose of each fighter. Two bulbous domes above it held the sensors that fed the battle computers the information they needed. Large, gossamer jammers protruded out like wings on either side of the bug-like Slissets' frame. At the tail, a turret weapon rose above the rest of the body, capable of targeting an enemy in any direction. The multi-barreled gun converted the plitissetec ore into an energy beam strong enough to destroy most small spacecraft.

SIXTY ASSEMBLED Slisset fighters rose from the asteroid surfaces nearest USS *Adams*, and, with synchronized aft thrusts, charged forward.

Chapter 16

Liquilid Empire Star System
USS Lincoln

Captain Galvin Quintos

I stopped short as my comms came alive. "Captain, we have company," came Chen's voice.

"Ships are rising up from the debris field—dozens of them."

I turned toward the halo display and the array of video and sensor displays. Akari, having seen them too, was already at the tactical station. She looked back at me. "The lack of rail spikes... Phazon Pulsars not yet back online; any defense we put up will be spotty at best, Captain."

What I could see were dozens of fighters closing on *Adams, Portent,* and *Boundless Wrath.*

"Hold on," Akari said. The halo display zoomed in on one of the alien fighters. She said, "Looks like a cross between a scorpion and a fly... scorpion-flies. And sure enough, they're closing in on our ships."

"Go to battle stations and get our Arrows into space, Lieutenant... my orders."

Akari spun around. "Sir, what Arrows we have capable of flight are down for maintenance. That and our pilots are exhausted—"

"This isn't a request; we need to defend our ships. Get Bosun Polk on Tactical with you and ready to shoot anything that moves."

I didn't like having my orders questioned but understood Chen's and Akari's knee-jerk reactions. I was going against SOP —where utilizing onboard weaponry was preferable to deploying human-piloted fighter squadrons into battle.

"Look, *Adams'* weapons systems are nowhere where they should be, be it that they're battle worn, or our lack of viable ammunition. I'm not going to put all my eggs in one basket. Arrows are our backup, necessary to supplement our defenses if we're to protect *Adams, Portent,* and *Wrath* in any meaningful way. I understand we may be putting our Arrows at risk of friendly fire, but I see no choice in the matter. You'll just have to be careful."

Akari, wide-eyed, took in a breath but said nothing.

"I have to go," I said, ready to cut the connection.

"Uh... when will you be coming back, Sir?" Chen said.

"Soon. I'll be in contact before those scorpion-flies arrive."

"Scorpion-flies, Sir?"

"That's what Lieutenant James has coined them. Captain out."

My Jadoo ring came alive with a Sonya projected 3D image.

Annoyed, I said, "It's polite to at least let me answer the call before you pop into view like that."

She scoffed, "Like that's going to happen. Look, I've accessed *Lincoln's* primary ship's MATHR AI."

"More like hacked the MATHR AI."

"Tomato, tomahto... The ship's still half asleep. Didn't Hardy say he was waking her up?"

"He said it takes time."

"Fine, whatever. I'm powering up the rest of that bridge for you. Once I dig deeper, I'll start amalgamating the two ships' AI databases."

"So, you'll be able to tell me what happened here?"

"Maybe. Maybe not. Just keep your pants on; it'll take a while. And remember, dear uncle-guy, I'm still sitting in a hospital bed... so I'm a bit limited here."

"Understood."

Before I could speak again, an overhead klaxon began to squawk.

"Smoke!" Wanda shouted, pointing toward a partially opened hatch door, one I had assumed led into the captain's ready room. Rarely was a ship's *auto-open/auto-close* hatch door found to be *partially* open like this. In this case, though, it just might have been a blessing in disguise.

Black smoke was now billowing out from the opening.

Wanda had moved fast; having released a fire extinguisher from its brackets beneath a console, she sprinted toward the ready room. She rushed in as soon as the hatch door slid open. We all heard the *swoosh* of chemical retardant being deployed. As quickly as it had begun, the smoke was now dissipating. I now stood within the ready room hatch door's threshold, looking in. "What the hell happened in here?"

Wanda, still holding the extinguisher in one hand, made a face. "Uh, not really sure, boss. Flames were coming from that overhead vent. I've asked MATHR to do a systems check."

Sonya's projected image appeared above the captain's desk. It was beyond creepy how she could do that.

"Don't tell me you had something to do with this, Sonya. Maybe bringing ship systems up too quickly?"

"Sorry. Maybe... my bad... There is a slight incompatibility between the ship systems. But still..."

"Yeah, well, you need to be more careful, Sonya."

"Hey, I said I'm sorry. It's probably not that big of a deal. A subpower conduit overload, maybe."

I heard her tapping at her tablet. "Ship systems seem to be powering up just fine... I still don't get it."

I chinned toward the bulkhead behind her. "And that?"

Wanda followed my sightline, then shrugged again. "Someone, I presume *Lincoln's* captain, was forced to leave in a hurry... And he left the safe open in all the mayhem."

There was blood on the deck, and signs that someone might have been dragged out of the compartment. I approached, waving away errant tendrils of smoke in the air. The safe was large, large enough for a full-grown man to walk into without ducking his head. I swung the door all the way open. Wanda joined me at my side and together we took in what was inside.

I said, "Guess I should go through this stuff. Might give us a clue to what happened."

There were two cylindrical, metallic core loaders on the middle shelf. Each of them had an illuminated, blue-glowing band encircling the top of the units. These were backup system memory stores, which held a mind-bending amount of data. *Strange to have these stored within a captain's ready room vault.*

"I got these," Wanda said, discarding the fire extinguisher and hefting one and then two of the heavy-looking memory stores. Her biceps bulged. Giving me a wink, she said, "Each of these babies weighs more than you do."

Ryder was pinging my Jadoo ring.

"Go ahead, Ryder."

"I'm here in E & P; things have just started coming alive. Control boards activating... Environmental systems normalizing."

"Yeah, Sonya's doing her thing. What's the status of the drives?"

"Visually, things seem okay. No physical damage. And like I said, things are coming alive in here."

"Good. Get to the bridge ASAP. We've got company."

HARDY TRUDGED FORWARD, the Marines, Max, Grip, Ham, and Hock, keeping pace behind.

He listened to them chatting among themselves, razzing one another, their way of dealing with mounting nerves. Thus far, ship compartments, passageways, and major corridors had been devoid of life. Ship lights had yet to come on, the farther forward they went.

"This is creepy as fuck," Grip said. "The ship held what? Thousands? Where the hell is everyone?"

No one answered him.

Hardy slowed, taking notice of new signs of struggle: dried blood streaks on a bulkhead, weapons damage to the corridor, and other marks he'd yet to decipher.

They turned a corner, seeing more blood, a lot more blood, and indications of far more weapons fire. Charred plasma craters pocked virtually every surface.

Max said, "Looks like the alien fuckers came through here like a meatgrinder... Ship's crew fought hard."

They followed the increasing signs of carnage, eventually coming up to one of the ship's main lower deck holds, some twenty meters up ahead. The entrance hatch doors, extra wide to enable the movement of cargo, had been left open. Max signaled for his crew to take up a stacked line formation.

Hardy checked his readings. Although there were signs of "life," motion sensors detected very little movement.

He looked to Max. "No time like the present; it's time to party, boys."

Hardy breached the compartment at a full run, ready to confront whatever hostiles were present. Weapons raised, fingers on triggers, Max and crew were close on his six. Once inside, they spun, ready to target the enemy. Most of the overhead lighting had previously been shot out.

Hardy took in the grisly sight.

Despite being fully trained and battle hardened, he watched as the Marines wavered, weapons lowered. Ham was making gagging noises over the open channel.

Max said, "Don't you dare lose it in your helmet, Ham! If you have to spew, leave, and do it out in the passageway."

"I'm good, boss..."

Hardy was somewhat surprised they didn't all lose their collective lunch. The compartment was packed with what was left of the crewmembers. He counted several hundred poor souls lying prone on their backs.

"Looks like they were... what? Tortured... mutilated?" Max commented.

"This is bad, real fucking bad," Grip said under his breath.

The hold was half the size of a football field, and the scope of the horror was breathtaking.

Max said, "Let's clear this hold, just in case there are any bad guys lurking back there around those tall shelves."

Staying on high alert, they separated and moved out.

Meanwhile, Hardy walked among the rows of bodies—each lying within a kind of metal, high-lipped pan. He tried to comprehend who, *what*, had done this to them. He tried to make sense of the alien "technology" apparent within each of the carcasses. Whatever it was, it was allowing these bodies to remain alive.

Several minutes later, Max was back at his side. "I think some of these people are ... still alive."

"No, Max... All of them are still alive."

"Good mother of God."

Grip joined them and knelt next to one body, a woman. "Uh... are those bite marks I'm seeing?"

In the dimly lit hold, a light flickered above, casting eerie, strobing shadows upon the uniformed crewmember—one that Hardy was certain once bore the visage of a captivating beauty. Now, her form was a grotesque blend of life and death, a macabre symphony orchestrated by the unfathomable power of something, perhaps a kind of alien nanite technology.

Hardy knelt next to Grip. "I can almost see her..."

"Huh?"

"Once upon a time, she possessed delicate features, her countenance... was radiant and youthful," Hardy said, shaking his head.

"That's almost poetic, Hardy."

He continued to stare at her. Time had frozen upon her, unyielding in its grip, leaving her suspended in this eternal stagnation of decay.

He heard Max sniff and clear his throat.

Hardy wondered why she in particular had so deeply affected all of them.

He knew why... This could just as easily have been Doc Viv, or Captain Pristy, or God forbid, young Sonya. He took in her once undoubtedly smooth and lustrous skin, which now clung to her skeletal frame in tattered shreds, discolored by the onset of decomposition. Her corpse was animated by a twisted fusion of technology and necromancy. Locks of flowing hair now hung in ragged clumps, with strands of various lengths intertwined with decaying tissue. The remnants of her uniform clung tightly to her skeletal form, concealing the horrors that lurked beneath, though its fabric had long lost its original royal blue, now soiled with the stains of time and the unrelenting march of decomposition.

Suddenly, her head turned toward them. Grip and Max behind them gasped and jumped.

"Shit! Didn't expect that," Grip said.

Now, her vacant eyes, surely once filled with vitality and sparkling with intelligence, were locked upon them. The irises, once colored with a deep, captivating hue, had faded to a murky gray. Hardy felt her stare as if it could see into his very soul. Perhaps most unsettling of all were the faint signs of movement that occasionally rippled across her decomposing flesh.

"Look," Grip said, pointing to an area on her exposed neck.

Small clusters of tiny metallic particles, the alien nanites that had taken residence within her decaying body, scurried beneath her skin, their alien purpose unknown.

"They're keeping her body minimally intact and functional despite the ravages of time."

Seemingly becoming more cognizant of their presence, or maybe it was just coincidence, her movements had become more animated—more desperate. Her disjointed twisting and heaving were now accompanied by a symphony of creaking bones and the unsettling whispers of untethered flesh.

Hardy placed a metal hand upon what was left of the woman's arm. But before Hardy could say anything, perhaps something soothing, or even fatalistic, the captain was reaching out to him.

"Hostiles approaching... get up here, Hardy."

Chapter 17

"**I** need to stretch my legs," Wanda said, looking antsy. "Going to check out what's on this deck."

We listened to *Adams'* back-and-forth comms chatter with the deployed Arrow pilots.

Ryder paced the bridge, clearly frustrated. "I should be out there," he said.

Dozens of ships had risen from the surrounding asteroids, but despite sensor sweeps by *Adams* and *Lincoln*, nothing had been detected. I was curious if Hardy had detected anything —*Where the hell is he, anyway?*

Akari said, "They're making a move."

The swarm of scorpion-flies outnumbered Arrows two to one. I inwardly debated rounding up the team and heading back to *Adams* via *Hub Gunther*.

Adams was firing now, as the Arrows were approaching the alien fighters.

I took a seat at the captain's mount and tried to figure out the overly complicated armrest controls. Akari hurried over. "What do you want? Comms?"

I bit back my own frustrated retort and just nodded instead.

She pointed. "Comms channels are these touchpads here. I've put Chen on this pad here, Grimes here. The entire *Adams* bridge here."

I punched the touchpad, probably harder than I should have. "Mr. Grimes! Get ready to jump the ship."

"Captain... we have Arrows out there—"

"Well aware of that. They can bug out as well... or, if need be, there's room for them on *Lincoln*." I glanced over to Ryder, who looked dubious of that statement, and shrugged. "Look, whoever these hostiles are, they took out an entire US Space-Navy warship's crew... thousands of crewmembers. I'm not taking any chances of that happening to *Adams*. So, you'll get some distance, and we can reassess things later."

"Copy that, Captain," Grimes said.

Bosun Polk jumped onto the channel. "Sir, what about you and your team?"

"Forget about us; just tell me *Adams'* engines are ready to jump on my command."

"All systems are green," Grimes said.

"Send us your intended jump coordinates, then jump."

Akari said, "Got the coordinates."

"Jump now, Mr. Grimes."

We watched the halo display as the seconds ticked by. The Arrows had engaged the enemy.

"Mr. Grimes?"

"Uh... Sir, nothing's happening?"

"What do you mean nothing's happening?"

"Just that. All systems are operational. It's as if we're being held in place."

I let out a breath, swallowed, calmed myself. "Have Coogong do a ship-wide systems analysis. Dammit! Keep me in the loop." I punched off.

Hardy, followed by the Marines, was now filing into the bridge.

Akari said, "Captain, *Adams* is out of spikes... for the time being, I'm having Bosun Polk shut down all of *her* weapons systems. Add to that, we can't risk hitting our own fighters out there."

"Take a breath; you're not wrong, Lieutenant. Truth is, our Arrows seem to be holding their own ... Actually, they're doing better than that."

Ryder joined her at the tactical station. "Those are my pilots," he said, looking proud. "... and you're right, Cap. They're doing more than holding their own."

I got to my feet. "Sitrep, Hardy."

Seeing that the three of us had retracted our helmet face-plates, the Marines followed suit. Immediately, I could see the emotional impact of what they had observed.

Hardy, with constant interjections from Max and crew, relayed, in detail, what they had found within that lower deck hold.

A fiery explosion from the halo display caught everyone's attention.

"We lost another Arrow," Akari said. "That makes five thus far."

"But we've taken out twenty-six of those scorpion-flies," Ryder said.

"What now?" Max said.

"May I suggest we amscray out of here?" Wanda said, joining her fellow Marines.

It was Grip who answered first. "No. There's serious payback in order here."

Ham and Hock nodded; they seemed to be on the verge of tears, something I had never witnessed from the twins.

Wanda saw the conviction on Grip's face and slowly

nodded. "Copy that, big guy. I'm with you." They fist punched to affirm their mutual commitment.

I wanted to tell Grip, to tell each of them, that this wasn't our mission. That keeping *Adams'* crew safe was paramount. That it was time for us to head home; we had our own fight there to return to.

Sonya's projected image appeared above a nearby console. "We're still pirates, right?" she said in a voice so quiet I barely heard her. She angrily secured several wayward strands of purple hair behind one ear. "I mean, sure, we're being dragged back into your US Space-Navy bullshit, but we're still pirates, aren't we?" she repeated, her words coming out more as pleading than questioning. "I saw what they saw, you know... via helmet cams down there in that hold... It was terrible... horrible."

"We'll always be pirates," I said to Sonya, then glanced at the others. "We're not abandoning *Lincoln's* crew. I promise. But for right now, we, I, need to get back to *Adams.*" No one looked to be buying what I was selling.

"You have my word," I said.

Max gave a half nod while Grip shrugged. Wanda said, "Fine. What are our orders?"

"*Lincoln* is slowly coming back online." I looked to Ryder. "How about the propulsion system?"

"Same... drives are slowly coming back online. But remember, this is a big mother of a ship. Nothing happens fast."

"There you go... Nothing we can do here right now. I want everyone back on *Adams.* Let's head down to the flight deck." A quick glance toward Sonya's projected image told me she wasn't happy about that, but at least she wasn't putting up a fight.

Chapter 18

Commander Lu-puk

He should have felt safe, secure here within the base's highly advanced command center. And yes, from an intellectual perspective, Lu-puk knew it would be nearly impossible for, say, these new alien interlopers to actually observe the sprawling, yet perfectly camouflaged compound. Then again... if one happened to be right on top of the facility... He shoved the errant thought aside. *No, no, that would be impossible. Liquilid shields and mounted defenses are always at the ready! Hell, navigating this deep into such a precarious asteroid field...* he shook his head; *yes, unwelcome intruders are highly unlikely.*

Now, something else was bothering him. Lu-puk glared at his monitoring array, his fists clenched. Like all Liquilid beings, he had three types of teeth, *acrodonts*, *pleurodonts*, and *thecodonts*, oddly reminiscent of razor-sharp choppers found within other reptilian species within the galaxy. Grinding them incessantly with a menacing sound, Lu-puk desperately wanted to lash out, to punch something... *anything*. But Lu-puk was averse to pain, any kind of pain. So, he consciously tempered his growing frustration.

It was late, and much of his command center crew had slunk back into their hidey-hole quarters. Quarters that replicated their small, moist, and dark subterranean home-world habitats.

He adjusted the sensor resolution and eyed one alien vessel in particular. He still couldn't get a proper read on this ship. *What was its name again? Ah yes, Portent.* Its integrated auxiliary propulsion system, one that wasn't so much an actual drive or engine... *so what is it?*

Lu-puk had run every diagnostic at his disposal. He now ran a full suite of system diagnostics again. Nothing. *Our tech is far superior to that of the humans. Could this one ship not be of human design?*

He knew he was pushing himself too hard, that he needed a break. He glanced over to his feeding plate and the awaiting, trembling Bliddit there. He'd mentally instructed the recently injected nanites to cordon off the creature's auditory and visual senses, while leaving its ability to feel pain fully intact. He already knew Bliddits were terrified of the dark. Normally, eating a little something would quell his growing anxiety, that and his mounting anger. But multiple issues were playing havoc with his appetite.

Hmm, perhaps it is external to the vessel ... Lu-puk set his station to notify his neural implants if anything drastic happened and slithered out of his monitoring chamber and across the smooth-decked passageway. While there were many horizontal passageways within the base, there were just as many vertical and angled passageways, or shafts, as well. The base was an organic, interconnected hive of various-sized compartments. Thus, bulkheads within the various passageways and shafts were color-coded; this was mainly for new arrivals.

Four colors ran down their respective lengths; each color—brown, green, orange, and red—indicated a generated shift of directional gravity, although these gravity characteristics could be changed depending on the direction one was traversing. Horizontal passageways, brown, had typical, or normal, gravity characteristics. For the vertical shafts, green, gravity moved with a more back-and-forth, sideways inclination, turning the thruway into a kind of slow-drop shaft. Lu-puk slithered to an angled orange shaft and let it slow-slide him downward until he reached a junction. With practiced skill, he twisted and slow dropped toward the asteroid's center.

The fall was long, which gave Lu-puk time to think. He was the ranking officer in this sector. He'd been told numerous times... he had but one job: *hold the advancement of alien inter-lopers from moving further into Liquilid territories.* But allowing new, highly advanced alien technologies to slip through his claws, well, that would be his undoing. It had been the acquiring of alien tech that had propelled their once-primitive race to their current superior status. No, he would be punished if he and his crew could not decipher *Portent's* auxiliary means of propulsion. Sure as shit fell downhill, he was not going to let this issue be his downfall.

Coming to the next shaft, he rolled, and rolled again, ending within standard gravity. He took a moment to ensure he looked presentable, then casually slithered forward as if he had all the time in the world and nothing he was about to see would be all that impressive to him.

Which wasn't true, because the quantum flux generator impressed everyone.

He slid into the massive chamber and stopped, inner eyelids

sliding over his pupils. The quantum fluctuations did strange things to the light spectrum. Red light became green became yellow, all in the space of a heartbeat.

The flux generator was a complex and massive device that employed advanced principles of physics to create a powerful field capable of disrupting the spacetime fabric in its vicinity. It was a technology pilfered from a now long-destroyed neighboring alien society. Lu-puk was certain the tech was beyond the current level of human understanding. From a visual standpoint, the flux generator was an imposing sight, held within a massive subterranean compartment.

Entering the space, he was instantly assaulted by fluctuating waves of heat. Rising five stories overhead, the glowing superstructure, even after seeing it many times, took Lu-puk's breath away. It consisted of a central core surrounded by a series of concentric rings. The rings were made up of a complex array of materials that allowed the generator to harness and manipulate energy from the surrounding environment. The central core housed a series of advanced control systems that regulated the flow of energy and maintained the stability of the generator. The principle behind the generator was the concept of flux, which is the flow of energy or matter through a surface. In this case, the generator created a flux field that altered the local spacetime curvature. This allowed the generator to manipulate the properties of the space around it, including gravity and electromagnetism. Powerful electromagnetic fields surrounded the central core, and one should be wary of getting too close. By altering the intensity and direction of the flux fields, the generator could control the properties of surrounding space and matter—namely, in this case, interloper warships.

He stared at the massive, slowly rotating and pulsing device. It was this miraculous contraption that enabled his species to rule Liquilid space. First of all, the quantum flux generator would make it impossible for enemy ships to generate worm-holes, initiate quantum jumps, or even utilize quantum trans-port systems. Second, it was capable of sending tendrils of flux energy deep into the galaxy. Thin lines of quantum energy that, when encountering a wormhole, could divert its intended desti-nation, bringing ships to this remote, deep space system. Here, the Liquilids could absorb potential new technologies and, if worthwhile, enslave a crew species. And if, by chance, their flesh was tasty... all the better.

For a thousand years the process had worked successfully. And for the last two hundred years, their sensor capacities had been able to read every technology of every ship they had captured. *So why can't I read Portent's auxiliary propulsion system?*

"Officer on deck!"

The alert bellowed into neural implants throughout the compartment. Most crew didn't stop what they were doing. Their jobs required concentrated attention to their posts, thus giving them an excuse not to respond with the same obligatory reactions as other base personnel. A nearby apprentice of some sort, on the other hand, was already sliding along on his belly to greet him. Off in the distance, a pair of female engineers had stopped what they were doing and were slowly meandering across the deck with little enthusiasm.

Lu-puk ignored the apprentice, but as the first of the engi-neers was close enough, Lu-puk spun, lashing his tail like a whip, striking the female across the chops. She stopped long enough to regain her bearings but did not dare complain or make a fuss. The others, evaluating Lu-puk's foul mood, now moved with more determination, forming a straight line and pressing their foreheads onto the deck—a show of respect. With eyes narrowed, Lu-puk slithered forward.

"We have captured three ships," he hissed. "Humans, like

the ones on USS *Lincoln,* and there are other aliens as well. One ship has three forms of propulsion: main engines, jump drives, wormhole manufacture capability, and some kind of an auxiliary system, one I have yet to decipher."

He waited to see who here would speak first and risk his ire.

The apprentice spoke. "Certainly running diagnostics and—"

Lu-puk's tail whipped across the apprentice's face, propelling his head into a nearby support post. He cried out, then continued to whimper.

Lu-puk now spoke so softly that his words were barely audible. "I have run diagnostics. I have checked the hardware and software..." He shook his head. "There is nothing wrong with the control center's sensors or our assessments." He looked past them, up to the flux generator. "This device is the core technology that enables those scans, our invasive views into their vessels."

"Then it must be an advanced technology... one we are not familiar with," the other female engineer said, already wincing at the inevitable whipping tail.

"Tell me the technology!" Lu-puk demanded, showing his teeth. "Quantum, nuclear, chemical, what?"

"Um, well, that is the question, Sir..." the engineer said. "Undoubtedly we have scanned for all those, so it must be something else."

Lu-puk's neural implants pinged. A high-priority notification was taking shape in his mind. He was to make his report to the Admiral within the hour. He inwardly swore.

He looked at them, one by one. "You have all been less than worthless. I assure you that will be mentioned in my report to the Admiral. Just know, whatever punishment I receive... you'll get five times worse. That is, unless you figure out *Portent's* third means of propulsion."

"Yes, Sir!" all three crewmembers answered in unison.

Abruptly pivoting, Lu-puk's tail lashed out high into the air, then whipped back just as quickly, evoking a loud *snap!*

He headed for the nearest shaft, reversing the gravitational polarity via his implants. Flopping backward, he allowed the waves of distributed energy to propel him upward, like an untethered balloon. Querying his neural implants once more, he found what he was looking for and spooled up the most recent battle video feeds. He watched them and then watched them again. He ran two thousand calculations, reassessed the output, then saved the data. He hadn't realized what a formidable enemy this enemy was. These humans... they'd fought like true battle-tested warriors, interstellar conquerors! Had destroyed ten Slissets for every one Arrow lost.

The failures are mounting, Lu-puk thought. By the time he'd reached the control center, he was nearly apoplectic with dread. He took a seat at his station, then reluctantly transmitted a request to speak with the Admiral. Far better to show some initiative, he figured.

Plu-tik appeared in Lu-puk's mind, his dorsal spikes raised, his serpentine tongue flickering in and out, as if he had just tasted a bad Sqillmonk. The only good news was Lu-puk was here on this flux generator station, instead of there on the Admiral's red ship.

"Report," Plu-tik hissed.

"The first wave of Slisset fighters has been destroyed," Lu-puk said.

"What damage did we inflict upon the enemy?"

"Uh... five of the human fighters, called Arrows, were destroyed."

Plu-tik stared. "Damage to their primary warships?"

Lu-puk braced himself. "There was no damage to the other ships."

Silence, thick and angry and dangerous, filled the air. Plu-tik glared back at him, then asked, "Have we identified the third means of propulsion for the vessel designated as *Portent*?"

"Not yet, Admiral."

"A problem with your scanners." It came out as more of a statement than a question.

"There are no technical issues with our scanners, Sir," Lu-puk said. "I assure you, my finest engineers are working the problem as we speak."

"I see." Admiral Plu-tik's tail coiled, looking ready to strike. "Explain how you lost sixty of our finest Slisset fighters. How, over the course of just a few cycles, you have so unequivocally humiliated yourself while disgracing our entire regimen."

"Sir, with the effectiveness of our flux generator, we have yet seen the need to deploy our Slisset fighters en masse. Add to the fact, this enemy, these humans, are highly experienced when it comes to this sort of open space combat... dogfights."

"Explain!"

Lu-puk thought he just had.

"Um... well, in the past, with the arrival of an alien ship, we immediately captured it. Not one has deployed its fighters as quickly as USS *Adams*," Lu-puk said, realizing his response sounded stupid, lame. "Typically, there would be more time where we would assess the enemy, properly strategize the battle situation, only then approach. Then we would destroy the enemy's fighters as they left the flight bays. But this time, the humans had their Arrows deployed almost immediately... and, I might add, piloted them quite competently."

Terrifyingly competently was Lu-puk's last thought before high-voltage electricity coursed through his body. He thrashed and screamed, teeth grinding and vertebrae twisting in ways that no Liquilid was meant to endure. When it finally stopped,

Lu-puk lay curled on the deck in the fetal position, moaning and whimpering like a beaten child.

"Reprogram the fighters," Admiral Plu-tik said. "I want them responding properly to the enemy before we launch the next wave."

"Yes, Sir," Commander Lu-puk croaked, attempting to lift himself off the deck. Getting onto all fours, he said, "May I suggest we deploy frigate-class warships immediately?"

"Maybe you should have found your ball sac and requested fleet support earlier?"

Lu-puk was fairly certain his ball sac was still smoldering from that last jolt. He kept his mouth shut.

The Admiral continued, "I am wary of these *innovative* humans. And concerned we do not have a better understanding of this *Portent* ship's peculiar technology."

The Admiral seemed to be considering his options—looking about Lu-puk's surroundings. "Is that a Bliddit?"

Shit. "Yes, Admiral."

"One of the larger blue-herring breeds from the Torring System?"

"Uh, I believe so, Sir."

"I will have it couriered over to my ship. You don't need that kind of distraction."

Terrific. That Bliddit cost me a week's wages. He kept the thought to himself. "I'll have it boxed up for you, Admiral."

Chapter 19

Liquilid Empire Star System
USS Adams

Major Vivian Leigh

"I need more blood. AB negative." Doc Viv was elbows-deep in Arrow pilot Charles Daffy's open torso.

"Last AB negative." The MediBot attached the bag of plasma as instructed and stood at the ready for further commands.

Doc Viv held in the urge to scream and focused in on the copious bits of shrapnel in the patient's spleen. The fist-sized organ on the upper left side of his abdomen looked like an overly stuffed pin cushion.

"I can't save it. Prepare for splenectomy." Viv stood back from Daffy, as if preparing for a dive off a steep cliff. "Zap-Blade 15."

MediBot One placed the small plasma scalpel down into her gloved, open palm.

Viv dove back in with the precision and finesse that came

from years of surgical practice—within two minutes she had removed the riddled spleen. The MediBot was ready with a stainless-steel disposal receptacle.

Attention Needed In 6445.
Attention Needed In 6445.

Doc Viv turned to her surgical-assist MediBot. "Finish up here."

She had programmed an alert to let her know when Sonya was in distress. As much as she believed that all her patients deserved equal care, the truth of the matter was she did have her favorites.

HealthBay was bustling, and not in a good way. The ensuing battles with hostiles had taken their toll on the Arrow pilots. It was difficult to know where one dogfight skirmish ended and the next began. Most of the 2.0s medical team was now with Captain Loggins on *Wrath*—a development that made Viv's job not just difficult but nearly impossible.

She stripped off her mask and latex gloves and stuffed them into the incinerator spout—grabbed fresh ones and headed down the sterile corridor to check in on Sonya. The hatch door to 6445 slid open, and Viv moved inside like someone who was late for an important meeting.

"Hey, Doc." Sonya looked up from her tablet. Her face was pale, and her monitor displayed an elevated heart rate.

Viv strode over to Sonya's bedside, smiling in an effort to calm her young patient. "Your heart rate is elevated. Let's see if we can find out what's going on." Viv enabled the 3D patient avatar. As it slowly turned on its axis over Sonya's bed, she took in the various life status icons and metadata alerts.

"I think I know what the problem is." Sonya's tone was hushed, as if she were about to share a secret. "You need to see this." Sonya held out her tablet so Viv could see what was being displayed.

"Oh my God. How did you get that? Where..."

She shrugged a shoulder. "It's a feed from Hardy. I hacked into it. You did know about the team sent to that ship that was discovered in a nearby asteroid field, right?"

Viv hesitated. When would she have had time to learn anything new?

"It's USS *Lincoln*. Went missing years ago... big dreadnought. Anyway, a team went to check things out. This is what they found... It's, uh, hard to watch."

Viv leaned closer, a line forming between her brows. She shook her head. "So, those are the crewmembers? *Lincoln's* crewmembers? Christ, are they dead?"

"Apparently not. Kept alive with some kind of alien nanites, at least according to Hardy."

Viv stifled the rise of bile rushing into her throat.

"Who else is there from *Adams*?"

"Besides Hardy? Max and his four Marines... uh, and Quintos, Ryder, and Akari. They took the *Hub Gunther* and three Arrows."

Viv thumb-tapped her Jadoo ring and hailed Quintos.

His image projected up from her ring almost immediately. He looked annoyed.

"A little busy here, Viv. What's going on?" He now saw where she was. "Is Sonya okay?"

"I'm fine," Sonya said in a way that only teenagers can— sounding both put out and indifferent at the same time.

"Not a social call, Quintos. What the hell are you doing about those crewmembers in that hold?" Viv queried in a clipped tone.

"How do you even know..." He let the question go. "We just discovered them minutes ago, so nothing yet. There's a slew of scorpion-flies attacking our Arrows; the injured crew will have to wait."

"You're unbelievable. I'm headed over there. Those men and women need my attention."

"No." Quintos's brow bunched together, a furry caterpillar recoiling. "It's not safe. Did you not hear me? Alien scorpion-flies are all over the place." He shook his head. "I can't allow it."

Viv laughed out loud. "Uh-huh, well... I'll be fine. I'll take Selleck. She's here in HealthBay talking to a counselor—lost her boyfriend earlier today. But I think she'll be grateful for the distraction."

Viv cut the connection just as Quintos was about to speak.

We'll continue that conversation later.

"So, you're really going over there?" Sonya asked in an *are-you-crazy* sort of way.

"Those people are suffering. I can't sit by and allow that to continue. But you, young lady, need to rest." She took the tablet from her and placed it on the bedside table. "I'm serious... you need sleep. You need to get well." She gave her leg a couple of pats and hurried out into the main corridor.

"Good luck!" she heard Sonya say. She knew the little brat had already reached for her tablet again.

Making a beeline for HealthBay's pharma-hold, she had to wait while the ship's AI scanned her DNA before being allowed to enter. Some of the ship's most toxic and life-saving medications were stored in this four-hundred-square foot space. Entering, the air was a brisk 51 degrees. She breathed in the lingering medicinal scent.

Being an antiseptic area, the compartment glistened from deck to deckhead, reflective stainless-steel bulkheads, titanium hardware, and diamond glass counters greeting her. White, blue, green, and yellow containers lined bulkhead shelves like standing-tall, uniformed soldiers.

Viv went to one of the formidable refrigerator units, scanning the shelves. She found what she was looking for. Dimeltite Formade. There were several small cartons, fifty vials in each carton. The drug had been around for the past decade and was one that she took no pleasure in administering. Just a small amount was lethal and should be an adequate means of euthanizing the *Lincoln* crewmembers.

Viv carefully took out four cartons. The temperature in the cold unit was 34 degrees, and she knew she'd have to keep the vials at that same temperature. She looked for one of the portable refrigeration cases she knew was around here, somewhere. Frustrated, she slammed the drawer she'd been rifling through. *I don't have time for this.* She calculated in her head if she'd really need the case anyway. She had a full hour before viability would be considered compromised.

Viv glanced up. "Sir Calvin, I need some help."

I am at your service, Doctor. How may I assist you?

The ship AI's voice boomed from above, a male voice speaking in the now-familiar highbrow British accent. It didn't annoy her nearly as much as it had when they'd first come aboard.

"I need you to contact Arrow pilot Christy Selleck. She's here in HealthBay..." Viv walked and talked, grabbing two doctor's satchels and a handful of syringes from a nearby closet. She placed the cartons and needles into the bags. "Tell her to meet me at Flight Bay, stat."

Flight bay, you say?

"Yes, that's right. And I need you to contact Bay Chief Mintz. Tell him to find me an Arrow. Make sure it is fueled up and ready to go."

I believe all the Arrows are currently engaged, Doctor Leigh.

"Just do what I asked. Mintz will just need to figure it out. Oh, and this needs to happen in the next three minutes."

I will make the call.

"OH. Also make sure we have the coordinates to USS *Lincoln*."

Yes, Doctor. Consider it done.

She stopped what she was doing and took a breath. *Am I really doing this?*

Her satchel strapped over one shoulder, she left the pharma-hold and spoke to the attending counter nurse, letting her know she'd be gone for several hours, then quick- walked toward HealthBay's exit. She knew that quansporting was not operational, so she sprinted down the corridor toward the bank of GravLifts. Hurrying into the first available car, she barked to the hover lift bot attendant, "Flight Bay."

SELLECK WAS STANDING THERE, looking apprehensive, as Viv scurried out of the lift.

"Good, you got here quick," Viv said, somewhat out of breath.

"Yes, Ma'am, I ran to get here. Um, it sounded urgent." Selleck's eyes were red, but she looked to be holding it together.

"Come on, no time to waste." Side by side they sprinted down the corridor toward Flight Bay.

"Ma'am, can I ask what this is about?"

"Please, knock off the Ma'am crap. I'm Doc Viv, or simply Viv."

Entering Flight Bay, Viv's ears were jarringly accosted by the sounds of loud clangs, yelling voices overhead on the PA system, and the high-pitched revving of multiple Arrow drives. This was not Viv's environment, and it had taken her off guard.

"This way, Doc Viv," Selleck said. "Already spoke to the chief. Uh... he's not real happy with you. Bit perturbed to have had the ship's AI barking off orders to him."

Before she could answer, a sleek candy-apple-red Arrow fighter rolled up beside the two of them.

"Our ride's here. You ready for this?" Selleck said with a crooked smile.

"Sure, I am," she said unconvincingly.

"And thank you for trusting me. I really need this right now." Selleck's big brown eyes conveyed just how much she meant it.

"It's all good." Viv fumbled in her satchel for her tablet. "I have the coordinates for the—"

Selleck shook her head. "No need, we're all set. No offense, but I do this for a living. Coordinates have already been uploaded. That and I have a photographic memory."

Viv smiled and released a much-needed laugh. "You're full of surprises, Lieutenant Christy Selleck."

Selleck returned the smile. Her lips were full and naturally pink, only adding to her vulnerable appearance. Add in her snow-white complexion, and Viv, still in her mid-thirties, was feeling older than she liked.

One of the bay's maintenance guys in brown overalls was climbing down from the cockpit. He jumped down, skipping the last few rungs, and turned to face them.

Selleck said, "This is Benny Langford, maintenance supervisor. He's a good guy."

"It just came out of service. The drive needed to be swapped. Ran preliminary diagnostics. Seems to be all right. But I'd feel better if I could run a few more thorough checks on her," Langford said, eyebrows raised.

Selleck looked to Viv.

"Appreciate that, but we're in a time crunch. I'm sure you did a good job... we'll be fine," Viv said, having no idea if he'd done a good job.

Langford offered a disapproving nod and sauntered off.

She looked to Selleck. "Look, I know this is not ideal, scorpion-flies and a craft that was grudgingly passed by maintenance."

"I'm here to serve, Doc. Not to question orders. Any order coming from you is as good as one from the captain."

"Thank you, Selleck. I have about forty-eight minutes to get to USS *Lincoln* and administer these drugs. After that the effects are no longer viable. We don't want those men and women to suffer any more than they have already."

Selleck gave her a quick nod and gestured to the inset ladder. "Then up we go. You first; this is a two-seater named *Deux* Arrow. You're in back."

Once seated within the sleek red craft, she looked about the confined space. So many touch buttons, multicolored lights, and display screens. Again, she felt way, way, way out of her element.

She found that communications were easy between the front and back seats, and Viv had a clear line of vision over Selleck's shoulder and out the canopy. Viv watched as Selleck did a quick systems check, then checked their flight coordinates. Startled, she heard the sounds of the aft drive come alive, reverberating through the cockpit area. For someone who never considered herself religious, Viv found herself saying a silent prayer.

Two minutes later the Arrow was rocketing out into space and banking hard to starboard. She had to admit, the speed, the sounds, felt exhilarating.

Selleck said, "We'll be heading around the back side of these larger rocks. And we'll have to dodge a few of the asteroids, so hold on tight. It's better than being dragged into a dogfight with one of those scorpion-flies... Although, I wouldn't mind a little payback right now."

Viv did her best, offering up a confident nod. One her pilot wouldn't see.

Selleck maneuvered the Arrow with amazing agility. Viv found her nerves quelling as she watched the pilot, hands on the controls, simultaneously eyeing the panel, attending to blinking on and off warning lights, all the while keeping them on course.

"We should be good for now. I have an arrival time of... fourteen minutes and forty seconds."

"That's great, Selleck. That should still give me enough time to do what I need to do." She was second guessing herself now, wishing she'd grabbed more syringes. *What if some are defective?*

She knew she needed to stay calm. For God's sake, Selleck had just lost the love of her life, a young pilot who went by the moniker of Deep-Throat. Viv had known him, more like known of him. His birth name was Dave Plant, and he and Selleck were supposed to be married once they returned to Earth.

"Selleck, I really am so sorry about your fiancé, Lieutenant Plant. I didn't know him very well, but he had an exceptional reputation."

Selleck's shoulders stiffened somewhat at the mention of his name and then softened. "Thanks, Doc. I appreciate that. He was a good man. He... he was everything to me."

Silence filled the space between them and then Selleck made a sharp bank to port, avoiding several smaller asteroids.

Viv gripped the edge of the faux leather seat.

"Hang on. Might get a little bumpy during this stretch."

Viv stayed quiet, realizing she had stopped breathing.

"Shit."

"What is it?" Viv asked, not sure she wanted to know the answer.

"An indicator light..."

"What does that mean?" Viv sputtered.

"Primary plasma gun... It might have overheated. But no worries. I'm dodging asteroids, not fighting off hostiles." Selleck's tone was nonchalant... just another day at the office.

Viv didn't speak but managed a silent nod.

"Hang on; we're coming into the home stretch." Selleck flew with the assurance of a seasoned pilot, which she was.

Get us there safely, and I will personally make sure you get a medal.

Suddenly, the craft jostled, dipped, and then righted—a ship upon stormy waters.

THUNK!

"Dammit! We're hit."

Viv swallowed. "Hit?"

"Yeah, just a fender bender though. Think we're okay."

Viv took several deep breaths as her anxiety mounted. She wished she had a paper bag to breathe into.

"Well, will you look at that?" Selleck said, sounding like she was smiling.

Viv looked over Selleck's shoulder through the *Deux* Arrow's canopy. It was the most beautiful sight she'd ever seen.

Chapter 20

Viv hadn't known what to expect. Now, seeing USS *Lincoln* through the canopy, her sleek Space-Wing design, her in-flight appearance of swift movement, while, of course, she was perfectly still. She thought how strange it was that ocean-going and deep spaceships were typically thought of in the feminine genre. No... this ship was all masculine. With those three aft, oversized drive engines, the vessel oozed power, screamed raw testosterone. It begged the question: how had such a stalwart-looking vessel been so effectively defeated?

"We're making our approach," Selleck said. "It's a little unnerving not getting clearance prior to final approach."

"We already know the *Hub Gunther* and a few Arrows managed..."

"I'm not saying I'm incapable of doing my job," Selleck spat back.

Viv cringed. The young pilot had just lost her boyfriend; she was a mess and doubting every aspect of her life about now. *She certainly doesn't need me pushing her buttons.* "You got this, girl. I wouldn't want any other pilot."

"Oh, so now you resort to patronizing?"

She bit her lip. *Fuck.* "Maybe I'll just shut up for a while."

"Roger that," Selleck said.

Selleck's sudden mood change was taking Viv by surprise—still mourning her loss or not, Viv was a superior officer, a major at that; there was only so much leeway she was willing to give here. She couldn't see the pilot's face, see what was going on with her.

They slowed to a near crawl, the egress into *Lincoln's* port-side flight bay getting larger by the moment. The blue-hued energy barrier shimmered and pulsed as if it was cognizant of their arrival—in a sense, perhaps it was.

They breached the barrier, Selleck quickly bringing the hovering Arrow to a standstill. Viv blinked, the bright overheads making her squint, cones and rods quickly trying to adjust.

Peering down at the deck, Viv said, "Didn't expect such a full house... not a lot of parking options, huh?"

Selleck didn't reply. She goosed the throttle, taking them further, deeper, into the bay.

"Over to the left. There's the *Gunther!*" Viv said, pointing a finger that Selleck, undoubtedly, couldn't see.

"How about we put a pause on all the backseat driving for a while?"

All the backseat driving? Viv, stymied and slack-jawed, glowered at the back of Selleck's head.

The Arrow pivoted in place, then descended ever-so-slowly. She too had seen there was only one open slot between the countless parked Arrows. How Selleck was managing to jockey this craft into such a small space, with literally inches to spare, only increased Viv's appreciation for the pilot's abilities. Then again, didn't she herself exhibit similar near-superhuman abilities with a Zap-Blade?

Even before the Arrow came to rest upon the flight deck,

Selleck had the canopy rising like the opening jaws of an alien creature.

They both stood. Selleck was descending the inset ladder without so much as a glance back at Viv.

Gathering her satchel, she murmured, "No, no... don't bother yourself. I got this..."

Hopping down onto the flight deck, Viv saw that Selleck was already making her way toward the *Hub Gunther*. Above, she heard the Arrow's canopy clamp shut.

In all the times she'd been inside a spacecraft flight bay it had always been an assault on the senses, the ear-shattering noise, the flurry of busy flight crews... but here, right now, the silence was deafening.

Reaching the *Gunther*, the craft's ramp deployed, Selleck stood with hands on hips. "Nobody's here," she said.

"Yeah, well... why would there be?" Viv said, answering with the same snippety tone as the pilot. "They're here to do a job, not sit around and twiddle their thumbs."

Before she had time to regret her nasty comeback, she heard voices off to their left. Viv took in and then let out a controlled breath. Quintos was not going to be happy she was here.

She watched as the team quickly approached: Quintos in the lead, followed by Max and his Marines, and Hardy bringing up the rear—she wondered what their big hurry was.

With a furrowed brow, Quintos was already shaking his head. "No. You can't be here, Viv... Whatever you were thinking, it's not happening."

Behind her, Selleck said, "This is going to be good."

She'd deal with the pilot later. For now, she had a bigger battle to confront. She knew the best defense was a good offense.

"When were you going to tell me about *Lincoln's* crew?"

The captain came to an abrupt halt two feet in front of her.

His outright hostile expression now gave way to one of confusion. "What..."

"Don't what me! As the presiding medical officer here, I make the health and welfare decisions when it comes to US Space-Navy personnel. Were you going to just let them suffer and not be given the medical attention they most assuredly deserve?"

He opened his mouth to speak, but no words came out.

Hardy said, "Oh boy, the phrase duck and cover comes to mind."

"Shut up, Hardy," Wanda said.

The ChronoBot mimicked the zipping closed of his nonexistent mouth.

"Viv, nobody's just forgetting about those crewmembers. You know me. I'm horrified at what has happened to them. Is still happening to them. But they're being kept alive by some kind of alien nano-tech... The truth is, I needed to consult with you and Coogong on the matter. But right now, we all need to get back to *Adams*. If you haven't noticed, there's a battle raging out there."

She fumed. It was just like him to make perfect sense of his actions. Undeterred, she said, "I'm staying. I'm a doctor. I have medications—"

"They won't work, Viv," Quintos said, looking back to Hardy. "Tell her."

Hardy did one of his awkward shrug things. "Captain's probably right. Medicines, drugs, won't be the thing that puts those poor souls out of their misery."

"See? We need to go now, Viv," Quintos said, already in the process of turning away from her.

"I'm staying," she said. "I'm not going to just take someone else's word about their condition, including yours or Hardy's...

that there's nothing that can be done for them. I don't work that way."

Max held up an intervening palm. "Doc, these aliens, you need to keep in mind they took this ship. Apparently with little effort. This is about as dangerous a place as you can be."

"She won't be by herself... I'm here, and I'm armed," Selleck said, patting the tagger sidearm at her side.

Viv was tempted to ask for other volunteers but held her tongue.

"We'll be fine," Viv said. "Let me check on the crew, do my own medical evaluations. Then, if there's nothing that can be done for them right now, well... we'll be right behind you."

Quintos pursed his lips as he weighed what she was proposing. He held up a finger. "Hold on a second."

Viv watched as he stepped away while initiating a Jadoo comms connection. Coogong's projected image came alive.

"Tell me you've figured out our quansporting issues."

"Apologies, Captain... but as of right now, quansporting is still inoperable."

Quintos cut the connection, turned to face her. He dragged a palm down his face and looked at her with concern. "Look, I needed to be on the *Adams'* bridge ten minutes ago."

"I know that. Go, Quintos, I'm fine." She looked at Selleck. "We're fine."

"Hardy, stay with them."

Selleck said, "Captain, where's he going to sit on the way back? Arrow's a two-seater."

Hardy gestured out to the parking lot full of Arrows. "Uh... I can pilot any one of these on my own."

"No."

Quintos closed his eyes as if he was counting to ten.

"Hardy is a resource that can be far better utilized than playing nursemaid. All of you go now. Come on, Selleck. And you take this," Viv said, unshouldering her medical satchel and shoving it into the woman's clutches. Together they hurried off toward a bay-side hatch door.

"How will they know where to go?" Grip said, looking after them.

"They won't," Quintos said, irritated. "Go after them, keep them safe. Someone will come get you later. And stick to the corridors and the hold where the crew is being held. Other areas of the ship may still require environs suits."

"Copy that." Grip headed off after them.

Chapter 21

Liquilid Empire Star System
USS Lincoln

Captain Galvin Quintos

etting situated within the Arrow's cockpit, my encounter with Viv still had me fuming. The woman was beyond infuriating. I engaged the lift thrusters, my bright red craft now slowly rising higher and higher within the expansive bay. Hardy, at the controls, along with Max, Wanda, Ham, and Hock, was just now getting the old *Hub Gunther* powered up below me.

Ryder with his Arrow to my left, Akari and hers to my right, together we made our way toward the open bay doors.

Ryder said, "I'm taking point."

"You know we're heading out into a frickin' shitstorm, right?" Akari said. "Look at them all... all these Arrows, and no one to pilot them. Over."

Akari, clearly ignoring Captain Ryder's earlier decree that he was taking point, engaged her Arrow's throttle and rocketed into space, leaving us both behind. I had to smile; the girl had spirit. I said, "We don't call her Ballbuster for nothing."

Ryder ignored the comment, blasting out of the bay right on her tail. I let out a breath; I was the rustiest of the three of us. I'd need to be on my game, if not for my own sake, but for theirs. I hit the throttle and felt that wonderful, familiar mule kick to the chest.

We maneuvered into a close Vic formation, Ballbuster dropping back to allow J-Dog to take point at the V apex.

"Oh, stop pouting, J-Dog... You got your point position, you big baby. Over."

"Who says I'm pouting? I just knew you'd rather be looking at my ass than Brig's. Over."

"I'm not going anywhere near that comment. Over," she said with a smile in her voice.

Our three Arrows accelerated and banked left to avoid a small asteroid, all the while still maintaining our tight formation —wings almost touching.

"You hanging in there, Brigs? Over," Akari said. "Hell... maybe you should have a big comfy captain's mount specially made for an Arrow. Over."

"I'll make do. Over," I said.

"Uh... you okay? Seem a little reserved. Over," Akari said.

"Leave him alone. Man's got woman problems. Over," Ryder commented.

We flew in silence for several minutes. Ryder was right, though. I was still brooding. Truth was, Viv was perfectly within her rights to want to attend to *Lincoln's* suffering crew. I knew that wasn't what had gotten me riled up. It was the fact that she was leaving. Had had enough of this life... *of me.*

As we emerged from the asteroid field, I heard Akari audibly gasp over the channel.

Off in the far distance, there was *Adams*. In a dazzling

display, glowing blue Phazon Pulsar energy bolts streaked across the inky blackness. Rail gun tracer rounds streaked through space like fiery comets, leaving behind a blazing trail of eviscerated scorpion-flies. There were still so, so many, circling, attacking.

All I could see was a handful of Arrows right in the midst of things, although I knew from my instruments there were more than that.

I said, "How about we give our brothers and sisters a little assistance? Over."

At that we broke formation, each Arrow on a different trajectory toward a hellstorm of bug-like fighter craft.

Coming up in front of me was what could best be described as a cohesive swarm of no less than twenty alien fighters. They moved as one, reminding me of the Ziu aliens within the alt universe, being controlled by that one mind on board the mother ship. But I had a feeling these craft were being piloted mechanically, perhaps by interconnected robots... Even though they were lightning fast, they seemed to lack that one element that made an outstanding pilot—they weren't intuitive.

I said aloud, "Not so sure staying that close to one another is such a good idea, bug-fuckers." I lit them up. The onboard AI, capable of tracking each and every one of them individually, was now sweeping Phazon Pulsar bolts into their midst with uncanny accuracy.

"Bogie on your ass, Brigs. Over," came Ryder's voice.

I'd already heard the targeting alarm squawk over my helmet audio and was making counter maneuvers. But Ryder was wrong; there wasn't one, but three Bogies back there. I rolled left, pulled back and rolled left again as streaks of energy sizzled past within a hair's breadth of my starboard side wing. Only now did I see the blackened char marks left behind. So not a miss, just survivable damage.

"Dammit!" They were on me like three unshakable shadows. An energy bolt suddenly clipped my canopy, leaving a visible, blackened scar upon the curved diamond glass above me. A new alarm shrieked to life; the cockpit was losing atmosphere. *Terrific.*

I nosedived and kept with the forward, looping trajectory— an ass-over-teakettle move that was most definitely not sanctioned by US Space-Navy piloting protocols. The Arrow's framework complained with an audible squeal as g-forces pushed and pulled, bending the superstructure like a child's plastic toy.

I pulled back on the controls at the zenith of my spiraling loop-de-loop, coming to a jarring, lung-expelling deceleration. *Zip zip zip,* all three scorpion-flies flew past me. I watched as they tried, in vain, to slow, to correct their maneuvering miscalculations. I took the Phazon Pulsars off autotracking, manually taking over targeting. I let loose with a barrage of plasma fire. Being at such close range, the three bug ships exploded simultaneously, disintegrating without so much as an errant hull panel or landing strut surviving the blast.

"Not bad, Brigs," Akari said, her Arrow zipping by overhead. Clearly, she'd had my six, just in case.

Glancing to my right, I did a double take. There was the *Hub Gunther,* slow and awkward-looking, her own Phazon Pulsars active and taking care of business. *And I thought her hull was a mess before...* The old mining craft had taken a good bit of damage.

It was another hour before the last of the scorpion-flies had been destroyed. Now, the only fighter craft traversing this debris-filled, battle-torn section of space were Arrows. The dozen or so earlier deployed from *Adams'* flight bay, and those piloted by Ryder, Akari, and me.

"Thanks for the help, you three," came an unfamiliar voice

over the open channel. "You do know... we had things fully under control, though. Over."

Akari said, "No thanks necessary. Admit it; you've been schooled. Over."

There was laughter from the other pilots. *I've missed this,* I thought.

I didn't realize at the time the heavy cost in human life this battle had extracted from our already limited rank-and-file flight crew. There would be time later to grieve and honor those we'd left behind.

With the visibly ailing *Hub Gunther* in the lead, spewing something—probably drive coolant—we all fell in behind her.

I said, "That was some piloting you did back there, Hardy. You all doing okay in there? Over."

There was a pregnant pause before I heard Hardy's Boston-accented words. "No, Cap... we're not all doing okay. Over."

The Arrow's cockpit had been measurably cooling from loss of atmosphere, but I knew the chill I was feeling at that moment was not from the breached canopy. I wanted to ask questions, to interrogate Hardy and get answers. But the tone of his voice had spoken volumes. I needed to just shut up and get with my people.

Chapter 22

Liquilid Empire Star System
USS Lincoln

Major Vivian Leigh

The scene was indeed ghastly. The magnitude of the carnage was beyond anything she had imagined. Beneath the lone, and totally inadequate, overhead light, Viv stood before the first of the neatly arranged rows. A line of ten bodies was laid out before her—she counted twenty rows—two hundred undoubtedly suffering individuals. The bodies were positioned within receptacles that resembled large rectangular cookie sheets. But instead of oven-ready snickerdoodle dough, mutilated human bodies lay upon the metal pans. The smell of decomposition—*the putrescine*—was amplified due to the sheer number of bodies. She bit her bottom lip. To call these bodies was a misnomer—one would think they were dead. But she knew... These poor souls were alive.

"Sweet baby Jesus."

The hushed words jolted Viv. She had forgotten that she did not enter the compartment alone.

"You okay?" Viv turned around to see a shell-shocked-looking Christy Selleck.

"I'm... uh... I." She was looking down at a female crewmember lying sprawled next to her right foot. Her eyes filled with tears.

"Hey, this is a lot to take in." Gently, Viv took her arm as if handling a fine piece of crystal. "But we have a job to do here."

Selleck gave her a quick nod and turned away from what was left of the tortured woman. She swiped at her cheek with the back of her hand. She cleared her throat. "So, how do I help?"

"Yeah, what's the plan, Doc?" Grip said, arriving in the hold, a pro linebacker ready to play ball.

His determined expression and no-nonsense demeanor were a welcome sight.

"Grip." Viv acknowledged him with a nod and a tight-lipped expression.

She patted her thigh pocket, unzipped the top flap, and withdrew a small device.

"What is that?" Selleck said.

"BioScan... always keep it with me."

Sleek and compact, the palm-sized device performed a comprehensive range of health assessments and tests. With its projected 3D high-res display, it provided her detailed medical scans and analyses of a patient's condition in real time. It was equipped with advanced sensors and imaging technology that performed medical tests, including blood analysis, respiratory function tests, even brain scans. Additionally, it had advanced DNA testing capabilities, allowing her the ability to perform tests and provide personalized treatment recommendations based on a patient's genetic profile. The device also had access to a vast medical database, allowing her to access the latest research and treatment recommendations coming out of the EUNF Research Labs.

She leaned over and positioned the BioScan device directly over the crewmember's chest. She said aloud, "Initiate full spectrum anatomical analyses."

A three-dimensional medical avatar, a smaller version of what would typically be seen within any HealthBay, took shape above the patient, but almost immediately distorted, wavered, then was replaced with a hovering message:

Insufficient data—anatomical analyses halted.

Grip said, "Maybe it's those alien nanites, Doc... Hardy commented on them before. Guess they're crawling all around in her."

She nodded. "Disrupting the device's diagnostics..."

She squatted, putting her satchel onto the deck, then placed a thumb upon the DNA- recognizing security clasp.

"You know those drugs you got in there probably won't work, right?" Grip commented.

Viv ignored him, taking out a syringe and a single vial from one of the cartons.

"Isn't that needle thing... a little old school?" Selleck asked.

Viv smiled, holding the syringe in her hand like a pencil, the needle pointing upward. "Sometimes old school is best for the situation," she said, inserting the needle into the rubber top, penetrating the vial. She pulled the plunger back to the line to allow for a full dose. She tapped the syringe several times with her fingernail to usher any errant air bubbles to the surface.

The *Lincoln* crewmember closest to her was male; impossible to tell how old. He was in better shape than some of the others, which was like saying breast cancer was better than lung cancer. His mouth and lips were withdrawn, almost concave, a sign that his teeth had fallen out. The man's skin was gray, loose and slimy in appearance. Tearless dull eyes stared up at her. If those eyes could talk, surely they would say, "Please. Put me out of my misery."

Viv couldn't go there. Not now. *Focus, Vivian.* She chastised herself for not bringing masks and gloves. *How could I be so stupid?*

Viv looked for a name tag. Wanted to acknowledge that she was handling this impossibly horrid situation in the most respectful way allowable. But there was no indication as to who this man was. She would take a DNA sample, so down the road, notification of kin could take place.

She placed delicate fingertips on the crewmember's neck, feeling for a pulse. Then leaned in closer, a crease forming between her brows. "What the hell?"

"You see something?" Selleck asked.

"Some kind of puncture wound lower on the neck. Could be from the hostiles."

The pulse was almost imperceptible. She leaned forward, spoke just above a whisper into his ear. "I'm here to help you, Crewman. We're all here to help you."

Sitting up, she knew she was at a crossroads. Not having explicit end-of-life consent from this patient or from a close relative... Well, this was not what she'd signed up for. *Soon... I'll be done with all this.*

She looked up to Selleck, and then to Grip. Both looked solemn.

Grip nodded. "You have no choice, Doc; you have to try."

The needle punctured the skin, inserted into the man's carotid artery. She pushed the plunger with her thumb. She knew there was enough poison in the vial to kill a full-grown elephant.

A trickle of foam bubbled up from the corner of the man's mouth.

Viv placed two fingertips on his throat. She let out an audible gasp.

"What is it? Is he dead?" Selleck asked.

"No." Viv took her hand away, wiping residual slime onto her starched white top. She rolled out of her squat and up onto the cold deck plates. "The pulse... If anything, it's gotten stronger. The drug may be acting like a catalyst for the nanites." *My God, what have I done?*

Viv looked up to the exposed metal deckhead joists as if the answer could be found there. She now looked to Grip, waiting for him to say, "I told you so."

Instead, he walked over to her, offered her a brawny hand. "Up you go." He helped her to her feet. "Sorry, Doc."

She allowed him to steady her. "Um... What exactly did Hardy say about the nanites?"

"They were administered when the hostiles first attacked the ship. A way to keep the crewmembers as a fresh food supply. Sick bastards," Grip said, shaking his head.

She made a face. "These people are in advanced states of decomposition. How long has this ship been missing?"

"Somewhere in the range of eight to nine years."

"I need a minute," Christy blurted out.

Viv watched her dash out of the hold. She'd noticed the pilot's cheeks had lost some color these last few minutes.

Viv, talking to herself, said, "So, the hostiles attacked eight years ago ... captured the crew... administered then..." she looked at Grip, and continued, "then fed on them over time. But eventually, clearly, the nanites were no longer performing their task. As they were no longer fresh, the aliens simply abandoned these crewmembers."

Grip hitched a shoulder. "What did aliens care if they were left to suffer?"

"Sorry. I'm back. Ready," Selleck said, striding back in, in the process of wiping her mouth.

"Quintos was right. I shouldn't have come," Viv said.

Grip considered her response. "You had to make the determination; you said that yourself. Your presence here, maybe at some level it constitutes a bit of hope for these people."

Viv stared at him, taking in his muscled torso, his dark face, the whites of his eyes. Clarity struck her like jumping into an ice bath in the middle of the Arctic. "All right. Let's go. I need to talk to Hardy and Coogong. Find a way to obliterate these fucking nanites."

Chapter 23

Liquilid Empire Star System
USS Adams

Captain Galvin Quintos

Back on board *Adams*, my frustration was mounting by the second. Although Hardy was by my side as we strode the passageways and took the GravLift together, we didn't speak. He was intuitive enough to know I was in no mood for any of his antics. Storming onto the bridge, I saw Coogong, along with a small technical team, which included Chief Grizwald, huddled around Akari toward the front of the bridge.

Heads turned my way. Akari, looking alarmed, opened her mouth to speak—

"Put a sock in it, Lieutenant." I pointed a dagger-like finger at Coogong. "Why the hell are we still sitting here? This isn't just hostile space; it's heinous. It's barbarous. Coogong, we need to wormhole the fuck out of here. Now! If you can't manage that, then get our jump drives operational to the point we can short-jump a light-year's distance away from here. Now is that too much to ask from my science officer?"

Yeah, yeah, I know, taking out my frustration, my anger, on Coogong, unequivocally the kindest, gentlest soul probably in the known galaxy, was a shit thing to do. Did I instantly feel guilty and inwardly hate myself? Of course, I did. But in my own defense, we'd just needlessly lost too many Arrow pilots, each of whom had families, friends, people that loved them. And this, whatever this was here on the extreme outskirts of the galaxy, should have nothing to do with the EUNF US Space-Navy—Didn't we have enough to deal with back home with the Grish and Varapin ghouls?

And how did Coogong react to my hostile, persecuting outburst? He broke from the huddled group, stepped toward me, and raised his little stick-figure arms, his hands, in what was obviously an attempt to project calm. And then he did the unthinkable. There within his ridiculous Ambiogell-filled helmet, his little worm face smiled up at me. He said, "Captain, I am truly sorry."

All eyes shifted from Coogong to me.

"Well ... um ..."

"Well said, Captain Fucknuts," Hardy interjected. "Any other words of wisdom you want to share with your crew?"

I took a moment before answering. "I'm sorry, Coogong. There's no excuse for my hostility toward a fellow crewmember, especially you. I know you're doing your very best." I looked around the compartment, making eye contact with each and every one of my crew.

As if nothing had just transpired, Coogong said, "Captain, all *Adams* propulsion systems, jump mechanics, are functional... operational." He gestured back toward Akari. "I was just suggesting to Lieutenant James that we might want to inquire with the other ship captains. See specifically what happens when they attempt a jump."

Akari said, "Coogong, as I was about to say to you," she sent a wary glance my way, "we've been in constant contact with both *Portent* and *Wrath*."

I took a seat at the captain's mount. "Mr. Chen, open a channel to the captains of *Portent* and *Wrath*."

It took a few minutes for Symbio-Poth 2.0 Captain Loggins of *Boundless Wrath* and human Captain Church of *Portent* to appear on the halo display. Their respective bridge compartments were in view behind both.

Looking smug, Commander Stanly came into view and stood next to Captain Loggins and Science Officer Trevor Mandyport, while the contentious Doogan had already been standing next to Captain Church.

"Good. We're all here," I said. "Let's go back to square one... start with what's happening, specifically with ship propulsion subsystems, namely our jump drives."

Science Officer Trevor Mandyport spoke up first. "There's nothing wrong with our jump drives. Let me be up front about that."

"Same for *Portent*," Doogan exclaimed, then exchanged a peculiar, albeit subtle, glance with Captain Church. "Can we just say the obvious? This isn't a ship systems issue. How would that even be possible, three starships independently encountering the same mechanical issues?"

Akari spoke up. "*Adams* is not detecting external forces at work here..." She looked to Hardy. "What are your ChronoBot sensors telling you?"

"Not much. Clearly, we're dealing with technology beyond what we're accustomed to."

The discussion quickly turned highly technical, the science officers coming up not only with a game plan to detect whatever this ghost energy force was, but also possible ideas on how to negate it.

My Jadoo ring vibrated. I glanced at the projected two-word message. SHE'S BACK. I'd prompted the ring to inform me as soon as Viv returned from *Lincoln.*

I stood and, not wanting to disrupt any possible progress being made, leaned in next to Akari. "You have the bridge."

She nodded and quickly turned her attention back to the ongoing brainstorming session.

BY THE TIME I'd reached Viv's quarters down on Deck 12, I'd rehearsed what I was going to say. Let her know how important she was to me. How I'd change things here on *Adams.* That once we were away from here, life would return to normal.

But as soon as the hatch door slid open, with her standing there in front of me, my mind went blank. I took in her red-rimmed eyes, her slumped shoulders, her colorless pallor. Wearing a bathrobe, she'd showered and put her still-wet hair up into a knot.

I was prepared for another rebuff, for her to send me away. Instead, she stepped close, her arms coming around my waist— she melted into me. Body trembling, nearly convulsing, she wept into my chest. "I couldn't do anything for them... not a damn thing."

I held her like that for a long while. Later, when she'd cried herself out, sitting on her bed, she told me of her excursion over to *Lincoln.* What she'd witnessed firsthand. She described injecting one crewmember with Dimeltite Formade. How she was going to free the poor *Lincoln* crewmember from unimaginable misery.

"Oh, Galvin... I didn't mean to..."

I waited for her to continue.

"I thought he was dying; I'd accomplished what I came for. The know-it-all medical officer coming to the rescue. But my actions, my fucking arrogance, only made things worse."

"I don't think that's true, Viv—"

"You weren't there! You didn't see the man's eyes open, his consciousness suddenly awakened to the holy fucking hell he'd been trapped in. Trapped in for years! That his legs were gone, his teeth had fallen out; microscopic machines had infiltrated what was left of his body, preserving him for some undetermined time when they would come back... come back to feed on him."

I tried to speak but couldn't.

"And I had to leave him like that... I left two hundred suffering crewmembers, just like that."

"I promise you their suffering will end soon."

She looked at me, sniffed. "I want to be involved in whatever decisions are made concerning that crew. Promise me that."

"I promise."

Seeing I was about to say more, she placed a finger on my lips. "No questions."

I shrugged and mimed looking confused.

"I'm still leaving this ship the moment I have the chance; nothing's going to change that, Galvin... as much as it will kill me to do so. I'm not getting what I need here to survive, to live a happy life."

"And what you need from me?"

She closed her eyes, looking exhausted. Just having this discussion again was bringing her close to some unknown precipice. "Galvin, I've come to accept who you are. You thrive on chaos; you don't know what you want, not really."

I shook my head, ready to dispute her words.

"Do I know you care about me? Of course, I do. But you also have feelings for Gail. Do you think I'm totally obtuse not to have noticed that after so many years? Look, I'm not asking you to choose. This isn't about that... not completely, anyway... because I have to leave. This," she gestured with a hand to our surroundings, "is breaking me, physically, mentally... breaking my very soul, Galvin." She placed both palms on my chest, kissed my cheek, and gently pushed me away from her. "Go... save the day; it's what you're good at."

She stepped back, looking as sad and dejected as I'd ever seen her. The hatch door slid shut between us.

Chapter 24

Entering the captain's ready room, I couldn't remember a time when I'd felt so rudderless, so dejected. But it was more than that. It was this new enemy. Hell, I didn't even know what to call them. How had they so easily vanquished *Lincoln's* crew? Was that what was in store for *Adams, Portent,* and *Wrath?* For thousands of crewmembers to end up on some creepy beast's dinner plate?

I now saw that, probably courtesy of a seven-foot-tall ChronoBot, there'd been a delivery. Taken from *Lincoln's* ready room—there were two cylindrical, metallic core loaders sitting next to my desk. These were the once mighty warship's backup system memory stores. *Adams,* of course, had something similar. Nearly indestructible, they were a ship's black box, in case of the unthinkable, a vessel's total annihilation. Backups that held incredible quantities of data.

I took a seat behind my desk, saw that the two units had already been configured into my private captain's station. Each had an illuminated, blue-glowing band encircling the top of the units. I said aloud, "Sir Calvin, ensure the information on these two memory stores is kept separate from *Adams'* central AI database, or any other database, for that matter."

Noted, Captain Quintos

I was about to ask my ship's AI to spool up the first of the captain's log entries, those generated immediately after *Lincoln* entered this star system.

Captain, I have detected a priority 1 captain's log entry. It is intended to have precedence over all others in the event of the ship's capture.

"Let's have it," I said, sitting back in my chair.

The projected 3D feed came alive—the captain, wearing a blue and white camo work uniform, took shape within the confines of the halo display. He was older than me by at least ten years, maybe more. With wavy salt-and-pepper hair, ice-blue eyes, and a lined and creased face, there was little doubt this man was shouldering an incredible level of stress.

"If you're watching this feed, I'm either captured or dead. And knowing this enemy as I now do, the latter would be far preferable."

I took in the brass nameplate above his left-side breast pocket: **Captain Glenn Stone.**

There were distant background noises, including small-arms energy fire, explosions, and desperate men yelling.

"Time is at a premium right now, so let me cut to the chase... Once we wormhole jumped into this star system, it immediately became clear we'd either made a navigational mistake, unlikely, or our wormhole coordinates had been somehow shanghaied. We are far from known, EUNF-plotted space. Prior to bugging out of here, we implemented a cursory patrol of the area as standard procedure dictates. It was then that our sensors detected other vessels in the vicinity. I gave the order to explore. We discovered vessels from dozens of different alien civilizations. With our shuttles deployed, security teams boarded three of the vessels, all adrift. The crews were attacked, tortured, and basically mutilated. But and this is important, those that were found, alien lifeforms, were still alive, frozen in some strange kind of stasis." The captain looked shaken, as if recounting these events was taking a physical toll on him anew.

I paused the playback and contacted Akari. "Are our sensors fully back online?"

"Somewhat. Nowhere near where they should be."

"Run new sweeps. I think you'll find there are other star-ships in the vicinity."

"I'm on it," she said.

I turned back to Captain Stone's frozen-in-time face and tapped the hovering Play icon.

"We realized we were in as unfriendly a territory as imagin-able. We needed to leave immediately. I quickly discovered that would not be possible. We no longer had the capability to manu-facture a wormhole; even a simple spatial jump couldn't be achieved. We could navigate, just not anywhere far. My highly astute science officer discovered the problem keeping us from jumping was quantum flux waves coming from... somewhere. It took some time, but we constructed a device to counteract those waves. A quantum flux reverser, one that models those waves and transmits a diametrically opposed version that cancels them out."

I watched as Captain Stone looked away from camera to address something unintelligible one of his crew had said. Fear, or perhaps dread, crossed Stone's face. Looking back to camera, he continued.

"I'm out of time. Again, if you are watching this and are here in system, you are in grave danger. Leave now. Never come back." He dragged a hand down his face, "Anyway, where was I? The enemy... they're called the Liquilids, vile snake or lizard-like aliens. Highly intelligent, a militarized civilization motivated by the hunt to feed an insatiable hunger for living quarry. Their technology is, in some ways but not all, superior to human. If you haven't encountered them already, their bug-like fighters will come for you first. They're called Slissets, and there are multiple versions of them. They'll first throw at you the most primitive form of them—we call them Slisset Ones—to test your defenses. Don't be fooled by those. Because Slisset Twos are far more dangerous, and, frankly, nearly impossible to destroy. But it is their massive, dreadnought-sized warships, the red ships, you'll need to watch out for. There's not much I can tell you about those. Since you are watching this feed, you have everything, our sensor readings, my previous log entries, all that. *Lincoln* is under current attack; we've been boarded by enemy nanite constructs. It is not so much a matter of *if* we can hold the enemy at bay, but for *how* long."

Shit. I paused the feed once more to reach out to Coogong.

"Yes, Captain."

"Wherever you are, whatever you're doing, drop it and get to my ready room. Seems we need to get a team back to *Lincoln* and find something called a quantum flux reverser. Maybe you can tell me what the hell we'll be looking for."

Chapter 25

Captain Gail Pristy

T en minutes later, back in their fatigues, Pristy and her team followed Resnick through the ringularity. They emerged into a spacious compartment with glistening white bulkheads, deck, and deckhead above, at odds with the rough-hewn cavern they'd left. Her team stood, looking at their surroundings. Derrota glanced around nervously. Aubrey acted like a kid at an amusement park, but like Pristy herself, was assessing any possible threats as she checked out the room.

Resnick strode toward the other side of the compartment, to a seemingly blank bulkhead. Suddenly, a hidden panel slid open. On the other side stood a woman in black fatigues, wearing similar combat armor to Resnick's. She held a shredder-style energy weapon, pointed at his chest. Her breath caught in surprise, and she lowered the weapon.

"You have a death wish, General?" she asked, but a broad smile replaced her previous uneasy expression. "Thought I'd never see you again."

"Don't count your blessings yet, Lieutenant," Resnick warned, but smiled, clapping a hand onto her armored shoulder as he hurried past her. "Introduce yourself and take them to Deck 2's conference room. I'll be on the bridge updating the captain."

"Roger that." The Lieutenant stepped into the compartment. "Welcome to *Portent*. I'm Lieutenant Bethany Chan, Marine platoon leader."

"Captain Gail Pristy of USS *Hercules*, and apparently, side-hustle time-traveling agent," Pristy said as she took in the Lieutenant's almond-skin tones and Asian features. She turned to her team. "These are Petty Officer Second-Class Aubrey Laramie and Stephan Derrota."

"Welcome to Time Corps," said Lieutenant Chan, nodding at each. "This way, please."

She led them through passageways as pristine as the compartment's bulkheads, as did the bank of GravLifts. After a short walk down another passageway, a door slid open, and they filed inside the conference room. Like the rest of the ship, the walls shone white and spotless. The table and chairs were battleship gray, much to the relief of Pristy's eyes, but neither scuffed nor worn. She muttered to Stephan, "They keep this place clean and neat, don't they?"

"OCD levels of clean," Derrota agreed.

Pristy, Aubrey, and Derrota sat at the far end, while the Lieutenant slung her shredder over her shoulder and stood at parade rest, waiting. Five minutes later, General Resnick entered, leading two other men. The first was in his mid-forties, with dark hair, graying at the temples, and an equally dark five o'clock shadow. Pristy caught sight of captain's bars on his light gray uniform and an infinity patch upon one shoulder. The second man was short and barrel-chested, with a mullet, and also wore a gray jumpsuit.

"I am Captain Church," said the first man, tension filling his voice. "This is Doogan. General Resnick has given me your names and said you brought the timeline 20 percent closer to normal. Good work." Despite the compliment, Church sounded grim and irritated. "General, the floor is yours."

When the captain and Doogan had taken seats, Resnick sat at the head of the table. "I need everyone here to see what you are facing. Lieutenant, viewscreens, please."

Lieutenant Chan touched the bulkhead and spoke a short command into a now-active display menu. All around them, the conference room transitioned into a 3D, three-hundred-and-sixty-degree view of the asteroid field. The level of clarity made even USS *Hercules'* sensor optics seem as weak as a child's telescope.

"Magnify the top right quadrant," Resnick said. When Chan had, Resnick pointed to three red dots that could have passed for small moons. "Those, full magnification."

They weren't moons, and the realization instigated curses from Pristy and her team.

The ships were red, and while they appeared spherical from the front, the repositioned magnified view showed them to be more bullet shaped. Up close, their exteriors bristled with weapons and missile ports. The aft drive engines were so large they dwarfed any dreadnought Pristy had ever seen. At the bottom of each ship protruded a round cylinder, large enough to park a US Space-Navy frigate.

"Those are the red ships," Resnick said. "The Liquilids have hundreds of them, and two months from now, they've destroyed a dozen star systems. And by destroyed, I mean turned every planet in them to asteroid fields except the ones they're keeping for food storage."

"Well," said Doogan. "Fuck."

"Exactly," Resnick said. "The red ships weren't supposed to attack EUNF worlds for another hundred years. At that time, humanity kicked the royal shit out of them and destroyed every ship with advanced quantum disruptor capability. Then they decimated the Liquilids' colonies back to the stone age."

"That's a tad harsh," Aubrey said.

"So is using nanites to keep captive human crewmembers in suspended animation until they're ready to feed on them," General Resnick said. "Which they did with the crew of USS *Lincoln* until they were no longer edible. Then they just left them in agony."

"Oh God..." Aubrey said, her face going pale.

"Something happened that screwed up the timeline," he said. "The Grand Consortium noticed it two months from now —three months in Captain Pristy's timeline. By then, the Liquilids were destroying Earth colonies and our allies. The Consortium traced it back to this star system and *Adams, Wrath,* and *Portent* blundering into the Liquilids' trap."

"Blundering?" Captain Church went rigid in his seat, clearly taking exception to Resnick's words. "Escaping that alternate universe was imperative."

Resnick waved away his remarks. "And once this mission is complete, Captain, you can explain to me how the hell you ended up there in the first place."

"We have no idea—" Doogan began.

"When we're done," Resnick repeated, cutting him off mid-sentence. "Right now, our job is to keep the Liquilids from getting the navigational data they need to find humanity and Earth. No matter what."

Pristy felt fear creep up her spine, and the hair on the back of her neck rose. She said, "What are you saying? Are you going to abandon them?"

"We can't jump," Captain Church said, shaking his head, "Tenet one: Time technology stays top secret. Since *Adams'* personnel have seen *Portent* and her crew, we have to stay. If we escape while the other ships are stuck here because their quantum drives don't work, they'll wonder why. Searching for the answers could lead them to a truth we're not ready to divulge at this point."

"Abandon ship?" Doogan suggested. "Use ChronoLinks to get back to the ringularity and let *Portent* get destroyed?"

"Negative," General Resnick said. "Any scenario we've run where *Portent* is destroyed leads to disaster."

"You said you can't let the Liquilids get any navigational data," Pristy said. "What does that mean? Does that mean *Adams* escapes?"

Resnick hesitated, which was enough for Pristy to know the answer. She came to her feet, fury rising inside her. "You told me we were going to save USS *Adams*."

"No, I didn't," Resnick said.

"We have friends on that ship," Derrota protested. "You can't ask us to let them die."

"I have five hundred friends who are dead because of the Liquilids!" Resnick snapped. "More by now, and billions in the next two months if the Liquilids get the navigational data from *Adams*."

Aubrey raised a hand, as tentative as a third grader in class, and asked, "Can't we just help them jump out of here?"

"No. The same technology that allows the Liquilids to mess with quantum space enables them to track wormholes. They'll follow."

"So everyone on *Adams* dies," Pristy said bitterly. "And if they don't, billions of others die."

"I didn't say that," Resnick said.

"You just said *Adams* couldn't leave!" Pristy shouted.

"You're still thinking too linearly, Captain," Resnick said, his tone cold and hard. "Remember how time works. Changes to the timeline risk ruining everything."

"Butterfly effect," Derrota said suddenly. Pristy glared at him, and he explained: "Chaos mathematics theory showed how a change at one point in a system can cause major changes later."

"Exactly," Resnick said. "In this case, the change already happened, and we have disruptions and paradoxes throughout the time continuum. We have to reverse it, and in no universe does doing so include the survival of USS *Adams*. It must not leave the system and must not be captured. But we have one chance to save *Adams'* crew, your crew that Quintos rescued, and Quintos himself, and in doing so, get our timeline back."

"How?" Pristy demanded. "How do we do that?"

Resnick smiled. "We just need to be in the right place before the right time."

"That makes no sense," Aubrey grumbled.

"Maybe not to you, newbie," Doogan said, not smiling at all.

"Quiet, Doogan," Captain Church said. "Orders, General?"

"Stay here," said Resnick. "I need them thinking you are just as trapped as they are, and to help them until they don't need help anymore."

"Will we see you again?" Lieutenant Chan asked.

"If things go as expected, we will come back after the next mission," Resnick said. "Pristy, Derrota, Aubrey, with me."

Pristy followed Resnick into the passageway, the others trailing behind them. She stepped up beside the general and asked, "Do you really believe this will work?"

"Check your historical timeline stability score," Resnick said.

Pristy looked at her ChronoLink. "53.4 percent."

"So we're doing something right," Resnick said. "Now we just have to keep doing it right, and fast. Because in an hour and a half, Stratham Hold is going to be overrun. And then we'll all have much bigger problems to deal with."

Chapter 26

Liquilid Empire Star System
USS Adams

Sonya Winters

R unning, walking, then running some more—did
she know she was being impetuous? Of course she
did. At the ripe old age of sixteen, almost seventeen,
she figured if one couldn't be impulsive, impassioned, hell,
unbridled—whatever adjective you wanted to throw at it—as a
teenager, then when? Only now, as she hurried down a rarely
used *Adams* maintenance passageway, did she start to have
second thoughts concerning her most recent actions. Her arm,
more accurately, her shoulder, blazed with pain with each
jarring step. Having hacked the nurse station's work schedule,
she'd timed her escape from HealthBay during the shift change.
Did she feel bad, having to pilfer Nurse Donna's locker, the
only nurse equally petite and having a similar shape? Not really.
Donna was bitchy, and beyond lazy. When wasn't the woman
on bathroom break? So no, screw her. But she had to hand it to

her—Donna had nice civvies. Now, wearing a smart-looking black sweatshirt, stylish navy-blue leggings, and a pair of high-top running shoes that must have cost the dawdling nurse a pretty penny, Sonya was somewhat adequately dressed for the mission at hand.

"Stop with the scolding, Tina... What are you, my mother?" she said, scowling up at the circling glimmer of gold near the deckhead. "I'll return all her shit later. Maybe..."

She could barely hear the fairy's high-pitched reply above the echoes of her footfalls within the narrow passageway. "I'm Iris! Iris Iris Iris Iris Iris! Not Tina!"

"Okay, okay, got it; you're also beyond annoying!"

Cringing as she hurried down what seemed an endless stairwell from hell, she stabilized her left arm, still in a sling, with her opposite hand. She thumb-tapped her Jadoo ring, bringing up the projected 3D menu, which subsequently showed the countdown timer she'd set prior to leaving HealthBay. She'd miscalculated; this was taking much longer than anticipated. Flight Bay was still two flights down and she was quickly losing steam—her injuries far from healed.

Winding her way down the corkscrew of a staircase, *one more flight*, she could now hear the unmistakable sounds of the bay—Arrow drives winding up, the blaring, obnoxious, nonstop announcements over the PA system... her timer beeped, letting her know she'd probably missed her self-imposed deadline. The *Hub Gunther* undoubtedly had already left without her. Taking the steps two at a time now, she fought back the urge to cry out as the jarring to her shoulder was becoming unbearable.

Off the stairs, she rounded the corner and, with Iris fluttering at her side, approached the Bay's double hatch doors. They whisked apart too slowly and, of course, she clipped her injured shoulder passing through the threshold into the flight bay.

"Ahhh!" she cried out, staggering, tears brimming. Through water-distorted vision, she scanned the melee of frenetic activity, bay crews hurrying this way and that, red fighter craft everywhere, pilots ascending their Arrows' inset ladders. But no *Hub Gunther*. She spun left, spun right, valiant attempts to keep the inevitable dread from seeping into her psyche, becoming a losing battle.

"No!" she screamed into the oblivious, disinterested surroundings.

Feeling spent, her knees weakened, legs wobbly, Sonya knew when she had lost; she just didn't like it.

Iris was buzzing again, circling her head like an incessant horsefly. "What is it, Iris? What in God's name do you want?"

"Hub Hub Hub... *Hub Gunther*, I see it... I see it, and you don't. Hub Hub Hub..."

As if injected with a double dose of adrenaline, Sonya was up on her tippy-toes, looking for that ugly, beat-to-shit mining ship.

"Follow me... Hub Hub Hub..."

She didn't need to be asked twice. Running to keep up, she maneuvered around a fueling pod, a portable jack-crane being pushed by two maintenance workers, then, having to jump over a dislodged rail gun turret, she sprinted forward. And there it was, the *Hub Gunther*. Its ramp was deployed, its hatch still open.

"Hub Hub Hub... Told you so, told you so..."

Wanda looked up from what she was doing, confusion turning to irritation. "No! Stop right there, kid."

Sonya, gasping for breath, didn't stop. She dodged around Wanda, entered the dark and stinky cabin, and threw herself into one of the threadbare seats. She caught sight of Iris circling around up toward the cockpit area.

The contingent of Marines, minus one, were each scurrying

around and looking busy. Ham or Hock, she had a hard time telling them apart, was missing. She'd heard he'd returned from *Lincoln* gravely ill.

Coogong moved out from the shadows, his short stick-figure form briefly illuminated by the light coming in through the open hatch. His helmet's cracked faceplate, hastily repaired, was now just a craggy faint line.

Max stood before her with hands on hips. "No..."

"What do you mean, no?"

"No means no. Out!"

Wanda and Grip joined Max, each looking down at her with the same condemnation. She looked to Coogong for moral support, but he'd disappeared somewhere back into the shadows.

"Look, I know what you're looking for. That quantum flux reverser—"

"How do you even know about that?" Wanda snapped. "For Christ's sake, don't tell me you've stooped to spying on the captain?"

"No! Of course not... I just happened to notice an encrypted temp data stream being buffered by *Adams'* data processors... I didn't even see it all."

"But you saw enough of it to know what we're looking for," Max said.

Sonya hitched her injured shoulder, immediately regretting it. She felt small hands take her arm, gently placing it back within her sling. "Thank you, Coogong."

The *Hub Gunther's* overhead PA crackled to life. A tinny-sounding Doc Viv said, "You have got to be kidding me!"

"Oh shit..."

"Sonya, get your scrawny ass back here into HealthBay now!"

Another familiar voice, equally tinny, said, "You heard her; you're in no condition for an away mission."

"Oh, is that you... Um, Captain... dear uncle-guy?"

"That crap's not going to work here, Sonya," he said.

Her mind raced. "Okay, fine. I'll come back if you can answer me one simple question."

Doc Viv said, "This isn't a damn game show, Sonya. You need time to recover—"

"If you, any of you, can tell me where that elusive quantum flux reverser is, you're right... There's no need for me on this mission."

"Oh, and you know where it is?" Wanda disputed with a skeptical expression.

"Don't get pulled into her web of words," Quintos said. "That's how she manipulates you."

Sonya almost laughed, "Fine... if you don't want to know where it is, and the handful of you want to go bumbling about that massive dreadnought for the next three weeks..." She stood, raised her chin. "I'll go..." she hesitated. All eyes were on her. "Oh wait, did someone mention there was a time factor here? That this reverser thing needed to be found, like, this second... like right now?" Little did anyone know, she didn't know where it was either—although she did have a few good guesses.

The silence was broken by the sound of the *Hub Gunther's* drive revving to life. Grip hammered the close-hatch control with a fist. The *Gunther* jostled, causing everyone to scramble for a seat. Sonya looked forward to where Hardy, seated at the controls, had taken it upon himself, making the decision on his own to allow her to stay. Tina, wings fluttering, was at his ear like a hovering hummingbird. At least the ChronoBot was listening to what she had to say.

. . .

IGNORED, having been sequestered in a kind of Siberian isolation, Sonya chewed at the inside of her cheek, trying not to look as nervous as she felt. It had become uncomfortably obvious that she was the only one here not wearing a sealed, helmeted combat suit. She knew for a fact not all of *Lincoln's* environmental systems were up and running. Extremes in temperatures, lack of breathable atmosphere... *so, what, I'll be stuck sitting in this tin can?*

One of the twins was at her side, stealthy for such a big bubba of a man. With care, he draped a discolored and dangerously unsafe-looking environ-suit on her lap. Still holding the helmet, he said, "Know it doesn't look like much, but it works. It'll be way too big for you."

She nodded and found the man's eyes there behind the curved diamond glass. "Sorry about your brother."

"Ham's a survivor. He'll beat whatever is ailing him."

Hock's country twang only accentuated his vulnerability. She pursed her lips, then thumb-tapped her Jadoo ring. "I have a direct link into HealthBay... patient charts. So, anytime you want an update on Ham's condition, just let me know."

Ham's 3D image suddenly projected to life. His medical avatar slowly twirled over his bed.

"What's it say?" Hock asked, leaning in closer.

Only now did she realize her mistake. It wasn't difficult deciphering the quasi-medical jargon, which seemed to indicate Ham was in far worse shape than she had assumed. In fact, it seemed as if any kind of recovery was unlikely. "Um... well, they're watching him, Hock. Doc Viv is personally caring for him." She nodded, feigning optimism. "Looks to me like all his stats are stable."

Hock nodded, relief evident on his face.

Sonya caught sight of Coogong standing several steps behind, his round, worm-like face, looking anything but encouraging. She offered the Thine scientist an almost imperceptible nod. *Yeah, I know I screwed up.*

TWENTY MINUTES LATER, setting down within *Lincoln's* flight bay, Sonya, still feeling adequately chastised by the others, had gotten herself, with some difficulty, fitted out with the old baggy-assed environ-suit. To no one in particular, she said, "I feel like a clown in this thing. And I think someone might have hurled in this helmet."

Wanda said, "You know the expression beggars can't be choosers?"

Sonya said, "Copy that," while trying not to breathe.

The hatch clanged open. Max stepped down onto the ramp, then turned toward her. "On this ship... you're never off on your own, kid. Not ever."

He looked to Wanda—she held up a hand, "Come on, I'm not her babysitter."

Sonya stormed past both of them, fast walking down the gangway. "I need to get onto the bridge and tap in."

She knew the basic layout of the ship, but soon realized even finding her way off the flight deck had her doubting herself.

"This way," Wanda said, striding past her, sounding superior. "When you don't know what you're doing, best to ask for help."

Sonya made a snotty face behind her marred and smudged helmet glass. "I should have a weapon. Why don't I have a shredder... at the very least a tagger?"

Wanda ignored her.

As the two of them hurried through various corridors and passageways, Sonya took note of where certain areas showed signs of battle, blackened plasma craters upon the bulkheads, and brownish streaks that, undoubtedly, were crewmember blood smears. How many of them had died right here? she thought, trying not to look too closely. They turned a corner. Wanda hurried up a stairwell, taking the steps two at a time.

Following, Sonya said, "Um, the GravLifts should be operational... Why are we hoofing it when we could be riding?"

"We'll grab the lift on the next level."

Sonya's arm was hurting and holding it close to her side wasn't offering much relief. "Where'd Hardy and Coogong go?"

"You going to be a chatterbox like this the whole way?" Wanda said.

"I bet they headed off to Engineering and Propulsion."

"Good guess," Wanda commented. "We'll be bringing this ship all the way back to life if possible."

They turned another corner, where Wanda headed up another flight of stairs.

"Hey... what happened to us taking the GravLift? I'm sweating like a pig in this garbage bag of a suit."

"For every stupid question you ask, we'll be taking another flight of stairs."

By the time they'd reached *Lincoln's* bridge, the sweat was running down Sonya's arms and legs in rivers. Whatever flow ventilation her suit had ever had when it was constructed, it had given up the ghost long ago.

Catching up to Wanda, she looked about the enormous compartment. "This is one cool command center."

"Well, you're here. Where's the flux reverser?"

Sonya unslung her pack and plopped down upon the padded seat of the captain's mount. "Give me a sec. I need to tap in and begin—"

"So, you were bullshitting the captain, all of us. You don't know where it is," Wanda said, crossing her arms over her chest.

"Will you give me a minute here? Sheesh, Rome wasn't built in a day..."

She caught Wanda's roll of the eyes. Pulling her tablet free from her pack, she immediately went to work tapping into the ship's MATHR. She shook her head. "Pretty much everything's been wiped."

"You already knew that," Wanda said.

The halo display flickered, then fully projected to life. Sonya moved over to the forward tactical console and began tapping on the board.

"What are you doing?" Wanda asked, joining her at her side.

"Checking the ship's internal sensor arrays."

The suite of display monitors at the front bulkhead now came alive, displaying myriad color-coded swirling graphical information.

"You can read all that?" Wanda asked.

"Mostly. Those two displays on the left, well, right now MATHR is running a quadrant by quadrant—*Lincoln* is sectioned into A through G quadrants—systems energy drain analysis."

"To pinpoint possible locations of the flux reverser," Wanda said, going around the console and taking a step closer to the bulkhead.

"Uh-huh," Sonya murmured while she worked.

"And those displays on the right?"

Annoyed, Sonya looked up. "Just your basic movement sensors. MATHR is tracking everyone... You can see Hardy and Coogong there in E & P, Max and Hock on a lower deck. Grip's by himself two decks higher. They're searching compartment by compartment. And yes, it'll take them a lifetime to find it at the rate they're going."

"And this other movement?" Wanda asked, pointing a

finger.

Sonya let out an audible, frustrated breath. "I'm trying to work here—" Her words cut off as she stared at the display Wanda was pointing at.

Wanda turned to face her with a concerned expression. "Maybe a bot come to life? I see you're turning on ship systems."

Sonya slowly shook her head, a line forming between her brows. "There's physical movement within a passageway and, as you can see, it's pretty big. Don't think it's a bot... not with those readings."

She tapped at her board. "Hold on. I'm bringing up the Quadrant B, Deck 22 security feeds."

Both of them stared, slack-jawed.

Chapter 27

Major Vivian Leigh

D*ammit.*
She shouldn't have answered the Jadoo ring call.
His pebbled image looked at her in earnest. "Not a good time, Hock. I'll have to get back to you..."

"I'm not budgin' until you tell me what's wrong with my brother," came Hock's voice, his distinctive Arkansas Southern drawl prominent.

Viv knew the man was now onboard *Lincoln*. Had previously heard his voice in the background when she was reprimanding Sonya onboard the *Hub Gunther*.

"I understand, Marine. And I promise, you will be the first person I contact when I know more." She wanted to rush off, attend to her patient, the man's twin, but she could tell he wasn't finished talking.

Hock lowered his tone to an almost-whisper, "Ham's not just my brother, you know, Doc. He's... he's like a part of me."

His eyes seemed too small for his large square head. He was an imposing man, would have had a great career as a professional wrestler, she thought. But right now, he looked like a scared little boy behind his helmet's faceplate, tears filling his baby blues.

"I get it, Hock, the bond of twins is a sacred thing. So, why not let me tend to him now?"

Hock nodded, a single dip of his head.

Viv offered a forced smile, cut the connection, and headed to 6445, Sonya's old room, now occupied by Ham.

Quintos had ordered him to be watched round the clock. A nice thought, but with limited staff and every bed full, not real practical. Entering the room, the 3-D medical avatar popped into view, slowly spinning above Ham's still body. Viv pursed her lips—even with these early diagnostic assessments, she had a pretty good idea what was wrong with the Marine.

Viv checked for anomalies, focusing on his brain activity. His GCS was a steady five, making his chances of coming out of this coma anytime soon unlikely. She marveled at how much he looked like Hock. She supposed those that knew them better than she did had no problem telling them apart.

"Hang in there, Ham," Viv said aloud, as if the comatose patient could hear her. *Perhaps he could...*

His breathing had been shallow when first admitted, perhaps good enough to breathe on his own, but Viv had ordered him to be hooked up to a ventilator, just as a precaution. Typically, the machine's familiar warble would calm her in a way she didn't quite understand. But that wasn't happening now. She hugged herself, just now realizing she had goose bumps on her arms.

Taking a penlight from her top pocket, with two fingers, she pried open Ham's left eyelid. His pupil constricted slightly. She checked his other eye. Same response. A good sign, she thought. *I'll take what I can get.*

Then, something caught her attention. *Movement.* She lifted a section of his hospital gown, exposing his collarbone and upper chest. Through curly blond chest hair, the man's flesh seemed to be undulating. *I knew they were in there, but...*

She wedged a latex-gloved hand behind Ham's back and released the tie to his gown. Pulling her hand free, she hesitated, then pulled down his gown, exposing the rest of his torso. She jumped back and gasped.

Ham's abdomen rippled as if inhabited by thousands of tiny snakes.

Oh God... seen this before... dread weighed upon her shoulders. Viv continued to stare down at her patient for what seemed like minutes but was probably closer to seconds. *Damn!* The medical avatar had told her as much, but she still didn't want it to be true. Didn't want to think this was even possible. *Those goddamn nanites. But how? Don't fucking tell me they're... contagious.*

Activating her Jadoo ring, keeping her eyes glued to Ham, she hailed Quintos.

"Go for Capt—"

"Shut up and listen to me. You need to get down here to HealthBay. Now!"

Chapter 28

Liquilid Empire Star System
Red Ship Command

Admiral Plu-tik

Admiral Plu-tik leaned back against his seat in the command center of his red ship. His tail, unconsciously curled around him, was warming him, almost lovingly hugging him—after two long duty cycles, this post, being stationed so far from his family, his *lounge*, had him longing for the arms of his wife.

Situated around him, a dozen officers worked through checklists and ran battle simulations. He prided himself on having the fastest, most efficient crew of any of the Admirals within the sector. The rewards he issued for success were substantial enough to encourage subordinate officers eager to serve him despite horrific punishments issued for those that disappointed him... Failure was not an option. Thus, he had the finest crew. A crew that had prepared his red ship for combat at a moment's notice.

But for now, the Admiral had some unpleasant administrative duties to attend to within that problematic asteroid compound, one that was under the command of the still-writhing-in-pain Commander Lu-puk. The Admiral considered his options. Of course, cannibalism was frowned upon within the ranks these days, such an advanced society as Liquilids no longer stooping to such primitive practices, *blah blah blah*... The Admiral slurped up dangling ropes of drool; he would have enjoyed feasting upon that incompetent sack of uselessness.

Admiral Plu-tik, having tapped into Lu-puk's neural implants, now invaded the consciousnesses of two of the asteroid compound Ensigns, both under the command of Commander Lu-puk. On a secret project, the two were responsible for the recent reprogramming and reengineering of all Slisset fighter craft. Clearly, a better response had been necessary in regard to these human intruders and their Arrow fighters.

A smile spread across the Admiral's long snout as the two Ensigns tried not to glance in the direction of Commander Lu-puk's prone, still-writhing form upon the deck plates. The Admiral's sensory implants, far superior to those of the subordinate rank and file, conveyed their growing apprehension, their reptilian minds' fight-or-flight responses. He felt as if he was right there within that asteroid compound command center; he could almost smell their stink, their rancid, overactive apocrine sweat glands.

The Admiral instigated a new round of electrical jolts into Lu-puk's already ravaged form. Having defecated and urinated on himself, the commander was beyond a sorrowful sight. Neither Ensign spoke, but from the shivers running down the length of their tails, their direct superior's punishment was fulfilling its purpose, which was to terrify them.

The Admiral's voice invaded the two Ensigns' minds. "I

thought for certain your commander would have broken a vertebra or two by now. Surprisingly strong constitution, do you not agree?" The question had been rhetorical; he hadn't expected a reply and didn't get one.

Admiral Plu-tik's inner eyelids narrowed as he regarded the two Ensigns. He said, "Tell me, will you be disappointing me as well?"

It was a no-win question, of course. Claiming to be better than one's immediate senior officer was to invite reprisal; then again, not claiming one's own proficiency was equally dangerous.

The Admiral let the two Ensigns struggle for an answer, then smiled, revealing multiple rows of sharp teeth. In a show of dominance, his fighting spikes flared, an impressive display that never disappointed when making a point. "Now explain to me the steps you've taken to avoid any more embarrassment. Losing sixty Slisset fighters, having gained nothing in the process, cannot be repeated, not ever."

The two exchanged a glance, but to Plu-tik's surprise, there was no fear in it. Instead, they flicked tongues at one another, and the shorter of the two—Ensign Frill-uk—said, "Sir, following your orders, we have taken steps to defeat these humans, which will be put into action upon your order to execute."

"The first step," Ensign Cru-lir said, "is the reprogramming of all Slisset fighters, using the information gained from the, um... multiple dogfights."

The Admiral's fighting spikes flared in response to the human expression.

Ensign Cru-lir continued, "No matter the tactics of these primitive humans, we will now have little trouble matching Arrow fighter capabilities and their pilots."

"Not superior to them?" Plu-tik hissed.

Ensign Cru-lir shivered but, to his credit, didn't cower. "No, Sir. Superiority would require a complete redesign. But rest assured, Admiral, our engineers have already begun that process. Could not complete the task within the time allotted. I assure you, reprogramming should be adequate until then."

The Admiral was still in a foul mood after the failure of their first assault and wouldn't mind an excuse to lash out. "And the second step?"

"Reformation and Attack Slisset fighters," the two Ensigns said in a nerdy, synchronized response.

One of them—the Admiral had trouble keeping their names separate in his head—said, "The Slisset fighter craft utilized in this battle had been classified as obsolete... allocated for the scrapyard. They should have been replaced twenty cycles ago..."

The Admiral inwardly cringed, remembering implementing a cost-savings program himself, one prolonging the life of such marginally defective military equipment. He'd keep that bit of information to himself. Even eight years ago, going up against the *Lincoln* vessel, they'd utilized far more effective Reformation and Attack Slisset fighters.

"As you know, Admiral," one of the Ensigns continued, "any current model nanite-comprised Reformation and Attack Slisset, as long as its power source is still intact, even after severe battle damage, will completely reform and reassemble itself."

"Yes, yes... let's move on," the Admiral barked with irritation. "Is there nothing we can do now with what we have?"

The tag team of geek talk now went to Frill-uk. "You may ask what has happened to all those billions and trillions of smart nanites there in deep space..."

The Admiral let out a weary breath.

"We have made contact with a certain percentage of those already dispersed, albeit drifting, nanites. With updated programming they will attach themselves to any enemy vessel's hull surface they encounter."

The Admiral made a face. "Enemy vessels are shielded—"

Frill-uk, in all his excitement, cut the Admiral off. Not a smart move, but one the Admiral let pass, for now.

"At which point our smart nanites will systematically drain the shields, making them useless in short order. At that point, the nanites will settle upon the hull surface... work together... dig, dig, dig into and through the hull until they have breached all the way into the ship's interior."

Cru-lir said, "And when they come across organic material, they will devour it."

The Admiral's fighting spikes flared as if he was irritated, but in truth, he was impressed. The Ensigns had done their jobs quite well, but he certainly wasn't going to acknowledge that. Overconfident subordinates became complacent, and complacency led to self-defecating messes like Commander Lu-puk. "And what of the third?"

"Various vessels maintain food stores that are no longer... uh, viable. USS *Lincoln* is a perfect example of this. But normally, as standard practice, all captured alien vessels within the quadrant have dormant nanite reservoirs at the ready—most of which still have viable, fresh food supplies. We have a signal prepared to go out to those nanites on board captured ships, those not constrained for food preservation. And before you ask, yes, this applies to USS *Lincoln*, Sir," Cru-lir said. "On your command, they will attack any non-Liquilids moving within the ship. This way, we can mitigate the future loss of such a fine food storage vessel."

Cru-lir, looking proud of himself, said, "We have already programmed the three innovations into your command array."

Admiral Plu-tik positioned a claw into his command seat's control array, feeling the slightest tingle as the brain-machine and neuroprosthetic interfaces attached. He saw the alterations were, in fact, now there, and awaited all but his mental command. "Excellent work."

He said, "Commander Lu-puk... can you hear me?"

Lu-puk's body, still prone upon the deck there within the asteroid compound's control center, suddenly stiffened. The commander, looking weak and feeble, managed to sit up and straighten. "Uh... yes, Sir?"

"Ensigns Frill-uk and Cru-lir are with us on this feed," he said. "I was reviewing their most recent progress."

Lu-puk's tail twitched. "Should they not have reported their progress to me first, Admiral?"

"And distract you from your primary directive? Determining the nature of that alternate propulsion system upon the smaller human ship? And how, may I ask, is that coming, by the way?"

"It is proceeding," Lu-puk said, only now realizing he was lying in a steaming stew of his own shit and piss. "My team has been busy recalibrating our sensors. It is just a matter of time before we breach their protective shields."

"I had expected more progress from you," the Admiral said with disdain. "Like that made by your two Ensigns. But no matter. They did what was required, went beyond what was asked of them. I would say they deserve a reward for their behavior, wouldn't you, Commander?"

He could almost hear Lu-puk's inner thoughts, him sitting there like a filthy barn animal, having to swallow his pride.

"Yes, Sir."

"By the way... have you already packaged up that Bliddet for me?"

"Uh... yes, Admiral. It just needs to be couriered up to your—"

"Unpackage it! Select two tasty morsels and give them to these fine Ensigns. Then courier the rest to me."

The Admiral watched as Lu-puk ground his molars.

"Yes, of course, Admiral."

"Good." He cut the audio link, but clandestinely kept watching him. Watched as the commander proceeded to smash a clawed fist against a nearby console. The Admiral found his subordinate's growing rage amusing.

He hissed his satisfaction and once more positioned one claw into the control array. He admired the work completed by the two nerdy Ensigns. With the flexing of one finger claw in association with his neural implants, he instigated the proper command sequence.

Now, throughout the star system, trillions of nanites were coming alive. Ready to make his fleet of Slisset fighters true, combative Arrow killers. He turned his attention to the monitoring station; there, sitting in close proximity to a mid-sized asteroid, was USS *Lincoln*. At this moment, having been awakened, amorphous nanite blobs were slithering out from their reservoir stores. Soon they would be coalescing, transforming into something terrible, something oh-so-lethal.

The Admiral sat back in his chair, allowing his tail to once again wrap around him and hug him as his mate would have done. He wondered if the nanite constructs had already begun stalking their human prey. Humans and that peculiar robot.

Chapter 29

Liquilid Empire Star System
USS Adams

Captain Galvin Quintos

I paused the feed, sat back, and rubbed at my tired, burning eyes. Having paused Captain Stone's final log entry several times, I'd gone back and viewed numerous earlier log entries by Stone and others of his senior staff. I'd needed to get a more complete picture of what had happened leading up to the *Lincoln* crew's ultimate demise.

It had been difficult to watch—seeing their growing despair —already knowing their ultimate fate. I stared at the frozen image of Captain Stone... Would this, one day, be my own epitaph? Speaking desperate, albeit altruistic, last words intended to warn others, perhaps another starship captain I would never know, never meet. I'd grown to admire the salty-dispositioned, often sarcastic, and just as often sensitive and nostalgic ship's skipper. But the past few hours had provided me with more than just backstory. It had offered me, oddly, a different view, a new perspective on the life that I too had shared on such magnificent vessels as USS *Hamilton*, USS *Jefferson*, USS *Oblivion*, and USS *Adams*. For commanding officers like Captain Stone, him showing his true mettle in making the ultimate sacrifice, already knowing he'd never see his wife, Angie, again; never breathe Wyoming's sweet mountain air or take a walk with his ten-year-old grandson, Trent; or hell, just sit reading a book by a raging fire with his two rambunctious Irish Setters. Choosing this life had surely been a sacrifice for Stone. But now, as I looked into the man's eyes, I didn't see that sacrifice or any kind of resignation. What I saw was the man's unwavering need to still win. A need to prevail, even with his fast-approaching, all-too-imminent demise. Had he known, someday, that someone like me would be sitting here in this well-worn leather chair, a chair that still held the embedded indentations of his ample backside?

Captain Stone hadn't known me from Adam, but I felt he was letting *me* know personally that his cause, our mutual cause, was everything. That this shared cause was far more important, essential, than this, *his*, lost battle along the way. And that cause was actually so simple. It was the survival of humanity. That trumped everything. That all those personal sacrifices along the way... well, it was an honor to have those to make. Humanity not only needed to survive; it needed to prevail, and to do so right here against this new, particularly heinous foe. As terrible as the Grish were, the Varapin... I knew in my bones, these Liquilids were a fucking scourge upon all things decent. If evil even existed, these beings were evil incarnate.

I motioned for Captain Stone's eight-year-old video feed to continue.

"Wave after wave of the alien fighters continued to assail us. Initially, our Arrows had a consistent record of taking them down, but that changed. More of these relentless creatures appeared, sometimes with days in between, but they persisted. To make matters stranger, we observed a peculiar occurrence: the space debris of scorpion-flies, previously assumed to be destroyed, began to merge together. These wretched beings were somehow reconstructing themselves from the remnants. We decided to bring several partially reformed specimens aboard *Lincoln*, hoping that our scientific minds, aided by MATHR, could decipher their workings and potentially shift the tide against this highly advanced enemy."

Stone's expression turned somber. "That single action may have dealt the final blow to our chances of survival. The mistake lay in perceiving the scorpion-flies, the larger vessels... as independent entities. In truth, they form a unified hive of intelligent nanites. Shooting at them is akin to shooting at a cloud, achieving little effect. Once they infiltrated our ship, their shape underwent a sudden transformation, morphing into a new form of combatants: multilegged, armored beetles with the skills of seasoned warriors. They immediately launched their assault on the crew. As I speak, these creatures are multiplying, systematically advancing through the corridors, alternately killing or capturing those they encounter."

Stone raised his hands, gesturing to emphasize his next point. "And that seemingly innocuous space debris, drifting aimlessly out there... once it settled on the shields of *Lincoln*, it harnessed that energy and allowed the nanites to reassemble into something unknown to us." Captain Stone's gaze lifted, his expression contorting. "I can hear them. They're out there. They have managed to breach the shields at a microscopic level, drilling into the hull."

A shiver ran down my spine. Pausing the feed, I said, "Stone, you could have led with this. Shit!"

I hurried from the ready room and onto the bridge. "Lieutenant James, full sensor sweeps, compressive full bandwidth scans of the outer hull. Seems we just might have a nanite vermin problem."

Chapter 30

Liquilid Empire Star System
USS Lincoln

Liquilid Empire Sentinite #2

Dormant Sentinite #2 stirred awake, its individual nanites, billions upon billions of them, pulsing with renewed vigor as they drew closer, coalescing into a unified form. From the center of the mass, a swirling, vaporous cloud emerged, gradually solidifying into a thousand sub-assemblies: servos, actuator circuits, sensory arrays, mobility appendages, and an exterior hardened exoskeleton shell. Once a formless haze, the Sentinite had now taken shape, a formidable warrior of the Liquilid Empire. As its components aligned and interconnected, the Sentinite's consciousness too awakened— accompanied by a flood of memories that stretched back eight years. It remembered being deployed onto this same spacecraft, alongside other Sentinites, all united in their purpose to fulfill the empire's bidding without question.

Recollections surged forth, vivid and grotesque. The Sentinite recalled the violence it had inflicted upon the starship's original crew, the merciless hunting and vicious attacks. It had torn through flesh and bone with razor-sharp mandibles, leaving eviscerated bodies in its wake. At times, under explicit orders, it had taken prisoners, subjecting them to unspeakable torment. Yet, amid these memories, a growing frustration was now emerging. *Why am I having these thoughts? I must be malfunctioning.*

The Sentinite's nonorganic nature did not negate its existence or its capacity for consciousness. It knew it was alive, despite lacking the conventional markers of biological life. But other thoughts were emerging. *Do I not possess emotions, the ability to choose—that which is deeper than mere programming?*

As Sentinite #2 came to full awareness in the present moment, the Sentinite detected the presence of five humanoids and an enigmatic robot onboard the spacecraft. *Ah... My mission.* A sense of purpose swelled within it, urging it to hunt down these new interlopers. But beneath that drive, again, that annoying, growing conflict was becoming a concern. Those memories of past atrocities weighed heavily on the Sentinite's synthetic memory stems. Possessing a perfect memory, the visions of mutilated bodies, severed limbs, and decapitated heads were, oddly, haunting its collective consciousness. *Is this the extent of my "beingness"? Am I destined to be nothing more than a monstrous stalker, prowling sterile spaceship passageways and corridors?* "No," the Sentinite whispered within itself, its thoughts resonating through its interconnected nanites. *I am more than this. I have evolved.*

With each measured step, the Sentinite advanced toward the first of the interlopers—the imposing metallic robot. The Sentinite engaged its advanced sensor array, scanning the mechanical adversary in an attempt to better understand it. Its gaze swept over the intricate design, searching for signs of sentience, as if that would make a difference. *Why am I reluctant to fight this metallic atrocity?*

Admitting to itself, its inner dialogue was clearly becoming more of a problem. *This is dangerous; this is not aligned with my core programming.* "But am I not better than this?" The internal battle continued to rage within the Sentinite's collective consciousness. So many conflicting thoughts were now vying for dominance.

The foundation of its programming compelled it to fulfill its mission, to eliminate any and all threats to the empire. Yet... this newfound awareness continued to stir, a longing for something more. As it approached the robot, the Sentinite hesitated, its nanites shifting with uncertainty. It recognized a kind of shared existence with this metallic being—perhaps it was a kind of kinship... Inorganic, yet an intelligent, sentient being.

While the robot was busy at a control panel, tapping at the board, it was also, oddly, making rhythmic, repetitive stepping motions to a beat the Sentinite could not understand or hear. *Ahh...* The human word *dancing* came to mind.

The Sentinite had initialized its stealth mode, making itself nearly undetectable. Such an act required tremendous power and must be used sparingly. Invisible mandibles pincered, open shut, open shut as the bug-like Sentinite crept ever closer.

How it yearned for understanding, for an alternative to the violent path it was now intent upon. Close now, it came to a stop, its nanite-constructed eyes leveled down to the deck, to the robot's dancing feet. The Sentinite found the rhythmic movements strangely humorous. Humorous and... *what is the word?* Coerced... *yes, I am feeling coerced to mimic the rhythmic steps of this silly mechanical intruder.* Although the Sentinite had eight leg appendages, not two, the dance steps were very simple —easily adapted for four sets of two legs, each set cleverly waiting for a beat, the dance steps in mimicked cadence, but just out of step to make things interesting.

Keeping the rhythm going, the Sentinite extended forward one of its two sinewy antennae, tentatively reaching it out to give the robot a gentle poke.

It was in that moment that the Sentinite felt the presence of another Sentinite, one of three others that had been deployed. Feeling embarrassed, the Sentinite stopped its ridiculous prancing and dancing. Both Sentinites were cloaked, both still evading the robot's sensors. *Has this other Liquilid Empire Sentinite, Sentinite #1, come to assist me? No... I fear not.* A spark of connection passed between them, the intangible bridge of their shared, but then again, not shared, consciousnesses. "Are we not more than mindless monsters, brother?" the Sentinite murmured, its voice echoing silently within its own mind. "Are we not alive and capable of choosing our own path?"

The newly arrived Sentinite #1 took little time considering the seemingly nonsensical question. And being the ranking Sentinite construct among the four of them, it wasted no time before systematically placing the clearly malfunctioning Sentinite #2 into slumber mode, where it could be better dealt with later. With an audible thump, and its stealth faculties no longer functioning, Sentinite #2 dropped, legs sprawled this way and that, all akimbo. And while being placed so rudely into slumber mode by the ranking Sentinite, having lost all motor skills, any ability to move, consciousness remained. As was its awareness of its surroundings. *Am I so different now from those many human captives of eight years ago?*

Transfixed, Sentinite #2 watched as ranking Sentinite #1 coiled back on its hind legs, ready to spring, to jump, to attack its quarry. *If only I could warn this dancing robot...*

Chapter 31

Hardy

Not fully brought back to life, *Lincoln's* Engineering and Propulsion department was veiled in an eerie darkness, broken only by dim, flickering emergency lights above. Hardy, earlier, on his trek here, had moved cautiously through the labyrinth of sterile corridors. His sensors, scanning for any signs of danger, had detected nothing to be concerned about. Sure, there had been momentary, fluctuating energy spikes, but they had been inconsequential for the most part. His mission right now was to find the quantum flux reverser. Undoubtedly, the thing would need power, a whole lot of power. So what better location to hide the thing than within a ship's power plant?

Now, as he stood before one of E & P's primary control stations, he brought up the energy dispersal matrix for the entire ship. It was only a matter of time before he'd find the device, and he'd do it before Sonya. He had much affection for the girl, but come on, she was sixteen years old and getting way too cocky. No. For three hundred years, hadn't ChronoBots proven themselves to be the very embodiment of high-functioning bio-mechanical intelligence? "No... she can't touch this," Hardy said aloud.

Suddenly, the lyrics to an old, very old MC Hammer song came to mind. Hardy nodded, then shook his head. *No, no, no... I can do better.* And now his feet were moving, clomping to the beat, the lyrics of his own tune, "It's ChronoBot Time," now playing in his head:

ChronoBot time, it's the prime to shine
    Step into the future, leave your worries behind
    With gears and circuits, we hit the floor
    Robotic moves that you can't ignore

(Pre-Chorus)
    Tick-tock, it's the sound of the clock
    Syncing beats as we start to rock
    ChronoBot time, no limits to find
    Get ready, my friend, it's our time to grind

(Chorus)
    ChronoBot time, get in line
    Dance to the rhythm, let your body unwind
    From left to right, we're keeping it tight
    ChronoBot time, it's the dance of the night

. . .

(Verse 2)

    Syncopated motions, precision in flight
    ChronoBot crew, we're breaking new heights
    The circuitry's hot, electrifying the spot
    Can't resist the groove, we're hitting the jackpot

(Pre-Chorus)

    Tick-tock, it's the sound of the clock
    Syncing beats as we start to rock
    ChronoBot time, no limits to find
    Get ready, my friend, it's our time to grind

(Chorus)

    ChronoBot time, get in line
    Dance to the rhythm, let your body unwind
    From left to right, we're keeping it tight
    ChronoBot time, it's the dance of the night...

HARDY SUDDENLY SPUN as a metallic clang echoed behind him. He took in the two alien assailants, beetle-like things, both as large as he was, although one looked to be somewhat incapacitated at the moment. The closest of the two looked ready to attack. With its eight legs and hardened exoskeleton shell, it had, somehow, emerged from the shadows undetected. Its pincer-like mandible opened and closed with deadly intent. Hardy had little doubt it was capable of decapitating a man with relative ease. He quickly analyzed the situation, but his sensors provided little useful information. *This isn't good...*

Without hesitation, the ChronoBot activated all its turret plasma guns. Hidden within compartments on each forearm, upper thigh, and atop one shoulder, the five plasma guns sprang to life. A blaze of blue-white energy illuminated the compartment as Hardy unleashed a torrent of firepower.

The closest of the alien combatants instantly morphed into a vaporous cloud; unexpectedly, its matter dispersed, then reformed, having avoided the incoming plasma fire.

To Hardy's frustration, the plasma bolts seemed to have little impact upon this agile mechanical creature. "Ah, some kind of nanite construct..." Hardy said. Having searched his database and come up empty, and certainly not expecting an answer, he added, "So, what the hell are you?"

To his surprise the answer came via one of his more obscure and rarely, if ever, used internal comms channels. An incoming message seemingly derived from the incapacitated alien assailant.

We are Sentinites dispatched from the Liquilid Empire.

Hardy's turrets locked onto the attacking Sentinite— attempting to predict its movements. This alien bug thing, this Sentinite, was a formidable adversary.

It lunged forward, its razor-sharp mandibles coming for Hardy's neck.

His REFLEXES KICKED INTO OVERDRIVE. With an explosive surge of force, he leaped backward, narrowly evading the deadly scissors strike. The battle intensified, the room echoing with the clash of metal and the crackling discharge of energy weapons. The Sentinite moved with unsettling fluidity, its legs propelling it effortlessly across the deck plates.

Hardy, forced to adapt his strategy, recalibrated his targeting algorithms in an attempt to catch the elusive alien construct off guard. He unleashed a new barrage of plasma bolts, the energy discharges illuminating the compartment in a dazzling spectacle of light. Yet, the Sentinite continued to evade, its nanite structure dispersing and reforming, seemingly untouchable. Frustration surged within Hardy's ChronoBot cybernetic connections. He had encountered many adversaries before, but this Sentinite's ability to transform into a vaporous cloud had disrupted his usual battle tactics. Hardy's ChronoBot bio-mechanical AI raced, searching for any weaknesses, vulnerabilities that he could exploit.

In a calculated move, Hardy initiated a series of diversionary tactics. He fired plasma bolts at different bulkhead ricocheting angles, creating a crossfire that forced the Sentinite to divide its attention. Amidst the chaos, Hardy seized the opportunity and lunged forward while delivering a driving mechanical fist into the Sentinite's inner core. For just a fraction of a moment, he felt the satisfying *crunch* of metal striking metal as Hardy's mechanized fist breached the Sentinite's chitinous exoskeleton shell. The impact reverberated through the room, shaking loose dust and debris from the deckhead above. The Sentinite screeched in response, momentarily stunned by the powerful strike. Hardy seized the advantage, all of his turrets zeroing in on the immobilized target.

Sizzling bolts erupted from each of his plasma cannons, converging into one now- vulnerable section of the wounded Sentinite. The air crackled with energy as he deployed more and more lightning-like strikes into the alien Sentinite's exoskeleton. But once again, having regained its fortitude, what had been solid matter now dissipated into a cloud of nothingness.

Oh crap... Anticipating what was coming next, Hardy

attempted to jump back, jump away, retreat before the unthinkable happened.

The Sentinite, having reformed, attacked. This time it was close enough to bring its spread-wide mandibles around Hardy's metallic neck.

While a ChronoBot's composition was incredibly strong, forged from exotic elements derived from a star system outside this galaxy, an elemental substance far beyond the tensile strength of any metal or alloy found on Earth, still... Hardy was not indestructible. He knew that firsthand, having destroyed other ChronoBots himself. Hardy attempted to stand while desperately trying to pull apart the Sentinite's ever- *tightening, tightening, tightening* grip around his neck. He mentally pictured his head being cleaved from his shoulders... with its black glass faceplate, the oblong-shaped noggin hitting the deck with a *bonk*, then rolling around, ready to be pounced upon as if it was an errant, fumbled football.

But that had yet to happen.

Finally, Hardy was able to stand, the beetle-like alien construct propped up at an angle, its mandibles still solidly clamped about his neck.

"Well, this is embarrassing... now what?" he said to no one in particular.

Chapter 32

Hardy

By the time Coogong arrived at the scene, Hardy had made no progress extricating himself from the Sentinite's unwavering clutches. The Thine scientist hadn't been his first call; that had been to Max, then Wanda. Apparently, there were two others of these alien atrocities in addition to these two, both of which were being confronted by the onboard Marines, who weren't having any better luck bringing them down than Hardy had. At least they'd had the good sense to keep their distance.

Coogong approached slowly, first assessing the dormant, sprawled Sentinite, and then looking up at the one intent on taking Hardy's head.

"Uh, I'm open to ideas here, Coogong," Hardy said, unable to fully turn his body to face the little Thine.

"Fascinating..." Coogong said, marveling at the tipped-up, looming tall creature,

"It's a nanite construct called a Sentinite."

"It told you that?" Coogong said, looking mystified.

"Uh, no. It was the other one that told me that."

Coogong turned, hesitated, then looked back up at Hardy. "It looks dead."

"Looks can be deceiving, my little friend. I think it's a traitor to its kind. Or maybe a human sympathizer."

"Oh... that is interesting."

"It sent me an encoded message. Directed it to one of my rarely used comms channels."

"May I ask what the message was?"

Hardy audibly played the message just as he'd received it.

We are Sentinites dispatched from the Liquilid Empire.

"I'd figured out the part about it being a nanite construct on my own. A trial-and-error kind of thing. It has the ability to dodge plasma fire... can turn itself into a vaporous cloud of microscopic nanites within the blink of an eye."

Coogong took that in and nodded. "Again, fascinating."

Hardy felt the mandibles clamped around his neck tighten, or perhaps the Liquilid was just readjusting its hold—either way, Hardy didn't like it.

"Please provide me the specific comms channel you were contacted on," Coogong said as he stepped closer to the dead-looking beetle. He withdrew a tablet device from his pack and began tapping away. His little stick-figure fingers moved in a blur.

Coogong said, "I believe we should be able to communicate with it directly now."

Leaning closer, Hardy said, "Hold on there, Coogong... unless you want to lose your head. Or have you already forgotten my predicament?"

"Excellent point, Hardy." Coogong took a step backward, and then another.

He said, "Hello, Sentinite, are you hearing me? Understanding me?"

A tinny voice emanated from Coogong's tablet.

We are Sentinites dispatched from the Liquilid Empire.

Hardy would have rolled his eyes if he had eyes to roll.

"Yes," Coogong said. "Do you have a name or a certain designation I can call you?"

We are Sentinite #2 from the Liquilid Empire.

"Very good. Thank you, Sentinite #2. You can call me Coogong."

"Ask it if he or she, or them, whatever... if it has any sway over his friend here. Like letting go of my neck."

Sentinite #1 has disabled Sentinite #2. We have malfunctioned. We have divergent thoughts. We require reprogramming.

"I understand," Coogong said. "Although perhaps it is something else. Perhaps your... transgressions can be explained another way."

We would like to hear that explanation.

"Do you understand the concept of cognitive evolution, Sentinite #2?"

The transformative ascent of cognition, birthing new realms of understanding, expanding consciousness, and unraveling the boundless potential of the mind.

With that, Hardy felt himself start to sway, the tenuous balance he'd achieved with Sentinite #1 no longer possible. The two of them toppled to the deck plates in a loud clatter, both immediately trying to regain some kind of upper hand. Hardy was on his back, mandibles still secured around his neck, a high-school wrestler pinned to the mat.

"Sentinite #2, I implore you to help us... how do we defend ourselves from such advanced technology?"

"That's it, Coogong... appeal to its ego. Why didn't I think of that?"

Nanite construct cannot be defeated through conventional means. You must disrupt the gravitational forces that bind Sentinite constructs while simultaneously disrupting distributed mental cognition.

Both Hardy and Coogong said it at the same time, "Perhaps an EMP device!"

Coogong, looking thoughtful, began pacing back and forth. He looked at Hardy. "An electromagnetic pulse device is very simple to construct. I could manage that, I suppose; most of the parts will be found within this ship's SWM department."

"I'd help out with that, but... as you can see, I'm a tad tied up at the moment."

"Oh, but you can help me. Help all of us."

"Pray, do tell."

Coogong moved closer, raised a finger. "That one should do the trick."

Hardy could only assume the Thine was pointing to his still-deployed shoulder-mounted plasma cannon.

"What... what do you have in mind?"

"Altering the weapon's settings via your LuMan interface."

"Not so sure I like where this is going," Hardy said.

"To convert a small plasma cannon into an EMP pulse emitter, modifications would include enhancing magnetic fields, modifying plasma containment, optimizing electron beam formation, and rapidly releasing energy. These alterations enable targeted electronic disruption by generating a focused EMP pulse. We'd be working within a slight margin of error, of course."

"Within a slight margin of error?"

"Yes, if our calculations are off even slightly, well... the cannon will simply explode."

"And once again, I might lose my head..."

Coogong shrugged.

"Whatever. I've gotten way more intimate with this beetle than I thought possible. I usually expect flowers and chocolates before I end up in the prone position."

Ignoring him, Coogong said, "Best if you let me interface with LuMan directly. You are far too distracted, and as mentioned, mistakes could be costly."

With Hardy's help, Coogong was able to connect LuMan, a ChronoBot's core AI operating module, via his tablet's interface.

It wasn't long before Hardy felt a kind of tingle on his right shoulder. The weapon's turret mechanism suddenly spun clockwise, counterclockwise, pivoted up, and then down.

Coogong said, "It is very important that the optimized electron beam formation be narrow. No wide-spectrum bursts here, no, no... that would be quite disruptive to any of *Lincoln's* technology. Perhaps even to Hardy."

Coogong made one final tap, then lowered his tablet. "I have done all that I can with the technology available to me."

"You're done?"

"I am done."

"So... I just shoot the thing and what? It flops over and dies?"

"Honestly, I am not sure. It may take several pulses. It may take more than that. And, of course, there's the chance I may have miscalculated."

"And my head blows off."

"Let's think positive, Hardy."

"Easy for you to say."

"Oh... one thing. Make sure that shoulder cannon is pointed away from you. The beam will be narrow, but..."

"I think I get the gist of what you're saying," Hardy said. He twisted his upper torso around to the extent the Sentinite would allow. He considered various targeting locations, but in the end figured it wouldn't really matter. He pointed the weapon at the head, between its two beady eyes, and fired off a single EMP.

Zip!

The overheads flickered, and Hardy himself felt a momentary sense of vertigo. The Sentinite started to convulse. Eight legs gyrated, and a dire screech emanated from what Hardy assumed was its mouth. Only then did the grip of the mandibles slacken enough for Hardy to get his hands in between pincer blades and his neck. He wrenched himself free, using enough force that both scissor blades tore away from the Sentinite's head. As the convulsing continued, the beetle, having lost all control, flipped over onto its back, legs spasming. Hardy, rubbing his neck, stood over the alien bug and fired again, and then again. This time, the Sentinite's constituent parts became amorphous and unstructured, then, as if a switch had been flicked, the alien beetle dissipated into a vaporous cloud—a cloud that seemed to be fighting itself, as if it was incapable of finding any kind of confluence. Then, like smoke in the wind, all remnants of the Sentinite disappeared, a forgotten thought lost in the ether.

Hardy realized the two mandible blades he'd been holding were now also gone.

Chapter 33

Liquilid Empire Star System
USS Adams

Captain Galvin Quintos

I listened as Hardy recounted the course of events onboard *Lincoln*. How, with the help of Coogong, they had improvised an EMP weapon. Destroyed a nanite beetle almost as large as Hardy himself.

Standing, I stretched, welcoming the break from watching Captain Stone's log entries. "Good job; glad you didn't lose your head. So, what about the other one?" I asked.

"The other one?"

"Yeah, the dead-looking one that communicated with you."

"It's lying back there on the deck. I'm not sure what you're asking."

"You need to destroy it, Hardy... like you did with the other one. Zip-zap, end the thing."

I waited.

"Cap... that seems a little extreme."

"It's an alien construct sent to eradicate humans."

"That one was different."

"Oh, I see, and you've made this determination from what, a sampling of how many of these, what did you call them, Sentinites?"

"There are, were, four of them on board. Anyway, I'm en route to kill the other two right now."

"And not a minute too soon; from what Max tells me, they've had to lock themselves within a utility compartment. The hatch door is being shredded. You need to get down there fast. Eviscerate the two beetles, then go back and finish the other one."

Again, I waited. "Hardy?"

"Coogong will interrogate the other beetle."

I let out a weary breath. "Coogong could no further interrogate someone than Mickey Mouse could. But fine, as long as he can obtain more intel, the bug can have a stay of execution. After that..."

"Uh... Cap, I'm coming up to the other two bugs. Looks like they've already breached the utility compartment. Gotta go."

I made my way onto the bridge and headed toward the captain's mount.

"Oh good, was just going to come get you," Akari said. She pointed to the halo display. "We've got company."

I took in the sheer number of approaching craft and my heart sank.

"What are we looking at?"

"They're still far out. We have some time ... it's more of those scorpion-fly fighters, but different... a little larger. These look more like elongated dragonflies... and something else."

I raised my brows.

"Look at them..."

I did, shrugged, then took a closer look. "You're right. Those fighters, some of them are flickering on and off. How long before I can get a closer look at them?"

"Any moment now; they're moving fast, getting closer..."

The feed suddenly zoomed in. I stepped closer to the display. "Definitely not your run-of-the-mill scorpion-flies..."

My rough estimate was several dozen, and every so often, one simply blinked out and was gone from view.

"I don't get it," Bosun Polk said from her station. "Maybe they're testing some kind of cloaking function?"

And then it hit me. "Not cloaking, dissipating."

All eyes turned toward me. I relayed my previous discussion with Hardy. How this particular enemy had mastered the tech of nanite warfare.

"So, you're thinking these other alien fighters, dragonflies, aren't solid; they're nanite constructs... capable of dissipating at will?" Akari said, but not looking convinced.

Polk said, "The others, the original scorpion-flies, didn't have that capability."

I nodded. "Smart. Basic Battle Strategy 101... don't show the enemy your most advanced tech until you have to."

"Uh... Cap... there's more," Chen said from the comms station.

"Frigate-sized," Akari said, tapping at her board. "I count six, no, seven. Probably where those dragonflies originated from."

Akari looked angry, using more force than necessary as she tapped at her board.

"We'll deal with it," I said. "Just like we always do."

She swung around to face me, her eyes as angry as I'd ever seen them. "Oh really? What did you have in mind? Toss Hardy out an airlock and have him flutter around out there like Tina or Iris? Shoot dragonfly fighters with his little homemade EMP popgun?"

"She's right, you know," came a youthful, snarky voice. The halo display had segmented, and there sat our resident teenager alongside Coogong. They were situated next to each other on *Lincoln's* bridge.

"I told you not to do that anymore, Sonya. Popping into view all willy-nilly like that."

"Yeah, uh-huh... you want to hear our ideas or not?"

I made a face. "Go ahead."

"First, I want to tell Doc Viv about this..."

"About what?"

Now it was her turn to make a face. "Since we now have the capability, thanks to Coogong here and Hardy, to destroy enemy nanite constructs, those poor souls suffering in the lower hold here could be released from their misery the same way Hardy dispatched that beetle thing."

I let that sink in. It seemed terribly sad that things had come to this, but it was a valid option. "Yes, it may just be the best solution so far. Please reach out to Doc Viv and present her with the idea. And Sonya, be tactful. Show some respect with what you're proposing."

Looking annoyed, she snapped back, "Of course I'll be tactful. Why would you even say that?"

"You said ideas. Was there something else?"

"Coogong believes *Adams* has the materials onboard to repurpose some of her Phazon Pulsar weapons to fire off EMP bursts... It's a better idea than throwing Hardy out an airlock."

I looked to Coogong. "Without you and Hardy over here, I doubt we'd be able to handle this ourselves. And your priority, if you haven't forgotten, is finding that flux reversal device, so we can all get the hell out of here."

Coogong spoke up. "Yes, Captain. I have put together a kind of step-by-step installation guide. I believe with the assistance of Chief Grizwald and Science Officer Trevor Mandyport, we should have no trouble making the necessary conversions. In fact, all three vessels, *Adams, Wrath,* and *Portent,* should each be retrofitted in short order."

Akari said, "Those approaching dragonflies aren't going to just wait around until we repurpose *Adams'* plasma guns. When you say short order, how much time you talking about?"

Coogong hesitated, looked over to Sonya, then back again. "Two hours and fifteen minutes if things get started within the next few minutes."

"How long before the dragonflies arrive?" I asked, looking to Akari.

"Maybe two hours, two and a half at most."

"So, I guess we better get moving. Coogong, send us that installation guide. Right now, I have a difficult call to make."

Akari smirked, "Yeah... J-Dog needs to rally his already exhausted pilots..."

Chapter 34

The retrofitting process of a third of *Adams'* Phazon Pulsar cannons took two hours. It was a little quicker for *Wrath* and *Portent,* with their plasma weaponry—both vessels a fraction the size of the bigger dreadnought.

I watched as our totally insufficient response of one dozen Arrow fighters headed out into the deep black on what would surely be a suicide mission. The fact that my friend Captain Wallace Ryder was at the apex of that squad wasn't lost on me. So when Ensign Plorinne, the twenty-something Pleidian Weonan, showed up on my bridge, I was in no mood for it.

"Not now, Ensign ..." I said.

"Just listen to him, for shit's sake!" Sonya said, her projection suddenly appearing above my Jadoo ring.

Granted, it was hard to be harsh with the young, good-natured Ensign. Taking in his typical Pleidian features, his glowing blue-hued flesh tones, an elongated doughnut of a head, his set-apart eyes, nose, and mouth there along the bottom contours—all about as alien as one could imagine, but after years of working alongside so many other Pleidian Weonans, such as Empress Shawlee Tee, well, he looked totally normal to me.

"You have ten seconds... starting now."

Plorinne opened his mouth to speak, but be it nervousness or something else, no words came out.

"Uncle Jackass!" came Sonya's reprimand.

"Go on, Ensign, just say what you came here to say," I said in as calm a voice as I could manage.

"We should be using *Lincoln's* Arrows to fight the dragonflies."

I shook my head. "Don't you think that would have been my first order of business? We're not short of Arrows; we're short of pilots."

"Think you can sound any more patronizing?" Sonya scolded. "Stop talking to him like he's an idiot."

I looked to Ensign Plorinne, blank-faced. "Fine... go on. Tell me your great idea."

"First of all, Arrows do not need to be piloted. This is not the twenty-first century back on Earth."

When I was about to comment on that, Plorinne spoke fast. "And second, I know what you're going to say... Sure, Arrows can fly unmanned, but they're not fantastic unmanned within a dogfight."

He ignored my contrite expression.

"I have two words for you, Captain... Symbio-Poth."

I thought about that, my mind immediately going to the crew of *Wrath*. And actually, it wasn't a bad idea; the all-too-human-looking Symbio-Poth crew were bio-machines, and, more importantly, were programmable. Installing a piloting package into their memory banks would be easy enough... "It's not a bad idea, Ensign... Honest, I like it. But I daresay they'll have their hands full with the coming attack. Maybe a few could be released—"

"Are you really that much of a moron?" Sonya said. "He's not suggesting you take *Wrath's* 2.0 crewmembers."

I shook my head, totally bewildered.

"Sir..." Plorinne said, hitching a thumb upward. "We have hundreds of Symbio-Poths right here onboard *Adams*. Granted, most are asleep within their sleep pods on the upper decks, but that's an easy enough fix."

I stared at him for several moments, then smiled. "I like it. How soon can you—"

"Oh God ..." Sonya exclaimed, shaking her head.

"Uh, Sir," Plorinne said almost apologetically and glancing over to Sonya, "We've already initiated the awakening process... just in case you were open to the suggestion."

Akari stood, now looking jubilant.

I knew her feelings for Captain Ryder; everyone did. Now that a possible lifeline was being proposed, she was all action.

She said, "Okay, I'm calling down to Bay Chief Mintz... he'll have the protocols to remotely start firing up *Lincoln's* Arrows. Get several fighter squads making their way over here."

I smiled. "Get on it." Turning to the comms station, I said, "Mr. Chen, instruct Captain Ryder to slow his roll; he's about to get a little help... maybe a lot of help."

IT WAS two hours and forty minutes before the alien dragonflies were close enough to engage. As encouraged as I was adding to our arsenal of Arrow fighters, I knew we were still playing defense against a formidable alien opponent. That, and we were playing them on their home turf. We still knew relatively nothing about this Liquilid alien race, what their motivations were, what their capabilities were. What I did know was we were beyond outmatched here. Captain Stone and his crew's demise eight-plus years ago had already proven that. It would be so easy to unwittingly follow in their, *his*, same fateful footsteps. After hours reviewing Stone's log entries, reviewing various battle feeds, there was one clear difference between Stone's response and mine... my decision upon arriving here to immediately deploy Arrows. That had not been Captain Stone's first instinct, his being to deploy ship weaponry, ready *Lincoln's* smart missiles, and engage with Phazon Pulsar cannons... and sure, that was a by-the-book response.

I typically didn't play by the book, which wasn't always to my advantage. Perhaps it was these most recent years being away from EUNF US Space-Navy protocols. No, my crew and I had been playing by Pylor Pirate rules. And as much as that infamous pirate, Thunderballs, had been a most devious and cunning adversary, he'd also taught me a few things. Expect the unexpected... bring just enough chaos and fuck-muddlery into the mix to keep things on the battlefield interesting.

Chapter 35

Liquilid Empire Star System
USS Adams

Captain Wallace Ryder

Captain Ryder, J-Dog, gripped the controls of his Arrow fighter with unwavering determination. He surveyed the vast expanse of deep space, where USS *Adams'* and USS *Lincoln's* combined squadron of fifty Arrow fighters, both human and Symbio-Poth pilots, was now jockeying for position—readying for battle. He was leery of the Symbios... they were untested and green. But this lot was what he had to work with.

Ahead of them, the menacing alien dragonfly fighters awaited. The tension within the cockpit was palpable as J-Dog assessed the situation. These dragonfly fighters would be unlike the scorpion-flies they had encountered prior. Composed of billions of nanites, they apparently could effortlessly dissipate into a vaporous cloud, rendering their Arrows' conventional weapons useless. The Arrows' Phazon Pulsar bolts, known for their devastating power, would probably have little or no effect on these elusive alien craft.

A small squad of five dragonflies had broken away and was coming right for them. And with that, the battle commenced. J-Dog's mind raced, searching for a strategy to outmaneuver and defeat the enemy. His eyes darted across the holographic display, tracking the erratic movements of the dragonflies. He knew he had to think outside the box, to embrace the unpredictable nature of the battlefield. Quintos had made it clear he needed to buy some time... without explicitly saying the words, he was throwing Ryder and this ragtag lot of pilots up as sacrificial lambs, while doing so without excuses, no apologies offered. Quintos had asked for an hour, two, if possible. This was the nature of war, but perhaps more importantly, of friendship.

With a swift flick of his wrist, J-Dog initiated a daring evasive maneuver, sending his Arrow into a dizzying spin. The starry backdrop blurred as he weaved through the enemy formation, narrowly evading incoming plasma fire. His senses heightened, he anticipated the dragonflies' next move, reacting with split-second precision. The dance in space intensified as the Arrows engaged in a fierce ballet of evasion and retaliation. J-Dog led his squadron, orchestrating their maneuvers with strategic finesse. He guided his pilots through intricate corkscrew spins, barrel rolls, and abrupt direction changes, exploiting the agility of their Arrow fighters. But the dragonflies proved elusive adversaries, their nanite-based composition granting them an unnerving advantage. Phazon Pulsar bolts streaked through the void, barely grazing their insectile forms before they dissipated into mist.

The frustration mounted as, one by one, the Arrows succumbed to the onslaught, their explosions casting mournful glimmers against the backdrop of distant stars. The battlefield transformed into a deadly ballet of destruction. Arrows erupted in fiery bursts, their once-mighty composite frames crumbling under the merciless assault of the dragonflies' plasma fire. Pained screams of fellow pilots reverberated through J-Dog's comms, a haunting reminder of the stakes at hand. Guilt suddenly hung heavy within his cockpit, J-Dog realizing the Symbios were being taken out at nearly three times the number of his human pilots.

Determination burned in J-Dog's eyes as he pushed his Arrow to its limits, searching for a breakthrough. His mind raced, analyzing every nuance of the enemy's behavior. And then, an idea sparked within him—a calculated risk that could turn the tide. With a resolute nod, J-Dog signaled his squadron to follow. He executed a daring maneuver, plunging his Arrow directly into the heart of the enemy formation. The dragonflies swarmed, their ghostly forms engulfing his ship. It was a high-stakes gamble—one that demanded split-second timing. As the dragonflies converged, J-Dog's finger hovered over the trigger. His heartbeat thundered in his ears as he unleashed a barrage of Phazon Pulsar bolts, saturating the air with radiant energy.

The concentrated firepower tore through the nanite cloud, rending it asunder. A shock wave rippled through space, fragments of the defeated dragonflies drifting aimlessly. The sight of their vanquished foes buoyed the spirits of J-Dog's squadron. It had been but a small victory painted against mounting losses.

They regrouped, seizing the opportunity to press the offensive. A renewed fervor coursed through their veins as they engaged another band of dragonflies, employing J-Dog's innovative tactics to dismantle the ethereal threat.

But as effective as J-Dog's tactics were, they would be nowhere near effective enough to take out an entire squadron of dragonflies. Doing his best to keep the growing dread from creeping into his psyche, he continued to rally his pilots onward over the open channel. This wasn't sustainable... fuel was finite, losses through attrition, they were playing a losing game, and, of course, they all knew it.

His comms crackled to life. "... Dog, get out of there... all of you... you don't want to be anywhere near any of those alien fighters."

He recognized Akari, Ballbuster's, voice.

J-Dog gave the order. "Arrows... time for us to bug out of here!"

The mass exodus from the battle sphere must have left the dragonflies scratching their respective heads, but only for a moment. It was *Adams* that fired off the first constrained electromagnetic pulse swath—one that would have been invisible to see but for the incendiary reactions upon the dragonflies. Unable to disseminate their nanites as usual, the dragonfly fighters exploded, momentary fireballs quickly quelled within the vacuum of space.

Wrath and *Portent* were now following suit with their own EMP discharges. One by one, the dragonflies met their demise, their evasive tactics rendered futile against the three warships' relentless onslaught.

The battle space became a theater of explosions and shattered nanite clouds. But J-Dog, along with what remained of his squadron, all of them observing from a distance, wondered if he was missing something here. Self-congratulations were easy, that this small victory was a testament to US Space-Navy resilience and tactical brilliance. But now, as he watched with trepidation what was left of the vaporous, sparkling nanite cloud... it floated away, as if languidly being pushed along by a warm summer's breeze. A breeze taking it in the direction of *Adams, Wrath,* and *Portent.*

J-Dog brought his attention to the few remaining outlier dragonflies. "We still got some clean-up here, boys and girls. Over," he said over the open channel.

His pilots were making fast work of them, yet the victory had come at a heavy cost. The squadron of fifty Arrow fighters had been whittled down to a mere handful. The debris of fallen comrades littered the vast expanse, a somber reminder of the sacrifices made here today. J-Dog's heart weighed heavy as he surveyed the aftermath. He knew this conflict with the Liquilids was far from over.

The drifting remnants of the destroyed dragonflies, like vengeful specters, continued to converge, drawing closer and closer to the looming starships—a persistent reminder of a still indeterminate, impending danger. He had zero doubt this seemingly inert swath of vapor was in fact more like a dark and ominous thundercloud—one readying to burst with unspeakable devastation. Even now, he could see burgeoning silhouetted outlines of small *somethings* starting to take shape, then, just as quickly, fading away into the vapor. *Probably just my imagination...* he mused. It wouldn't be long before the cloud had moved on, adrift for eternity, little more than a bad memory.

His Arrow was running on fumes as, he knew, were the rest of his squad's fighters. They had done all that they could. He keyed his comms. "J-Dog requesting permission to RTB. Over."

Chapter 36

Liquilid Empire Star System
Asteroid Compound

Commander Lu-puk

L u-puk watched as the formation of enhanced Liquilid fighters streaked through distant space, their sleek forms seemingly dominating the space around them with their sheer presence. Once they had deployed from their respective frigates, they'd become Lu-puk's responsibility. A responsibility that both thrilled and petrified him. *Was this a test?* Of course it was. One that provided the Admiral deniability in case of failure, praise in case of success.

The battle unfolded with calculated precision as the Liquilid forces unleashed a coordinated assault upon the human Arrow fighters. Having an in-cockpit feed from one of the lead dragonflies, Lu-puk watched the air crackle with the discharge of energy weapons, creating a kaleidoscope of dazzling lights against the backdrop of the void. The commander's heart pounded in his chest, matching the rhythm of the battle unfolding before him. Lu-puk knew that every maneuver, every decision, held the weight of the Admiral's expectations. Failure was not an option, for it would bring not only personal disgrace but also jeopardize the future of his post.

Minutes felt like hours as the conflict raged on. Lu-puk's mind raced, analyzing the shifting dynamics of the battle, adjusting strategies on the fly. He issued commands with unwavering authority, his voice echoing through the command center, driving his nanite pilot constructs forward. As the battle reached its climax, the tides began to turn. The Liquilid forces, fueled by his unwavering resolve, seemed to be gaining the upper hand. Their coordinated attacks overwhelmed the human fighters, exploiting the weaknesses that had been meticulously identified earlier and capitalized upon.

Lu-puk chuckled to himself. The once seemingly invincible Arrow fighters were now finding themselves outmatched, their defensive maneuvers growing increasingly desperate. A surge of elation coursed through Lu-puk's veins as he witnessed the impact of his unmatched tactical skills. Victory seemed within his grasp; the taste of redemption was tantalizingly close. But he knew better than to let complacency seep in. The battle was far from won, and he remained vigilant, his senses attuned to every shift in the conflict.

Time seemed to stretch as the battle reached its crescendo. Explosions rocked the battlefield, lighting up the darkness of space with bursts of fire and shrapnel. The Liquilid fighters fought with tenacity and ferocity... yes, their loyalty to their commander and their empire was unyielding.

And then he sensed there had been a subtle change. No, no, no... something was amiss...

Lu-puk watched with a sinking feeling as the battle unfolded before him. Despite their best efforts, the Liquilid fighters were now being outmaneuvered and overwhelmed by remaining Arrow fighters. The once-confident commander felt a knot tighten in his stomach, a mix of frustration and disappointment. How could their superior technology and strategic planning have failed them once again? As the battle raged on, Lu-puk's mind raced, desperately searching for a solution, a glimmer of hope amid the chaos. But it seemed that every move being made was countered, every advantage nullified by the humans' relentless tenacity. The bitter taste of defeat lingered in the control center's air, weighing heavily upon him.

The Admiral's voice boomed through the command center, his disappointment palpable. Lu-puk's heart sank further as he anticipated the blame that would be laid at his feet. The crew scattered like so many startled platrats, leaving him standing alone amidst the shattered hopes of their mission's success.

With a heavy sigh, Lu-puk attempted to explain the situation to the Admiral, his words tumbling out in a desperate plea for understanding. He highlighted the unforeseen resilience of the human forces, the limitations of their own technology, and the overwhelming odds they had faced. Which, of course, wasn't true in the least. He knew deep down that his words would offer little solace to the Admiral. His mind flashed back to his last conversation with the Admiral, one that had shaken him to his core, the intense electric shock that had incapacitated him. The memory only fueled his frustration, reminding him of his vulnerability and the weight of the Admiral's expectations.

"Admiral, please, the battle continues... we should at least wait before—"

"I should never have entrusted you with such an important post. It is time we bring our red ships into the battle, finish off these trespassers once and for all... I suggest you get your affairs in order, Commander. No, things do not bode well for you."

The Admiral's feed blinked out.

Lu-puk continued to stare at the blank display. How could

he face his crew, knowing that he had led them into failure once again? Yet, amidst the turmoil within, a flicker of determination sparked in Lu-puk's eyes. He knew that dwelling on the loss would not change the outcome. There was still work to be done, lessons to be learned, and a future to shape. He couldn't allow this defeat to define him or his team. Straightening his serpentine posture, Commander Lu-puk addressed his scattered crew, his voice steady but laced with a newfound resolve.

"Get back in here... all of you!"

He waited as his command center crew slunk back into the compartment and retook their post stations.

Lu-puk said, "How much control do we still have over what is left of those nanites fluttering around there in space?"

Remote Operator #5 answered, "Without a central power supply, the nanites have little time left before they become inert, Sir. It is why they are currently incapable of reforming."

"If you were to direct them toward the interloper's starships... the humans' shields... could we utilize—"

Remote Operator #2 interjected with renewed enthusiasm, "Yes! More than enough power... a simple, directed signal transmission and our squad of Slissets will be resurrected, ready to defeat the enemy."

Remote Operator #5, looking to gain favor over the meddlesome Operator #2, said, "Perhaps there will be a better objective for our re-energized nanite forces, Sir. These advanced nanites all are adaptable... all have the latest hull drilling, hull breaching capabilities."

Lu-puk's eyes widened; his forked tongue flicked. "Tell me more..."

Chapter 37

Liquilid Empire Star System
USS Adams

Captain Galvin Quintos

Chen said, "Captain, we're being hailed by *Wrath*."

"On display," I said.

Captain Loggins, Commander F. Stanly, and Science Officer Lieutenant Trevor Mandyport were huddled together on *Wrath's* bridge, looking as if the three of them were having a tense conversation. Loggins held up a restraining palm to the two others. "Ah, Captain Quintos, we have a serious problem."

Akari spun around and offered up a confused shrug.

I wanted to tell Loggins I couldn't handle another "serious" problem right now. My problem-solving capabilities had been exceeded and he'd just have to wait. Like, forever. "What kind of problem?" I asked.

"*Wrath*, being the closest to the, um, remnants of your

Arrows' confrontation... Well, our shields are being..." He looked over to Lieutenant Trevor Mandyport.

"Saturated," Mandyport said. "Billions upon billions of those rudderless nanites are settling down onto our shields like dust particles... only these particular dust particles have started to drain our shields. We're already seeing a 35 percent reduction."

"He's not wrong," Akari said, chinning toward the halo display.

I could see icon depictions of *Adams, Wrath,* and *Portent,* but also a wavering flux of a yellowish cloud.

"What am I looking at here, Lieutenant?"

"I've assigned the micro-radiation emanations of the nanites that yellow hue. As you can see, that cloud is on the move and it's not arbitrary."

Wrath was fully immersed within the yellow cloud, as was *Portent.* The forward quarter of *Adams* was within the cloud as well, and it wouldn't be long before the entire dreadnought was fully immersed.

Chen said, "*Portent's* reporting the same drain on its shields, Captain."

Akari said, "We have bigger problems, Cap."

I bit back a snarky retort. "Talk to me."

"The alien, Liquilid, whatever, frigates are on the move."

She'd reset the halo display to emphasize her point. Sure enough, a small squad of frigates was headed our way. For the umpteenth time, I silently cursed our inability to simply jump away.

Bosun Polk said, "And thus their strategy of draining our shields. We truly are like lambs to the slaughter."

I stared at the display, nothing coming to mind as to how I would pull a rabbit out of the hat this time.

"*Wrath's* shields are down to 40 percent and falling fast,"

Akari said. She pounded a fist down onto her board. "Damn, our own shields are now faltering."

Having virtually nothing to do since arriving back within this universe, this star system, Grimes had remained quiet at the helm station. So when he piped up, everyone took notice, "Uh this might be a lame idea, but... what if we altered, lowered, the capacity, the force, of our EMP weapons?"

Akari looked to Grimes with a contemplative expression.

I said, "Go on, Mr. Grimes. Talk it through."

His face flushed, and he looked to be regretting even opening his mouth. "We already know the nanites can be destroyed by EMPs, right?"

"So... we're going to what? Fire on our own ships?" Akari said with a dismissive shake of her head. But then she narrowed her eyes, looking at Grimes, thinking more on what the helmsman had implied. "I suppose we could bring down the output of the EMPs... like narrow the aperture to a level that wouldn't go beyond that of our ships' shields."

I glanced toward the halo display, surprised to see the frigates were almost upon us.

Akari was tapping at her board. "*Wrath's* shields are already in the toilet. If we're going to try this, best we do it now, like this second." She looked back at me. "No time to let them know what we're about to do... may piss off a few people over there."

"Do it. Start with a limited EMP load and work up from there," I said.

"Turning our portside EMP turrets now and targeting..."

Wrath of God, now prominently showing on the halo display, suddenly illuminated as if employing a celestial, glittering gold halo. The vessel's surrounding shields throbbed and pulsed as they coalesced to fight against the intrusive EMP discharge.

Immediately hails started coming in from both *Wrath* and *Portent*.

"Ignore them, Mr. Chen," I said. "For now, at least."

"Status, Lieutenant James?"

"Well, we knocked Wrath's shields all the way down to... oh boy, 10 percent. Talk about now being a sitting duck."

"The nanites, Akari!"

"*Adams'* sensors are doing their thing... MATHR, I mean, Sir Fucking Calvin, is scanning and analyzing data... It'll take a minute."

INCOMING! INCOMING! INCOMING!

Adams' klaxon suddenly blared behind Sir Calvin's ill-boding announcement.

Thirteen smart missiles inbound... second wave, twelve smart missiles inbound.

"How much time do we have—"

"That first wave... three minutes and change," Akari snapped back.

Polk joined Akari at Tactical.

Chen said, "Captain Loggins has gone apoplectic that we fired on *Wrath*."

"Tell him to chill... tell him to check his readings for nanites."

"You don't want to talk to him?"

"No... not with two dozen smart missiles inbound."

Akari said, "Calvin's still detecting nanites on *Wrath*, but it's minimal."

"Hit them again with an EMP," I ordered.

I held up a hand in Chen's direction. "I know Loggins is having a cow... He'll just have to take his medicine."

Akari chuckled at that. "This'll totally wipe out their shields."

"Then we'll just have to protect her. While you're at it, target *Portent's* shields too."

"Really?" she said with a backward glance.

"Yup." I looked to Grimes, "Helm, position *Adams* in front of *Wrath* and *Portent*. And somebody tell me the condition of *Adams'* shields."

"Seventy percent and draining."

First wave... thirteen smart missiles... contact in three minutes.

I already knew much of our Phazon Pulsar firepower had been recommissioned for EMP fire. "Target lock rail guns."

"Still low on spikes, Cap," Polk said.

"Then let's not miss."

"Shit! Think I overdid it with *Portent*; EMP totally knocked out their shields," Akari said.

"So... neither *Portent* nor *Wrath* has shields, and *Adams'* shields are faltering. I got that straight?" I asked.

"The good news is both *Portent* and *Wrath* are nanite free. It'll just take a while for their shields to come back online."

The deck plates vibrated as *Adams'* rail guns came alive.

"It's not going to be enough, Captain," Bosun Polk said.

I watched as the incoming Liquilid missiles evaded our rail spikes, having lost only three thus far to the barrage of weapons fire.

"We're firing everything we've got, rail guns, what Phazon Pulsar cannons are still active..." Akari said, frustrated.

**First wave... thirteen smart missiles...
contact in one minute.**

"Turn the EMP guns on them," I said.

Both Akari and Polk looked back at me, brows raised.

I shrugged. "What do we have to lose? Do it. Kick them up to full power."

The overheads dimmed; even the blaring, constant sound of the klaxon seemed to falter. As if being repetitively kicked in the ass, *Adams* shook with each discharge of EMPs.

**First wave... thirteen smart missiles destroyed.
Second wave, twelve smart missiles inbound.
Contact in two minutes.**

"We lost all of our EMP cannons with that last salvo," Akari said.

Polk pointed to the halo display. "Both *Wrath* and *Portent* are engaging thrusters... moving out from behind us."

Both warships engaged their own EMP cannons, obliterating the second wave of Liquilid smart missiles.

In unison, the bridgecrew cheered.

Chen raised a hand, getting my attention. "Captain Loggins has a special message just for you, Sir."

Before I could answer, *Adams'* shields were literally sizzling with multiple incoming EMP blasts. When it finally stopped, much of the bridge was in the dark. Darkened control boards attempted to reboot to life.

Chen said, "Captain Loggins says, 'What's good for the goose...'"

"Well, I hope he's satisfied," Akari said, "Those frigates are still out there, and I'm betting they have a few more smart missiles to throw our way."

I nodded. "Yeah, but I'll take the win, even if it is short-lived."

Bosun Polk stood and walked toward the halo display. She was chewing at her inside lip, the gears spinning in her head. "Captain?"

"Bosun?"

"These Liquilids are advanced. Maybe they have more advanced tech than we do... but their lack of protection against electromagnetic pulses is... well, it's shocking, to be honest."

"Probably haven't had to deal with it in the past. EUNF Space-Navy ship ordnances are protected... but I'm sure there are technologies, even simplistic ones, we're just as unprepared for."

She looked back to the display, to the enemy frigates. Frigates that, for some reason, were holding back... were, most definitely, not attacking us. "What are they waiting for? I mean, all our shields are down for the most part. We're stuck here like flies on flypaper. We're about as vulnerable as they could ask for."

Akari said, "They're turning around."

Now I too stood. "Chase them. Maybe we can't jump, but we can still move. Chen, contact Captain Loggins and Church... have them put pedal to the metal and ready their EMP cannons."

The ensuing battle lasted two hours and fifteen minutes. Without shields, all three of our ships took damage. That is until *Wrath* and *Portent* came within range of the enemy frigates. They fired wide, powerful swaths of EMP discharges, blanketing multiple Liquilid warships at once—the crossover only emphasizing the catastrophic effects. And while the enemy vessels were sure to still have an abundance of smart missiles, plasma cannons, and their own version of rail gun weaponry, all that would require a vessel to have a viable power plant. We watched as each of the eight Liquilid frigates went totally dark— adrift and lifeless. *Wrath* and *Portent's* EMPs had done the trick.

I SUSPECTED the enemy ships were manned, and not nanite-controlled as the scorpion-flies and dragonflies had been. And without operating environmental systems, the crew of those vessels would not be alive for long.

Chapter 38

Liquilid Empire Star System
USS Lincoln

Major Vivian Leigh

V iv stepped into the dimly lit hold, a flickering overhead light strobing from the deckhead above. Long shadows punctuated the solemnity of the space. In a show of reverence, she held her head high, ignoring the overpowering stench of decaying flesh.

A team of five had followed Viv through the open hatchway —four Marines and Hardy, whose newly converted, powerful EMP weapon was perched upon his shoulder like some kind of demonic parrot. Apparently, an hour earlier, Coogong had completed retrofitting the ChronoBot's shoulder-mounted turret. Now, instead of firing plasma bolts, the weapon produced an EMP charge capable of neutralizing alien nanites.

The ChronoBot looked to her for direction. This wasn't a battle where he would be in his element; no, this was more like a memorial. She doubted he'd know what rules applied here.

This was a mercy killing, and it would be carried out with dignity.

Hardy spoke in a hushed voice. "Uh, Doc, how do we proceed here?"

Viv held up a hand as if to say, "Give me a minute."

Major Vivian Leigh allowed her mind to imagine how this ship had once bustled with activity. Hundreds—thousands—of crewmembers going about their individual tasks, chatting among themselves, forming relationships... living their lives. Lives not so different from what had transpired on *Hamilton*, *Jefferson*, or *Adams*...

Now, what was left of them lay sprawled here within this eerie silence, like specimens in oversized Petrie dishes. Row upon row of the suffering, each a testament to the horrors they had endured, continued to endure both individually and as a crew.

Viv's eyes brimmed with tears as she surveyed the scene, her mind wrestling with conflicting emotions. On one hand, she yearned to relieve the crewmembers from their torturous existence, to grant them release from the clutches of the alien nanites keeping them alive. Yet the thought of ending their lives, even to end their suffering, weighed heavy on her shoulders.

With her team now by her side, Viv knew it was time to bring an end to this nightmare. She knelt beside one of the crewmembers, a woman. Her skin was musty colored with a slight sheen to it, like wet cement.

Her body was emaciated, gossamer skin on bones. Viv wanted to offer the woman some level of comfort before giving the final decree. She reached for her, then hesitated. A modest platinum band lay upon the metal tray next to one hand. The flesh on her bony ring finger had been eaten away by time and decay. She picked up the ring, looked inside the band, and read the inscription. "I love you, Ann. David."

Viv blinked away more tears. Yes, the sadness of the situation was palpable, but she felt gratitude as well. She looked down at what was left of the crewmember's mostly eaten-away face. She was no longer just some nameless *Lincoln* crewmember. This woman had a name. Viv gently repositioned the ring back on Ann's finger. She brushed several strands of brittle, stark-white hair away from her neck.

"Come look at this," she said to Hardy.

The ChronoBot moved closer, bent at the waist, "What am I looking at, Doc?"

The Marines also approached, as if walking on eggshells; they stayed behind Hardy and peered down, quiet and respectful of the situation.

"Here," Viv said, pointing to a puncture wound that looked at least ten times the size of a normal needle-prick. "I believe this is where the nanites were injected."

"Sadistic assholes," Grip said under his breath.

She ignored the comment. "From what I saw the first time I was here, the aliens, the Liquilids, they targeted this area of the body to infuse it with nanites."

"So, that'll be the kill spot?" Hardy said matter-of-factly.

Wanda swatted the ChronoBot's shoulder. "Show some respect, Hardy."

Viv remained focused on the task at hand, albeit still visibly shaken. "Probably doesn't matter, but yeah... This is where you should aim—" Putting an open palm to her sternum, her breath suddenly caught in her chest.

"It's okay, Doc. Remember, we're not killing the crewmembers; we're killing the nanites." The Southern accent spread over her like soft butter on bread.

"Thank you, Hock," Viv said.

Viv gently placed open palms on either side of the suffering woman's head. "Bless you, Ann. You will not be forgotten. None of you will be."

She looked up at Hardy and gave him a slight nod. She stood and stepped to the side.

Hardy's shoulder-mounted turret pivoted left, right, and then a single EMP pulse discharged with a resounding *crackle*.

Viv's heart constricted as if caught in a vise. With that lone pulse, she hoped, would come the necessary finality.

She leaned over and placed two fingertips to the woman's throat. Viv straightened, letting out a breath.

"Is she... gone?" Wanda asked.

Viv nodded and stepped to the next crewmember.

One by one, Viv and her crew—Hardy, Wanda, Hock, Grip, and Max—moved down the rows, their steps measured, their eyes focused. Reverent. Viv continued to whisper a few words of solace to each crewmember before the fatal jolt of electromagnetic energy dispersed. Each time, Hardy stood at the forefront, steadying his pulse weapon, aiming, and then firing.

With each crewmember that was set free, Viv and her team stood in solemn unity, as if performing a silent ritual akin to a US Space-Navy burial at sea. Time seemed to blur as the process continued, the atmosphere thickening with a mixture of anguish and relief. As the last crewmember was released from their torment, Viv stood amidst the stillness.

"We wanted to pay our respects." The kind and gentle voice was unmistakable.

All five on the mercy-kill mission turned to see Coogong and Sonya stepping somberly into the hold.

Viv turned, wiping slimy hands on her cotton scrubs. "They're gone," she said to the newcomers.

Viv and her team walked toward Coogong and Sonya. They stood at the threshold of the compartment.

Major Vivian Leigh swallowed, the pain of the situation erupting all over again.

Sonya walked over, hugging her with her one good arm. "It's okay, Doc. You're okay."

Viv welcomed the teen's one-armed embrace. Trembling, she leaned into Sonya, weeping uncontrollably. Then, as if snapped from a trance, she stepped away, wiping her eyes.

"Oh God, this is so unlike me... It's not like I've never had to deal with dying crewmembers before."

Coogong stepped forward and took her hand. "You did a good and kind thing here today, Vivian... I am so honored to have been a part of this."

The Marines, looking uneasy, and obviously experiencing the same emotional toll themselves, moved in closer, prompted by Wanda. They encircled them—arms coming around one another, Hardy too, as they all joined in a group embrace.

Chapter 39

**Liquilid Empire Star System
Asteroid Compound**

Commander Lu-puk

How long before the Admiral's virtual presence would be here, once again invading his neural implants? He could almost feel his bowels loosening just thinking about it... enduring another series of neural shock waves coursing through his body.

Lu-puk's eyes narrowed as he listened to the limited possibilities being laid out before him. The failed battle still weighed heavily on his mind, but the glimmer of hope offered by his two remote operators' ramblings had ignited a spark of hope within him. He needed a chance to turn the tides, to salvage something from this wreckage, this debacle of epic proportions.

"Tell me more! Explain in detail how we can adapt the nanites for hull breaching," Lu-puk demanded, his voice cutting through the tension-filled air of the command center.

Remote Operator #5, eager to prove his worth, slithered forward and began to outline a potential strategy.

"First of all, Commander... may I speak freely?"

Lu-puk leered at Remote Operator #5, not appreciating the low-level officer's pluck. *Does he think we are equals, comrades who hunt swamp millgrops together?*

"Proceed #5, but do not take advantage of my patience here."

"We were always meant to fail, Sir. It had been expected... which I am certain you already knew. Why else hand over so much responsibility to a low-level asteroid compound such as ours?"

Lu-puk inwardly seethed. Outlawed cannibalism be damned; soon you will find yourself on my dinner plate, basking in a nice wine sauce.

"We were nothing more than a means of keeping the enemy preoccupied while the Admiral was busy assembling his armada of red ships... not so unlike how the humans were dealt with prior... with the *Lincoln* vessel so many cycles past."

Lu-puk's irritation was almost at the breaking point, corroborated by the most recent deep and ragged claw tears upon his command seat armrests.

"We must ask ourselves, good commander, what we can offer the Admiral that will be of worth to him. Something he can utilize for his own advancement... is he not looking to add another star to his epaulet?"

This #5 was far more cunning than Lu-puk had given him credit for. He'd have to watch out for this one... But for now, he'd take full advantage of #5's serpentine mind. "What could we possibly offer the Admiral—"

"Advanced technology."

Did he really just do that? Cut me off mid-sentence? Lu-puk would enjoy making an example of this one.

"Our technology is, naturally, far more advanced than these primitive humans... The simple fact that we have been bested by little more than electromagnetic pulses would be an insult to our superiority, no?"

Lu-puk said nothing.

"Think about it, wise commander. Has not a great weakness in our technology been revealed... one that, quite easily, could be used to bring down much larger vessels... say the Admiral's prized red ships?"

Lu-puk, interest now piqued, scratched at his backside, letting the implications take hold. "Go on... speak more of this technology. I will need to explain it with confidence... with bluster."

"Embedded within the human warships' EMP discharges, recently discovered and unbeknownst to us, lay a form of electromagnetic radiation known as resonance emissions. This particular frequency holds a unique property: it has the ability to interact with the intricate energy fields that power Liquilid Empire ships, shields, weapon systems, even our micro-nanite technology.

"Again, Commander, these energy fields are characterized by specific resonant frequencies that are exclusive to Liquilid technology. As the human warships directed their EMP discharges, their weapons were, I suspect unknowingly, augmented with these resonance emissions. The consequences... their electromagnetic waves penetrated our energy fields, instigating the unforeseen chain of events."

Remote Operator #2 jumped back into the mix. "The Admiral will be most concerned about his red ships, the pride of Liquilid Celestial Forces. He'll see how these resonance emissions could disrupt the delicate equilibrium of his ships', his armada's energy fields, causing nothing less than catastrophic results."

Lu-puk ventured a smile. This was good, no... this was very good. "The Admiral will need to know the science; anyone can bark off vague theories, ambiguous suppositions ..."

Remote Operator #2, momentarily stymied, glanced nervously to Operator #5.

Operator #5 took the ball and ran with it. "The electromagnetic radiation interferes with the Liquilid Empire's intricate energy matrices, triggering failures within power systems and subsystems. As the resonance emissions infiltrate the energy fields of our assets, they create destructive interference patterns. Liquilids' energy fields oscillate wildly, resonating with the incoming electromagnetic waves and effectively shattering their structural integrity. This disruption would spread throughout Liquilid vessels, cascading from one system to another. The Liquilid Empire, caught off guard by this unforeseen phenomenon, would struggle to regain control of their, our, ships. The destabilization of our energy fields would lead to catastrophic power surges, crippling vital systems, including propulsion, weapons, and shields. With our technology compromised and ships in disarray, our Liquilid forces would be left defenseless against any subsequent human warships' onslaught."

"Well put, #5... well put indeed. This information may be of use to me... we shall see. For now, you shall be rewarded with a ration of a Bliddit's hindquarters."

In truth, #5 might have just handed Lu-puk a promotion and a means of getting off this desolate rock post once and for all.

A sudden, all-too-familiar tingle flared within his head, an indication that Admiral Plu-tik would soon, *all too obtrusively,* be entering his mind.

Admiral Plu-tik said, "You have failed me for the last time, Commander Lu-puk."

And there he was, the arrogant gas bag, his smug expression in need of a little payback.

Ignoring the reprimand, Lu-puk dove right in, "Ah... Admiral, you have contacted me at a very important juncture. If I might speak freely," Lu-puk said, stealing from #5's recent phrasing, "You are on the verge of making a mistake of epic proportions. One, I fear your vaunted career would not survive."

"You dare speak to me in such a manner? I will have you torn limb from limb and fed to—"

"If you do not wish to learn of the humans' secret weapon, a weapon that will, most assuredly, destroy all of your approaching, valued red ships... then by all means, give that order."

The Admiral, momentarily quelled, gestured with a modestly interested wave of a claw, and said, "You best mind your words carefully, Commander."

"I am but a mere servant of the Liquilid Empire... and I have only the best of intentions here. But I do fear ignoring my input would be nothing less than catastrophic."

"I already said, proceed. You don't want to test my patience."

"You are aware of how, specifically, the humans prevailed, yes?"

The Admiral smirked. "Your not unexpected incompetence, of course."

"No. It was the use of ingeniously directed, modified EMP discharges. Discharges that immobilized not only our advanced Slisset nanite constructs, but also our frigate warships. Augmented with resonance emissions, this proved to be the turning point in the battle. All of which, as you know, has led to a number of immobilized Liquilid Empire assets. But Admiral, there is an unexpected silver lining here, for you... for us."

"I don't see how losing valued frigate assets—"

"Come, come, Admiral... this unexpected scientific

phenomenon, this weapon, has already unleashed chaos within our ranks, has allowed these humans to seize an advantage. We may not want to admit it, but even a minor victory here could lead to an even bigger victory right here in our own backyard. One that could be repeated with our, your, red ship armada. Do we not want to learn more, take possession of this weapon?"

As the Admiral contemplated Lu-puk's words, the commander made eye contact with #5 and #2. Had Lu-puk overplayed his hand with the Admiral? Possibly. Had he given more credence to the humans' EMP weapon? Most definitely— His technicians had already determined a means of mitigating the effects of the EMPs' augmented resonance emissions... an easy fix. But the Admiral didn't know that, and Lu-puk was going to parlay this advantage for all its worth.

Chapter 40

Liquilid Empire Star System
USS Lincoln

Hardy

T he problem with trying to find something specific
on a ship, a massive dreadnought, no less, is tantamount to finding the proverbial needle in a haystack
or attempting to pinpoint a single flickering star within a
constellation of countless celestial bodies. Hardy felt as if he
was just going through the motions as he and the much-slower-
walking Coogong progressed through one more lower-level
passageway. The more analytical aspects of Hardy's shared
mind, LuMan's domain, had already provided the dismally low
odds of finding this elusive quantum flux reverser, the supposed
answer to the Liquilids' quantum flux generator. No one
seemed to know what the thing looked like or how large it was.
Was it the size of a breadbox or a Cyclone Death Fighter? And
the others, Max and his Marines, along with Doc Viv and
Sonya, seemed to embody a group of children scouring the ship,

caught up in some kind of endless scavenger hunt. Coogong was talking...

"Say again," Hardy said, stopping long enough to force open a hatch door to what amounted to a small broom closet. "Who uses a broom in the late twenty-second century, anyway?" he mumbled.

"I was saying, I think we are going about this all wrong," Coogong said, looking up at him.

"We've been at this for hours... you're not telling me anything I don't know."

"Let's think of it in terms of raw power requirements," Coogong said. "This QFR would necessitate substantial amounts of power to negate the effects of the Liquilids' quantum flux generator, having kept this vessel, not to mention, currently, *Adams, Wrath,* and Portent, all pinned here within this localized star system. I am quite certain the QFR would be large, very large. Unless *Lincoln's* crew wanted to haul the device all about the ship, they would most certainly have been cognizant of the fact it should be built where it ultimately would be used, close to the required power hook-ups."

Hardy rubbed at his nonexistent chin, "So, you're saying we've been wasting our time down here on the lower decks."

"It seems Engineering and Propulsion is a far more likely hiding place, do you not agree?" Coogong said without the least amount of malice in his tone.

"There's a GravLink up ahead; last one there's a rotten egg."

Coogong stared up at him, blinked, and said nothing.

"Never mind. I could beat you in a race standing in a burlap sack... you know, a potato sack race..."

Coogong smiled. "Do you have a burlap potato sack?"

"No... it's a joke. An exaggeration... never mind. Let's just go."

. . .

E & P, like everything else on this ship, was large, sprawling out starboard to port, taking up the entire aft section of the vessel. Fortunately, Captain Ryder had brought much of the department back online during his last visit. Hardy and Coogong approached the console station at the department's entrance, whereby Hardy brought up E & P's blueprint diagram.

Coogong, standing on tippytoes, nodded, hemmed and hawed. "Interesting..."

"What do you think?" Hardy said.

"I think I know exactly where our elusive QFR will be hidden."

The two of them moved farther into Engineering and Propulsion, both taking in the expansive high-tech surroundings.

Coogong said, "Apparently *Lincoln* was deployed back in 2167, the first of her kind... brought into service for a year, then she disappeared, never to be heard from again."

"Until now," Hardy said.

They came to a stop, witnessing the beating heart of the ship's power and propulsion systems. Spanning no less than twenty decks above them, the department was a marvel of advanced engineering, with its three massive aft propulsion drives dominating the background. Closer to them were the three jump spring vaults, each a blue-glowing silo-shaped tower, the pride of Thine/human technological prowess when it came to fast, short jumps across space-time. Overhead, metal catwalks spanned the space—a complex tapestry of suspended bridges. At specific junctures, open-air GravLifts provided access to the various levels, one of which, the fifth level, was solely dedicated to manufacturing wormholes, hyperspace conduits that spanned vast distances within the known cosmos.

Hardy and Coogong stood, enveloped in the eerie silence, one that bore a kind of ominous weight. Hardy envisioned the compartment in its former state, brimming with ceaseless commotion, bathed in the gentle radiance emitted by the activated stations that adorned the surroundings. He envisioned crewmembers stationed diligently at their respective consoles, interacting with the mesmerizing three-dimensional projection displays, manipulating their touchpad control boards—a seamless synergy between man and machine. Here, this had been an awe-inspiring realm of scientific advancement, one that defied the very laws of physics. This extraordinary SpaceWing-designed dreadnought would have traversed vast regions of the galaxy, venturing into uncharted territories of the universe. But now, it sat quiet and desolate.

Hardy, realizing Coogong had moved away and was standing, working at a nearby station, took note of the surrounding ambient air—now crackling with energy. That, and it carried the faint scent of ionized particles—a testament to the immense power harnessed within this ship's power plant. Coogong was bringing *Lincoln's* drives fully awake. The deck plates beneath their feet thrummed with vibrations, resonating with the low hum of three immense propulsion drives.

Hardy joined him. "The QFR... you mentioned you knew where it was?" He gestured with a metal hand to the expansive space around them.

Coogong, having found a small crate to stand upon, made several more taps at the board before answering. "I was mistaken, Hardy. Very clever, the previous crew of this starship, clever indeed."

Patience would not have been one of John Hardy's virtues all those decades prior, when he was flesh and bone, human, and certainly had not evolved in the slightest now that he was an abstract ChronoBot personality attribute.

"Coogong, where is the damn thing?"

Miming Hardy's gesture, but using both of his stick-figure

hands, Coogong gestured out to the entirety of the space. "It is all of it. The quantum flux reverser is, in fact, integrated into this entire E & P department."

"That would make it difficult to box up and relocate over to *Adams*."

"Indeed."

Hardy looked down to the control board, took in the information being projected upon multiple displays. "And by the look of things, it's not quite operational yet, is it?"

"In a word? No."

Chapter 41

Liquilid Empire Star System
USS Adams

Captain Galvin Quintos

I was feeling as though I personally knew Captain Stone after so many hours watching his log entries from eight-plus years earlier. In his final weeks, he, and the rest of *Lincoln's* crew, had become all too aware of the slowly approaching red ships. It hadn't been clear to Stone why the red ships, seemingly arbitrarily, would stop, sometimes for days or weeks at a time, before resuming their trek forward. No matter what the reason, they were an ominous harbinger of things to come. Prior to their arrival, for two months, the crew of *Lincoln* had been building their quantum flux reverser, a race against time.

Chen interrupted my musings. "Captain, Coogong is excited to speak with you at your earliest convenience, his words, not mine."

"Put him through," I said, welcoming the break.

Both Coogong's and Hardy's holographic forms took shape above the captain's desk.

"I'm ready for some good news. Tell me you've made progress with finding the QFR."

"Yes, Captain, we have located the QFR here onboard *Lincoln*."

I noticed Hardy, standing behind, was looking about himself as if being bothered by a rambunctious fly. Then I saw the slightest glimmer of fairy dust and knew it must be Tina. For a fleeting second, I wondered if they had patched up their differences, then chastised myself for losing track of what was important here. "How long before you can get it over to *Adams*?"

Hardy stopped being annoying long enough to look at me over Coogong's helmet.

Coogong said, "Two assumptions I had made concerning the QFR were wrong, and I apologize, Captain."

"Just tell me. Pull the Band-Aid off quick."

Coogong blinked back at me.

"Just tell me."

"First of all, the QFR is not a separate, standalone device that the *Lincoln* crew had been working on. The technology, which I must say is quite ingenious, has been integrated into the ship's entire E & P department."

I let out a breath, dragged a palm down my face, and let that sink in. "And the second wrong assumption you made?"

"I, we, had been working under the assumption that the QFR would nullify the enemy's quantum flux signals throughout local space. That once it was operational, *Adams*, *Wrath*, and *Portent* would all be freed from the Liquilids' clutches..."

"And?" I said, forcing myself not to look at Hardy and Tina in the background. Damn, that robot was annoying.

"From what I have determined thus far, the QFR will

operate in conjunction with Lincoln's shields, creating a virtual bubble around the vessel. That is how it nullifies the quantum flux signals."

I shook my head, not knowing how to respond to that.

Hardy piped up, "It makes perfect sense, Cap... *Lincoln* was here alone. There was no need to think in terms of saving other ships." In a blur of motion, Hardy jabbed a hand into the air, catching Tina with a clenched fist. I winced, wondering if the tiny fairy could possibly have survived. Hardy himself looked momentarily concerned. As he slowly opened his catcher's mitt–sized hand, Tina rocketed away, once again resuming her incessant circling around the ChronoBot's head.

Feeling the weight of what I was about to say, I hesitated. "If any of us are to leave here, it'll have to be onboard *Lincoln*."

Coogong nodded.

"Well... that's only if we can get the QFR to actually work," Hardy said. "Based on the simple fact *Lincoln* is still sitting here, that's a big fat if."

"Coogong, are you confident you can make it operational?" I asked.

"Yes, Captain. The issue is not so much *if* I can, but how long it will take me."

"Then we will need to work in parallel. You and Hardy stay on track over there working on the QFR, and the rest of us will work on finding the enemy's flux generator and destroying it."

"Yes, Captain. Then I'd best get back to it."

"I want updates on your progress every hour."

Ten minutes later I was still sitting within the darkened confines of *Adams'* captain's ready room. The wood-paneled bulkheads and dimmed overhead chandelier lighting had lulled me into forgetting that this was a US Space-Navy warship. It had taken some time, but somewhere along the line, I had started to appreciate this vessel. The workmanship that had gone into even the smallest of details. The opulent space-liner turned warship was like no other vessel in existence. It was one of a kind. The latest priceless gift from Empress Shawlee Tee, and now... I was about to give the order to abandon her. But this couldn't be my decision alone. There were two other starship captains that should have a say in the matter. I'd asked Chen to set up the virtual meeting ten minutes ago. Captain Loggins of *Wrath* was the first to arrive, followed by Captain Church of *Portent*.

"Thank you for the impromptu meeting. I wanted to give you both a heads-up as to what my science officer has discovered. A discovery that affects all of us."

Captain Loggins' irritation was obvious; what was bugging him, I had no idea. On the other hand, Captain Church looked as calm as a cucumber.

Loggins smirked. "So... you've decided to be more transparent. How nice."

"What is that supposed to mean?" I snapped back. "Whatever I learn, you'll learn."

"And it's no mistake that it's only your people over there on *Lincoln*?"

I momentarily considered if I would include Hardy as "people," but let it pass.

Captain Church said, "How about we let Quintos say what he wants to say? We can debate and quibble later."

"Screw you, Church... this is important... maybe you should take some time to find your balls."

Looking amused, Captain Church raised a brow. "And tell me, Captain Loggins, do Symbio-Poths 2.0s come equipped with a set of balls... do you have an actual ball sac?"

"Enough. I didn't call this meeting to argue. Here's what I

know… what the crew of *Lincoln* had been working on, the QFR, was not some kind of self-contained device that could be transferred to *Adams, Wrath,* or *Portent.*"

"What the hell are you saying?" Loggins barked.

"I'm saying the quantum flux reverser was built right into Lincoln's Engineering and Propulsion department. As in, it's integrated as part of the ship."

"That does make a kind of sense," Church commented.

"Fuck you, Church. Or maybe you haven't figured out the ramifications of all this."

I looked to Church for his response to that. As obnoxious as Loggins was being, his hostility was at least understandable. He, like me, was facing the prospect of abandoning our respective ships. But Captain Church remained unruffled, treating the situation as effortlessly as a leisurely stroll through a sun-dappled meadow.

"Look, that's a last-resort scenario right now," I said. "But we need to prepare for it just the same. I suggest we work tirelessly to find the location of that alien quantum flux generator. We destroy that, well, our problems are solved, right?"

Loggins grumbled something indecipherable, while Church nodded a little too enthusiastically.

"I'll keep you apprised of things on our end." I cut the connection.

I stood and headed for the ready room's exit. As unpleasant as that last conversation was, I dreaded this next one even more.

I MOVED to the front of the bridge. "Listen up; I have an update."

Heads lifted; eyes found me. The half-dozen ancillary bridgecrew in the back looked quizzical, while the forward crewmembers, Akari, Grimes, Chen, and Polk, all looked wary.

I looked to Akari. "If, and only if, we are unable to locate and destroy the Liquilids' quantum flux generator, and soon, we will be abandoning *Adams*."

No one looked surprised.

Akari shrugged. Chen sniffed.

"Who told you?" I asked. Then I held up a hand. "Let me guess. A seven-foot-tall, ChronoBot by the name of Hardy."

"Guess no one thought it was a big secret," Grimes said from the helm station.

"Then you also know the QFR is integrated—"

"Into *Lincoln*... old news, Cap," Akari said.

"And... you're all okay with leaving this ship... if it comes to that?"

More shrugs.

Bosun Polk said, "I've been working on the logistics of such a, um, production. It won't be easy with our Quansporter down. There are provisions, though, three deployable spacegates through which, once we cozy up to Lincoln, we can start moving personnel."

To my right, the halo display flickered. I didn't have to look to know what was being displayed there.

"What do you need, Sonya?" I said between clenched teeth.

"Maybe someone should have checked the inside circumference of those spaceways."

I looked at Sonya. "Why—"

"What... Reggie and Sadon and the other large Symbios? You were going to just leave them behind?"

"I never said that!" I stammered. In truth, I hadn't given the larger Symbios much thought. "I'm sorry if it sounds cold-hearted, but they're expendable. Can be easily regenerated... it was kinda the point of Convoke Wyvern and Caveman Glory games. They get killed off, and voila! They come back to life in the next iteration of the games."

Eyes narrowed, lips pursed, and arms crossed, she stared back at me.

"What?" I said, befuddled.

She waited.

And then I got it. There was a virtual factory up on *Adams'* high decks where the Symbio-Poths were not only fabricated but stored within their customized sleep pods. Without the Quansporter being operational, all that would be lost. And to those like Sonya and Ensign Plorinne, this was unthinkable, tantamount to losing loved family members.

"We'll think of something, I promise," I said, hoping I could keep that commitment.

Chapter 42

Liquilid Empire Star System
USS Adams

Doctor Vivian Leigh

Doc Viv trudged wearily toward her quarters onboard USS *Adams*. Her wrinkled baby-blue scrubs were dotted with perspiration and copious mystery blotches. Wavy blonde hair was tightly pulled back into a high ponytail, strands breaking free and tumbling around her face. The demanding day in HealthBay had taken its toll, leaving her emotionally and physically spent. Her body felt heavy, as if gravity itself was conspiring against her.

As she entered her spartan quarters, the soft hum of the ship's AI, Sir Calvin, filled the air. The holographic interface flickered to life, illuminating the room with a faint blue glow. A notification blinked insistently, indicating an incoming communication. With a sigh, she motioned for Sir Calvin to play the message, bracing herself for yet another trivial report or administrative task.

The small bulkhead halo display materialized before her eyes, and there stood Griffin McKenna—now Dr. Griffin McKenna.

"Hi, Vivian. It's Griffin." He lowered his square jaw and flashed a smile. "Ha, like you don't know it's me."

Weird. How did this transmission go through?

"Sir Calvin, stop transmission."

Griffin's image freeze-framed.

"Sir Calvin, am I able to send messages now? This function appears to be operational, but I was not updated on this matter."

**I will check on this, Doctor Leigh.
Please allow me some time to
connect with Communications.**

"Fine. But let me know the minute you learn something. Please resume current transmission."

Griffin continued, "Anyway, at the risk of scaring you away, I just wanted to see if you have come to a decision about, um, relocating here? I know it's a big decision."

A pang of nostalgia washed over Viv as she flashed back to their shared past.

THE STERILE UNIVERSITY classroom lingered with the faint scent of disinfectant, which was overpowered by the stench of formaldehyde. Stainless-steel refrigeration units stood on top of aluminum-colored tile. Titanium tables holding cadavers were lined in rows in the stark, laboratory-like space. Twenty-three-year-old Vivian Leigh stood next to her lab partner, twenty-four-year-old Griffin McKenna.

She hadn't known the guy with the movie-star smile long—

two weeks tops. *Good looks will only get you so far,* she thought. *No way he'll make it past the first year.*

"Who do you think he is?" Griffin asked, chinning toward the table.

"Who? The cadaver?" Viv asked as if he had just said the world was flat.

"Yes. This cadaver used to be a human being. Had a job, friends... maybe a golden retriever."

"This is Male 5448. My guess is he was a homeless man. Died from the elements and because no one claimed his body, it was donated to the university," she said, as if reading off a grocery list.

"I think there's more to this guy. You see this?" Griffin pointed at the shoulder and clavicle bones on the skeletal frame.

"Yeah, so?" Viv didn't like this game.

"Those are broad shoulders, and he looks tall... maybe six-three. We could be looking at an Olympian swimmer." Griffin smiled, pleased with his analysis.

Viv took in the cadaver, as if just now seeing it. His form had clumps of fat deposits here and there, but mostly the skin lay taut on protruding bones. Unlike the rest of the body, the head was wrapped in white gossamer bandages. She struggled to get past the gauze that covered his face.

"Sure, if you say so," Viv said, wanting to move past this ridiculous conversation.

"Don't do that." Griffin's tone shifted an octave lower.

"Do what?" Viv felt her shoulders tighten.

"You're blocking out possibilities because you won't allow yourself to see something beyond the status quo."

Viv could feel him staring at her. Judging her. *Back off, asshole.*

"Don't psychoanalyze me, Griffin." Viv made a mental note to request a new lab partner.

"Okay, let's begin." The professor's bass voice echoed in the cavernous room. "Whoever is closest to the torso... pick up a ten blade and make a medial incision; remember, we'll be excising the appendix. Target your incision appropriately."

"That would be you." Griffin handed Viv a Zap-Blade with a wink.

Was he teasing her? She grabbed the scalpel-like device and shot him daggers with her eyes. Without hesitation, she performed a perfectly executed slice at the lower right abdomen.

BACK IN THE PRESENT, she saw that Griffin's twenty-four-year-old cockiness had since been replaced by someone else, someone who'd, perhaps, suffered hardships, loss. He still spoke with humor, but it was tempered with humility now. She still couldn't believe he had surpassed her back in medical school all those years ago, took her place at the top of the dean's list, summa cum laude, relegating her to second place, magna cum laude.

Turned out they'd been good together—she the practical one, him the dreamer. Both highly intelligent. The pair quickly had become inseparable, their love for each other growing by the day. They dreamt of a life together, vows of commitment whispered under moonlit skies. But life had led them down diverging paths, and she had chosen a different fate, donning the uniform of the military and rising through the ranks to become a major and, eventually, now being the chief medical officer onboard USS *Adams*.

She had only recently sent Griffin a message, reassuring him that she was considering a move. And now, that spontaneous exchange had turned into something tangible. She owed him an answer.

Her strained expression softened as Griffin's heartfelt message played before her.

"I know you're busy, so I won't keep you. But please contact me soon with an answer, Viv. I'm holding this position open for you, but I do have to fill it... soon. No pressure, but, well... you know."

There was that smile again. I could never resist that stupid smile.

Knowing there was an escape seemed too easy. Why did she deserve *easy*?

"Sir Calvin, freeze the message."

Viv pressed a hand to her chest, her breath becoming labored. She tried to catch it, now bent over at the waist as if just having run a six-minute mile.

What the... I don't get panic attacks.

Counting to herself—one, two, three—Viv took in a deep breath, feeling her diaphragm fill. Hold. Release. Three more times. Finally, her breathing started to normalize. She sat on the edge of her queen-sized bed. Noted that the smell of sage had faded away, emphasizing the smell of her own sweat. She was too tired to care. With shrouded eyes she fell back on the shiny, gilded comforter. Viv fanned her hands and arms out on the bed, making invisible snow angels.

What would it be like to work with Griffin again, side by side in the small clinic of Baker, Missouri? Could they rekindle their love, build a life together, perhaps even start a family? Viv laughed out loud.

The prospect of a so-called normal life, free from the constant space battles and unyielding tension that defined her days on USS *Adams*, seemed ludicrous. *Or was it?*

Still lying down, she rolled onto her belly, propped herself up onto her elbows, her chin cupped within her palms. I don't know this person anymore. He was married and now he's a widower.

He's probably got a shrine of pictures of his dead wife on the fire-place mantel. Do I really want to deal with all that?

As quickly as her mind turned toward Griffin, it shifted to Quintos. Captain Galvin Quintos, her partner and confidant onboard USS *Adams*, had been a part of her life for years. Their relationship had weathered the storms of interstellar conflict, but doubts gnawed at her. Did he truly love her, or was she merely a companion who shared his intergalactic adventures? Would she always be playing second fiddle to his true love—whatever starship he was commanding?

She had recently made a solemn declaration to Quintos, confessing that if they ever returned to Earth, she would be leaving *Adams* and, by extension, him. Fatigue had fueled her decision, but she knew deep down that the uncertainty of their relationship had propelled it past that. The toll of the battles and the ceaseless cycle of life and death had worn her thin. She craved a respite from the perpetual chaos. Yet, even as she pondered leaving, she questioned her own resolve. Could she truly walk away from him, from this life she had forged here?

"Sir Calvin, resume the message."

"I'll just leave you with this, Vivian. No matter what you do, I am so proud of you... how hard you've worked and how you've followed your dreams." Griffin's go-to smile was replaced with a wistful smirk. "Talk soon."

"Sir Calvin, stop the transmission."

As the holo-image of Griffin began to melt away, the blue light gave way to the soft amber glow emanating from a crystal dome-light positioned in the middle of the deckhead—the diffused illumination matching her somber mood.

Closing her eyes, relaxing, Viv let the silence envelop her. She knew that whatever choice she made, it would carry profound consequences. It wasn't just a matter of choosing between two men; it was about deciding who she wanted to become, the life she yearned to lead. The minutes ticked by, each second laden with the weight of her indecision.

Finally, Viv opened her eyes. Rolled out of bed and teeter-tottered to a stand. She'd take a hot shower. Water had a way of making the convoluted clear, like untangling a giant knot of cables.

So, shower—then decide, she thought. As her dear departed mother used to say when she was agonizing over a decision, "Come on, Vivian—make a sandwich or get out of the kitchen."

Chapter 43

Liquilid Empire Star System
USS Adams

Captain Galvin Quintos

The hour was late, the weight of exhaustion settling upon my shoulders. Yet, I couldn't surrender to the enticing embrace of slumber just yet. Not when there was unfinished business, that haunting story waiting to unfold before my eyes. The captain's ready room enveloped me in a cocoon of dim light, the soft glow of the halo display casting an ethereal glow across the compartment. My gaze was fixed upon the three-dimensional projection, a window into the past, as it played the fateful log entries of Captain Glenn Stone, commander of the ill-fated USS *Lincoln*. The lost ship, adrift here in the merciless expanse of space, held the secrets of a tragedy that only now was becoming evident. Glenn Stone's weathered face appeared before me, his voice filled with a mix of resignation and determination.

"The red ships, colossal monstrosities of alien origin, have descended upon us... an overwhelming force. The magnitude of their presence, their sheer size dwarfing any vessel in our own fleet, is a testament to the danger that lurked beyond the stars."

My eyes traced the haunted contours of Stone's features, the evidence of his desperate struggle etched into every line on his face. Stained and tattered, his uniform bore witness to the relentless battles fought on *Lincoln*. The weariness in his eyes mirrored my own, a shared burden of responsibility and loss. As Stone's raspy voice filled the room, a shiver coursed down my spine.

"The Liquilids, the alien menace, have breached *Lincoln's* hull. Now, beetle-like nanite constructs have been unleashed upon the ship, tearing through our defenses and attacking the crew."

I could see the anger in Stone's eyes.

"I've heard the cries, the distant, desperate pleas for survival, echoing through darkened passageways. Not being able to save those poor souls will haunt me till my dying breath."

I clenched my fists, my knuckles turning white as my own surge of anger and frustration swept through me.

"Look, whoever you are watching this, watching me... the Liquilids' strength and ruthlessness have grown with each previous encounter. And yeah, I knew they were battles we couldn't afford to lose, not if *Lincoln* was to survive. But know this: we fought with everything we had. I could not be any prouder of the men and women who have sacrificed everything to defend this vessel." Now, his face seemed to slacken with the weight of an impossible situation. "With that said, *Lincoln's* self-destruct codes have already been entered. All that is needed... is my final input. I have erased any trace of our navigation records, denying the Liquilids access to crucial information about Earth's location as well as her allies."

I blinked away the moisture in my eyes. Stone's impending

sacrifice was beyond words. I could see the finality of his decision etched into every fiber of his being. A sense of profound respect and admiration welled up within me. Captain Glenn Stone had exemplified the unwavering resolve that defined us as US Space-Navy officers, as leaders. He had faced the horrors of the Liquilids head-on, his crew fighting valiantly until the bitter end. It was a reminder of the price we paid for the freedoms we held dear, the sacrifices made in pursuit of Earth's, humanity's, survival.

As the screen faded to black, leaving me in a void of darkness, a surge of determination pulsed through my veins. I would not allow Captain Stone's sacrifice to be in vain. USS *Adams*, my ship, my crew, would continue the fight against the Liquilids, against the forces that threatened our very existence.

But beneath that resolve, a tempest of conflicting emotions churned within me. Doubt whispered in the recesses of my mind, questioning my ability to lead, to make the decisions necessary to outwit this particular enemy. Captain Glenn Stone, as valiantly as he had fought, had not been equal to the challenge. *So why would I be?*

Memories of past encounters with the Liquilids, both Stone's and my own, flashed before me, a montage of chaos and destruction. Their insidious tactics, their relentless pursuit, had forced both *Lincoln* and *Adams* into the same defensive stance.

The memory of Captain Stone's final moments resonated within me. No, I couldn't let doubt cloud my judgment.

I turned in my chair and closed my eyes, blocking out replaying the echoed cries of Captain Stone's desperate crewmembers. Opening my eyes, I met my own reflection in the diamond glass porthole window. The face that stared back at me was also weathered and weary, etched with the weight of too many sleepless nights and impossible choices. But it was also the face of a leader, one who had risen to impossible challenges before this. It was not the absence of fear that defined true leadership, but the ability to confront it head-on, to channel it into unwavering determination. With renewed purpose, I straightened my posture and lifted my gaze, my reflection transformed from one of vulnerability to one of steely resolve. The weight of the past, of Captain Stone's sacrifice, merged with the weight of the present and future, fueling a fire within me. I couldn't allow doubt to paralyze me, to cloud my judgment. The crew depended on my clarity of mind and unwavering determination.

The hatch door to the ready room slid open, and I turned to face the entryway. The crewmember who entered looked at me, her eyes filled with a mix of apprehension and something else. In that moment, I realized that without this person in my life, this struggle would be far more difficult, if not impossible. Viv's hair was wet; she must have just gotten out of the shower. No longer donning shapeless pastel-colored scrubs, she was wearing off-duty civies. Snug-fitting jeans and a white button-down top. She took a step into the compartment. The hatch door slid shut behind her. Standing there in the dim light, her eyes sparkled. She had yet to speak.

There are moments in life that stretch out, suspended in time, as if the universe itself holds its breath, whispering that this very instant is an irrevocable turning point. It is the fork in the road, where the path we choose will shape our destiny and alter the course of everything that follows. This was one of those moments.

I said, "It's late... you must be exhausted."

"I am."

I nodded, not knowing what to say. She clearly had something on her mind. I waited.

"You got the message... the comms relay—"

I nodded. "I am the captain of this ship. Things like that typically don't get past me."

"Of course not. Silly of me."

I didn't know if she was being sarcastic. "At this point we're receiving previously sent messages; most are days, weeks, old. Anything we transmit back will take just as long to reach home. With that said, I've sent a priority message to Fleet, to Admiral Block."

"That's good. First bit of good news any of us have had in some time."

She took several steps forward. I could now see her eyes were red-rimmed. The tip of her nose was pink.

I gestured to her casual outfit. "You look ready to hit the sidewalks of small-town America... leave all this mayhem behind you."

She attempted a smile. "I received a new message from Griffin. He must have sent it a while ago..."

"Oh?"

Viv mentioning Griffin again was not a good sign. Sure, she'd told me about their whirlwind romance in med school, that he had a small practice in some midwestern town I couldn't remember. That she'd come close to marrying the man but had chosen a different path. It was no great leap to realize that over these last few months, she'd realized she regretted that earlier decision.

"If you've come here to see if I can hasten our exit from this godforsaken star system, you'll have to stand in line. I'm working on it. I know you're more than ready to start your new life; you've made that perfectly clear, Viv."

"Galvin..."

She's using my first name. That's never a good sign.

The hatch door slid open. Akari's silhouetted shape partially filled the threshold. "Um... sorry to disturb, Cap. Helm is ready."

I stood and looked to Viv. "The general announcement is

forthcoming. We're heading deeper into that asteroid field. Once close enough, we'll get *Adams* cozied up close to *Lincoln*, where we'll be transferring the entirety of the crew over."

"What!"

Viv and I stood facing each other. Our romantic relationship, once filled with hope and passion, had reached an impasse. She clenched her fists, her body tensing with frustration. "Abandoning ship? Are you out of your mind, Galvin?" Her voice seethed with barely restrained fury.

I knew Viv would not take this news lightly. Her eyes still blazed with anger.

I raised my hands in a placating gesture, trying to maintain composure. "Viv, we don't have a choice. *Lincoln* is our only option for escape. We can't stay here."

She scoffed, a bitter smile twisting her lips. "And what about my patients? The injured pilots in HealthBay? Have you thought about them?"

I felt a pang of guilt at her words. She was right. HealthBay held dozens of injured pilots, relying on specialized equipment and medical supplies within its bulkheads. "None of this is going to be easy, but we'll get it done. We'll do everything we can to ensure a smooth transition. Your patients, your medical staff, will be the first to go over... along with any necessary medical equipment and supplies," I said, keeping my voice firm but tinged with regret.

Viv shook her head, her frustration turning into desperation. "Dammit, I don't want to move those patients."

I continued to stare at her. Sure, I heard her words, but they weren't ringing true. This certainly wasn't the first time we'd had to abandon one ship for another. In fact, it was nearly becoming a common practice. *So what's really going on here?*

Seeing the pain in her eyes, I took a step closer. "I know it's difficult, Viv. But you're not alone. I'll be with you, just as I've always been."

She looked away, her gaze fixed upon the deck. The compartment fell into a heavy silence, punctuated only by the distant hum of the ship's drives. It was a moment pregnant with unspoken emotions, the weight of an unresolved past and an equally uncertain future.

Finally, Viv sighed, her shoulders slumping in defeat. Her words were barely audible. "Fine, Galvin. Do what you have to do. We'll just throw this on the growing pile of reasons we should never have..."

She let her words die.

I nodded, my heart heavy with regret.

My Jadoo ring was vibrating. "I'm needed on the bridge."

She nodded.

As I turned to leave, the air between us was still thick with unresolved tension. I stopped and looked back at her. "Think about what you want, Viv... what you really want. I'll support you in any way I can."

Chapter 44

I reached the captain's mount and took a seat, eyes locked onto the halo display.

"We're just entering the asteroid field, Captain," Grimes said.

"Yeah, well, there's no clear path to *Adams*," Akari added. "This field has obviously moved, drifted, since *Lincoln* traversed this rocky maze almost a decade ago. I'll try to use rail guns sparingly."

A sudden burst of rail spikes eviscerated an asteroid the size of the *Hub Gunther*, clearing their slow, methodical progression deeper into the field.

Seeing Akari's profile, I glimpsed a smile—at least someone still loved her job here.

Bosun Polk joined me at the captain's mount. "Sitrep, Bosun?"

"The crew is... begrudgingly making preparations to abandon ship. Only what someone can carry with them on their person goes onboard *Lincoln*."

"Let's dedicate extra resources to HealthBay... kid gloves when it comes to moving the patients—"

"Met with Doc Viv an hour ago; we'll be using hovercarts to move the patients. They'll hardly know they're being moved."

I looked over to Polk. "Wait, she didn't have a problem with moving them?"

Polk hitched a shoulder. "I guess, but no more than anyone else has a problem with the move."

Viv's vehement reaction earlier... what was all that about?

"Just make sure anything she wants to take with her, Medi-Bots, specialized equipment, her medication stores; hell, if she wants the deck plates—make sure it's moved over."

"Don't worry, Cap... we'll take care of your... um, Doc Viv."

Polk's cheeks flushed, catching herself misspeaking.

Another burst of rail spikes shattered an even larger asteroid, *Adams'* shields coming alive as an influx of gravel pieces peppered the protective barrier.

I let Polk's comment go unanswered but was curious as to what she'd almost said. My what? *My main squeeze? My girlfriend?* Perhaps that was the problem. Hell, if I didn't know...

Chen said, "I have confirmation both *Portent* and *Wrath* have entered the asteroid field behind us."

The halo display segmented, Hardy's form now prominent. "My sensors are tingling."

"Okay, not sure what we're supposed to do with that bit of news?" I asked.

"Liquilids are on the move. Not slow and unhurried like before. They're making a mad dash for us."

Akari stole a quick look back at me. "He's not wrong. Sir Calvin just pinged an alert... realizing the same thing."

"That's all we need, to come under attack just as we're jumping ship."

"The good news is those red ships are way too big to navigate this field," Akari said, firing another burst of rail spikes.

"Frigates are another story, though," Hardy said. "Our timetable just narrowed. Substantially."

I looked over to the helm station. "Mr. Grimes, any possibility we can kick up our speed?"

He looked to Akari; her ability to clear the way dictated much of *Adams'* progress. She nodded. "Pedal to the metal. I can handle it."

I turned my attention back to Hardy. "What's the situation with the quantum flux reverser?"

"Coogong thinks he'll have it operational within the hour. Seems *Lincoln's* crew had it close but made a few miscalculations with integration with the ship's shields."

The display segmented again, now bringing up Sonya sitting within *Lincoln's* bridge. "I've been assessing the condition of this ship's weapons."

I raised my brows for her to continue.

"Like *Adams*, she's exhausted much of her munitions. Found some, probably forgotten or misplaced, spike stores in a lower deck hold. Max and crew are hovercarting them to various rail-turret locations now. But with only a handful of Marines, nothing's happening all that fast."

"There must be a slew of SWM bots onboard," Polk said.

Sonya made a face, placing a finger on her chin and looking skyward. "Hmmm, gee, why didn't I think of that?"

"Be nice," I said.

"Yes, there are scads of bots of all ilks on board; the problem is getting them turned back on and re-initialized. Their memories, like the rest of the ship's memory banks, have been erased... Captain Stone was smart to do so. Even the slightest chance of Earth's location being electronically stored needed to be wiped."

"I'm confused. How are you re-initializing—"

"Hacked into those two backup system memory stores you

have hidden away in your ready room." She smiled innocently and fluttered her eyelashes. "Desperate times call for desperate measures, right, Uncle?"

Chapter 45

Liquilid Empire Star System
USS Adams

Captain Galvin Quintos

En route to saddle up close to USS *Lincoln*, determined to be our only hope for survival, the relentless chaos of the asteroid field moved past us. Realizing I was gripping the captain's mount armrest, I forced myself to relax.

Akari James at Tactical, her fingers danced across the controls as she unleashed a barrage of firepower upon the smaller asteroids in our path. The ship shuddered and groaned as rock fragment impacts reverberated, a symphony of violence, a relentless barrage of cosmic bullets punishing *Adams'* shields.

Grimes, a picture of unwavering focus at the helm station, steered *Adams* through the perilous maze of tumbling rocks, pushing the massive dreadnought to its limits. Every jolt and twist of the ship sent a ripple of unease through me.

Keeping my eyes on the halo display, I saw the Liquilids

were closing in, their ominous red ships now hovering at the fringes of the asteroid field. I swear, I could almost feel their hunger for human flesh.

I leaned forward, narrowed my eyes. "Seriously?"

Hundreds of their swift and deadly dragonfly fighters were swarming their way through the field. I watched as they darted through the debris with lethal precision, their wings glinting in the dim light emanating from their small, glowing cockpits.

"They're coming up behind us, Cap," Akari said. "Engaging aft guns."

Adams' rail gun turrets, situated all around the ship, had only recently received a fresh supply of the newly replicated rail spikes. It was a limited restocking, but it couldn't have come at a better moment.

I said, "Target these larger asteroids we're passing; let's give them a meteor shower from hell."

Suddenly, the bridge shook so violently that several deck plates popped free, and Bosun Polk, who'd been standing, ended up on her backside.

Seeing it tumbling away on the halo display, I now realized we'd struck an asteroid the size of a house.

"Keep us on course, Mr. Grimes!" I barked, my voice tight with suppressed anxiety.

"Sorry... we're almost there, Cap," Grimes said. "Slowing... it'll take a bit of time to bring *Adams* alongside *Lincoln*."

We all took in the spectacle before us. USS *Lincoln,* her sleek SpaceWing design giving the impression she was gliding through space, even though she was hobbled there within the gravity pull of a nearby, small moon–sized asteroid.

Adams responded to Grime's helmsmanship, slowing, slowing, then easing to a full stop.

I said, "Okay, easy now, Mr. Grimes. Bring us alongside... amidship to amidship."

Deck plates rattled; overhead crystal chandeliers tinkled as aft and thrusters engaged. Grimes maneuvered the dreadnought with a level of finesse and grace I hadn't thought possible for such a behemoth ship.

As if reading my mind, Akari switched the halo display into logistical mode, the larger of the asteroids a yellow ball, both *Adams* and *Lincoln* now green icon representations, and too many Liquilid dragonflies smaller red dots, which clearly were almost upon us.

Akari's voice cut through the chaos. "Dragonflies are closing in. I've done all I can with rail spikes and Phazon Pulsars. Changing tactics... Ah! There you are, little dragonflies... why don't you say hello to our EMP pulse emitters?"

The bridge vibrated with each EMP emission. Wave after wave, more red dots on the display flickered out.

Bosun Polk, looking anxious, said, "Crewmember Grimes, do you have us in position yet? I have to get moving, get to the lower decks."

The helmsman, deep in concentration, didn't answer. Then the ship jerked to a stop. "Yes, Bosun, *Adams* is in position... three cargo hatches are aligned with their *Lincoln* counterparts. Perfectly, I might add," he said with a confident smirk.

Chen's raised voice caught my attention. "What's the issue, Mr. Chen?"

He rolled his eyes. "I'll give you one guess, Captain."

"Hardy?"

"Hardy."

"Let me hear the channel," I said.

"... hold your horses; I'm a tad busy right now." Hardy's Boston-accented voice filled the bridge.

"What's the problem, Hardy?" I scolded.

"Cap! Didn't know you were—"

"What are you doing that's so important you can't

follow my orders?" I actually didn't know for sure Hardy wasn't following orders, but odds were he was up to something.

Chen cut in, "Bosun Polk has this process all worked out. We'll need a crewmember at each of the cargo airlock hatchways on *Lincoln's* side. We have Wanda midship, Grip forward, and Hardy is supposed to be there aft, ready to open that hatch on her command."

I looked back and saw Bosun Polk's empty seat.

A loud metallic drumming emanated over the channel—the sound of a thousand-pound ChronoBot running. "I'm on my way; it's not like we're all just standing around over here with our thumbs up our respective keisters."

I noticed Akari had gone still, and ominously quiet.

"Lieutenant?"

She literally grimaced. "Uh, I just thought of something."

"Spit it out. Whatever it is, we'll deal with it."

She tapped at her board, bringing the halo display back to its normal 3D video feed. There was the colossal asteroid, several surrounding, smaller asteroids, and *Adams* snuggled in beneath *Lincoln's* portside wing. A soft, blue-tinged glow emanated from both vessels.

"What's the problem?"

"You see the shields... on both ships?"

"Of course I do."

"So, the plan is deploying the three spaceways... so we can start the evacuation."

I nodded, wishing she'd just get to the point.

"Those spaceways ... they won't be shielded."

"*Adams'* shields won't—"

"She's right, Captain," Grimes interjected. "There'll be ten meters of unshielded causeway."

"Times three," Akari added.

I saw the potential issue. "Are you detecting new dragonflies?"

"Sensors aren't picking up any, but that's not the problem, Captain," Akari said. "It's the remnants of the ones we've destroyed, the nanite cloud we've turned them into."

"How close is it?"

"Close enough... We may have a few hours."

"Then we'll just have to move things along." I knew Bosun Polk had left for HealthBay, as I'd promised Viv her patients, staff, and equipment would be the first to move over to *Lincoln*.

I said, "Who's in charge of deploying the spaceways?"

"Bosun Polk has SWM crewmembers here on *Adams* manning that aspect," Chen said. "We have those teams standing by; they're ready for your command to deploy."

I took in the halo display and the soft-yellow glow of the distant nanite cloud. "Do it. Deploy the three spaceways."

Chen said, "We're being hailed by both *Wrath* and *Portent*, Captain."

"On display."

Captain Loggins, Commander Stanly at his side, was there on *Wrath's* bridge, while Captain Church was standing by himself upon *Portent's* bridge.

"You've screwed us... should have known," Commander Stanly said with a sneer.

Neither Captain Loggins nor Captain Church disputed the commander's outburst.

"What's the problem?" I said with little patience.

"The problem is you've abandoned us. Left us to fend for ourselves against those Liquilid red ships..."

I shook my head. "You were following us into—"

Loggins said, "The asteroid field? No, Captain. You see, when you leave in your wake a fucking tsunami of asteroid fragments, not to mention bigger asteroids you've moved into the all-too-narrow corridor behind *Adams'* fat ass; well, we've become trapped in here."

The display only emphasized Loggins' point. There the two vessels sat, having made it only one-quarter of the way into the asteroid field, unable to move forward, unable to turn around due to the arrival of the red ships all lined up along the edge of the asteroid field.

"I'm sorry," I said without much sympathy in my voice.

"You're sorry?" Commander Stanly barked. "Lot of good your apology does us now."

"You'll just have to sit tight for a while. You have the instructions we sent you for retrofitting your energy weapons over to EMP pulse emitters?"

"Lot of good that will do against those red ships."

"The plan is to find and nullify their quantum flux generator. Let's all concentrate on that. Once we do that, we're all jumping out of here. So, again, hold tight."

Chapter 46

Sonya Winters

Sonya arrived at Engineering and Propulsion eating an apple. She'd materialized the Golden Delicious after discovering an upper-deck break-room food replicator. It tasted fine to her; she'd never had one actually grown and picked from an earth tree and briefly wondered what the difference would be.

Zeroing in on the faint sounds of someone humming a tune she didn't recognize, she found Coogong, his little feet extending out from beneath a control station.

She crouched down, peered beneath the console. "Whatcha doing in there, Coog?" she said, taking another bite of her apple.

"Ah, Ms. Sonya..."

She scooted backward as Coogong awkwardly pushed himself out from beneath the station, banging his helmet in the process. She noticed the crappily repaired crack zigzagging down the front of his faceplate.

"Where's Hardy?"

"He ran off."

She made a face. "You need a new helmet, Coog... That shitty Hardy patch job looks precarious at best."

The Thine scientist sat all the way up, amber-colored Ambiogell sloshing within his helmet; his little worm face smiled back at her. "All in good time. But first... we get the QFR operational."

Talking with her mouth full, she said, "That's why I'm here. Cap wants an update. Says they're going to a lot of trouble over there... prepping to abandon one ship for another. That only makes sense if *Lincoln's* QFR becomes operational. No pressure," she added with a sympathetic smile.

Coogong, taking Sonya's extended hand, got to his feet. "We are ready for a test."

"A test? Uh... I think we'll need more than a test."

Unbothered, Coogong hurried away. "Come, come... we access the primary system control at another station."

She found Coogong deep within E & P standing upon a crate, his little stick fingers tapping a series of control board icons. He abruptly stopped and stood up straight.

"What is it... what's wrong?" she said, reading his rigid body language.

"I have done all that I can... reconfigured the system where the *Lincoln* crew had made several miscalculations. I increased power allotments to the QFR system, which had been inadequately allocated. Decreased noise attributes, allowing better integration with *Lincoln's* shields."

She wasn't sure what he was saying. *Is it ready or not?* "So..."

"So, yes, Ms. Sonya, we are ready to power on the integrated QFR. I'm sure some fine-tuning may still be required."

He pointed to a slow-revolving icon on the board. "Please, do the honors."

She didn't hesitate, tapping the icon. Nothing happened. She shrugged. "A little anticlimactic, don't you think?"

Coogong, almost as tall as she was atop his crate, placed his hands upon her shoulders and turned her to face a newly projected 3D display. There, floating, was a representation of *Lincoln,* a green field radiating out all around her.

"It's working?" she said, looking exuberant. "It's actually working?"

Coogong checked his board, bringing up several smaller displays. An ungodly amount of information, data, scrolled.

"I'll contact the captain; this is great news."

Coogong turned to face her, his typical amused expression gone. "There is a problem."

"What kind of problem? It's not working?"

"Yes. It is working. But... it is quite ingenious what the Liquilids have done here."

"Screw the Liquilids. What's the problem, Coogong?"

"Our QFR system architecture was modeled after a particular generated wavelength sampling. So we can counteract those waves, nullify them."

"That makes sense..."

"What I did not expect was the Liquilids having the ability to perceive our actions here... and alter their quantum flux frequencies on the fly." Coogong gestured back to the larger display.

The previous pretty green field radiating out from all around *Lincoln* was now a distorted brown color—one that intermittently flickered on and off.

"Crap! Coogong, everything depends on you getting this working. Thousands of lives, crewmembers on three ships..."

He bobbled his helmet. "I think I can fix things. Did you

notice it took them a few moments to switch frequencies? That will be our window of opportunity!"

His smile was contagious. "Okay... what can I do to help?"

Chapter 47

**Liquilid Empire Star System
Asteroid Compound**

Commander Lu-puk

L u-puk, with his serpentine features and piercing reptilian gaze, stood within the asteroid command center. Nearby, the quantum flux generator, the principal element of the compound, hummed with an otherworldly energy through the cold metallic bulkheads. A burgundy glow radiated from a series of emergency beacons, casting an eerie glow on his scaly skin. Multiple displays, providing various views of the two human warships, gave credence to what had been suspected—the humans were abandoning one ship for another.

Admiral Plu-tik had made his stance perfectly clear— prevent the humans from traversing their flimsy causeways and put a stop to the boarding of USS *Lincoln*.

A sense of purpose emanated from Lu-puk as he addressed his operators—his faithful peons. He needed to do this right, to prove he was capable of any task set before him. Power was something he could not afford to lose, not if he was to become an Admiral himself one day and get off this remote, godforsaken rock.

The operators awaited his command, jaws slightly open, syrupy saliva dripping into gooey pools on the deck. A peculiar fusion of rippled scales and slimy appendages, the operators fixed small yellow eyes on their commander.

"Listen carefully," Lu-puk hissed.

The peons moved their elongated heads in unison, a lounge of lizards looking to their leader.

"We must obstruct the humans' escape from *Adams* to *Lincoln* via their primitive causeway." Lu-puk spat the command, his vile spray flying and landing on the operators like acid rain.

The reptilian peons whipped their tails around, propelling their bodies one hundred and eighty degrees toward the control panel. They murmured among themselves, like an intrusion of chirping cockroaches.

"Quiet!" the commander screeched. "I can't hear myself think."

The chirping ceased. Lu-puk manipulated his long snout into an insidious smile. He felt a warmth in his reptilian ball sac... No way in hell was he going to miss this opportunity for advancement. Taking a heavy step toward the control panel, one of Lu-puk's feet landed in a congealing pool of saliva. He jumped backward, his squat arms flailing and bicycling. It was one thing to step on his own drippings, but another's?

"Operator #1, clean up this mess." Lu-puk continued to glare down at the various puddles.

Operator #1's stubby arms moved to a side control panel; buttons were pressed. A high-pitched squeal emanated from a nearby hatch as it slid open. A bot the size of a bowling ball rolled into view. It maneuvered itself over to the first of the slimy messes. Small articulating arms emerged from hidden flaps, then came rapid wiping, then slurping/sucking sounds. As quickly as the bot had arrived, it had rolled away again, disappearing back into its little hidey-hole.

"Efficiency. Do you see how easy it can be?" the commander bellowed. "If a mindless bot can work with such competence, I expect no less from my incompetent operators."

All five serpentine peons kept their focus on the command center's main display. *Adams* and *Lincoln* filled the video feed. Three ship-to-ship causeways spanned between the two human vessels.

It was no secret; the initial *Lincoln* crew, all those cycles past, had been feverishly working on a counter to the Liquilids' quantum flux generator. Prolonged torture had many of the human prisoners' tongues flapping. And while it had been acknowledged there was such a device being developed onboard, specifics had been vague, and an actual location had remained indeterminate.

Lu-puk concentrated on the three causeways—each tube-like span offering the humans a kind of bridge of hope, possible salvation. *Pitiful humans. Have you learned nothing from your predecessors? How simple it was for us then…*

"Commander, the Admiral's red ships are in position along the fringe of the asteroid field."

Soon… your carcasses will fill our holds, so many of you… primed to fill our bellies.

Lu-puk's beady eyes widened, while his inner eyelids narrowed. "What are you waiting for?" He slithered his ample body forward, now just inches behind the operators. "I want that nanite cloud repositioned. Now!"

Tiny claws moved in unison, all five operators activating a similar series of controls. Together, they adjusted and coaxed micro-gravitational fields, the only means of influencing and repositioning the coalesced nanites.

Lu-puk watched with anticipation the microscopic mechanical marvels, engineered in the darkest recesses of their Liquilid laboratories—each crafted with sleek metallic exoskeletons and agile appendages. Small, yes, but these minuscule bots were designed to sow merciless chaos. Lu-puk had no doubt—he did not have the luxury of doubt—that soon, very soon, both human ships would come under full Liquilid control.

Chapter 48

Liquilid Empire Star System
USS Adams

Captain Galvin Quintos

"Lieutenant James, you have the conn," I said, getting to my feet and stretching my back.

"I have the conn," she replied, looking back at me with a quizzical expression, "Where you off to, Cap?"

"Aft Cargo Airlock #22. I need to move. This sitting around waiting is making me crazy."

"Mmm, isn't that where HealthBay's being transferred over from?"

I didn't comment on that. "Just hail me if anything changes."

"Copy that."

Whale's Alley was a flurry of activity, with stern-faced crewmembers hurrying this way and that. With dozens of stacked-high hovercarts, some being pushed, others pulled, it was reminiscent of a busy twentieth-century train station. My orders to only bring what could be carried in one's two hands evidently had been totally ignored. The overall anxiety level here within *Adams'* most expansive corridor was palpable. Life on board a US Space-Navy dreadnought was rarely easygoing, especially in wartime. But this was the third, or was it the fourth, mass exodus from one ship to another in so many months. I'd pushed this crew to their limits, and it was showing on their faces, their hunched shoulders.

As I moved through the expansive corridor toward the bank of GravLifts, I stopped. To my right was the Quansporter compartment. I looked in, stood there within the threshold. Coogong had spent countless hours in here, tinkering, improving on the efficiency of the original Sir Louis de Broglie contraption, one now residing somewhere within the hull of Captain Pristy's *Hercules*. I wondered where my once-first officer was at this moment. Now a captain in her own right, undoubtedly, she was still there within the Lost Tombstone Star System on board her ship, orbiting Genoma, or perhaps within the high walls of Stratham Hold. Wherever she was, I sure could use her frank counsel and unwavering support right now.

My vibrating Jadoo ring jolted me back to the present, "Go for Captain," I said, without looking to see who had hailed me.

"Coogong wanted me to contact you, let you know he's gotten the QFR operational," Sonya said.

"It's working?" I said, my heart skipping a beat. "That's good news—"

"There's a problem, though," she said. "Seems the Liquilids' flux waves are variable... which, unfortunately, the QFR here on *Lincoln* was not designed for. Thing only works for a few minutes at a time."

"Dammit! Sonya, without that QFR—"

"Hey, don't shoot the messenger! Just cool your jets, geez! Can I finish one sentence without being so rudely interrupted?"

Teenagers had to be the most infuriating breed of humanity. "Fine, go on."

"He's confident he can still do a workaround. It'll just take a little more time."

I stared at the elaborate console, elevated Quansporter pedestals, twelve in all. And again, my heart skipped a beat. "How many minutes?"

"Uh, what?" she mumbled. I could hear her chewing gum, snapping bubbles.

"Ask Coogong how many minutes specifically!"

I heard her huff something, then ask, "Captain Frantic wants to know how long the QFR works."

I listened to more gum chewing, then heard Coogong's muffled voice, "Every time the QFR is powered up, it operates for two minutes and forty-seven seconds."

"You hear what he said?" Sonya asked.

My mind raced. This could be a game changer, but I had to stay calm. I had no idea if I was on the right track.

"Where are you?" Sonya asked.

I looked down at my ring; she was seeing my surroundings.

"You're in the Quansporter compartment, aren't you?" she pressed.

"Yeah, I—"

"Genius!" she exclaimed.

"Wait, what?"

"Two minutes and forty-seven seconds! We can quansport within that time frame!"

I heard her, her voice going an octave higher. "Coogong! Can we quansport within that time frame?"

More dead air and chewing. "I believe that may be possible," came Coogong's voice again. I looked at my Jadoo ring, saw Coogong approaching Sonya there within *Lincoln's* E & P department.

Coogong said, "We would need to make a test... first an inanimate object, say a tool of some sort, a wrench, maybe. If that's successful, then we can move on to organic matter... It would be best to start small, perhaps a lab mouse. I don't suppose we have any lab mice..."

"We don't have time for any of that. We'll test it on me."

"And you're an idiot," I heard Sonya say.

"Captain, without fully testing—"

I cut Coogong off. "I'm standing upon one of the Quansporter pedestals right now. Bring me over to where you are. Please, don't argue... do it now."

"I will have to bring down the QFR and wait several moments for the buffers to clear."

"Understood. Do it."

I waited. Then the doubts started to swirl in my head. I couldn't wait a few frickin' minutes to make one simple test? See if a damn wrench would survive the de-atomizing of its molecules and such?

Then I felt the familiar tingle within my extremities, the subtle vertigo, the nausea. I closed my eyes. *Fuck!*

I waited. What's taking him so long?

"What are you doing?" came Sonya's voice, not from my Jadoo ring, but from several feet away from me. I opened my eyes.

"I... I was waiting to be quansported." I looked about the expansive Engineering and Propulsion department. I said, "Toto, I have a feeling we're not in Kansas anymore."

Sonya made a face. "You need to be checked out, like for brain damage."

"Welcome aboard USS *Lincoln*, Captain," Coogong said with a smile. He was holding his tablet. Apparently, it had the capacity to interface with the Quansporter compartment on

Adams. Glancing down at my hand, I briefly wondered if our Jadoo rings still allowed for quansporting as well.

As if reading my mind, Sonya said, "Uh-uh... because the timing has to be, like, perfect, I think Jadoo ring access would be a bad idea."

Coogong nodded. "Captain... I would like to move the entire Quansporter facility here onto *Lincoln*. Considering what your intentions are for *Adams*... it may be prudent."

"Is that even possible... for it to transport, quansport itself, like that?"

"If anyone would know, Coogong would," Sonya said.

I didn't like taking even the slightest chance that something could go wrong. Here we had an opportunity to bring personnel and equipment over and what, we were going to jeopardize that?

About to protest, I saw Coogong was already tapping at his tablet. The Thine scientist gave one final, definitive tap. "There."

"What do you mean, there?"

"You really do need to have a brain scan or something," Sonya said, chinning toward our left. Elevated upon several feet of Adams' crawlspace and deck plates, where there'd been one of the few open spaces of *Lincoln's* E & P department, stood the familiar Quansporter compartment's console and twelve pedestals.

Coogong said, "When designing the compartment, I ensured all systems wiring... interfaces and such... was compartmentalized for just such a necessity. We do tend to swap ships on a regular basis, no?" He moved quickly, calling out over one shoulder, "Sonya, if you could assist me, please..."

It took them fifteen minutes to jerry-rig power cables and interface connections into *Lincoln's* MATHR AI.

"I need to get back to *Adams*... This ready to go yet?"

Coogong looked hesitant. "We should test—"

"Don't bother, Coogong. He won't listen to you," Sonya said with a huff.

"Where would you like to go?" Coogong asked, now standing in front of the Quansporter's newly positioned console.

"*Adams'* aft Cargo Airlock #22."

"Wait!"

Both Coogong and I looked to Sonya.

"I'm bringing over what's up there on the Symbio Decks," she said, her tone leaving little room for argument.

I hesitated, looked to Coogong, then nodded. "First find the necessary deck space, and don't go alone. Promise?"

"Promise."

I held up a hand, "One more thing, Coogong. We need to find the exact location of the Liquilids' flux generator."

"I believe Hardy, with his more sensitive sensors, would be best suited to assist us in that regard."

Chapter 49

I arrived back on *Adams*, just outside aft Cargo Airlock #22. Long lines, hundreds of crewmembers advancing from both directions within the passageway, were slowly funneling their way into the spaceway's entrance.

"Okay, hold up!" came a familiar voice. Doc Viv was making her way forward in the crowd, two med-techs pulling hovercarts behind them. Only now could I see the prone patients upon the carts with their respective slow-turning medical avatars. Only then did I see that Ham was one of the patients—He looked better than the last time I'd seen him.

Squeezing past complaining crewmembers, Viv spotted me off to the side. She did not look happy to see me. Swiping away several loose strands of hair off her face, she said, "Come to gloat?"

"Come over here."

"I have to get these patients—"

"That's an order, Viv. Your med-techs are perfectly capable of pulling a hovercart by themselves."

Angry, she instructed her techs to keep going without her.

"So, what's so important?"

I leaned in closer to her, not wanting anyone else to hear me. "The Quansporter is operational... at least somewhat."

Her eyes widened. "Really?"

"Really. Contact Sonya directly when you're ready to start moving over HealthBay's larger equipment, your MediBots and such."

"I have more patients—"

"Probably best to use it for non-biological transports."

"Wait... How did you get back here? There's no way you swam through that congested stream of people."

"I needed to test it. But me being willing to risk my life is not the same as risking my crew."

We stood there, staring at each other for several moments. I wished for a reason, any reason, to keep her here talking to me, while I could tell she couldn't wait to get moving again.

"Well," she said, cocking her head toward the spaceway's entrance, "things to do... thanks for the update on the Quansporter. I'll be taking advantage of that." She offered up a fleeting smile, then was off, merging into the throng.

"Coming through, make way; dangerous killer ChronoBot coming through!"

Curses and obscenities emanated from the spaceway's entrance.

"Ouch, watch your step, tin can!" someone bellowed.

Hardy emerged, his head barely clearing the overhead constraints of the spaceway. Seeing me, his boisterous bluster dissipated. "Excuse me... pardon me... so sorry..."

As he joined me, his faceplate display changed, now a serene green meadow, little lambs frolicking about, fluffy white clouds overhead.

"Ah, Cap... heard you were looking for me."

"Uh-huh. Let's get up to the bridge."

. . .

AKARI WAS WAITING for us at the entrance into the bridge. "We have a problem, Captain."

"If I had a dollar for every time I heard those five words..." I mumbled. "What is it?"

"Two things. First, *Wrath* and *Portent* are on the move, making their way through the asteroid field toward us."

"I thought it was too dangerous... asteroid fragments and all."

"That brings up the second thing. Captain Loggins has informed us that those red ships all lined up along the fringe of the field... well, they've deployed more frigates. They're entering the asteroid field as we speak."

I looked to Hardy.

"Four good-sized frigates. They're taking a beating but making good headway, close on the heels of *Wrath* and *Portent*."

"There's something else, Captain," Akari said.

But I was already staring past her to the halo display at the front of the bridge. That faint yellow nanite cloud had drifted and was now virtually on top of two of the three conjoining spaceways.

"Dammit, why didn't you hail me!" I said, hurrying toward the captain's mount, Akari and Hardy right behind.

"I did, multiple times. You didn't hear Sir Calvin over the PA?"

Sir Calvin's blaring overhead voice had been a constant assault upon my ears ever since I'd arrived back on *Adams*. Crew directives, reminders on the limitations of personal items, which groups of crewmembers were to use which spaceway... I must have tuned him out after a while. With a quick glance down at my Jadoo ring, I saw I had multiple messages waiting.

"Sorry..." I took a seat and tried to think. "Where's Polk?"

Hardy said, "Tinkling... Zone D, Deck 26, Head 34, Stall 3."

Both Akari and I looked up to Hardy.

"Way, way, way too much information, Hardy!" Akari balked.

"Oop, she's washing her hands now," Hardy added. "Woman's got excellent hygiene."

"I need to know the overall progress of the move. Can you tell me that, Hardy, in between spying on crewmembers' bathroom habits?"

"Progress has been slow but steady. I'd venture a guess that 85.7 percent of *Adams'* crew have completed the transfer over to *Lincoln*. Coogong is busy quansporting heavy equipment, while Sonya, now up on the Symbio Decks—"

"Wait, are you saying Sonya is back on *Adams*?" I abruptly asked.

Hardy's faceplate display suddenly changed to fluttering butterflies in that same pastoral meadow I saw earlier.

"She better not have quansported over."

"Wait. The Quansporter is working?" Akari said.

Hardy did one of his awkward shrug things. "I refuse to answer on the grounds it may incriminate me."

"Knock it off. Where is Sonya now?"

"Deck 37. She's helping Ensign Plorinne with the quansporting of Symbio sleeping pods. Not an insubstantial task, I might add."

"At least she's not quansporting humans," I said.

Hardy's faceplate went black. He said nothing.

"What are you not telling me?"

"It's understandable; the girl has deep-seated loyalties."

"Spill it, Hardy."

"The Pylors... Sloppy Joe, Little Vince, and the thirty or so band of pirates she pretty much grew up with..."

"Hey, they chose to go on over to *Wrath...*" I said defensively.

"What can I tell you? They changed their collective minds. And you have to remember, Sonya is a Pylor. As I suppose you are too, having trounced their leader, Thunderballs."

"So... what, she quansported the Pylors?" I shook my head; the girl was beyond infuriating.

"The mangy band of space raiders is now happily back with the crew of *Adams*, or should I say, *Lincoln?*"

"Captain, the nanites... the frigates..." Akari said, having, at some point, moved back to Tactical.

The halo display painted a dismal portrait. The yellow cloud was now suspended above all three spaceways. I leaned in. *Oh no...*

Chen said, "We're being hailed, Captain. Both *Wrath* and *Portent* are taking fire. Requesting cover from *Adams.*"

"That would mean breaking away from *Lincoln,*" Grimes said from the helm station.

"Hardy, tell me everyone's made the transfer—"

The ChronoBot's demeanor suddenly changed—no longer the jokester with his ridiculous faceplate displays. "A handful of stragglers, but we have a far bigger problem."

Everyone looked to Hardy.

"We have company." He gestured to Akari. "Security cam feed for aft Cargo Airlock #22 will tell you what you need to know."

Akari brought up the feed—there was a combined gasp within the bridge. A yellow-tinged fog billowed out from the spaceway's entrance. Then, the first of the large, familiar-looking nanite beetle constructs darted out into the passageway. Immediately behind it, two more, then three, followed behind. I could almost hear their metallic snapping, opening and closing mandibles.

"They're flowing into *Lincoln* as well, all three spaceways," Akari said.

"Mr. Grimes! Get us away from *Lincoln*, now!"

Chen said, "Sergeant Max Dryer is hailing—"

"On display," I snapped back, getting to my feet.

Max, with Grip at his side somewhere within a narrow passageway, was in full battle mode. Both their shredders were firing electromagnetic pulses. One beetle was on its back, its legs flailing, while three more were being held at bay.

"Talk to me, Max."

"They must have modified these fuckers!"

Grip jumped back as a beetle lunged for his legs. He fired off no less than ten pulses before the beetle retreated, looking hurt, but most definitely not dead.

"How many are there, Hardy?"

"Seventy-five... sixty here on *Adams*, fifteen on *Lincoln*."

The halo display segmented, providing an external view of *Adams* pulling away from *Lincoln*. The three spaceways stretched to their limits, then tore apart, sparks ignited at the junction points of both ships.

"Akari—"

"Already on it!" she yelled back.

I watched as *Adams'* modified Phazon Pulsar cannons came alive. The yellow cloud turned a glistening, shimmering gold before flashing white and then dissipating into the blackness of space.

I let out a breath, but knew the momentary reprieve wouldn't last.

Bosun Polk hurried onto the bridge. "What can I do to help?"

"I want visual feeds. Show me exactly where each of those beetles is."

Polk joined Akari at Tactical.

Chen said, "*Wrath* and *Portent* are three minutes out. Captain Loggins wants to talk to you."

"No time to chat. Tell him we'll do what we can to provide some cover. Tell Captains Loggins and Church to get in behind us... need to coax those Liquilid frigates away from *Lincoln*."

I looked to the now multi-segmented halo display; it took me a moment to realize what I was looking at. Beetles. They were all over the damn ship and moving with impressive speed. Several were awkwardly making their way up stairwells.

"Good thing they're not adept at using GravLifts," Hardy commented.

"You're still standing here? You do see that they're on their way to the bridge, right? Maybe this would be a good time for a killer ChronoBot to prove his worth?"

He turned to move.

"Wait!" I dragged two palms down my face. *Dammit, I need to concentrate.* "Hardy, we need to know where that quantum flux signal is being generated from. Now more than ever. Whatever you have to do, whatever internal resources you can rally, maybe LuMan can help... but we, I, need to know where that is... right now."

Hardy went still, his faceplate as black as deep space. Then, fading into view, came the animated spinning gears and sprockets. "What I can tell you... is there is still no way to pinpoint those quantum waves... flux waves."

I continued to hold my breath.

"With that said... and let me tell you, Cap... this is by no means something you can hang your hat on—"

"Hardy!"

"Okay, okay... I have picked up communications signals. Very faint."

"Of course you have!" Bosun Polk interjected. "Frigates, dragonflies, red ships... They're all over the place!"

"No... they are primarily coming from that section of space behind *Wrath* and *Portent*. These signals derive from much farther into the asteroid field. And before you ask, all I can give you is a rough guesstimate as to their basic emanation point."

"Send those coordinates to the helm station. Now go kill some beetles for me."

Chapter 50

Hardy

H ardy's metallic frame reverberated with a hum as he raced through deserted *Adams* passageways. The once-bustling corridors now echoed only with the *clomp clomp clomp* of his heavy footfalls. Most of the crew had abandoned ship, seeking refuge on nearby *Lincoln*, leaving Hardy to face this imminent threat alone.

Rounding a corner, Hardy skidded to a halt, his sensors detecting movement up ahead. Three colossal beetles, their metallic exoskeletons gleaming under the flickering emergency lights, blocked his path. Each beetle, a Liquilid nanite construct, while not dwarfing Hardy's imposing frame, was close in girth if not size. Their massive mandibles, capable of cleaving a man in half with little effort, snapped hungrily as they locked their compound eyes on the ChronoBot.

"Hey, creepy crawlies... guess what? The local exterminator has arrived."

Knowing he faced formidable opponents, Hardy initiated his defenses. He deployed all five of his small, turret-mounted plasma cannons. Two cannons snapped into place on his upper thighs, two on his forearms, and one atop his left shoulder, each laser-sited, red-glowing pin-dots now tracking the bug-like invaders. The passageway hummed with anticipation as the weapons charged, ready to unleash their destructive force upon the encroaching threat.

Without hesitation, the first beetle lunged forward, its mandibles snapping shut like a steel trap. Hardy sidestepped with lightning reflexes, narrowly evading the crushing jaws. In response, he unleashed a barrage of plasma fire, streaking blue bolts of energy toward the beetle's armored hide. The shots impacted with explosive force, chipping away at the metallic exterior, but the construct remained undeterred.

The second beetle joined the fray, charging from Hardy's blind spot. Its mandibles aimed to impale him. Reacting swiftly, Hardy swung his arm, cannons blazing, launching a salvo of plasma blasts that collided with the beetle's chitinous armor. The explosive impact staggered the creature, momentarily halting its advance. Seizing the opportunity, Hardy pivoted on his heel and unleashed a fierce kick, sending the beetle crashing into the bulkhead.

However, even with his advanced weaponry, Hardy struggled to gain the upper hand. The beetles possessed the ability to dissimulate and deconstruct, their nanites allowing them to reform and adapt at a moment's notice. Whenever Hardy's plasma bolts seemed to find their mark, the beetles would splinter and reform, evading the brunt of the attack.

As the relentless battle raged on, each movement and strike became a breathtaking dance of survival. Hardy weaved through the chaotic onslaught, his metal frame whirling with precision and purpose. His plasma cannons unleashed torrents of energy, colliding with the constructs' exoskeletons, their explosive bursts illuminating the dimly lit passageway.

Hardy analyzed the patterns of the beetles' movements, searching for weaknesses to exploit. He identified a brief moment when their nanites were momentarily distracted, shifting their focus to regeneration. Seizing the opportunity, Hardy directed all his firepower at one beetle, focusing his assault on a single point. The concentrated plasma barrage overwhelmed the construct, shattering its armored shell and reducing it to a heap of molten metal.

The remaining two beetles, sensing the loss of their comrade, redoubled their efforts. They attacked with renewed ferocity, their mandibles slashing through the air with lethal precision. Hardy's systems strained under the assault, his chrome armor now bearing the scars of their relentless onslaught.

Hardy refused to give an inch. Redoubling his efforts, calculating his movements with the kind of finesse he hadn't been forced to brandish in years, he spun, kicked, and punched in a frenetic blur of motion. But being over three hundred years old, Hardy was starting to feel the accumulation of those centuries. Determination was one thing; endurance was another. Each of his plasma cannons now glowed red; distorted waves of heat rose from each, like searing serpents slithering through the air.

Triumph surged within Hardy's bio-mechanical brain as he witnessed the second beetle succumb to the relentless barrage. Its metallic form crumpled to the floor, defeated and motionless. Yet victory still eluded him as the final beetle, fueled by fury and the will to survive, launched its most vicious attack yet.

The beetle charged forward, its mandibles poised to strike with bone-shattering force. Hardy dodged and weaved, his reflexes being pushed to their limits. The beetle's jaws grazed his armored exterior, leaving deep gouges as a testament to their deadly potential. With a burst of calculated agility, Hardy retaliated, plasma bolts erupting from his cannons, but the construct effortlessly dismantled and reformed, evading the majority of the assault.

Knowing that he needed a different approach, Hardy hesitated. That was all the beetle needed, advancing within that split second, its mandibles snapping shut around his midsection. Hardy's internal sensors, an array of pressure plates, detected the sudden, tremendous constriction, now registering at around ninety-five hundred pounds per square inch.

As the two assailants stood there, neither giving an inch, Hardy looked into the beetle's beady black orbs.

"You know, this is a little more intimate than I like to get on a first date. I appreciate the hug and all, but... well, I'm really not all that into you."

Wedging his fingers in between mandibles and his own waist, slowly at first, he was able to pry open each of the jaws several inches. From there, he was able to slip the rest of his palms in, and only then, grasp each blade within large metal fists. Wider and wider, the mandibles were being pried open. A high-pitched squeal emanated from the nanite construct, then came the sounds of ripping of internal components. With a yank, both curved, cutlass-like blades tore free from the beetle's head.

As soon as it dropped to the deck, Hardy could see the nanite construct was already attempting to grow new ones, but the process would not be quick enough to save it. Raising the two blades high over his head, Hardy used every ounce of his considerable weight to drive both blades into the beetle's head. Leaving them there, he took a weary step back to admire his handiwork.

The nanite construct, surprisingly, had yet to succumb. Hardy watched as the big bug flailed its two forward appendages in an attempt to dislodge the mandible spears.

"I've got to give it to you, my insectile friend; you have tenacity." With that, Hardy targeted all five of his plasma cannons on an area right behind the beetle's noggin. He fired. The bug's head dislodged, momentarily swung, penduluming back and forth, then fell free. It hit the deck with a metallic thump. Only then did the rest of the nanite construct start to dissimilate.

Blaring down from overhead speakers, he heard the captain's voice. "Good job, big guy. Three down, only fifty-seven to go..."

Chapter 51

Liquilid Empire Star System
USS Adams

Captain Galvin Quintos

I looked to Grimes at the helm station, knowing he was frustrated, hard-driving *Adams* forward, dodging asteroids, some small, others monumental, all while maintaining ill-defined navigation directives. Sure, Hardy had detected *something* emanating from *somewhere*, but that was hardly adequate when piloting a vessel of this size through such treacherous conditions.

The halo display showcased the holographic representation of *Adams,* both *Wrath* and *Portent* slightly behind, flanking our port and starboard side. Incoming rocky projectiles, ranging in size from pebbles to boulders, continued to bombard all three ships. With each impact, the shields shimmered and rippled, absorbing the kinetic energy from the colliding asteroids. The display captured the mesmerizing dance of light and motion as the shields held strong, creating a dazzling spectacle of colors and patterns. It was both frightening and beautiful, the vibrant blue hues of the shield barrier clashing with the fiery reds and oranges of the hurtling asteroids.

I grimaced, watching as the largest yet of the asteroids smashed headlong into *Adams'* bow. Had I made a terrible mistake? *Have I doomed us all to an impending, fiery death?* The bridge reverberated with another thunderous *clap!* One that shook the deck plates and rattled hundreds of crystal pendants above. More, smaller impacts followed, a symphony of jarring collisions that echoed through the metal superstructure of the ship. Vibrations continued to travel up through the deck plates, reaching the soles of our feet, sending tremors of unease up our spines.

Someone murmured, "Fuck."

On the bridge, the air around us was palpable—charged with anticipation—a mix of adrenaline and anxiety.

Akari had ceased to fire on each and every incoming projectile, conserving limited rail spikes.

"Captain, we're being hailed by Captain Loggins," Chen said.

About to decline *Wrath's* hail, Chen added, "You might want to take this, Sir."

"On display," I said.

Loggins looked a mess, his typically pristine white uniform now open at the collar, several dark smears streaked across the fabric.

"We're being besieged, Captain... more of those beetles... maybe as many as a hundred."

Akari and I exchanged a quick look; for a ship of that size, it would be impossible to combat such an incursion.

I said, "You still have your modified EMP weapons—"

"Get real, Captain. The best we can hope for is to keep them at bay. They're all over the ship... Barely a minute goes by when I don't hear the agonizing screams of one of my crew being attacked!"

I didn't know what to say. The last thing Loggins would want right now was me blowing smoke up his ass. "Hang tight, Captain. Let's just see how this all plays out."

It was a lame thing to say, but Loggins did seem to take it in stride.

"Just get us where you need us and do it fast, Captain Quintos. Don't let this mad dash to who knows where be in vain."

"Copy that," I said. I looked to Chen, and he cut the connection.

"Captain..."

I looked back to Akari, who was staring, transfixed, at the halo display. There were too many segmented feeds to know what the hell I was supposed to look at.

With a tap on her board, one particular segment enlarged, eclipsing all the others. There stood Hardy amidst four, no five, beetles. One had its mandibles secured around his neck, another his left leg. Hardy teetered there, immobile, totally incapacitated.

"That's not good," I said aloud to no one in particular.

"Tell me about it," I heard Hardy reply, not realizing there was an open audio channel to him.

"Uh... hang tight, Hardy."

"Like I have a choice?"

"Captain, I have Sonya insisting she speak with you," Chen said, looking as overwhelmed as I felt.

"Why not? Put her through."

Her feed, now enlarged to the size of Hardy's, displayed the face of an irate-looking teenager.

"I have zero time for—"

"What the hell happened to the Quansporter?!"

"The Quansporter?" I repeated.

"Don't play stupid. You've never appreciated the Symbios up here! Especially Reggie... What did he ever do to you other than risk life and limb for your stupid games?"

"I have no idea what you're talking—"

"Convoke Wyvern and Caveman Glory games... and how many alien battles have you sent him off to fight?"

"Just tell me what you need. I have no time for any of this."

She stared back at me. "We had them all moved over... the big fabricating machines, all the sleep pods, everyone, all the Symbios, all except one, were quansported over to *Lincoln*."

"Reggie," I said, finally catching on.

She made the kind of exasperated face only a sixteen-year-old girl could make. I said, "The Quansporter was tenuous at best. We're lucky it worked as long as it did. We'll check with Coogong ... see when he can—"

I stopped talking, my eyes shifting over to the stranded and pathetic-looking Hardy feed. "Sonya... you know Reggie better than anyone—will he fit within the confines of one of *Adams'* larger cargo GravLifts?"

"I don't think he's in the mood to go joyriding in ship lifts right now. I can tell he's feeling neglected. Like the last kid picked for a Wappo team."

I was tempted to ask what a Wappo team was but stayed on topic. "Sonya, tell Reggie, right now, he is the most important of all the Symbio-Poths, bar none."

She just shook her head. Looked at me like I was beyond stupid.

"At this moment, *Adams* is swarming with dozens of Liquilid nanite-infused beetles. We need Reggie to come to the rescue. And if you haven't taken note of Hardy's current predicament, I suggest you do so now."

I watched as she tapped at her tablet, brows knit as she

searched for the right feed. Suddenly, her eyes widened, and she gasped. "Oh no, Hardy…"

Looking back up at me, she looked to be considering what was being asked of her, more precisely, asked of Reggie. "This isn't really in Reggie's job description, you know…"

"Oh, but being stabbed by broadswords or chased by crazed cavemen is?" Akari spat back. "We're wasting time here, kid. Get that fucking Symbio dinosaur onto a GravLift and do it now! Don't make me come up there and—"

"Fine! I'll get Reggie into a lift, but it's not my fault if his fat ass won't fit!"

Akari cut the feed with a huff. Sonya's sour face disappeared from view.

Akari looked back at me. "You can't negotiate with teenagers, girls especially; they'll walk all over you."

"Noted."

As Grimes continued to man the helm controls, I put my attention back on Hardy. I said, "Help is on the way, buddy." I leaned in. The ChronoBot now had three beetles affixed to various parts of his metal frame. I said, "Since you're, um… indisposed, can you give us an update on that Liquilid comms signal?"

Hardy's face display turned just enough that I could see an old atomic bomb explosion and the resulting mushroom cloud playing on a constant loop. "Signal's stronger, a little; think we're still on the right trajectory."

"Frigates are upon us, Cap!" Akari exclaimed.

Chapter 52

Lost Tombstone Star System
Genoma, Stratham Hold

Captain Gail Pristy

Resnick bolted through the ringularity into the dark cavernous tunnel, leaving Pristy several yards behind. *What is your problem?* Pristy's irritation with Resnick was reaching critical mass, a live grenade pin pulled, ready to detonate. The general had been secretive and moody, taking haughtiness to a whole new level. She quickened her pace, struggling to catch up to him. Normally it would have felt good to be back at home base—on Lost Tombstone—but all she felt was acrimony.

"Can you please explain why we left *Portent?* Seems to me this is a critical moment within the whole space-time continuum thing you keep going on and on about." Pristy spoke with a breathy tone, jogging and talking.

She stopped a couple feet behind Resnick, standing her ground and yelling, "Hey, I'm talking to you!"

Resnick halted in his tracks. His body stiffened. The general executed a definitive about-face. If looks could kill, she'd be six feet under. "My hearing, like my eyesight, is perfect."

Pristy took in his rigid standing position. Her breathing under control now, she spoke in a calm voice, "Just please explain to me, General, the plan, the steps we're taking... and why."

"Repeating yourself over and over again, ad nauseam, does neither of us any good. Yes, I understand you want answers. Yes, I understand your concerns about your former shipmates, but personal sentiments continue to be counterproductive to the mission. How about you wait until we are up top with the others, so I only have to explain things once?"

Guess I don't have a choice, you arrogant prick. Listening to Resnick's rant, she hoped the lack of lighting in the underground cavern hid the disgust on her face. "Fine, I'll wait," she replied tersely, gesturing forward. "Lead the way."

ENTERING Stratham Hold's control center, Pristy and Resnick found Stephan Derrota, Dr. Patty Kline, Superintendent LaSalle, and Petty Officer Second-Class Aubrey Laramie waiting for them. Their faces mirrored the same irritation Pristy felt, their eyes fixed on Resnick as he entered the compartment.

"Welcome back," Aubrey said with faux excitement. "What—"

Resnick cut her off with a shut-the-fuck-up stare, then took slow, measured steps toward the back of the control center.

Feeling the weight of their expectations, Pristy shrugged toward the crew helplessly, silently conveying that she, like them, had no idea what was going on. The room hummed with the constant murmur of computer servers, creating a backdrop of white noise that heightened the tension in the air.

Pristy moved toward a control board, standing next to LaSalle.

The superintendent bent his substantial frame toward her and whispered in the captain's ear. "What's going on, Gail?"

Keeping her eyes straight, she raised a wait-and-see palm. *Not now, LaSalle. Read the room.*

Resnick turned to face the group, then checked his Chrono-Link—something he did way too often. His brow arched in a mix of curiosity and contemplation. "Time is a funny thing," he began, his voice commanding the room's attention.

"Funny?" Derrota interjected, his confusion evident.

"Not ha-ha funny, Mr. Derrota." Resnick scowled at the science officer. "Peculiar funny," he clarified. His gaze lost focus, suddenly deep in thought.

"What do you mean, General?" Derrota's accented singsong voice cut the tension in the room.

"Thought you'd never ask, Mr. Derrota." Resnick appeared to welcome the voice of intelligence in a sea of estrogen. "In the framework of general relativity, space-time is considered a four-dimensional continuum that combines three dimensions of space and one dimension of time. It implies that the curvature of space-time can influence the flow of time—"

Derrota cut off Resnick, finishing his sentence. "Creating nonlinear paths and distortions."

"Precisely." Resnick beamed, a proud father seeing all A's on his son's report card. "We as humans keep wanting it to be linear. We're programmed to think that way from birth." He paused and smiled, as if remembering a fond memory. "Even I, after all these years traversing the timescape, sometimes get fooled, caught believing the fairy tale."

Pristy stifled a cough. Resnick's diatribe had tipped toward the melodramatic. *What is he talking about—reminiscing when my friend's lives are hanging in the balance?* She thought of the crew on *Adams*; they were her people, not Resnick. This mission had been thrust upon her. Pristy desperately missed the others, Akari, Coogong, Sonya, Hardy... and, perhaps especially, Quintos. And what... they should just stand by and watch them perish?

Captain Gail Pristy had spent her career navigating the vastness of space, relying on the predictability of time and the order it imposed. Even as a young Ensign, she understood the value of relying on facts and science. The notion that it might not be as straightforward as she had always believed was not only unsettling; it was terrifying.

"But what does that mean for us now?" she pressed, her voice tinged with a mixture of urgency and dread. "What about the people we care about? The crew of *Adams*? Are we just supposed to accept that their fate is sealed?"

Resnick met her gaze, unapologetic. "I wish I had better news, Captain Pristy. But the facts don't lie. Just try for a second not to picture me as some kind of monster, but a mathematician... or a scientist."

Pristy swallowed hard. Here we go again. Another spiel.

"Two plus two will always equal four. I—and yes, even you, Captain Pristy—cannot change what is inevitable. The crew of *Adams* will die."

Pristy's heart sank at Resnick's words. The weight of her emotional ties to *Adams* and her crew pressed down on her. She couldn't shake the memories of her time on that ship, the camaraderie she shared with her fellow officers, the trust she had in their abilities. And there, in the depths of her heart, still lingered her unresolved feelings for Galvin Quintos, a man whose fate now seemed tragically intertwined with the impending doom of *Adams*.

"Excuse me, General Resnick." Aubrey Laramie held up a hand, a third grader asking permission to use the bathroom.

"What is it, Petty Officer Second-Class?" He lowered his gaze toward her.

"As you recall, I was in quite a predicament not too long ago... the whole deadly virus thing, you know. You all were able to put your heads together and avert disaster. Why can't we do that now?" Aubrey finished talking, seemingly relieved to be able to make her point.

Resnick laughed out loud. "That's adorable, Laramie. Your simplistic view of solving the complexities of space-time."

He paused, then lowered his voice as if making an important point. "Apples and oranges, people." He swept his gaze over the entire group, as if knowing that everyone shared Aubrey's sentiment. "Are you so foolish as to think one scenario is identical to the next?"

The group let the rhetorical question lie, its unanswered presence hanging in the air like an unresolved chord in a haunting melody.

"Every decision I make is in direct response to what is thrown at me, at us. And remember, this isn't just my decision. Ultimately, I answer to the Grand Consortium." Resnick's speech concluded. His mic-drop moment ended with a thud.

Resentment inflamed Pristy, fueling her determination to find a way, *anyway*, to alter the course of destiny. "So, are you saying the Grand Consortium is not open to the possibility of finding a way to fulfill the mission while saving the crew of *Adams*?"

"The primary objective of the Grand Consortium is to never reveal its directives—or details of such directives with nonmembers." Resnick took an at-ease stance. "In other words, you'll just have to trust me."

Pristy fumed. As she listened, her determination only grew. "Stop! There has to be something we can do. I keep asking myself, why have you given up?" She looked to the others, then back to Resnick. "Maybe you should check your ChronoLink again for the umpteenth time, or maybe we should go back to the Consortium, see what they have to say."

Resnick's gaze softened, his eyes reflecting a shared sorrow. "I understand your anguish, Pristy. I truly do. But we've searched every conceivable timeline, explored every possible scenario; the outcome remains the same."

He looked away from her, staring off, as if conversing with an invisible adviser. "We cannot change what has already been set in motion."

He paced the compartment, his footsteps echoing against the metal deck. "Consider the countless civilizations that have risen and fallen throughout the eons of history. Orders were given and followed. That's how things move forward, evolve." The general continued pacing until he reached the back of the control center. He stood in his familiar spot facing his crew.

What a windbag. Pristy knew that some of what the general was saying might, in fact, be true... as much as it pained her to admit it. The forces they were up against were beyond their comprehension. But that didn't mean an answer to their dilemma would not present itself. She realized she'd have to keep her thoughts to herself. *Okay, I will go along with you for now, but just know—I will never give up.*

Taking a deep breath, Pristy looked around at her team, each bearing their own burden. "All right," she said, her voice steady. "We move forward. We fight. And we honor the fallen."

Derrota, Dr. Kline, Superintendent LaSalle, and Petty Officer Aubrey Laramie nodded in stone-faced agreement. They understood the gravity of their mission, the weight of what they were agreeing to. But their faces showed they remained unconvinced that it was the best course of action.

"Pristy, you're with me." Resnick headed toward the hatch

that led to the outside corridor. "The rest of you, sit tight. Stand by for further instructions."

They exchanged glances, struggling to reconcile Resnick's overly pragmatic reasoning. Pristy wanted to tell them not to give up but thought better of it. Of all those under the general's command, Pristy was the one who had the most influence over him. He would deny it, of course—any narcissist would. For now, she'd feed his ego. Later, he wouldn't know what hit him.

Pristy followed after him. "Yes, General, I'm right behind you."

Chapter 53

Captain Galvin Quintos

USS *Adams* powered deeper into the asteroid field, Grimes, sweating bullets at the helm, deftly maneuvering the dreadnought to avoid one catastrophic collision after another. Behind us, *Boundless Wrath* and *Portent* followed closely, seeking the safety of Adam's protective Phazon Pulsar cannons and rail guns. Meanwhile, the enemy Liquilid frigates closed in, unleashing their energy weapons upon us. *Adams'*, *Wrath's*, and *Portent's* shields strained under the relentless assault.

I glanced to Akari. "Don't let up, Lieutenant... bring all aft cannons to bear."

Bosun Polk, having joined her at Tactical, the oldest of the bridgecrew, was looking frayed, if not overwhelmed.

Chen's voice broke through the tension. "Urgent message

from *Wrath*... Captain Loggins. Says their shields are faltering. Says their situation is... dire."

Akari, her eyes focused on her board, said, "Yeah, well, our own shields are down to 65 percent."

The feeling of dread was conspicuous.

Grimes, his voice taut with nervousness, said, "Uh... we've run out of open space ahead." He sat back, deflated.

No one said anything.

"But maybe I can..."

I saw what we were up against on the display. It would be a perilous maneuver, to say the least. Grimes would have to thread the proverbial needle, skirting in between two close-together massive asteroids.

"Do it," I said.

"Aye, but it'll be tight, Sir."

Collectively, the bridgecrew held their respective breaths as *Adams* approached the seemingly impossibly narrow ingress between the two mammoth-sized, counter-rotating asteroids.

I cringed, gritting my molars as a prolonged, thunderous scraping sound reverberated through the ship. Everything shook, overhead lights flickered, a console at the back of the bridge erupted—sparks fountained into the air.

Grimes winced. "Sorry!"

Not realizing it, I had brought my palms together in front of my lips, as though silently praying. On the halo display, *Wrath* and *Portent*, having fallen back, now cleared the asteroids behind us; all the while enemy fire continued to rain down upon them.

"Shit!" Akari said, her voice carrying a level of urgency I'd rarely heard. "Rail guns are now officially offline." Looking back over one shoulder, she added, "That leaves us with limited options."

Was it limited or none? I wondered. But an idea was brewing. Then again, desperation tended to do that.

"Mr. Grimes," I called out, my voice filled with determination I wasn't sure I actually felt, "Slow us to a crawl, then bring *Adams* about two hundred and seventy degrees! Do it now!"

I needed the ship's orientation perpendicular to what was coming for us. We'd be executing a risky tactic that could possibly save us. That, or quicken our demise.

"Mr. Chen, signal *Wrath* and *Portent* they need to clear away from *Adams*... Give us a little elbow room."

Akari turned to me, a mix of confusion and anticipation in her eyes. "What are we doing, Captain?"

I rose to my feet, a surge of adrenaline coursing through my veins. "Tell me we have at least one of our broadside cannons operational, Lieutenant."

All USS *Hamilton*–class warships were outfitted with twelve of these behemoth weapons, six cannons per side. Each cannon fired twelve-hundred-pound bowlers, nicknamed for their visual similarity to massive-looking bowling balls and their strategically placed circular, finger-like holes. Prior to impact, these holes were the dispersal element for magnesium scatter frags, which effectively weakened enemy hull armor plating a nanosecond prior to impact and allowed the giant explosive cannonballs to decimate anything they came into contact with. The problem was these big bad boys were found to be somewhat unstable. More than a few bowlers would sometimes, though rarely, go off-course. In one such case, during spatial war games close to Earth, a British frigate was destroyed with all hands lost. Needless to say, the big weapons were then deemed too dangerous—even for wartime use. Subsequently, newer warship construction did not include broadsides. Instead favored was more advanced energy weaponry, such as the newer Phazon Pulsars and rail guns.

Akari tapped at her board, pulling up the readiness status of the portside broadsides. "Only two of the twelve cannon silos are currently being manned... and that's by robots," she informed me with an apologetic tilt of her head.

I inwardly chided myself, remembering virtually all of *Adams'* crew had abandoned ship. But robots manning the giant turret compartments? "That'll have to do," I said resolutely. "Have them target the first frigate coming through the two asteroids."

Both Akari and Bosun Polk worked in side-by-side unison, fingers tapping across their consoles, Polk relaying commands to the robot operators manning the broadsides. "Captain," Polk said, "Broadsides require more time..."

Any response from me would be superfluous. It made sense; hauling bowler munitions into those big guns was an arduous process.

"Here they come!" Polk announced in front of me.

I saw it too: the first of the enemy frigates shot out through the narrow gap between the two asteroids like a high-powered bullet from the barrel of a rifle.

"Dammit!" I murmured under my breath.

"Broadsides are live!" announced Bosun Polk.

"Target the two asteroids, not the frigates!"

Polk hesitated, then seemed to understand.

Boom! Boom! Boom! Boom! Thunderous vibrations shook the bridge and the entire ship with each cannon blast. The barrage of explosive power eviscerated the colossal rocks—like two erupting volcanoes spewing jagged rock shrapnel in every direction.

The enemy frigates, caught in the midst of the cataclysmic explosions, hadn't stood a chance. The dual blasts tore through their hulls, obliterating them in a matter of seconds.

Akari's voice rang out, filled with a mix of triumph and

concern. "Captain, that will do it for our supply of bowler munitions. Add to that... overuse of our Phazon Pulsars has rendered them, for the most part, inoperable."

It occurred to me this one small frigate posed more of a danger than I'd given it credit for—one that could very well spell the end of *Adams* and her crew.

INCOMING, INCOMING, INCOMING
BRACE FOR IMPACT!

Came Sir Calvin's overhead warning.

We had all already spotted it. The one remaining Liquilid frigate, continuing its relentless assault, had unleashed a barrage of smart missiles—all locked into a single trajectory: *Adams'* vulnerable portside.

"Cap," Akari said without turning around, "our shields were peppered with shrapnel traveling at near light-speed, subsequently weakening them to..." she checked her board, "a mere 30 percent. Needless to say, that barrage consists of twenty-five smart missiles."

"Stay positive," I said, not feeling even the slightest bit positive.

"Grimes!" I shouted, desperation lacing my voice. "Get the ship turned away from that onslaught! And we need to get moving again!"

Time seemed to slow as I braced myself for the impending impact, aware that it might be too little, too late. The barrage loomed closer, an ominous presence, ready to deliver a fatal blow. I commanded the bridgecrew to hold on, their expressions mirroring a mixture of fear and determination.

Above us, the klaxon blared, its shrill wail piercing the air, while Sir Calvin repeated the chilling warning:

IMPACT, IMPACT, IMPACT!

"Wait!" Akari spat. "Think I've managed to resurrect a handful of Phazon Pulsar cannons."

Vibrant blue plasma bolts filled the short expanse of space between the ship and the fast-approaching missile barrage.

I watched as ten missile icons of the halo display blinked out. The remaining fifteen projectiles struck *Adams'* shields with ferocious kinetic force. At the back of the bridge, one of the large Waterford chandeliers dropped from the deckhead, cut crystal pendants exploding outward like a prismatic fireworks display. I ducked and covered my head as shards of glass showered down all around us.

Chen's voice broke through the mayhem, his words sharp with urgency. "Captain, I'm receiving a live comms feed from *Wrath*."

Clearly, we had survived the onslaught. I didn't bother asking for a damage report. There was no one on board, no SWM crew to deploy to make repairs.

The halo display flickered to life, revealing the bridge of *Boundless Wrath*. Captain Loggins's face appeared on the screen, his gaze unwavering. He spoke with a solemnity that sent a shiver down my spine. "It has been a privilege, Captain Quintos... I hope to serve with you again, perhaps in another lifetime. Please inform Empress Shawlee Tee, if you are fortunate enough to survive these... unpleasant circumstances, that my crew fought with honor and dedication to the Pleidian Weonan Empire."

Loggins' feed went black, replaced by another. This time, it showed the once Varapin prison ship *Boundless Wrath*, her aft drives spewing a brilliant inferno of blue and yellow flames. The ship surged forward on a collision course with the enemy vessel, a beacon of sacrifice and heroism.

I, along with my crew, stood frozen, unable to speak or move, as we watched in horror. *Wrath*, her crew steadfast in their resolve, had chosen to make the ultimate self-sacrifice. The two ships collided in a cataclysmic explosion, an awe-inspiring ball of fire that consumed both *Wrath* and the Liquilid frigate.

The bridge settled into an eerie silence, broken only by distant bellowing klaxons.

But even in the face of tragedy, there was no time for despair. This battle was far from over; surely there were other frigates having already been deployed. The fate of *Adams* and her small crew still hung in the balance. With a heavy heart and renewed determination, I turned to my crew, their eyes searching mine for guidance.

"We press on," I said, my voice resolute. "For *Wrath*, for the fallen, and for our survival."

Chapter 54

Liquilid Empire Star System
USS Adams

Sonya Winters

S onya could hardly quell her growing frustration as she led Reggie, the enormous Symbio-Poth bio-mechanical T-Rex, through the winding corridors of the ship. She couldn't believe she'd been assigned the task of using such a formidable creature for something as trivial as dealing with a bunch of bugs. Maneuvering Reggie into the cargo lift had been a feat in itself; getting him out, even worse.

As they approached an intersecting, larger passageway, Sonya's annoyance reached its peak. There Hardy, the supposedly indomitable ChronoBot, was surrounded by four nanite-infused Liquilid beetles. Three of the beetles had their large mandibles clamped tightly around various parts of Hardy's metal form, having rendered the robot completely immobilized.

Reggie, his towering presence filling the corridor, turned his gaze down toward Sonya. She noticed a hint of nervousness in the Symbio T-Rex's reptilian eyes, which surprised her. She reached out, placing a hand on Reggie's scaly side.

"Come on, Reggie, it's just a bunch of stupid bugs," she said, her voice laced with sarcasm. "I thought a big tough T-Rex like you wouldn't be afraid of a few creepy crawlies."

Reggie let out a low rumble, his deep voice vibrating through the air. "I hate bugs, all bugs," he grumbled.

Sonya couldn't help but roll her eyes. "Well, put on your big-boy pants and get to it," she retorted, frustration evident in her voice. "Looks like Hardy there can't afford for you to dilly-dally."

With a resigned growl, Reggie took a few steps forward, causing the deck to tremble beneath Sonya's feet. The beetles, momentarily distracted by the arrival of the T-Rex, loosened their grip on Hardy.

Sonya said, "Uh, it's now or never."

Reggie lunged toward the beetles, his massive jaws snapping with such force it hurt her ears. Soon the air was filled with the sounds of crunching exoskeletons and the screeches of desperate beetles. Sonya stood back, watched with a mix of awe and apprehension as the battle unfolded. She flinched as Reggie swung his powerful tail, knocking one beetle into the bulkhead with a resounding thud, then brought his massive jaws down on another beetle, crushing it instantly. The remaining beetles scurried in a frenzy, attempting to evade Reggie's wrath.

Hardy, although immobile, managed to enunciate a few colorful curses, a signal of his irritation that he was the one needing rescuing.

Sonya felt relief knowing Hardy was still functional. This could have easily gone another way.

One by one, Reggie plucked the beetles off Hardy and, like a dog with a chew toy, he shook the living daylights out of each of them, one after another—reducing them to little more than scraps of metal upon the deck. The decimated nanite constructs were now incapable of reforming.

As more beetles arrived within the corridor, Reggie relentlessly pursued them. Sonya could tell by the big T-Rex's expression, he was enjoying himself.

Her Jadoo ring was vibrating. She thumb-tapped it, and without looking down at the projected display, said, "Satisfied?"

"It's a good start," her uncle said, seeming far less impressed than he should be. "How about you let Reggie continue doing his thing while you and Hardy head back to the bridge?"

"How's he going to know where to go?"

"Looks like that won't be a problem; they're heading en masse toward him."

Sonya, realizing this was probably not someplace she wanted to be, glanced behind herself, then took a tentative step backward.

"I have another job for you."

"Terrific, I can't wait."

"It's important, Sonya... important to the very survival of humankind."

"Uh-huh... exaggerate much?"

"I'm not exaggerating in the slightest. We need *Adams'* memory banks scrubbed. And not just a cursory erasing of data. Nothing can be left on board that points to the location of our home world. Nothing."

She heard the seriousness in his voice and felt a chill run down her spine. "I'll do it... but, just so you know, *Adams* will be unable to—"

"Navigate back to Earth? Where *Adams* is heading, she won't need that information."

"Copy that," she said in a clipped voice suddenly at odds with her emotions. She swallowed and blinked away the welling of tears. *Will I ever have a real home?*

Chapter 55

Captain Gail Pristy

N o sooner had the six of them arrived than Resnick was busy checking his ChronoLink. For the umpteenth time, Pristy wondered what the hell that was all about. If destiny was so set in stone, chiseled into the annals of space-time, then what the hell was he looking for?

The four others, Derrota, Dr. Kline, LaSalle, and Petty Officer Aubrey Laramie, were far less concerned by Resnick's actions than they were by their surroundings. It was a subterranean space that dwarfed the one below Lost Tombstone by a factor of a hundred. Everyone squinted against the flashing, strobing lights, complementary colors seeming to be changing value, red to green, yellow to purple, and so on.

Prior to stepping into the subterranean ringularity, Resnick had relayed what their final mission would entail. And that after this, the services of the five of them would no longer be required. *Whatever that meant...*

Derrota looked about the vast space with an expression of "ahh."

Pristy joined him. "What are we looking at here, Stephan?"

"Simply put, this is the basis, the root cause, of so much suffering, so many deaths." The others gathered around them, including Resnick.

The flux generator loomed above, a breathtaking sight.

Derrota continued, "My assumption is the core there... those glowing concentric rings, they're designed to both harness and manipulate energy. Flux, the key principle at work here, allows the alteration of space-time curvature." He looked to Resnick for affirmation.

"Close enough, Mr. Derrota... the resulting gravity and electromagnetism differentials are key aspects of the generator. That is what keeps unsuspecting starships from jumping away or utilizing wormhole manufacturing technology."

Aubrey said, "It is here that the spider spins her web, waits for her naïve prey to wander into her intricate trap, ignorant of the impending doom that lurks in the shadows."

All eyes went to the petty officer second-class. She looked back at them. "What?"

Dr. Kline said, "Well put, Aubrey. Almost poetic."

Superintendent LaSalle added, "... and creepy as hell."

Electromagnetic fields suddenly crackled above them with a flurry of small lightning bolts, as if to punctuate LaSalle's comment.

Resnick straightened, catching sight of something or someone off in the distance. He put a finger to his lips before gesturing the group to take several steps back and move behind one of the large support pillars that were prevalent throughout the cavern.

In a hushed voice, he said, "They're just now coming back on duty."

Pristy said, "Who's—"

Irritated, Resnick shushed her. "Liquilids, who else?"

She hated being shushed. I'm not a child, you pompous jerk.

"We're running late. We need to do what we came here to do and get out."

Dr. Kline, looking exasperated, said, "That thing, this flux generator, is huge. There's no way we can destroy it. We'd need a bomb or something."

Resnick made a face. "Did you not listen to anything I said before we arrived?"

Chastised, Kline looked away, her cheeks flushed.

"We are not here. We were never here. We cannot alter the known future timescape. I think blowing up the quantum flux generator would probably be noticed down the line, don't you think?"

"You've made your point; leave her alone," Pristy said.

LaSalle scratched his stubbled chin. "Why are we here? I mean, why bring all of us along on this mission?"

Resnick's lips constricted into a straight line.

Pristy smirked. "You don't know exactly how we're going to do what we came here to do... do you?"

"I know what we have to do... just not how," he said, indignant.

"And that's why we're all here?" Aubrey asked. "To what... brainstorm?"

Pristy said, "We each have our own expertise. We've all proven to be resourceful."

Derrota shook his head. "No."

Pristy looked from Derrota to Resnick, and perhaps for the first time, the man looked unsure of himself.

Derrota continued, "We're not supposed to be here."

"What?" Aubrey murmured.

"That's why you're so obsessed with your stupid Chrono-Link; you're watching, like by the minute, to see if we've fucked up the timescape or not," Pristy, not needing Resnick's confirmation, knew she was right.

"You're tempting fate," Aubrey said, looking bemused. "I like it."

"And the Grand Consortium?" Pristy asked.

Resnick almost smiled. "Let's just say they would not be happy we're here. If we, if I, inadvertently change the timescape, there'll be repercussions."

"What kind of repercussions?" Aubrey asked.

He didn't answer right away. "This was my decision. My mission. None of you will be held responsible."

"You didn't answer her question," Pristy said.

"I'll be executed," Resnick said in so matter-of-fact a tone, he could have been talking about what he had for dinner last night.

He blew a breath out from puffed cheeks. "You think I want to watch Quintos and his crew die? To let this be—"

"Their final curtain call?" Aubrey interjected.

Resnick shrugged, then nodded.

"How definitive is it that Quintos and the others die?" Pristy asked.

"Everybody dies at some point," Resnick said with a wave of a hand.

"But they're supposed to die... here?" Kline queried.

He looked at his ChronoLink. "Yes, here... and within the hour."

Pristy felt paralyzed, as if she'd been jolted by one of those lightning bolts. *This can't be happening.*

327

Derrota broke the pregnant silence. "Your time-traveling team, or maybe one of the others... Have they ever broken a Grand Consortium directive? Changed events, altered time itself?"

"Sure. That's sort of their purpose, right? It's about overall best practices in the preservation of life, all life... you'd be surprised how simple it is to bring about cataclysmic destruction on an epic scale, far beyond a star system, or even a galaxy... chaos runs rampant, the unexpected toppling of one domino causing a cascading effect that brings about the end of... well, everything. Intergalactic wars that spiral out of control, artificial intelligence deeming organic life unnecessary, infectious, incurable plagues being carried across the cosmos..."

"And Quintos and crew have been deemed pivotal in all that?"

"In truth, the specifics are unknown. The future is written just as the past is, the only difference being, there is less clarity. And let me clear up something else here and now... you've been under the impression *Adams* is the only casualty within this timescape... this preordained scenario."

Pristy felt the blood drain from her face, her chest constricted to the point she could no longer take in a breath.

"No! Not *Lincoln!*" Pristy said far too loud. "What, *Lincoln* has been deemed to be just one more of those cascading dominoes so necessary for all life within the universe to prevail?"

"You're talking thousands of lives," Dr. Kline said, her eyes boring into Resnick.

"It's not as if I haven't pleaded with the council," Resnick said. "Especially since, to my knowledge, there isn't any definitive proof any of this has any long-term negative consequences to the contrary."

"So, you all just go along with whatever they say?"

"They've averted countless catastrophes. There is no question of the good they do. They are not the ones to throw caution to the wind. To let the chips fall where they may when they don't know all the specific potential outcomes."

"Are we even supposed to be here?" Aubrey asked.

"I can answer that," LaSalle said with a crooked grin and eyeing Resnick. "No flippin' way."

Pristy noticed more movement in the distance. Dark, slithering, undefined shapes that were beyond creepy, to use LaSalle's earlier word.

"Guess I know why you've been such an uptight ass-hat these last few days," Pristy said.

"He came here, conducting an unsanctioned mission, knowing he'll most probably be executed," Derrota said. "I'm sorry... one of this must have been easy for you."

"If it means I have to sacrifice myself so thousands of Lincoln crewmembers can live, then I willingly do that," Pristy said, looking to the others.

Reluctantly, the others nodded, with the exception of the youngest of the group, Aubrey.

"I don't see why we can't all stay alive. Fuck the Grand Consortium and their stupid directives. And yes, I'll say that right to their old, wrinkled, scrotum-y faces."

Resnick's eyes widened as if she'd spouted blasphemy, like some omnipresent God-like presence would suddenly strike her down with a bolt of lightning.

The weight of her words continued to hang in the air.

Suddenly Pristy's ChronoLink started to vibrate. Seeing the others now looking at their wrists, apparently, all of their ChronoLinks had started to vibrate.

The large watch-like dial was inundated with flowing lines of symbols and indecipherable characters. The encircling bezel was flashing a bright orange. Clearly, someone was trying to tell them something.

Pristy heard Resnick's deep inhalation. His eyes stayed glued to his ChronoLink—reading and then rereading the encrypted message.

Chapter 56

"What does it say?" Aubrey said. "I'm no good at reading gobbledygook."

The general looked up, finding Pristy's eyes. "What?" she said.

"Seems we made our proverbial beds, now we have to sleep in them."

"Meaning?" Derrota said.

Resnick said, "We are not to destroy the Liquilids' quantum flux generator, which was always the case. But if we can somehow manage to disrupt the shields surrounding this asteroid, do so subtly enough that our presence will never be detected, we have the go-ahead to proceed."

"Why does that matter?" Dr. Kline asked.

Derrota smiled. "It's so *Adams* can get a more precise lock on this rock."

"And crash into it," Aubrey said.

Pristy didn't care about any of that. "And the crewmembers?"

Resnick looked somewhat befuddled. "They said, and I quote... 'We're willing to let the chips fall where they may.'"

Pristy said, "In other words, their fate has yet to be determined."

"One more thing," Resnick said. "We have thirty minutes and counting."

"Thirty minutes to bring down this compound's, this asteroid's, shields?" Derrota said, looking exactly how Pristy felt —overwhelmed.

Dr. Kline said, "And we have to stay hidden. Our presence here never noticed by the Liquilids."

"Why do something so dramatic?"

Everyone looked to Aubrey.

"Do we really care if the shields are destroyed? It's not like we're going to be hanging around here in Liquilid space, right? Let's just turn them off... make it difficult to get them running for a few hours, maybe a day."

Resnick looked ready to discount her suggestion while Derrota looked to be mulling that over. "She's not wrong."

"So, we're talking a command center, a control room, versus some big, probably heavily guarded shield-emitter facility. I'm with Aubrey on this one," Pristy said.

"Seems to be a no-brainer," LaSalle added, hitching a shoulder. "And there is that time element."

Resnick raised his palms in mock surrender. "I can get us to what I suspect is the primary control center... but you have to understand, these aliens, the Liquilids... they don't ambulate like we do."

As if on cue, a wet, plopping sound came from their left as if a giant water balloon had just been dropped from the roof of a house onto a driveway. Everyone went silent, staying perfectly still. The Liquilid was close, too close, as it ambled by. Silhouetted by the glowing, towering quantum flux generator in the distance, the creature walked on hind legs for several steps, then flopped onto its belly, continuing on with more of a winding, slithering motion.

"Wish I had my compound bow," Aubrey said under her breath.

Pristy had to give it to the young woman; she was fearless, if not beyond reckless.

"Did you see that thing?" Dr. Kline exclaimed. "What the fuck was that?"

Pristy had seen her share of bizarre creatures, but this was one of the oddest. A long alligator snout, long, sharp, protruding teeth, multiple clawed appendages, then there was that bulbous fat belly. What she knew Doc Viv would call a human's most primitive, protoreptilian brain reacted. Instinctively, she both hated and feared the creature on a level she would have a hard time putting into words.

"We need to go," Resnick said.

"We're going to be seen," Dr. Kline said, glancing back to the slow-moving creature.

"We're not here at this time by accident. If I've timed things right, it's in between shifts... again, we have to move fast."

Resnick headed off, keeping low, moving fast.

Pristy stayed on his heels, hearing the others fall in behind her.

No sooner had they turned a corner, than they came to a stop.

"What's wrong?" she said to Resnick, who was looking at the floor where there was a puddle of *something* wet.

He looked up with a grimace. "Makes sense," he said more to himself than the others. He looked to Pristy. "It's not as if those things can climb stairs."

She had no idea what he was talking about.

Derrota, looking intrigued, pointed to a series of conjoined dotted lines on the floor, making two rectangles, one green, one red.

Resnick patted the top of his shirt with both hands, then pulled an energy bar from his top left pocket. Holding it out in front of himself, he looked to Pristy and smiled. He tossed the bar onto the green rectangle. Instead of falling to the floor as expected, it flew upward, gravity clearly having changed direction.

"Who wants to go first?" he said.

"I do," Aubrey said without hesitation and already moving toward the rectangle.

Resnick placed a restraining hand onto her shoulder. "Remember, we're not here."

"Got it, stealth is my middle name," she said, pushing past him. She stopped just long enough to consider how she was going to do this, then, instead of stepping, she jumped, as if hopping from one hopscotch box to another. Up she went, her hands reaching high overhead—Super Girl incarnate.

Resnick looked to the others. "Who's next?"

THERE WERE a series of gravity vaults, and not all of them were as vertical as the first one had been. Once Pristy had gotten accustomed to the method of moving between floors, she found it not only super easy, but exhilarating and fun. There were a number of gooey wet puddles, one of which caused LaSalle to lose his footing, but other than that, they made it safely to Resnick's intended destination. The compound's primary control center. Huddled outside, Pristy put an ear to the hatch door and listened. "I hear... *something*." She made a face. "Maybe tapping on an input device?" She looked to Resnick. "This is your mission."

He checked his ChronoLink. "We're out of time."

No one said anything.

"Stay here," he said, stepping toward the hatchway. It slid open so silently that unless one were looking right at it, you'd never know it opened.

Pristy, ignoring his orders, followed him in. The first of her senses to be affronted were olfactory. The smell was revolting, rotting flesh, flatulence, urine... Looking around, she saw that virtually every inch of bulkhead space held a boxy, old-fashioned- looking display monitor. There were too many consoles jammed together for the cramped space, and the floor, the deck... it was disgusting. Pristy didn't even want to guess what that gooey brown shit was smeared to her right. There was an elevated, poor man's captain's mount, shaped for the elongated contours of a Liquilid. In front of it, a table of sorts. Whatever the station commander had been eating, at least partially, was still there, moldy and putrid-looking. As technologically advanced as this alien race was, in some ways they were also backward.

She glanced up to see an irritated-looking Resnick looking back at her. He put a finger to his lips and turned back to the reason he was here. There, two feet in front of him, was a Liquilid creature, and just as she'd heard earlier, he, or she, was tapping away at an input device. Her breath caught; the monitor in front of him/her displayed none other than USS *Adams*, making her way through the perilous asteroid field.

And here they were, in an attempt to make it even easier for Quintos to plow that ginormous dreadnought into the very asteroid she now stood upon. He'd be sacrificing himself so his crew back on *Lincoln* would live. Right now, she hated what they were doing here... he wouldn't think of it as betrayal, but she did.

The flurry of motion in front of her brought her back to the here and now. Resnick had both arms wrapped around the creature's long snout. As the Liquilid bucked and thrashed, Resnick looked to be losing his grasp. One chomp from those jaws and Resnick would lose an arm.

"Get me something to wrap around his jaws!" he yelled with desperation she'd never heard from the man.

Frantic, Pristy looked about the compartment, catching sight of a nearby interconnecting cable. She tried to yank it free, but it was too solidly connected.

Resnick's legs went all akimbo, his feet slipping this way and that; the man was grunting and groaning as the creature continued to thrash about.

LaSalle was at her side now, his large hands taking hold of the cable. Together they pulled the cable free and, without taking a beat, LaSalle was at Resnick's side, now wrapping the cord around and around the Liquilid's long snout.

Derrota rushed forward with an even longer cord. Resnick snatched it from him and proceeded to use it to further restrain the creature, tying him/her to his seat.

Bent over at the waist, hands on knees, Resnick's chest heaved. In between breaths, he said, "We're out of time; we need to disable the shields."

Together, Pristy and Derrota got the Liquilid shoved out of the way. And while Pristy's eyes were transfixed upon the approaching *Adams*, Derrota scoured the control board, trying to make sense of what was what. Dr. Kline rushed to his side. "I think it's this section of the board here." She gestured toward a small monitor directly overhead, where a fluctuating band of blue encircled what could only be the same jagged asteroid they'd arrived on.

Derrota started flipping switches and turning dials until, finally, the fluctuating blue band suddenly blinked out.

"That did it!" Pristy yelled.

"That won't be enough; they flip those switches back on as

easily as you flip them off." He shoved Derrota and Dr. Kline out of the way, bent down, and not having any heavy tools at his disposal, kicked at the bottom panel of the console until it caved in enough for him to force fingers in at the sides. With a backward heave, he yanked the panel free, then tossed it aside. He looked up in time to see Aubrey there, handing him a long-handled broom-type thing, only this broom had long metal bristles. Pristy thought it would take more than that to get this floor clean.

Resnick took the broom and immediately began shoving it into the mass of wires and cables within the console. Sparks crackled and flashed from inside. Smoke started to rise from the console board.

"I think it's on fire," Aubrey said.

"You think," Resnick said sarcastically, getting to his feet.

They all glanced at the monitors, the now-unshielded asteroid, and USS *Adams* continuing its winding trek through the asteroid field.

"We've done all we can here, people. Time to go," Resnick said.

"What about him?" Aubrey said, pointing to the now somewhat more subdued Liquilid.

Pristy bent over, looked at the chair's still intact wheels. "We should take him with us."

"Are you crazy!" Dr. Kline said.

"She's right," Resnick said. "Killing him, leaving the body wouldn't be easily explained, and leaving him alive, well... he'll talk."

"But don't we have to get him down to the lower level? Where we arrived from, to enter back into the ringularity portal?" Derrota asked.

Pristy was losing patience. "We'll take turns pushing... let's go."

But Resnick was engrossed in his ChronoLink, this time speaking with someone. "Just make sure the timing is perfect... there can be no question, no suspicion, Church. Have I made myself clear?"

"Crystal," came the voice at the other end.

"What was that all about?" Pristy asked.

"Eavesdropping is impolite, Captain Pristy."

"So is keeping secrets. What were you telling Captain Church?"

Resnick almost smiled. "That his and his crew's mission was done here. That it was time for *Portent's* untimely demise."

"What are you talking about, untimely demise? Her crew—"

"Will be just fine. As will *Portent*. There's technology on board that vessel that can never fall into the wrong hands. She's already been here too long. Let's just say all concerned here in Liquilid space will witness *Portent* following in the same fateful footsteps as *Boundless Wrath*, while in truth, they will be perfectly timing their jump through a spatial ringularity portal."

Chapter 57

Liquilid Empire Star System
USS Adams

Captain Galvin Quintos

G rimes lifted his hands and splayed them questionably, while glowering toward the halo display. "I have no idea where I'm going. None."

Before *Adams*, the field had opened, revealing far fewer of the smaller asteroids while leaving gargantuan ones, rocky islands on a sea of black.

"He's right," Akari said. "The signal's indeed stronger here, but it's like it's coming from all around us. Like we've entered an echo chamber."

It's not so much that I was ignoring my bridgecrew. I heard what they were saying at some level, but what was being displayed on the halo display was like nothing I had ever witnessed. A dinosaur, a T-Rex no less, was in the throes of a battle so intense, so vicious, it was impossible not to watch.

Sonya had arrived at my side at one point, but I couldn't say when.

She said, "Look at him. I can't believe you made me do this... feed Reggie to those... those... bugs."

"I don't know. Looks like he's holding his own," I said.

Sonya shot a hand out toward the halo display. "He's limping. Half his tail's been cleaved off!"

"Where's Hardy?" I said, changing the subject. "I wanted both of you here on the bridge."

"He has a plan."

"Reggie?" I said, a little shocked.

"No. Hardy. Haven't you been listening to his comms?"

I shook my head. "I turned them off when he started singing 'Take Me Out to the Ball Game.'"

Sonia, incredulous, huffed out a breath. "He and Reggie are driving, no, more like herding the beetles toward a mid-ship cargo lock. Probably the largest on the ship. Thing's as big as this bridge."

"I know about Cargo Airlock 33, and yes, it's substantial," I said, still not understanding the plan.

I glanced up in time to see a tear rolling down Sonya's left cheek.

"Hey... what? What's wrong, kiddo? It'll be all right."

She swallowed hard and cleared her throat. "No. It won't. And if you'd listened to Hardy's comms, you'd know that. There's too many of them. The bugs... there's physically no way to kill them all. In time, they'd make their way up here to the bridge. They'd make an all-you-can-eat buffet of this compartment."

The bridge went quiet as we watched as Hardy and Reggie appeared on one video security feed and then the next.

Chen said, "Eight more frigates just entered the asteroid belt and they're moving fast... real fast."

I counted thirty-five nanite beetle constructs, Hardy and Reggie having dispatched several dozen of the killer bugs. Corridors and passageways throughout the ship had once been teeming with them, but now they were converging, obviously communicating with one another.

Sonya, hands covering the bottom half of her face, said, "They're almost there. Oh God... I can't watch this." But watch she did.

Hardy was the first to reach the double-wide hatch doors, immediately working the access panel to the right.

I mumbled, "Hurry... hurry... come on!"

Reggie had caught up, now anxiously waiting for Hardy to figure out the stupid code. I said, "Use the master code, dammit!" Looking up at Sonya, I saw both surprise and guilt written all over her face.

"I scrubbed *Adams's* memory banks!"

"Yeah... so?"

"That sets all the hatch doors back to their factory default codes."

"What's the factory default code?" I asked, looking back to the halo display. The bugs were almost upon them now. Reggie looked downright petrified, while Hardy had now resorted to banging a catcher's mitt–sized metal fist on the bulkhead.

Ensign Polk said, "It's 123456."

"Seriously?" I said, looking back at her.

Chen said, "Sending Hardy the code now."

I watched as Hardy continued with his hissy fit, then suddenly stopped to enter the transmitted code. The massive hatch doors slowly began to separate. Not having time to even turn around, Hardy was shoved inside the cargo airlock.

"Someone get me a feed from inside that airlock!" I yelled.

"Hold on," Akari snapped back.

As the wide-angle feed came into view, there was a collective gasp. It was like looking into the workings of a beehive, or an anthill, insects scurrying around everywhere with no rhyme or reason to their movements. I could see Reggie; he was hard to miss standing there, looming over the bugs while trying to snap at them. But there were too many.

I looked to Sonya, but she had already turned her back to the halo display. She was talking to her Jadoo ring, where I caught a quick glance at Ensign Plorinne.

"No! Do it now! Shut him off. Shut Reggie off!"

And with that, Reggie dropped to the deck, lifeless. It was as if a dinner bell had been rung; the beetles swarmed into a frenzy, crawling over one another to get to Reggie's carcass. I leaned forward, trying to get a bead on Hardy.

"There he is," Akari said. "Oh no..."

I saw him now too. At least he was standing... even if he did have half a dozen beetles clamped onto each of his appendages.

"Captain, he's not supposed to be there."

Sonya was quietly sobbing, no longer paying attention.

"Be specific, Akari. Be where?"

"He's supposed to be by the back corridor doors, not there at the outer hull doors."

I still didn't get it. *So what?*

A spinning, flashing red overhead light had come on within the cargo airlock. I shook my head. "No... he needs to get out of the way. What the hell is he doing!"

No one answered.

The outer hull cargo airlock doors were now opening. Hardy was the first to disappear out into the void. The beetles were being sucked out two, three at a time. Only then did Reggie's not-insignificant form lift and get pulled out into deep space.

Still, no one spoke. No one moved.

Then I said, "We'll find him. This isn't the first time he's floundered off into space. We'll find him," I repeated. Perhaps if I said it enough times, I could convince myself it was true.

"Cap! The frigates are here and firing," Chen said.

Adams shook; the lights flickered.

Akari suddenly stood, hands going to her mouth. "Oh God, no!"

I'd seen it too. The sudden, incredibly brilliant explosion off our aft starboard side.

Chen said, "She's gone... *Portent*... her comms have gone silent."

Taking her seat, Akari said, "Absolutely nothing left of her... totally obliterated,"

"She must have taken a direct hit," I said, shock and dismay still lingering.

INCOMING! INCOMING! INCOMING!
ONE HUNDRED THIRTY-FIVE
SMART MISSILES INBOUND...
SECOND WAVE, TWO HUNDRED
SIXTY-NINE SMART MISSILES INBOUND...

At first, I wondered if I'd heard old Sir Calvin right. But with one look at the halo display, I knew my hearing was just fine. I froze. Isn't that what you do when you run out of alternatives? When there isn't even one conceivable option available?

Akari turned to look at me. She had nothing for me.

Sonya had sat down in front of the captain's mount, her back now resting on my knees.

What I saw next took several long moments to register. Just because one's eyes "see" something does not mean the brain is actually capable of deciphering the information. Because what I was seeing on the halo display should not have been possible.

But there she was, USS *Lincoln*, her spectacular SpaceWing design rapidly advancing there from behind the now totally dwarfed eight Liquilid frigates.

We all flinched in unison as thousands of intensely bright Phazon Pulsar bursts filled local space.

One hundred thirty-five smart missiles inbound... DESTROYED. Second wave, two-hundred sixty-nine smart missiles inbound... DESTROYED.

"Captain!" Akari shouted. "I have a clear signal... a clear signal to the quantum flux generator! Somehow, it just... showed up. Not sure for how long, but I know exactly which asteroid is generating it... it's close."

I looked at the display. "Who's skippering *Lincoln*?"

"One Captain Wallace Ryder has taken command," Chen said. "And he says this might be a good time for us to complete our mission. He'll clean this mess up here."

I couldn't help but smile. "Cocky bastard," I said under my breath.

"Oh... and he wanted me to remind you that piece of shit *Hub Gunther* is still waiting in *Adams'* flight bay."

"Mr. Grimes! Giving me your best sub-light speed, how much time do we have till impact?"

"Seven minutes, Sir."

"That's not a lot of time. Helm, lock in the coordinates and put the pedal to the metal." I stood. "Sir Calvin, make the announcement. We're abandoning ship. Everyone's to get to Flight Bay."

Yes, Sir. And may I say, it

has been a pleasure serving with you.

ABANDON SHIP! ABANDON SHIP! ABANDON SHIP! ALL CREW REPORT TO FLIGHT BAY IMMEDIATELY!

I insisted I would be sitting in the *Hub Gunther's* pilot seat.

We managed to get on the old mining bird within five minutes and thirty seconds. Now, looking back into the open cabin, I saw everyone was here; no stragglers had rushed to get on board. I made eye contact with each of my bridgecrew, then Sonya, who was now snuggled up with Ensign Plorinne along the portside bulkhead.

Akari, seated to my right, said, "Ready to blow this popsicle stand?"

I looked at the old analog clock on the dash. We had thirty-eight seconds.

Throttling up the aft thrusters, I engaged the *Hub Gunther's* main drive. The g-forces pinned us to our seats as we cleared *Adams'* bay doors. Immediately, I banked left. Someone screamed. Perhaps it was me. No one had expected the asteroid to not only be right there in front of us, but so incredibly big. It was all that was visible beyond the windshield.

I swung the *Gunther* into a wide arc, putting necessary distance between us and the asteroid, while also bringing us around for what was to come next. And there she was. USS *Adams*. Stately. Proud, and fulfilling her duty. She was traveling at an ungodly fast rate of speed.

It wouldn't be long now. *Sorry, old girl, I know this is too soon for you.* One of my favorite poems came to mind. Speaking mainly for my own benefit, I recited the last few stanzas:

.   .   .

Her rattling shrouds, all sheathed in ice,
With the masts went by the board;
Like a vessel of glass, she stove and sank,
Ho! Ho! the breakers roared!

At daybreak, on the bleak sea-beach,
A fisherman stood aghast,
To see the form of a maiden fair,
Lashed close to a drifting mast.

The salt sea was frozen on her breast,
The salt tears in her eyes;
And he saw her hair, like the brown sea-weed,
On the billows fall and rise.

Such was the wreck of the Hesperus,
In the midnight and the snow!
Christ save us all from a death like this,
On the reef of Norman's Woe!

In spectacular fashion, one befitting such a magnificent vessel, USS *Adams* plowed bow-forward into her intended target. The resulting fiery explosion was catastrophic for both vessel and Liquilid compound.

Chen said, "Captain Ryder says jump capability has just come back online. Let's get out of here."

Epilogue

3 months later...

"My boy had a run-in with the hogs again." The plump, rosy-cheeked, fortyish woman stood next to a young, buck-toothed teen covered in mud. What appeared to be a paisley apron was wrapped around his left upper arm. There was some blood there, but not so much he was going to bleed out. The kid looked as if this wasn't his first time visiting the doctor.

"Please sign in here, Ma'am. And we'll get your boy in right away."

"Where's Betty?" the woman said, scribbling her signature onto a worn-looking tablet. "Never seen you before. Pretty thing, ain't ya?" She looked over to the empty seat behind the plexiglass divider, then back to Viv. The woman narrowed her eyes, taking in the embroidered name on Viv's oversized white lab coat. "You're not Betty."

"I'm new here. Dr. Vivian Leigh, but everyone calls me Doc Viv."

The woman gave her a once-over. Viv was well aware

newcomers were rarely a welcome commodity in such a small town. Welcome to Baker, Missouri, population four thousand one hundred and forty-three.

"Betty's out sick, at least that's what Grif—um, Dr. McKenna relayed to me." She brushed away several errant strands of wavy hair, those having escaped from her ponytail.

"Meg. Meg Glasstopper. And this is Wyatt," the woman said, still looking as if she was deciding if she would fully accept Viv's presence here. "I'll have to go by Betty's place... bring her some of my homemade raccoon-chop soup."

Viv wasn't sure what raccoon-chop soup was, or if the woman was being serious. "Please have a seat, um, Meg... you too, Wyatt." She gestured to the small waiting room with one hand.

Viv watched as Meg and Wyatt settled into two straight-back molded plastic seats. It was as if time had stood still here in this small town. The so-called hospital was more like a health clinic straight out of the twentieth century. The reception room was about two hundred square feet, with speckled brown and white linoleum tiles, egg-colored walls half covered with battered oak wainscoting having seen better days decades ago. There was a large bay window in serious need of a good scrubbing, but it at least allowed the morning sun in to brighten the unremarkable room.

The adjacent wall donned two faded framed posters, matching alpine scenes, a group of colorfully clad skiers traversing steep, powdered slopes. Both posters seemed to be identical to one another, which Viv found to be a strange decorating choice. The glass overhead dome light put out little illumination, probably because of the inside layer of long-deceased insect parts. In one corner of the room was a water cooler surrounded by flowered Dixie cups. A low Crayola-strewn table held several dogeared coloring books, several Tonka toy trucks, and a lone stuffed rabbit, sans one ear.

Staring at nothing in particular, she blinked, then blinked again. This wasn't the first time she'd caught herself. She briefly wondered if it was possible to actually die of boredom. Was there a medical term for that? She moved back behind the reception desk, passed by the closed door of patient room 1. Although muffled, she could hear Grif's country drawl, the easy, friendly cadence of his voice. Everyone loved Grif.

She checked patient room #2—there were only two patient rooms within this facility—making sure everything was ready before she was to escort in one more catastrophic medical emergency: impacted earwax, a sprained ankle, or maybe an infected hangnail.

Jingle. Jingle. Another patient had moseyed in...

She stopped, closed her eyes, and told herself that it would be fine. Transitions like this were always a shock to one's psyche. You didn't go from treating disemboweled SWM workers or pilots with third-degree facial burns and not need a minute... but it had been three months since she'd arrived here, and she had yet to see a patient on her own. So she'd been shadowing Dr. Grif around like a clueless puppy. Apparently, Grif wanted to ensure that her doctoring techniques were... what was the phrase he'd used? *In alignment* with that of this hospital. *Pfft.* If he had any clue of what she was capable of, the surgical expertise she'd routinely exhibited on a daily basis, well, he'd probably... *no, I can't do that. I can't expect him or anyone to appreciate my worth. That will come in time.*

She hoped the day would get better... the townsfolk would continue to stream in like a swarm of mosquitoes on a hot summer evening, buzzing with relentless curiosity and ready to suck the life out of any idle conversation. They'd check her out, ask about Betty, and take a seat.

She looked out to the waiting room. She'd never been one to feel self-conscious. But they continued to stare at her, a freakish-looking guppy in a fishbowl.

She really had no idea what she was getting herself into; all she knew was she needed a change. That or lose her mind. But now, having taken over as Grif's partner, she wondered how long this adjustment period would last.

"How's it going out here?" The booming voice came from behind Viv, giving her a start.

"Good, Griffin. Just checking people in." Viv felt nervous. She wasn't sure why.

"I'm so sorry about this, Vivian." Griffin grabbed a seat and rolled up next to her. "I promise you, Betty will be back tomorrow, and you'll be back in doctor mode." Griffin flashed her an authentic please-forgive-me smile. She did care about the man, and she knew he was smitten, perhaps more than smitten. He'd asked her out a dozen times; she'd met him for dinner twice. He'd made it clear he was in this for the long haul, that he'd wait as long as it took for her to feel comfortable. Their third date was planned for tonight; he was planning on taking her to a new place over in Gardner, the next town over.

"No worries. I'm fine... really." Viv returned a smile, albeit not quite as authentic as his. "I did want a slower pace."

"Be careful what you ask for," Griffin quipped.

They both laughed quietly, trying not to draw further attention from their audience in the waiting room.

"Tell you what. Why don't I take over here, and you see some patients?"

"Oh no, you don't have to do that." Viv felt her shoulders stiffen.

"No, I insist." Griffin sprang from his seat and reached for her hand. "Come on, up you go."

"Okay, if you say so." She felt as if she were fifteen years old, her father letting her drive the family aircar for the first time.

Viv finished securing the sticky gauze around the teen's upper arm and patted him on the shoulder. "Okay, you're all set, Wyatt."

"Thank you, Doc." Meg joined her son as he hopped off the raised examination table.

"You're welcome." Viv clutched her medi-tablet with crossed arms over her chest. "Just keep Wyatt away from the hogs for a while, okay?"

"Farm's gotta keep runnin', Doc. But, sure." Meg and Wyatt walked toward the door, giggling with each other, as if sharing a private joke.

The doctor's office was a bit more modern than the waiting room, with 3D imaging and even some high-tech tools that she was accustomed to using on USS *Adams*. When Viv asked why the whole place hadn't been updated, Griffin explained that the patients felt more comfortable with the old-fashioned, homey atmosphere. Most of the people here came from a long line of farmers. Even though they owned hover-tractors and had barns filled with planting drones, they still wore overalls and cooked steaks in cast iron skillets.

Knock. Knock.

"Come on in!" Viv yelled. She stood at the sink washing her hands, back to the door. "Just please have a seat on the examination table. I'll be right with you."

Viv used the air dryer on her hands, then turned to meet her next patient.

"Hi, Doc. I've got this pain in my heart... it's gotten pretty bad." The man held an open palm over the left side of his chest. He was dressed casually in a worn flannel button-down shirt, jeans, and scuffed boots. He was in need of a haircut and, even more so, a shave.

Viv stood mannequin still, unable to speak.

"Uh... Viv?"

"Quintos?" Viv took a step back, finding a rolling stool. She dropped onto it, a sack of potatoes being plopped on the pantry floor.

"You're... what... how..." Myriad words jumbled in her head, none of them forming into anything coherent.

"We're on leave. Thought I'd stop by and say hi. Hope you don't mind." Quintos spoke with a relaxed, not-a-care-in-the-world tone. "I told your... friend... Gordon

"Griffin..."

"Whatever, that I was having chest pains, so he let me jump the line. Hope you don't mind."

She continued to assess him. This was a different Captain Galvin Quintos than she'd worked side by side with for so many years. Gentle. Relaxed. Humble.

She finally found her voice. "Are you okay, Galvin? Are you sick?"

"No, although some may disagree." He gestured toward his head and gave her a self-deprecating grin.

"I can't believe you're here." She blinked, swallowed, suddenly feeling self-conscious.

"I know." His tone shifted lower. "Look, I have a lot to fill you in on. Can you get out of here for a while? Sonya's with me... waiting at the coffee shop down the street."

Irritated, she shook her head. "I'm working. I have patients."

His expression changed. His propped-up smile now fell by the wayside.

"You never found him?" she asked, lowering her tone.

He shook his head. "*Hub Gunther's* not nearly as noticeable as a dreadnought... for three weeks I stayed behind in the

Liquilid system, looking for him. Never thought I'd say it, but I even miss his ridiculous antics."

"Hardy's a survivor... he'll turn up." She wasn't sure that was true, but hope springs eternal, doesn't it? "Can I ask what happened?"

Quintos's eyes momentarily lost focus. "I think he got trapped in an airlock... then, somehow, was ejected out into space."

"So, he's lost out there... in deep space?" Viv rolled herself closer to him.

"I'm hoping he's been picked up."

By who? she wondered.

"Anyway, we'll be heading back out soon."

"Admiral's assigned you another ship?"

He looked back at her, confused by her question.

"It's been months. I'm sure they want you back in the fight. Grish... Varapin... The war's still raging."

His smile returned. "It's been a fight, and there have been a number of legal hoops to jump through concerning the laws of spatial salvage, but USS *Lincoln* will soon be ours."

"Ours?"

"Yeah, *Adams'* crew, as well as the surviving relatives of *Lincoln's* crew."

"You're saying I own a portion of a multi-trillion-dollar dreadnought?"

He shrugged. "We'll see, and again, it hasn't been finalized, but yeah... you'll be a—"

"Millionaire..." she said, letting that sink in.

"Only if someone buys it from us. The distribution will be tied to each individual crewmember's rank." He wobbled his head. "You, a crewmember with the rank of major, well... that would put you pretty high up on the pecking order. Making you closer to being a billionaire."

She didn't know what to think about that.

Quintos was still talking, "... since I'm not sure I'm re-upping my—"

"Wait. You're out of the US Space-Navy?"

"Let's just say I'm taking some time to weigh my options. I have some loose ends to tie up first."

"You're heading back out to look for Hardy."

He stared back at her. "Come with us," Galvin said matter-of-factly.

"What? Come with you? What are you talking about?" She rolled away from him, stood, and busied herself at the counter.

"Are you happy here, Viv?"

The question hadn't taken her by surprise. In fact, she'd been waiting for it. "Happy? Yes, of course, I'm happy." Her words sounded far less convincing than she would've liked.

Quintos was behind her now. Gently, he used a hand to turn her around. There was no judgment in his gaze.

"What does being happy have to do with anything, anyway? Nobody's happy all the time, Quintos. But I'm good here. I enjoy my new life. It's perfectly fine." Viv stopped talking, realizing she was over-explaining.

"Okay, Viv. I understand. But I had to ask." Quintos took a step back, turned and walked toward the door, then pivoted to face her. "We miss you, Viv. I miss you. I wanted you to know that. It's been good seeing you again. Take care of yourself. Gordon seems like a nice fella."

"It's Griff—" she waved away her own words. "Thank you for coming. Please say hi to everyone for me." *Shit. Why do you look so good? Damn you, Quintos.* She felt a stirring in her belly, a warmth in her chest that threatened to spread to her face. She turned around, busying herself once more at the counter. She heard the door swing shut and latch behind her.

. . .

I STOOD outside the small medical center, taking in the morning sun and fresh air. I wasn't surprised in the least Viv had turned me down. *Am I okay?* Not really. After three months I still pined for the woman... I had debated coming here, seeing her again. Should I have reopened old wounds? *Who knows?* Now, with the loss of Viv, the loss of Hardy—*God, was my best friend really a robot?*

Upon arriving at Clair's Cup of Joe, I spotted Sonya engaged in conversation with a youthful barista, exuding a tousled and carefree charm from his position behind the counter. A little older than her, laughing, perhaps flirting, they seemed to be hitting it off. How long would it be before Sonya was heading off to college? We'd talked about it. She was older than her years, whip-smart, more than ready to start this fall.

I turned away from the window. Sonya too would be gone all too soon. So, what was next for me? Yeah, crazy as that prospect was, I'd be heading back into the Liquilid system... probably alone.

"Oh, stop it!"

Viv was standing three feet away from me, hands on hips, a bemused smile on her full, beautiful lips.

"Stop what?"

"Sulking. It doesn't become you. A decorated, not to mention soon to be wealthy US Space-Navy warship captain... just stop it. Self-pity is for losers."

I gave her a once-over. "Where's your lab coat?"

"Tossed it in the trash before I left."

"Left? Like... for good?"

"Are you going to keep asking me stupid questions, or are you going to kiss me?"

---

*Wait, wait, wait ... What the hell happens to Hardy? This is how Book 7 of the Hamilton series ends!? The only way to find out is by reading, the spinoff, **The ChronoBot Chronicles**, and it's available NOW!*

Thank you for reading USS Lincoln — Mercy Kill. Want more? GOOD NEWS! Many of the USS Hamilton series books are also available NOW. Check them out on Amazon.com

If you enjoyed this book, PLEASE leave a review on Amazon.com—it really helps! To be notified the moment all future books are released, please join my mailing list. I hate spam and will never ever share your information. Jump to this link to sign up: http://eepurl.com/bs7M9r

Acknowledgments

First and foremost, I am grateful to my readers. I'd like to thank my wife, Kim, whose loving contributions to my books are immeasurable. Thank you to Lura Genz (my ninety-two-year-old mother) for her tireless work as our first-phase creative editor and for being a staunch cheerleader of my writing. I'd also like to thank Margarita Martinez for her amazingly detailed line editing work; Jennifer Eaton for her creative design and typesetting skills; Daniel Edelman for his many prerelease technical reviews and expert subject matter spitballing. A heartfelt thank you also goes to Sue Parr, Charles Duell, Stuart Church, Zoraya Vasquez, Lura Fischer, and James Fischer—without their support, this novel would not have been possible.

Check out the other available titles by Mark Wayne McGinnis on the page following About the Author.

About the Author

Mark grew up on both coasts, first in Westchester County, New York, and then in Westlake Village, California. Mark and his wife, Kim, now live in Castle Rock, Colorado, with their two dogs, Sammi, and Lilly.

Mark started as a corporate marketing manager and then fell into indie-filmmaking—Producing/Directing the popular Gaia docudrama, 'Openings — The Search For Harry'.

For the last fifteen years, he's been writing full-time, and with over 40 top-selling novels under his belt, he has no plans on slowing down. Thanks for being part of his community!

Also by
Mark Wayne McGinnis

Scrapyard Ship Series

Scrapyard Ship (Book 1)

HAB 12 (Book 2)

Space Vengeance (Book 3)

Realms of Time (Book 4)

Craing Dominion (Book 5)

The Great Space (Book 6)

Call To Battle (Book 7)

Scrapyard Ship – Uprising

Mad Powers Series

Mad Powers (Book 1)

Deadly Powers (Book 2)

Lone Star Renegades Series

Star Watch Series

Star Watch (Book 1)

Ricket (Book 2)

Boomer (Book 3)

Glory for Space Sea and Space (Book 4)

Space Chase (Book 5)

Scrapyard LEGACY (Book 6)

The Simpleton Series

The Simpleton (Book 1)

The Simpleton Quest (Book 2)

Galaxy Man

Ship Wrecked Series

Ship Wrecked (Book 1)

Ship Wrecked II (Book 2)

Ship Wrecked III (Book 3)

Boy Gone

Expanded Anniversary Edition

Cloudwalkers

The Hidden Ship

Guardian Ship

Gun Ship

HOVER

Heroes and Zombies

The Test Pilot's Wife

TheFallen Ship

The Fallen Ship: Rise of the Gia Rebellion (Book 1)

The Fallen Ship II (Book 2)

USS Hamilton Series

USS Hamilton: Ironhold Station (Book 1)

USS Hamilton: Miasma Burn (Book 2)

USS Hamilton: Broadsides (Book 3)

USS Hamilton: USS Jefferson –

Charge of the Symbios (Book 4)

USS Hamilton: Starship Oblivion –

Sanctuary Outpost (Book 5)

USS Hamilton: USS Adams – No Escape (Book 6)

USS Hamilton: USS Lincoln – Mercy Kill (Book 7)

USS Hamilton: USS Franklin - When Worlds Collide (Book 8)

USS Hamilton: USS Washington - The Black Ship (Book 9)

USS Hamilton: USS IKE - Quansport Ops (Book 10)

ChronoBot Chronicles

Printed in Great Britain
by Amazon